A SEAHORSE YEAR

BOOKS BY STACEY D'ERASMO

A SEAHORSE YEAR

TEA

A
SEAHORSE
YEAR

STACEY
D'ERASMO

A MARINER BOOK
HOUGHTON MIFFLIN COMPANY
BOSTON • NEW YORK

FIRST MARINER BOOKS EDITION 2005

Copyright © 2004 by Stacey D'Erasmo

For information about permission to reproduce selections
from this book, write to Permissions, Houghton Mifflin Company,
215 Park Avenue South, New York, New York 10003.

Visit our Web site: www.houghtonmifflinbooks.com.

Library of Congress Cataloging-in-Publication Data

D'Erasmo, Stacey.

A seahorse year / Stacey D'Erasmo.

p.   cm.

ISBN 0-618-43923-4

ISBN-13: 978-0-618-43923-2   ISBN-10: 0-618-43923-4
ISBN-13: 978-0-618-61887-8 (pbk.)   ISBN-10: 0-618-61887-2 (pbk.)

1. San Francisco (Calif.)—Fiction. 2. California, Northern—
Fiction. 3. Runaway teenagers—Fiction. 4. Lesbian
mothers—Fiction. 5. Problem youth—Fiction. 6. Teenage
boys—Fiction. 7. Gay fathers—Fiction. I. Title.

PS3554.E666S43 2004

813'.54—dc22   2004042724

Printed in the United States of America

Book design by Robert Overholtzer

MP 10 9 8 7 6 5 4 3 2

FOR INVALUABLE HELP IN WRITING THIS BOOK,
I would like to thank Jennifer Carlson, Michael Cunningham, Esopus,
Gloria Fisk, Jayne Yaffe Kemp, Cammie McGovern, Catherine E. McKinley,
Laurie Muchnick, Roy Parvin, Elaine Pfefferblit, Laura Pinsky, Dr. Michael
Rendel, Peter Rock, Robyn Selman, the Ucross Foundation, Michael Warner,
and Jacqueline Woodson. Thanks to Jeanne Fury for the rock education.
And most of all, thanks to my dear Elizabeth.

For Rose D'Erasmo,
1917–2003

MY LOVE WILL STAY
TILL THE RIVERBED RUN DRY.

—PJ Harvey

Hal walks uphill. My son is mad, he thinks, and turns a corner, passing a coffeehouse where three women in sweatshirts sit at an outdoor table. It's cool, gray, and damp: summer in San Francisco.

"Hey, Hal," says one, a client. Hal waves.

"Yeah, he's great," she says to a friend as he walks on. "He got me back a thousand dollars last year."

My son is mad, thinks Hal. I am dying. He almost stops to call Nan and say that — I am dying, I am dying — but he knows that she will reply, calmly, "You are not dying, Hal. Did you talk to the police today?"

Sometimes he just can't handle her — her persistence, her smooth face, the way she occupies any chair as if she has just built it herself out of a tree she felled with her little saw. I am lost, he thinks, I am sure that I'm dying, my son is mad, and his mother won't admit that she can't carry him by herself.

Hal walks on. No one has found Christopher yet, no one has called to say that they've seen him, no one — not even Nan — has come in from the desert or the mountains carrying him. Hal looks up at the sky, as if Christopher might appear there, but the sky is blankly bluish gray. Back in Christopher's room in Hal's house, Christopher's saltwater fish tank is burbling to itself. Expensive fish circle through the carefully tended water: a lionfish, a snowflake eel, three temperamental tangs, and a bamboo cat shark who spends most of its time lying on the bottom of the tank, looking malevolent and morose. Since Christopher has been gone, it has fallen to Hal to take care of Christopher's fish. This morning, Hal noticed that the tank seemed warm and the fish sluggish, that they were swimming slowly, like a carousel winding down. Hal felt a panicky rush. He believes in omens and portents and signs of all kinds. He immediately set out for the aquarium store, the good one in Noe Valley where he had opened an account for Christopher. He thought he might see an omen or sign on the way, but so far there has been nothing, nothing at all, but that random, friendly hello and miles of sky without a break.

Hal looks down again, at the street. A not uninteresting man with a squashy nose looks Hal's way, but Hal doesn't look back.

Hal, walking uphill, is equally certain that Christopher is alive and that he is dead. Either way, he is certain that it will fall to him to carry Christopher — who, at sixteen, is much too heavy and tall now to be carried even by Hal — in the end.

Nan works in her garden. It is a long, narrow plot of land containing four square beds of flowers outlined by planks of silvered wood; around the beds is grass. Around the garden is a fence, also silvered. Trumpet vines tumble wantonly over the fence toward earth. Midway down the garden is a slender, deep purple, flowering plum that has never flowered or plummed but maintains a hopeful, leafy look. A few feet away from the plum tree, nestled in some tall grasses and a few wayward daisies, is the stone head of Sor Juana. Nan pulls a few weeds from around the pansies. She chews on a shred of chive. Her right hip aches, a tedious reminder of being forty-five, of the car accident at eighteen that broke her hip in the first place, and of the doctor in Mexico who didn't set it right. She picked up the statue during that trip, before she even knew who Sor Juana was or had a garden to put her in. She just liked Sor Juana's melancholy, downturned stone eyes, her stone wimple; feeling like Orpheus, Nan lugged her back over the border on the bus, placing her heavy stone head on the next seat.

Nan's body remembers everything and retells it to her from time to time whether she wants to hear it or not. She taps a loose end of a plank into place with her spade.

Marina said, over dinner the night before, "He's all right. I feel that he's all right."

Nan had stared at her plate, willing herself not to think. She found her hand closing and willed her fingers to open. She willed herself not to say, "You couldn't possibly feel him. You didn't bear him or raise him." She put her plate in the sink and walked outside to stand in the dark garden. But what was worse was the fact that Nan didn't feel anything either. She had no idea at all where Christopher could be. No breeze stirred the dark leaves.

Today the garden is calm. Nan stands up, holding the spade: a hopeless, foolish tool against the wide world. She thinks how foolish she herself must look, a short woman with short, gray-streaked hair, in dirty jeans, armed with nothing but a spade. She sighs, dirty fingers clenched around the dirty spade. She closes her eyes for a minute, thinks ChristopherChristopherChristopher, then opens them again. The garden remains empty.

Nan leans down to pick a few small green tomatoes for the windowsill. She tugs at a weed. Her hip complains. The cool, damp air washes over her. She tries to feel comforted by its purity. She listens intently for some sound or cry, perhaps from a great distance, but the only sound is the chink of her spade in the earth.

Marina paints the branch of a tree. The light in her studio is muted. The studio is in a converted church in the Mission; now it's a church of art. She works in the choir room, a boxy space with rickety windows and the ghost of the smell of wet wool. It's a mess: scattered around the room are, among other things, her bicycle, canvases in various states of use, work boots, cans of powder paint and acrylic, squashed tubes of oil paint, archival glue and Elmer's glue, a jigsaw, a drill, sketchbooks, a box of old snapshots bought at a flea market and another two or three overflowing with cut-up old books and magazines from her collage period, a hunk of dried-out clay, a kid's bead loom in a box that says

AMERICAN INDIAN LOOM, a ruler, a bunch of mismatched baby shoes, a sculpture leaning against one wall — an exchange with another artist — which looks something like a side of cured beef. A big plastic bucket is filled with clipped pictures of nineteenth-century valentines. Hearts and the empty shapes where hearts used to be are tangled together. The bucket sits under a table with curlicue white metal legs and a glass top, meant to be patio furniture; the glass is covered with swirls and blobs and streaks of paint, years of it in a multicolored, perpetual storm. Tacked onto the wall next to Marina's worktable is a yellowed postcard of an Agnes Martin painting: rows of white lines like stitches traced vertically across a slate background, determined and lonely and earthy. When she first met Nan, she thought Nan was like that painting.

Scotch-taped to the upper frame of one window are three dried seahorses, a gift from Christopher: one, two, three little rocking creatures with fixed rococo stares. There is a rent notice lying on the floor near the door, along with a note from Turner, a printmaker who has the studio directly beneath Marina's. The note says, *The cow Roberta won a Prix de Rome. She's a cow. COW.* Marina can hear Turner below her, laughing and talking on his cell phone. Through the old porous floorboards, she can smell the etching acid he uses.

Marina dots the tip of the branch. It's okay. Today the tree is okay, not so bad, she won't have to scrape it off and start again. Probably. She looks at it, wrapping a lock of hair around her finger: a schoolgirl habit, though this schoolgirl has a head of silver hair cut in a bob that just grazes the nape of her long neck. Marina is only thirty-eight, but her hair has been silver since she was twenty-five. She would no more have bothered to dye it than she would have bothered to iron a wrinkled shirt or mend a sweater with a hole. She has always preferred a life of casual accretion. In fact, she believes in it, almost as an *ars poetica*: what accretes naturally always turns out to be exactly what's needed. Painting should be like riding a bike with no hands, a mixture of velocity and trust.

For instance, this tree that she's been making for the last seven years: it hasn't been that well received, but she has persevered for reasons she can't quite explain. She's made the tree big; she's made the tree small; she's made the tree in oil, watercolor, gouache, collage, tinfoil, Polaroid, and acrylic; she's repeated identical trees in suspiciously regular rows on a single canvas; once she made an entire forest of trees from fabric remnants. This is a tree in oil, dense and telegraphic. She might have to scrape it off after all. There's another tree, a tree she can see clearly in her mind's eye, that will not fail, as this one suddenly seems in imminent danger of doing. The tree at this point has become fairly representational, close to the tree she drew over and over again when she was ten. It's a leafy, spreading, eastern sort of tree that seems quite specific, though if one were to look at it more closely, one would see that it isn't actually any particular organic species at all. Its branches bend strangely; its leaves are an uncanny shape. There are suggestions of faces in the bark. When she first drew it as a child in Los Angeles, it was a tree she had never seen, except in a dream. In the dream, it was the most beautiful tree in the world. She woke up needing to draw it. That was all she knew. In many ways, she thinks it may be all she still knows. She begins on another branch, with guarded hope.

When the wind blows, the rickety window shakes and the three seahorses, loose in their old tape, rap very faintly on the glass. It is, to Marina, an unbearable sound. In one corner of her studio, a boom box splattered with paint rests next to a wooden tray full of a random collection of CDs: some opera, some Depeche Mode, a boxed set of Patti Smith with crushed corners. She doesn't turn on the boom box. She listens hard for the tiny, unbearable rattle of the seahorses. It seems important.

Christopher has been gone seven days. Day by day, the time accretes with other events, events of much greater magnitude that have affected many more people: an earthquake in El Salvador; a change of power in Israel; the rise of the temperature of the earth by a fraction of a degree. Those events, however, are bearable. What is not bearable is the silence, punctuated by that tiny, almost imperceptible rapping. How will they survive this? Marina has no idea. A leaf appears, then another.

Nan parts Marina's thighs with her hands, buries her hands, her tongue, in Marina, as desperately as if this is their last fuck on earth. Marina shakes, but doesn't come yet. She pulls Nan up beside her in the twisted sheets. Nan is sweating and crying at the same time, and her lips feel rough and hot. Marina kisses Nan with deep, purposeful kisses, wanting to draw the poison out, but they are both poisoned, so she can't. They can only pass the poison between them. Nan reaches into the drawer of the night table and pulls out the old cracked maroon cock, slides it up inside Marina, whose glue- and paint-stained shirt is still half-buttoned on her body. Her silver hair is snarled and sweaty. Nan says into Marina's ear, "Give it here," and when Marina does it's like a wall falling down and on the other side of the wall is a rushing wind.

Marina starts to cry. Nan sits up, running the heels of her hands through her hair. She looks at the clock and sees that only twenty-one minutes have gone by.

Somewhere near Denver, Christopher hitches a ride with a truck heading south.

BLOOD

N AN STANDS IN LINE at Celestial Coffee, the alternative Starbucks, behind a teenage Goth girl and a woman in running clothes with a baby in a jogging stroller. Celestial Coffee has signed posters of jazz musicians on the walls, vegan baked goods, and one visible employee, a meditative young man in a Keep on Truckin' T-shirt. Nan hates Starbucks, but needs coffee, especially now, so Celestial is her compromise. She makes it with a kind of wry despair. O, San Francisco. Sometimes she finds it funny; at other times it makes her want to weep. When did the city of free love become the city of cash? Though the headlines insist that the bubble has burst, there remains an overcaffeinated fantasy, a bewitched atmosphere. Parades of people in khakis instead of parades of men in dresses, on roller skates. The minititans are jobless but still smiling. Lattes are being made all over town. She watches the procession go by, feeling like the only disenchanted one.

The woman with the baby in the jogging stroller has blond hair, pulled back in a ponytail and tied with a piece of purple yarn; the color in her cheeks is high, though her eyes look tired. The baby is sleeping peacefully, its tiny pink fists folded on its chest. In the aerodynamic wedge of stroller, he looks to Nan like a modern Moses in a polypropylene basket, floating down the river. She barely resists the urge to adjust his exquisite, sapphire blue

Polartec blanket, saddle-stitched around the edges in white, the Patagonia label showing. The Goth girl, despite the thick eyeliner and witchy dyed black hair and bits of metal studding her face, has a tentative expression, a skittish manner, as if this is her first time out as a Goth. She orders a double mint cappuccino. The woman with the baby orders a chai tea with steamed soy milk.

"Coffee, large, black," says Nan to the meditative young man behind the counter as he steams the soy milk, then, to the blond woman, "How old?"

"Twelve weeks," she says proudly. "He was up all night last night." She gazes at the baby with exhausted wonderment. "We tried everything." The young man hands the woman her tea in a plain white paper cup.

The Goth girl, sitting at a table nearby reading the *San Francisco Weekly* and drinking her double mint cappuccino, says, "Have you tried holding him on your knees, you know, on his stomach, while you rub his back?"

"Oh," says the blond woman. "No."

"Try that," says the Goth girl.

The woman laughs and looks at Nan complicitously. "Well," she says.

"It's true," says Nan. The young man hands her the large black coffee; the cup is warm and heavy in her hands. She was up all night, too, again, and now has the transparent, vertiginous feeling that coffee shreds but doesn't soothe.

"Oh?" says the woman, tightening her ponytail. "Are you a doctor?" Her eyes drift over Nan's face.

"I'm a mother," says Nan, and she knows her tone is aggressive. She tries to smile. "But my son is sixteen. A big boy."

"Ah," says the woman, tucking in her baby, who is still sound asleep. "So you're past all this."

Nan abruptly turns away, panicked by a strange thought. As she fumbles to open the door, she blows into the little sip hole in the plastic coffee lid, then burns her tongue on the hot coffee. She rubs the warm cup on her cold forehead, feeling defeated, which makes her only more focused. If she could stay awake all the time, she would. In her mind, Hal tuts, *"Hard-ass,"* and Marina, more tenderly, tells her that she's *"hypervigilant,"* but they're not, Nan thinks, mothers. They're not her. Demons walk right past those two all the time and they don't even notice, but she does. She sees demons every day, as ordinary as dirt — except, of course, that she didn't see this one coming at all. Which makes her no different from the ponytailed blonde, no matter how little soy milk she puts in her coffee.

The strange thought is this: maybe it was the otters.

When Christopher was ten, she took him for a treat to the Monterey Aquarium. He was already a fish expert. Marina had just sailed into Nan's life, silver flags flying. When Marina left Nan's house early — a Saturday morning, she remembers — Nan went into Christopher's room and woke him up. "Hey," she said, "let's go see some fishes."

He blinked at her, sleepy, faintly suspicious. "Who was that?" he said.

"Who?"

"Who left."

"A friend. Come on."

They drove down the 101, past the crowded suburbs to where eucalyptus trees lined the road and signs advertised cherries and garlic. Christopher was wrapped up in the big *Complete Guide to the Undersea World,* which was open on his knees, but Nan was still wrapped in Marina, who was, she had told Nan without any irony or self-deprecation, an artist. Nan could tell that Marina was younger, but by how much she didn't know. Marina's skin was unlined; her hair was silver; her gaze was somehow both frank and elusive. *Marina Sweeney,* she had said, holding out her hand. Marina Sweeney was almost waifish, but at the same time not: a wise child, with a long neck and a deep laugh. Taller than Nan. She wore a cheap ring with a little cartoon Mao star on it, a wrinkled, untucked blouse over a strange short corduroy skirt appliquéd with a leather flower, and her hair was messy — in fact, everything about her was messy, half-wild, but beautiful, like a fire. The skirt looked like a hand-me-down, but somehow that was the sexy part. Nan, who hadn't even wanted to go to the party and had thought she'd leave early, was surprised to find that she was already burning as she shook Marina's hand. Nan was on the hunt then, but without any particularly keen hunger. It was a rough hand, Nan noticed, which was strange on such a pretty, almost waifish woman. Marina also had a little smirking smile, the smile of a woman with a secret. Nan's senses awoke; she immediately wanted to know what the secret could be. "Oh, an artist," Nan had said, thinking: Just what this city needs. She was still burning the next day. The hills, on the way to the aquarium that day, were brown and flammable, too. It was hot September: fire season. Christopher, his chest neatly crisscrossed by the seat belt, studied the pages of *Undersea World* as if he hadn't already read them a hundred times before. Hot air blew in on him, reddening his cheeks. The car's air conditioning had long been defunct. He didn't seem to notice.

Nan took his hand in the ticket line. He danced at the end of her arm, happily mother-bound and dreamy, with his white, white skin, cloudy blue eyes, and a delicate clear drop of snot coming down from one nostril.

"Christopher," said Nan, "wipe your nose." He purposely wiped it on the sleeve of his jean jacket, which was identical to hers. "Oh, silly," said Nan indulgently, and he laughed his exhilarated little boy's laugh. She handed him a tissue.

Nan paid the admission fee. She had meant to save this expensive treat for his birthday, but today she was in love. Their lives were about to change. "Don't let go of my hand," she said. "It's very crowded."

Christopher nodded, already craning his small neck to peer into this simulated undersea world. "Where are the otters?" he asked intently.

"I don't know." Nan led him forward. The cool exhibition spaces were dark, the only light coming from the tanks. Myriad configurations of people swirled around them: a blond family of four in matching T-shirts from Disneyland; two Asian women, holding hands, and a teenage girl who was probably the daughter of the shorter one; four gay men with tattoos and little cameras; a straight black couple with a tiny baby all in blue, facing out in his Snugli from the man's chest; a loose group of deaf kids, their hands making faint slapping noises as they roamed from tank to tank; a middle-aged white man and woman obviously on a date, making conversation about the fish. Nan held Christopher's hand, feeling nervous: one small boy, so many strangers, yards of dark, carpeted corridor that would muffle the sound of his footsteps. In clumps or clutches of two and three, everyone crowded up to the glass, where the dim shapes of fish could be seen swimming slowly through the artificial deep.

"Isn't that one glamorous!" said the woman on the date.

How different these people were, Nan thought, from her own terror-spotted family. On a day like today, someone — probably her mother, that helpless beauty — would already be crying. Nan and her brothers would be communicating out of the sides of their eyes, with the hunch of their shoulders, the way they walked. Not that there was an aquarium in their Texas town; not that there was any wildlife to watch except dogs and their father. Nan knew it was irrational, but still, grown as she was, she always half expected him to rise up out of all shadows, to burst at her from around a corner.

Leaning against the wall outside Celestial Coffee, Nan wonders if she should have known then. There were dangers in the world, even here, where predators seemed to swim peacefully together in the same tank.

Instead, she said, "Look at the octopus!" She pointed to a huge, orange, many-limbed creature lolloping over a hunk of coral.

"No," said Christopher sternly. "That's a squid." He watched the squid, deep in its squid funk, for a long time. Only the squid's head moved in the current. The current moved around it, making the plants sway.

"Let's give someone else a turn," said Nan. She let Christopher lead. He was confident, as if he had been there before. Nan started to explain ecosystems to him, but he stopped her.

"I know that," he said with some impatience. They wandered upstairs and into a small atrium with a domed ceiling. Inside the dome, hundreds of silver anchovies swam around and around in circles, like a silver tornado. The light fell on Christopher and Nan's upturned faces. Christopher laughed. Nan smiled. The silver tornado was Marina whispering all around her. A silver tornado, but with small, rough hands, and an unearthly chemical scent. In the morning, Nan found that Marina had left a smear of lilac paint inside her elbow.

Sipping her coffee, Nan thinks, Was I distracted back then? Dreaming about lilac paint when I should have been noticing even smaller, more important signs?

But she didn't let go of his hand. She wouldn't have; she was always so careful. His was a little damp with excitement as he pulled her on, to see the turtles. No, she did let go of him for a second. He got as close as he could to the mammoth sea turtles lumbering through the deep. He spread his hands on the glass, staring, as did every other child there. They all ran to put their hands on the glass. A little girl in stretchy red shorts who smelled of candy bumped into Nan, eager to see what Christopher saw.

"Say excuse me to the man," said her mother. Nan turned around; the woman blushed. "Oh," said the woman. "Oh. Sorry." Nan looked at Christopher. In deep communion with the sea turtles, he didn't seem to have heard. Nan was sure, however, that he had heard; recently, he had a way of darting in and out of comprehension when it suited him. She kissed him on the ear, gently moving him to one side so the little girl could see.

"Are we gonna touch 'em?" asked the little girl, wistfully. Christopher shook his head.

He and Nan made their way to the sharks. "I wish I had a shark," Christopher told her as they watched the malevolent faces and unblinking eyes skim the other side of the glass.

"Do you think they're happy in an aquarium?" asked Nan.

He shrugged coolly. "They're okay, I think."

His nose was running again. Nan took out a tissue and wiped it.

"Where are the otters?" Christopher asked.

"Oh, right," said Nan. "Let's get some lunch first."

He nodded. "Don't forget."

When they reached the cafeteria, Nan must have released Christopher's hand again — so that was twice — as he sauntered in his little jean jacket down the hall and into the food line, picking up a plastic tray and setting it onto the metal runner in the practiced manner of a child who goes to public school. He extended his arms onto the tray and attempted to hang from it, picking up first one sneaker and then the other in a way that Nan should have reprimanded him for but didn't. She was letting him get away with everything today because she had fallen in love with a silver-haired woman and she could tell already that Christopher wasn't going to like it. He preferred the women who came and went like social studies units at school: anthropologically interesting but forgotten as soon as the test was over. It was not, Nan reflected, so different from what her own attitude had been until today. I'm sorry, Chris, Nan thought, joining him in line. Our lives are going to change.

She bought them both greasy fish sticks and listened as he identified all the fish on his paper placemat. Nan thought it was oddly cannibalistic to serve fish sticks in an aquarium, but Christopher was sanguine. The border between looking at the fish and eating them, between love and ingestion, seemed to be irrelevant to him. Why not have the creatures you love inside you as well as outside you? She looked at the fish on her own placemat, thinking that if someone made a paper placemat of her ex-girlfriends, they'd all be the same breed: *Femina aenigma*. Prone to migration, sleeplessness, and a compelling faraway expression. Marina, in bed, let her in. They were inside and outside together. Marina's rough hands were surprisingly strong.

"Bat ray," said Christopher loudly. The ocean tumbled outside the large cafeteria windows.

"You said that one."

"In seahorses," Christopher informed her, "the boys have the babies."

"Then if I were a seahorse, I guess I'd have to be a boy so I could have you," said Nan.

"They eat plants."

"I like plants."

"Every day? Three meals a day? Plant cake?"

"Sure. Like Sharon — she's a vegetarian."

"All right." Christopher nodded, satisfied, and set his small milk carton into the center of his empty, greasy paper plate. Then he drew his eyebrows together, poised on the brink of a question.

Nan didn't feel like answering questions about Sharon today; Sharon was irrelevant now. But just then a man at the next table glanced out the window and said, "There are two sea otters."

Christopher jumped up and stood on his chair.

"Chris." She tugged the back of his pants.

"I don't see them!" He leaned, Nan tugged again, and he sat back down reluctantly.

Nan crumpled her napkin. "Let's go around, then we'll come back and see the otters."

They left the cafeteria and walked on, strolling beside the walls of sea life. Nan's feet were already getting tired. Christopher gazed soberly at each tank, as if he were a small scientist. The little girl in the stretchy red shorts was ahead of them, glancing at the tanks, then, excitedly, back at Christopher to see if he was watching her watch the fish, which he wasn't. The girl's mother, who had a sober face and slender arms, looked at Nan once, twice, in a quizzical way. Nan rested her hand on Christopher's shoulder; her palms were sweaty.

"What?" he said.

Nan didn't reply. She looked at Christopher, who was gazing into the kelp forest. Thick strands of two-story-high kelp breathed gently underwater. In the tank light, Christopher's face was perfect; he was an illuminated boy, a hologram. It occurred to Nan that maybe she loved him too much, maybe she had damaged him in some deep and subtle way by holding him so tightly in her heart. Maybe, she thought, she should have another one, to dilute her passion.

That was the only danger she saw that day: that she might love her son too much.

"Hey, I wanted to see the jellyfish," Nan said. "They're just across there."

Christopher looked unhappy.

"Then the otters. I promise." She held out her hand.

"They feed them at three," he mumbled grumpily, taking her hand.

In the jellyfish halls, backlit tanks contained both enormous and tiny jellyfish in incredible colors, neon pink and daffodil yellow and cerulean. Each tank was a moving painting. The transparent bonnet tops of the jellyfish undulated, gently turning inside out, then reinflating. To Nan, they were the discarded shifts of bare-breasted mermaids, slowly floating down from the surface, where the mermaids combed one another's long, wavy hair. Marina Sweeney, with her small, white feet, would be the mermaid who lost her comb, dropped her lyre, had a tangle in her hair. She would sit just a little bit apart from the other mermaids, lost in some thought of her own, chewing on her nails. Nan would wait behind the next rock, watching. After Marina left in the morning, Nan had found a barrette in the bed. It was a kind of shimmery opal color that had almost disappeared in Marina's silver hair. So now Marina had a reason to call: *I left a barrette . . .* Nan had closed the barrette and set it on the bedside table, next to the phone. Surrounded by jellyfish, she let go of Christopher's hand then, too, she thinks — that was three — to reach out and touch the glass where the mermaids' dresses drifted down.

A few feet away, Christopher stood in front of a large tank where a vast constellation of little greenish jellyfish swam. He squinched up his eyes in the dark, tilting himself left, then right, as if he were an upside-down pendulum. Nan knew that he was making the jellyfish into crazy visual streaks. He had just started loving to draw that spring. Nan thought she might tell Marina that later. She wondered if Marina had noticed yet that she'd lost her barrette.

By the time Nan and Christopher left the jellyfish halls, they had missed the otter feeding. Christopher's head drooped. The interior otter pool was empty, the crowd dispersed. Nan felt frantic and annoyed, then had an inspiration. "Hey," she said, "I think they go outside, too." Christopher brightened. They went through a door, ascended a wide wooden staircase to a deck overlooking the otter pool. The Pacific Ocean crashed and spit on the rocks. The wind was sharp.

"Do you smell the salt?" said Nan.

He stuck out his tongue. "I taste it. Where are the otters?"

They went to the edge of the deck and stood by the railing. Nan read the otter information plaque aloud to him, but he wasn't listening. He was scouting. The otters weren't confined to the pool; they swam from the sea to the pool and away again, as they wished. The surf was very rough and it sprayed lightly at Nan's face; it was cool on the deck despite the sun. Nan turned Christopher's collar up. "I don't know, Chris," she said. "The otters might be sleeping."

"No," he insisted. "They're coming." He seemed tense, and Nan worried that she had gotten his hopes up only to dash them again. She shouldn't have stayed so long in the mesmerizing jellyfish hall. Now they might be in for a late-afternoon mood tailspin. She put on her sunglasses, rested her forearms on the upper rail, and perfunctorily watched the horizon, thinking: Five minutes, and then we're starting for the car. He gripped the lower rail, frowning.

Nan silently cursed the lazy otters, cursed the expensive aquarium for its impeccable environmental sense that let the otters appear and disappear like movie stars. If you're going to have kids here, she thought, put the fucking otters in a pen and shut the gate. "Hey, Chris," she said, "let's go get ice cream sandwiches —"

"No," he said in the burdened tone that she and Hal called *cranking*. Nan put her arm around his small, tense, denim-covered body. One of his shoulders still fit in her palm. The salty wind toyed with his fair hair.

Mercifully, miraculously, not just one, but a cluster of sleek, wet otter heads appeared in the surf. "Look!" said Nan, but Christopher had already spotted them and was jumping up and down in place. He waved his arms frantically as the otters tumbled toward them. As they got closer, Nan could make out their opaque black eyes, their strangely human fists, curled on their furry chests. They looked to Nan like fairies, advancing through the waves — she'd always thought fairies would be half-animal, half-elf, not those flossy Tinkerbell things. A real fairy would have paws.

Christopher was entranced; Nan held onto the back of his jacket as he hopped around in his red Nike sneakers. "Hey!" he yelled to the otters in his reedy voice. "Hey, look! Over here!"

Nan knew that the otters hadn't really looked; the subtle movement among them, the slight turning, must have been the current. One fat otter picked up his head, as if listening, then dove underwater. Christopher leaned over the lower rail, watching the otter go. Nan kept hold of his jacket, but every muscle in his body was straining away from her.

A cloud crossed in front of the sun. The ocean turned gray. Nan looked ahead as far as she could, to where the water disappeared into the sky. She thought, then, He will be a sailor and sail away from me one day.

Now she wonders what the otters knew that she didn't, and if they came because she let go of his hand three times. It couldn't have been more than three.

Christopher crouches below an underpass, waiting for the rain to stop. The highway is wide, dirty, and loud. The blue crayon is broken, but there's still enough of it to fill in a good bit of the inland sea.

Nan is late for work, but Peta sits faithfully, if somewhat arrogantly, at the counter, pert and smart and green-haired. "Hal called," says Peta.

"Okay. Did those returns go back?"

"Of course." Peta regards Nan compassionately through her young, heavy-lidded eyes. "I've got it covered."

Nan ignores this last comment and goes into her office in the back, hangs up her coat, turns on the computer. LET GO. BREATHE. KNOW THAT YOU ARE LOVED, says the screen saver — not her idea; it was left on there by the petty, pretty woman she once hired to do inventory who was going through a grueling divorce and "borrowed" a raft of self-help books that she never returned. The sentiment is punctuated by a spinning globe, as if God set it there. Nan hates the platitudinous screen saver but hasn't bothered to change it, though it seems particularly ridiculous situated among so much businesslike stuff: books and catalogues and faxes, dust jackets mounted on cardboard for window displays, stacks of *Publishers Weekly*, menus from local take-out places, memos from distributors. Pictures of Marina, Christopher, Hal. A generic green metal trash can into which she tosses her empty coffee cup.

It all adds up to a middle-aged, middle-manager stability that Nan, even after so many years, finds shocking. She was the traveler, the seeker, the runaway brother. When she dropped out of high school, she found the whole long, incredible road right there to meet her. It was a revelation to discover that it didn't end in Texas: it only started there. One day she followed it and a skinny woman to San Francisco. The skinny woman left her, but she had a friend who worked at Western Books, and the skinny woman had left the friend once, too. Nan and the friend used to break up empty book boxes in the back alley and talk about that skinny woman, how fucked-up she was, how impossible. And what *was* it with her, anyway? What was her problem?

Whenever Nan walked into the store, the books stacked in the dim interior light all looked like sleeping dogs to her, some brown, some red, some spotted. It was as if she worked in a pound. She picked up these stray volumes the way she would have petted a lonely dog. She hoped that in the end, with a little random affection from a stranger, they'd go to good homes and not get pulped. The atlases were the ones she brought home. Their shadowy mountain ranges and rivers made good company. Her favorites were color-coded by elevation: green and blue along the ragged coastlines shading to yellow, then brown, in the center. There were so many places she could be: Bandar 'Abbās, Córdoba, Bucharest, Nairobi. From Nairobi, you could take the boat to places even farther away.

But she didn't go to any of them. When the skinny woman's friend went back to the skinny woman, the friend did the gentlemanly thing and left Western Books. She shook Nan's hand apologetically, though also victoriously. Nan stayed on. She liked San Francisco. She rented a cheap house in the Mission with a backyard and a semi-demolished shrine containing a rusted Virgin Mary. She moved the Virgin Mary into the bathroom and hung towels on her outstretched arms. She took the ruined shrine apart, brick by brick. The bricks were perfectly good; she thought she'd make something with them sometime. On the afternoon that she carried the last brick over to the stack by the backyard steps, she could see that where the shrine had been there was now a sad bald spot. She stood in the bald spot, looking at the beetles running back and forth, kicking at the earth with the toe of her boot, and thinking about Texas. She still had some cool friends there; she missed Texas, sometimes. A beetle ran over her boot. She turned her head, watching the beetle go. The yard of the rented house was a simple rectangle, overgrown in some parts, scrubby in others. The fence was shot to hell and pockmarked in places as if it had, literally, been shot at. There was a gap in one part of the fence where a few boards were missing. Through the gap, Nan could see the yard of the neighboring house, a plain wooden chair sitting empty in the grass. Sometimes her neighbor, a longhaired guy, sat in the chair to sunbathe. He always seemed peaceful, his face turned up to the sun. Nan was pretty sure he was a fag. Everyone in San Francisco seemed to be a fag, though, including the straight people. She had gotten much more faggy herself, she thought, in the last few months.

Just then, though, the fag wasn't there. The chair was empty and sunless. Nan stood in the bald spot where the Virgin Mary had been and contemplated the overgrown, scrubby, shot-to-hell yard that wasn't hers. Her cat, Hash, prowled through the grass. Nan looked at Hash, who had been, up to this point, the sum total of anything like a family of her own, and who was beginning to go deaf. She picked him up and scratched under his chin until he purred. He was heavy and soft. His small animal heart beat in her hands. She was twenty-five, with no particular lover and no particular plans, or lots of lovers and lots of plans, depending on how you looked at it: she liked to think of herself as a liberated person. But just then the word *hydrangea* flew into her mind, from that time she worked in the nursery. She saw exactly where the hydrangea would go, in the far right back corner, and she saw it thriving. She saw a little tree, and tomato plants, and pansies. And she saw something else, too: her boy, playing there, and what his name was. She'd only been waiting for the right garden; now, here it was, right on time. Suddenly she didn't mind about the skinny woman anymore. The skinny woman was kind of like a car accident that tossed you onto the very road you were meant to take. Hash struggled out of her arms and began trilling with evil intent at a bird sitting on the fence. Nan contemplated the yard with pride. She had Hash for a long time after that, even though you weren't supposed to have cats with newborns, but Hash was so old by then he hardly seemed like a cat at all.

LET GO. BREATHE. KNOW THAT YOU ARE LOVED. Nan stares into space awhile. She should call Hal. Outside her office are the pings and clinks of commerce, and she knows she should be grateful for them, considering that she manages the Celestial Coffee of bookstores. She knows that she is privileged, in a poorly paid sort of way. Independence has a rare beauty; she's living in the last bit of a teak forest. On her computer the image of the little globe spins through space at a rapid speed: night and day would pass in very quick succession there. Where Nan is, it's just day, in its incredibly slow revolution.

Christopher, rigid in his chair in the soft-voiced therapist's of-

fice with the oil painting of ice skaters above the couch, had refused to speak above a whisper. He kept looking at the walls. His
hair was bright and unruly, and he smelled. When Nan woke up
the next morning, he was gone. The sketches tacked on his walls
— a bridge, a speeding car, his friend Tamara — fluttered in the
breeze from his open window, though he had, of course, simply
walked out the front door. His bed was made. Even before the police agreed, Nan knew, dismally, that no one had snatched him: he
was just gone. The only nonordinary element in the room, besides
his absence, was the carving knife plunged into the middle of the
floor and the wood's white flesh churned up from the otherwise
honey-colored surface. It is the knife, even more than Christopher's being gone, that keeps Nan up at night.

Nan, feeling electrocuted by caffeine without being exactly awake,
calls Hal. "Hey. It's me."

"Hey," says Hal. "Did you sleep?"

"No. You?"

"I took something. Let me give you a few."

"I can't. What if he calls?"

"You have to sleep, Nan."

"Later. Later." Nan rubs her eyes, puts on her reading glasses.

"I think we should hire a detective."

Nan sighs. "I don't know."

"It's been eight days. This country is full of missing kids and
they *never* find them. That cop already told us how little they can
really do."

LET GO. BREATHE, says Nan's computer. Nan turns the moni-
tor away from her.

Hal says, with some exasperation, "Why would you even
hesitate?"

"I don't want to scare him," says Nan, and she hears herself
mumble the words and knows how ridiculous they sound. "He'll
call." She wonders if she believes this.

"Nan."

"Hal, if he looks up from wherever he is and sees someone following him — come on. You know how he is." The coffee has

made the inside of her mouth taste bitter and raw. Her hair feels dirty, as if it, too, has been soaked in coffee. Her eyes are burning.

"I don't know anything anymore," says Hal. "I'm in hell."

Nan realizes that she is clenching her fists again, one in her lap and one gripping the phone. She makes an effort to unclench them. She is as exasperated with Hal as he is with her. She feels rushed, and that she doesn't have the time to explain to him what she knows, even though she doesn't know anything — that Christopher will call, that a private detective would be exactly the wrong thing to do at exactly the wrong moment. Nor can she draw Hal up from the bottom of his well. She has the dark sense that they are each on their own now, but she doesn't say so to Hal. He has been, after all, an exemplary father to Christopher, so much more than what she had ever imagined. And she loves him. She has come to love him, even to rely on him. She doesn't have the heart, or the time, to say *I'm sorry that you're not enough*, though this is how she feels.

"How are the fish?" asks Nan.

"Depressed," says Hal. "I think they know he's not there. Oh, and listen, you have to get me the figures for this year so far . . ." He pauses. "Nan. Do you . . ." He pauses again. It's quiet on his end of the line, the quiet of an office filled with the history of other people's money. It always makes Nan uneasy, that quiet, though she's also impressed by Hal's ease with it. Money is like another language he speaks.

"I think if something had happened, I would know," she says.

Hal sighs.

Before they hang up, they agree to give the police three more days.

Hal says, "Nannie, you've got to sleep. I'm sending Donna over with some of these pills."

Nan works her day the way a soldier ordered to dig a ditch would dig a ditch. Books come in and go out. Peta brings her a doughy wrap filled with hummus and vegetables, and Nan eats it the way a soldier would eat: for fuel only. She drinks another cup of coffee, a small one this time, and tosses the plain cup into the trash along with the other one. In the afternoon, she breaks up a heap of book boxes herself, in the back alley, though it's Peta's job now, not hers. She busts them open, flattens them, and when she sweats, the sweat smells of coffee and fear and exhaustion. She pulls off her cotton sweater; the T-shirt underneath is the same one she's been wearing for days. Her jeans are filthy. Stuffed into one pocket is the little clutch of sleeping pills that Hal sent over to her in a business envelope, embossed with HAL COOPER, C.P.A. on the flap. The letters are mauve and curly, as if accounting was Hal's fancy and not his bread and butter. Nan leans against the alley wall, breathing hard. The pills in her pocket feel good, though also like a lie. Nan reflects that she and Hal have each comforted the other with a lie today, and that both knew exactly what kind of lie to tell. She supposes that's intimacy, in its way.

Nan goes back into the store and gets her things from the office. "Peta," she says as she leaves, "you close up today, all right? There are some boxes out back to be tied."

As Nan drives home in her rattling car, she is unexpectedly pierced by the beauty of the fat, bewitched city. She goes over a hill, and the bay suddenly appears, framed by the graceful tumble of low white buildings on either side, gilded by an unexpected bolt of afternoon sun. The bay is like a mirror reflecting a child's drawing of heaven: solid blue and radiant. Nan imagines that the bay is a woman in a radiant blue dress, waiting to embrace her. She drives over hill after hill, trying to get closer.

Tamara is sitting on the front steps when Nan gets home. She's a tall girl with green eyes and straight brown hair and slender, arching eyebrows, slightly overplucked; she has the habitual look of skepticism on her face and at least one silver ring on every finger. She stands up in jeans that are long and wide at the bottom, as Nan gets out of the car. "Hey," she says.

"Hey," says Nan dully, closing the car door. "There's no news, Tam."

"Yeah, okay. I thought I'd hang with you a little bit. Help you with . . . stuff." She smiles tentatively.

Nan makes an effort. "Help me out back, then," she says, "since we have a little sun." Tamara follows her through the silent house, where Nan tosses her jacket onto a kitchen chair, and out to the garden. Tamara is taller than Nan, which gives Nan the impression that she is being followed by a flying milkweed. Nan squints, concentrating. Tamara sits down on the back steps. Birds twitter.

"We can stake the hydrangea," says Nan. She goes around to the side of the house and gets three long, thin pieces of wood, a hammer, scissors, twine, and a pair of gardening gloves for Tamara.

"I don't need those," says Tamara when Nan comes back. "My hands are really tough from volleyball." She holds up her hands, circled and double-circled in silver. A phone number is written on one palm in green ink. "You can have them."

Nan knows that Tamara is deferring to her advanced age, but she puts on the gloves anyway. They're yellow, frayed, and soft inside. Nan hands Tamara the hammer. "Okay, then I'm going to hold the stakes, and you hammer. Then we'll tie them up." Tamara nods politely.

They walk over to the hydrangea, which is large and sprouting exuberant purple flowers at every juncture. Branches of it are lying on the grass, full of purple blooms. "Fuckin' alien," says Tamara in an admiring tone, swinging the hammer lightly back and forth.

Nan can feel the sweat of the day on her skin; her hands inside the gloves feel grimy and grateful for the interior softness; her eyes still burn. Her cotton sweater smells. But, determined, she walks into the hydrangea with the stakes, struggling to right the springy branches that want nothing more than to recline in disordered splendor. The branches resist her. Purple flowers fall into her hair. Marina, she thinks, should be home soon. New sweat coats the old sweat, foul but reassuring. When she's in motion, the time seems to go faster.

Tamara, standing on the grass, rests the side of the hammer on her head. "I miss him," she says.

Nan, wrestling with the wayward hydrangea, doesn't reply, but Tamara continues, putting the hammer under her arm and picking aqua nail polish off one fingernail. "He was my first real boyfriend. He was, like, not a jerk. Did you ever read *The Second Sex*?"

"What?" asks Nan. A branch pokes into her sweater, then tangles in the cotton. Nan labors to untangle it.

"*The Second Sex*. The book. Did you read it?"

"Yes," says Nan, still working at the tangle of cotton and branch.

"Well, what did you think?"

"It was very important. It changed a lot about the way people thought about women." Nan sneezes.

"Yeah. Have you ever been to England?"

"Yes."

"Chris and I really wanted to go to England. I would have gone with him, and I can't say that about very many people. To go all the way to England with them. You know?"

Feeling old, Nan barely gets the branch out of the sweater. She takes the sweater off and throws it into the yard, then pushes the first stake into approximately the right place. The true right place is several inches over, but that spot is so dense with branches that nothing can be introduced into it. "Okay, come on," says Nan to Tamara, and the girl expertly knocks in the stake with three efficient blows of the hammer.

"Here, I'll do the twine part," says Tamara. She puts the hammer in her back pocket, pulls off a skein of twine with her ringed fingers, wraps the branch to the stake, and ties the twine in a bow. "Next."

Nan places the second stake. "What does *The Second Sex* have to do with you and Chris?" she says.

Tamara quickly whaps the stake with the hammer. "Nothing. I just wanted to know if you'd read it. I was making conversation. There."

Nan hands her the twine, holding back the branches with her body. Tamara leans forward, trussing the stake to the plant. Apparently she knows exactly what to do. Her straight brown hair flares out slightly at the ends. "I think I didn't tell you one thing," she says into the leaves.

Nan is suddenly tense.

Tamara ties another twine bow. "It was sooner than I said."

"What do you mean?" says Nan quietly. She places the third stake; this one fits exactly where it should. She can feel the coolness of the sun going down.

"The first time he seemed weird. It wasn't last month or whenever you guys got upset. It was before that — last spring." She taps the stake.

"Last spring?"

"It would be, like, if we went into a diner or bowling and there were people there, he'd say that he could tell they didn't like him. That they didn't like his face. I told him he was being paranoid." Tamara turns to peer at Nan through the hydrangea branches, and Nan sees that her green eyes, which are nearly the color of the leaves, are very steady, slightly defiant. She senses that Tamara hesitated before deciding to come over today. She sees Tamara staring out the window during a class at school, maybe calculus, trying to decide whether to tell Nan, whether Nan could handle it.

"Tamara. This is serious. What are you talking about?" Nan tries to stand up straight, but the hydrangea holds her fast.

"Hey," says the girl sternly, tying up the last stake, "I didn't even have to tell you, you know, and at the time it just seemed *goofy*, not like a big deal. If you thought about it yourself, you might remember some things, too. You're his mother. You see him all the time." Tamara steps outside the hydrangea and, red-faced, gathers up the scissors and twine. Hammer bobbing in her back pocket, she makes her way across the yard and puts the things away. Nan ducks awkwardly from under a branch and walks slowly toward the house. What had happened last spring? What had distracted her? Marina had a show up, so she had other things on her mind.

It was unseasonably hot. In Christopher's school picture, his eyes were closed and he needed a haircut.

"What else?" says Nan.

Tamara pauses at the top of the back steps, biting her lip. She shrugs.

"Tell me."

"Well, you know how guys are. They like to freak you out." She looks at Nan. "Trust me, they do. It wasn't what he said so much. It was more, kind of, his aura."

Nan breathes in, then out, before she ventures, "His aura?"

"Not his *aura*, not like with the colors. I'm not sure how to explain it. He was really jumpy. Did he tell you he failed English?"

"He didn't fail. I saw his report card."

Tamara looks pained. "Yeah. That's the thing. I helped him — sort of, make a new one. But that was the only class, the rest of it was good, and he didn't want you to be upset. So we fixed it."

"What?"

"On the computer. It's not that hard. I'm really sorry. It was the aura thing that was the weird part. Do you know what I mean?" Tamara gazes helplessly at Nan. She is at least a head taller than Nan; the step makes her a young giant. She clasps her hands in front of her in a childlike way, waiting.

Nan tries, and fails, to understand what the girl means. His aura? How could he have failed English? He always sailed through English. She sees that Tamara is waiting, guiltily, to be released. "It's okay, Tamara," Nan says. "It's not your fault. I'm glad you told me." Tamara smiles a relieved smile and clatters into the house and away.

Nan watches her go, hears the front door open and close. She retrieves her sweater from near the moderately upright hydrangea, then sits down on the top step. She doesn't put the sweater back on. She feels as if she has been sent a riddle she can't figure out: knife, aura, a failing grade erased. She wants to believe that this is adolescent churning, testing, but something about it bothers her. This business of auras. And how could Tamara have noticed some change in Christopher that she didn't? Tamara and Christopher were generally offhand with each other, simultaneously complicit and shy. Only once did Nan ever surprise them making out, their two sets of long legs tangled on the sofa. They liked to share packages of red Twizzlers while they watched *Stargate*. Nan sometimes heard the low buzz of Christopher talking to Tamara on the phone in his room at night. Talking and talking. For years.

Nan watches the light drain from the garden as the sun sets, watches the grass grow dark, watches the leaves on the trees grow dark, watches the flowers and the vegetables shrink and grow dark. Is Marina on her way home, or did she stop off at the house of the stupid girl Nan is sure she's sleeping with? That had started last spring, too. Then it had seemed okay, barely, but now — Nan isn't even sure where *now* is, though it's all now, everything is now, there is no past or future. The fence's hard silver dissolves; the twinkling sounds arise of her perfectly nice neighbors barbecuing something for dinner, and eating it. Her empty hands clench. She forces herself to unclench them.

Marina pulls Nan's wretched T-shirt up and off of her, helps Nan step out of the grimy jeans, takes off Nan's sneakers and socks. Little bits of sticks and dirt litter the bathroom floor. Marina helps Nan into the tub and when Nan is immersed to the shoulders, Marina slowly runs the soap over her, underwater. Nan closes her eyes. The tub water, under the soap bubbles, goes gray. Marina washes Nan's hands, moving the soap around each finger as if tracing it. She washes Nan's face with a washcloth and then, with the help of a plastic pitcher, she washes Nan's hair. The water from the pitcher runs over Nan's face. Nan begins to cry and she cries for a while as Marina holds her, plunging her arms up to the elbows in the water. Marina's blue shirtsleeves grow wet and cling to her. She presses her cheek against Nan's wet, soapy back. Marina finds the pills from Hal in Nan's pants pocket, the envelope with the curvy mauve writing now dampened and creased, and after Nan gets out of the tub and into bed she makes Nan take one. Just before she falls asleep, Nan notices how new the soap smells. Marina, turning a magazine page, smiles down at her.

Nan swims through heavy water. She flounders through caves, searching. Her arms are tired. Her legs are tired. Her ears fill with water. But she keeps swimming. Her mother and father are somewhere up above, and somewhere far below. She wants to embrace them, but their voices fade away as she swims. She sees her father reach out in rage for her mother, but both of them are drowning and so is she. Her hands fill with water. Jellyfish slip through her fingers.

She wakes up with her hands on Marina, one on the slope of her thigh, the other on her shoulder. The room is gray with first light. She sees that it is exactly eight hours since she took the pill. Their bed is a plateau on a rock face she's been clinging to all night; Nan's muscles feel pummeled. There's a chemical cloud in her head. Marina's scent is like food, and Nan buries her face in it. She puts her hand between Marina's legs and cups the curls and flesh of her. Then she rolls over and lies on her back, already exhausted by thinking. More than anything else, she needs to understand the knife. In the same way that it had lodged in Christopher's bedroom floor, it lodges in her mind. The failing grade, the sullenness: they make up a more or less coherent set. But she still can't think of any explanation for the knife. It was a kitchen knife: ordinary, completely uncharmed, with a dullish blade and a black handle. Looking at it stuck in the floor, she had the faintly ridiculous thought that she didn't know how to fix a knife hole. She wondered if wood putty would do it. She pulled the knife out of the wood, washed it, and put it away. Hal, when he arrived, was upset that she hadn't left it in the floor. And it was a clue, certainly, but not like that. The hole in the floor is still there.

What could the knife in the floor mean? The chemical cloud drifts to the left, to the right. Excalibur — but her sword or his? A warning. A message. Something for her to defend herself with, but against what? Some message about the floorboards? Or maybe it was love. Maybe Christopher fell in love with a knife, and his leaving it behind meant that he understood how dangerous a love it was. Maybe Christopher left to get away from the knife, and all of it — the things he said to Tamara, his strange glances and moods — circled around the point of that blade tip. She knows that doesn't make any sense. None of it makes any sense; her dread feels larger, more animal, than any of the facts. Nan gets out of bed, pulls on a fresh pair of jeans and a sweatshirt, and makes her way downstairs, barefoot.

The linoleum is cold. The kitchen is placid and shadowy, not seeming at all like an armory. Marina's keys and checkbook, a pair of her studio scissors, are scattered across the kitchen counter. Nan looks at the clock. Her brothers Henry and Robert — both lawyers, one in Boston and the other in Atlanta — will be kissing their wives goodbye for the day. The sun has risen where they are. The microwaves are dinging, the dogs whining and barking, the children laughing or fighting or already gone to school. Though Henry is an environmental lawyer and Robert a corporate one, they lead identical lives. But it's Jonathan — the one who, as a child, spent the most time suddenly naked and laughing, the one who later did the most drugs, the one whom their father always beat first and hardest — whom Nan wants to call. He lives in Los Angeles in a house full of guitars: vintage guitars, novelty guitars made out of bamboo or covered in red leather, electric guitars, acoustic guitars that speak with incredible antique sweetness. Jonathan slinks around L.A. like a cat, often working in studios until very late at night. He's a watery, secretive sort of person.

He answers the phone with his soft voice. "Yeah." He's never lost his Texas accent, though Nan sometimes wonders if it's one of his affectations. The Texan in L.A.: women love that.

"It's Nan."

"Nan? It's five in the morning."

"I know." As the chemical cloud drifts away in the cold San Francisco morning, she realizes that her right shoulder hurts from holding up the hydrangea. She rubs it. Her hands hurt, too. There's a splinter in her thumb, the flesh around it already reddening.

"Hello?"

"Jonathan, something's wrong with Christopher. Something's wrong, and he's taken off."

Nan can hear the small sound of Jonathan shifting in the sheets. He probably went to bed an hour ago. Jonathan's voice remains soft. "He's run away?"

"I don't even know if you can call it that. He had, I don't know, a freak-out, we think. He wouldn't wash, he was angry all the time, he was saying all sorts of strange stuff, and he just, he just wasn't Christopher. We took him to a shrink, which he hated. And. He disappeared the next day. Maybe that was the wrong thing to do. Taking him to a shrink." Nan stops talking. The Texas is sneaking back into her voice, too, the way it does with family. Jonathan is quiet on his end of the line, and she's extremely grateful that he doesn't ask her if she's told Henry or Robert. Holding the phone against her aching shoulder, she gets the coffee out of the freezer and ladles it into the coffeemaker. The fresh filter is bright white.

"You called the cops."

"Of course. But —"

"They're cops."

"Right." Upstairs, she thinks, Marina is still sleeping, warm flesh surrounded by pillows. Her silver hair is dim in the dimness, like a mirror in a dark hallway.

"Nannie. Jesus Christ."

"And there's something else." She tells him about the knife in the floor.

"People carry knives because they're afraid. You used to carry around that old busted jackknife, remember? But if he's afraid —" He pauses. "Why did he leave it behind?"

"I don't know," says Nan. The scent of brewing coffee rises. Already, the kitchen seems to be warming with the day's beginning.

"You ran away from home, too," he says. "Remember how you felt. Follow that."

They hang up. Nan sits at the kitchen table and drinks the coffee, glad of its bitter, sharp, unsugared edge. This is how a knife feels, she thinks, but she knows it doesn't: real knives really cut. When she ran, it was because a dark shape was chasing her. But nothing had ever chased Christopher, she'd made sure of that. If only she knew what he was defending himself against with that knife, she would run it to ground.

Hal taps on the glass of the saltwater tank. "José," he says. "José, José." The bamboo cat shark continues to recline, its ugly inverted mug resolutely shut. Hal taps in morsels of frozen squid, which float down through the water and come to rest on the pink and blue gravel. One lands on the shark's nose. Hal sighs, straightening up. On top of everything else, he thinks that the shark has an eating disorder because it eats only, apparently, when no one is looking. He won't touch the squid as they descend right past his nose, or whatever part of him that is, but by nighttime the squid are always gone. Are the other fish getting fatter? The shark is still alive, still alert, if sullen. As Hal turns away, he sees the miniature shark dig at the gravel, but the second he turns back the shark is motionless again. Hal wonders if the thing thinks that he, Hal, is some kind of bizarre predator: a balding fish on the other side of the glass, dribbling squid from its skinny fins as bait.

Hal picks up his keys and his black leather backpack and leaves the house. It's foggy, but he decides to walk to the police station for the air. The shark's name isn't really José — Christopher didn't name his fish. It's just Hal's private name for him, the name of someone he performed with in the Flytrap long ago. José, a.k.a. Not-So-Shrinking Violet, was sullen, too, and a picky eater. Hal, a.k.a. Orchidia Candelabrum, the Little Flaxen Waxen Flower of the Night, loved José, though they fought often, especially when the Flytrap was on the road.

As the last living member of the semifamous, cult, performance/glam rock band, the Venus Flytrap, Hal feels an obligation to memorialize the others in ways large and small: Not-So-Shrinking Violet, Giganda Lupinia, Rosa Rosa Rosa. And Adam, the first man, who wasn't in the Flytrap but brought it into being with his tremendous centrifugal force. Around Adam, grown men discovered that they had always wanted to be flowers, bellowing in leather lederhosen. Adam made the people he loved part of the glorious novel of his life, a novel that everyone he met longed to be in. When Hal thinks of that flare in his own life, he tends not to remember the somewhat hysterical performances so much as Adam, sprawled on Hal's bed in that tiny apartment in North Beach, legs spread. That's his image of 1979. And there was Hal, twenty-three, usually with mascara still running down his face from that night's show, fucking Adam hard in the skill-less Idaho way Adam claimed to like. Hal thought that meant that he had conquered Adam somehow, that he knew all about him. Afterward, Adam would sometimes read to Hal from his bad, actual novel in perpetual progress, *War* (he was a night writer, a night reader), and Hal would pretend to listen as he fell asleep.

Sometimes, such as now, Hal wonders if he is still a figure in Adam's life-novel, walking on past where the pages ran out. Despite the accounting business (dear God, just like his own balding, skinny-finned father back in Idaho), the jewel-like little yellow house, the lovers who have come and gone, despite Christopher and his own creased face in the mirror, Hal often seems to himself to have an unfinished quality, like a cartoon character who wasn't quite finished being drawn before escaping into the world. He wonders if that's the Idaho in him, the Boy Scout, the nervous high school basketball player, always being beaten to the tap: a man who needs to know that someone is watching. He thinks, really, that that desire to be watched is the faggiest thing about him.

As Hal walks along, he tries to imagine how Adam would have seen all this. If Christopher were Adam's son. Adam and Nan's, say, which would have made more sense because Adam lived next door to her, and they were so close, Brother Moon and Sister Sun. When he first met her, Hal thought Nan was like a cowpuncher who had just ridden into town. She had a dusty look, a gravelly voice, and a strangely — for her — delicate way of smoking, holding the cigarette in an elaborately effeminate manner that suggested she either didn't smoke that often or didn't really like it that much. She didn't seem to notice at all that she was short; she waved her arms around as if she were ten feet tall. She'd seen things, or so she said. The drifter, the Texan: Hal half expected her to spit tobacco instead of smoking it. He couldn't parse that bookstore she worked in at all because she certainly didn't seem like a bookish girl. She and Adam wore the same kind of thick leather cowboy boots, but they looked campy on him, dramatic Adam, with his crooked nose and head of long, sunflowerlike brown curls. On her, they looked like the real thing.

Hal was afraid of her, basically. He was afraid of both of them, the way they didn't want to be anything in particular, just to be in the moment. Adam worked as a drug counselor. Nan worked in a bookstore. But that had nothing to do with who they were: they were Adam and Nan, in boots. Everyone knew them. With Adam, Hal wanted to fuck his way to the secret. With Nan, he was sometimes sullen. He looked away when she was talking. He stood on the upwind side of her cigarette.

But then Adam died, and Nan marched through the gap in the fence as he was standing in Adam's ill-tended scrap of yard one afternoon, thinking, Now it's really over, and she had a determined look. She was direct. He could understand just how she felt: please let the novel continue. Who would they be as characters otherwise? He was tired and sad, too. He followed her back through the gap to her house, then jacked off into a plastic 7-Eleven cup in her bathroom, which was ornamented with that spooky rusted Virgin Mary heaped with odd-lot towels. When he got back to the bedroom, she had already pillowed up her hips, though she had summoned enough modesty to cover herself, badly, with a hand towel. She handed him a fat, needleless syringe — was it even clean? — saying, "It'll work better if you do it."

Hal, holding the syringe, looked at Nan. He hadn't anticipated this part, which woke him from his reverie: this was real, not an extravagant gesture. She wasn't kidding. She was going to be a mother? Her bedroom didn't even have anything in it except the bed, a chair, and a pair of jeans lying on the floor. The soles of her feet were smudged. She seemed defiant to him somehow, resting there on the black bedspread; it occurred to him that this might not be about Adam at all. He wondered if, had there been some other man in Adam's yard at the right moment, the meter reader, say, whether the meter reader would have been standing there instead of him. That would be like her. Suddenly the whole thing seemed comic; Adam definitely would have thought it was funny and put it in his novel. Hal laughed. Nan smiled. "His name is going to be Christopher," she said.

What a nut, thought Hal. Then again, he had gotten on that bus from Idaho, he had donned the leather lederhosen, he sometimes referred to himself, privately, as La Tumescia. Why not him? He was just over the crest of thirty, and he felt, more than ever, that he was a man. His manhood and his orchidity twined together in his mind, like a single strong root. He couldn't say which — the man or the orchid — was stronger in him as he poured the contents of the plastic cup in the syringe, holding his finger over the open end, and went toward Nan, lifting the hand towel.

It didn't seem in any way inevitable at the time; it seemed as accidental (at the time they would have said *improvisational* and been proud of it) as any man and woman falling into bed together. Anything could still happen back then. He didn't think she'd get pregnant at all, though at the same time, if she'd given birth to an antelope, he wouldn't have been much surprised. Also, compared to Adam, Hal was so secondary in the plot. How could Nan get pregnant on the first try from a minor character?

But she did, and it was Hal, and it's continued to be Hal, much to his surprise. When Christopher was a year old, Hal pasted glow-in-the-dark stars on the ceiling of Christopher's room in the Noe Valley house; when Christopher was ten, he installed the very expensive saltwater tank in Christopher's room; when Christopher was fifteen, he bought that neurotic shark with its cold green eye. It was Hal, the last living member of the Venus Flytrap, pulling off his garish yellow pigtailed wig sometime in the early eighties to realize that his hairline had receded nearly to where his father's had been the day Hal left home, and to wonder what people did for a living. (He tried, unsuccessfully, to wait tables.) It was Hal, holding the weight of Christopher in his arms, holding his hand to cross the street, then holding his hat, his scarf, his gloves, and saying, You have to put these on, it's getting cold. While Christopher, nine, darted around the darkening beach, his pockets clacking with treasure. Time to go home.

It was Hal in the rest of his life since Adam has been gone, and José, and Frank, and the rest, who, one by one, folded and died. Leaving Hal, a minor character, to bury them. To live. Hal wishes that that, at least, might have seemed inevitable, but it didn't. Luck isn't rational; neither, it seems, is bad luck. If Christopher had been Adam's son, this all might have made sense, because Adam was someone who summoned up the wild spirit of the universe. Adam and Nan were as thick as thieves. And Adam, Hal feels, would have understood what was happening now. He would have known what to do.

But Nan wasn't all that interested in the Flytrap. Hal didn't live in her backyard. They weren't as thick as thieves; they weren't thieves together at all. They were, in fact, scrupulously honorable with each other, fair about sharing time, fair about sharing work, about doctor's appointments and school plays. From the beginning, they had a rhythm. Nan, he discovered, might not be bookish, but she was straightforward: you need beans for protein, you need rice, bedtime should be pretty much inviolable. She'd bring Christopher over along with several large bags of groceries until she noticed that Hal's cabinets were filled with all the same things. They barely had to discuss the sugar issue. It made Hal laugh to find that, of course, two of Adam's closest friends were, in certain respects, more like one another than like Adam: how many sunflowers did one bouquet need? They've gathered warmth as they've gone along, he and Nan, slowly and steadily, rarely striking sparks. Some days, he still doesn't like her; he knows he irritates her, too. He thinks she's rash. She thinks he's poky. But they are like two people who have found themselves the only ones at some unprecedented natural event, like an island emerging all at once or a river suddenly running backward. Turning to each other in the night, united not by passion but by fate, equally changed: *Did you see that?*

Hal walks up the steps of the police station feeling ungainly and lost. These days, he doesn't understand anything. He doesn't even understand what the shark's problem is, though his fingers stink of squid. Adam is gone. His son is missing. Absence, Hal has discovered, is grindingly mundane. All he can do is the sensible thing. He pulls open the heavy glass door and goes up to the desk, where a dark-eyed, uniformed young man with one earring sits.

"I'm here to see Officer Suarez," says Hal.

"All right," says the young man, pointing down a corridor to the left. "That way." The young man is handsome, but Hal can only silently guess how many years older than Christopher he might be. Christopher, he thinks, would never want to be a policeman, he's too sweet-tempered and creative. Hal has always imagined him in some marine biology station somewhere, wearing a wetsuit and writing things down on charts.

Officer Suarez stands up from his desk when he sees Hal, holds out his hand. Hal shakes it, and they both sit down. Officer Suarez is a lithe man with a mustache. His arms are short. He exudes the strained, deferential prowess of policemen, that practiced, faintly menacing politeness. Unlike Nan, Hal doesn't mind cops, though he wishes this one was, in fact, less polite. All that politeness feels like barely concealed indifference.

"Mr. Cooper," says Suarez, "I wish I had some solid news for you. You really didn't have to come in."

"It's been nine days," says Hal.

"I know." Suarez sighs. "Believe me, I know how many days it's been. This is the problem with kids. They don't necessarily have resources, but they're clever. They find these out-of-the-way spots to hide in, underpasses or tunnels. They start breaking into houses —"

"Christopher wouldn't do that," says Hal flatly.

"With all due respect, Mr. Cooper," says Suarez, folding his short arms across his chest, "I don't think you know what Christopher would do, under these circumstances."

A silence falls between them. Hal looks away, toward the California state flag on the wall. The upper right-hand corner, unsecured, is sagging, revealing the greenish cinderblock behind.

Suarez says, "The good news, relatively speaking, is that he hasn't turned up in any hospitals or morgues." Suarez clearly expects Hal to bear the word *morgues,* and Hal does, holding Suarez's gaze steadily. "I know that may not sound like good news to you, but from a police standpoint it is, because it means that in all likelihood he's out there somewhere. And since you all say that there was no argument between yourselves and him, my guess is that he'll call when he gets hungry enough."

Hal knows that Suarez is sort of trying, in his way, to be reassuring. He knows that the term *yourselves* is generous, because Suarez, who wears a wedding band and told Hal he's from Fresno, can manage only to nod in the direction of the odd tangle of their lives. But he is, at least, managing that nod. In addition, there is the cold and unregenerate fact that Suarez does not know where Christopher is.

Hal hunches forward. "But he could be lying by the side of the road somewhere, he could be hurt."

"True," says Suarez. "The thing is, though, that hurt people have a way of turning up, because they're sitting in one spot. It's the people who are on the move who are hard to find. My gut says that your son is on the move."

"We've been thinking of hiring a detective," says Hal.

"Sure. Why not?" The policeman casually opens his hands, closes them again, a gesture that makes Hal quite sure that Officer Suarez doesn't have much hope for another runaway kid.

Hal picks Nan up at the bookstore, and they go down the block to a storefront sandwich place. They sit by the window, where an orange cat dozes on the wide sill. Nan is two years younger than Hal, but her determined manner always makes him feel that she is the older one. Or maybe it's motherhood, though she doesn't look like the mothers from either of their childhoods. She orders a meatball sandwich — she never cares what she eats — and he orders a salad.

"So," she says.

"Suarez thinks he's probably still, you know, out there, and that he must be moving around a lot."

"Like from place to place? Not hiding out somewhere?"

"No, he said Chris could be hiding out."

"That's helpful," says Nan as the sandwich shop girl puts their food down. "So he could be moving around or he could be just in one place. Want a meatball?"

"No, that's okay." Hal pushes at the salad leaves with his fork. "I don't even know if I want this."

Nan grabs Hal's hand, squeezes it. "Eat," she says. "We both have to eat. I took one of those pills you sent. It helped."

"He also said he didn't think a detective was a bad idea."

Nan pets the orange cat in the window. Her expression turns mulish.

"Nan?"

She makes a face; she eats a meatball.

"Nan."

She swallows. "Not yet."

"Nan." Hal wishes, not for the first time, that he could reach inside her brain and pull out the rock of stubbornness that's always rolling around in there.

She pushes her meatball sandwich away from her. "He'll call."

"Maybe." He purposely keeps his tone very light.

Still looking mulish, she says, "No." She throws a meatball onto his salad. "Not yet. Please."

"Nan," he says for the fourth time, like a sad refrain.

A burly man leans over awkwardly to open the truck door. The wind is blowing hard, with an edge of cold in it. "Come on, then," says the burly man. Christopher tosses the rolled-up paper in first, then climbs in.

On the way to his office, Hal detours to the aquarium store in hopes of getting some advice about the shark. It's very important to him that the shark not die. The man who runs the store, and who seems to know an extraordinary amount about all fish everywhere, is a beefy Vietnam vet named Howard. He has a soul patch and a multicolored eel tattooed all the way up one arm, wrapped around and around his flesh like a flowing ribbon. The eel also seems to be named Howard, or at least that's what's written along its first few curves. When Hal comes in, Howard is standing at the counter, emptying a medicinal-looking powder into a fishbowl containing a single vermilion fish. The fish is shaped like the end of a shovel and has both eyes on one side of its head; the powder turns the water electric green. The vermilion shovel fish hovers meditatively in the electric green orb, like a bizarre Christmas ornament. Being in the aquarium store always seems to Hal not unlike being a fish inside an aquarium. It's dark, with quiet boxes of light and exotic fish and gently waving underwater plants. He feels calmer there. He feels closer to an understanding.

Hal explains about the shark. Howard listens, tapping a little more powder into the fishbowl. The eel on his arm seems to twist.

"Did you try the silversides?" asks Howard.

"No dice," says Hal.

Howard peers in at the shovel fish, examining him. "Squid?"

"I'm not sure. Maybe."

Howard sighs. He doesn't look up from the fishbowl, which is changing in color from green to a charcoal gray, the powder's magic evaporating. The vermilion fish continues to float without visible motion. "You might try glass shrimp." He catches Hal's eye, and Hal notices, for the first time, that Howard's eyes are two different colors: one green, one brown. He wonders why he never noticed that before. Howard's eyes are two different fish, swimming in separate bowls. "You have to feed them to him live."

"Live?"

"Yeah. Just a second, I'll get you some." Howard shuffles to the back of the store and comes back with a plastic bag. As Hal is paying, both of the shovel fish's two eyes gaze at Hal, but Hal can't tell whether the fish can actually see him.

After lunch, Nan tries to concentrate. There are no boxes to flatten today; she forces herself to look at what she needs to order: more Harry Potter. The meatball sandwich was a mistake; it's heavy and dull in her stomach. She thinks again about what Tamara said, trying to piece it together. Just last year. She can't understand it, because last year she still felt blessed for having such a sweet guy. She felt as if she'd been waiting for the tsunami of adolescence, but it hadn't come. Christopher was no longer, of course, the delicate changeling who had welcomed the new millennium with them dressed up as some bewinged, alien creature of his own design with extravagantly curly painted-on antennae-eyebrows (Nan was a pirate; Marina was Patty Hearst, with a water gun; Hal was Janus, his other face gazing placidly from the back of his head at the party) and had fallen asleep before midnight, one orange wing askew over his shoulder, the other crushed beneath him. He put the wings away soon thereafter or more likely lost them; Nan can't remember when she saw them last. His shoulders broadened; his voice deepened. The way he used to have of tossing his longish hair out of his eyes changed from faintly kissable to almost rakish. (Nan was secretly proud of that, though she tried not to show it too much.) He chattered less. At a certain point, maybe when he was fourteen, he began maneuvering to make sure he was never seen in public with all three of them at the same time, as if collectively they added up to something more unpresentable than any of them did alone. Marina was the only one who didn't mind. She said, "Cut him some slack, he's that age. He's embarrassed when the wind blows."

It felt like a small price to pay, considering. He became handsome and more knowing, but he retained an unselfconscious pleasure in peaceful concentration that Nan had never seen in her brothers, or, indeed, herself. Maybe he got it from Hal, the way he could spend hours carefully shading in a drawing that he was working on, or keep an eye on one of his fish all afternoon to see if it was moving differently, or walk along a shoreline peering at things and collecting them in a little bag. She had been so grateful that it never seemed to occur to him that some boys would never be caught dead being so interested, so open, in the presence of their parents. As big as he was, he would happily curl up in a chair all day and read, doodling in the margins. He was still gangly at the wrists and ankles; his shirtsleeves and pants were somehow always coming up short. When Tamara started stopping by to watch the Sci-Fi Channel, Nan could hardly blame her: Christopher was the fledgling new man mothers wanted for their daughters and daughters wanted for themselves. A handsome, slightly awkward guy with just a drop of rakishness who didn't think it unmanly to be still, who watched over his aquatic charges with kindness, who slipped without armor from planet to planet. Nan couldn't figure out how the miracle had happened, that he didn't have that needing-to-prove-something air; did that mean he felt entitled? She didn't care. He was entitled to all of it: the sea, the sky, past the sky. She wanted him to have it. More.

Maybe that was her fault, maybe she was a female Daedalus. Maybe the heat of the approaching real world had melted the wax, sent the boy on a spiral. Maybe her father was right that boys needed to be tough, tougher, toughest.

No. She orders a bunch of Harry Potters in a daze, you can never order too many, anyway. No matter what the price, she would never trade Christopher's inherent gentleness. It was something she had never even thought was possible, not really, though it was what she most wanted for him. Was this turn of events, then, divine retribution for all her father's bad deeds? No god, minor or major, could be that cruel. She wonders what else Tamara knows. She wonders what she herself has forgotten, what she overlooked, what precious bit of information she dropped on her way between work and home or left by accident at the grocery store. Her own mother was so forgetful; she'd sworn to herself never to be like that. What Tamara had said to her — "You're his mother. You see him all the time" — was callous, but true. She'd been too late, she'd missed something, but it was the kind of thing no detective would ever find. She's going to have to find it. Of that, Nan is sure.

Hal spends the afternoon calculating numbers, an activity he is very good at. He began this years ago doing the books for the Flytrap, which meant keeping track of who had said they would pay them and then dividing the very small belated checks into four even smaller belated checks, which he passed out without fail. Somehow he was able to keep the group, in its way, solvent: there was always money for thrift store costumes. A framed photograph of Hal in a torn dirndl hangs behind his desk. What he began doing almost as a joke, a parody of his father, somehow became what he did for real. He didn't know how to do anything else, except sing loudly and badly. And then the money itself, once it started coming in, wasn't a parody at all. The tattered little house, painted black, that he bought from a nest of Hell's Angels has become ridiculously valuable; fortunes have been made and lost in this pretty city.

Hal framed the torn dirndl picture to remind himself not to take it all too seriously. But people in this city trust him with their money, in part, Hal thinks, because of the dirndl picture and all that goes with it. They like an accountant with a racy past; it gives them more faith in their own ability to make and keep money, and yet to live as if that were not what they were doing. As Hal works, a business card faces him, propped upright against the stapler. DAN JONES, it says, a name that seems fake. But Dan Jones was certainly real enough, a light-skinned black man who had lived for years in Florida before moving to San Francisco. Hal knows this because he picked Dan Jones up in a bar two nights ago.

Dan was quite slender, with a small, pointed face. His large apartment south of Market was windy. Dan's white shirt was exceptionally soft and fine, with buttons that seemed to be hand-carved from something — onyx? Hal didn't have time to figure it out as he unbuttoned them. Dan's pants were also made of some flowing, rich material; their buttons were white — ivory? Did people still have ivory buttons? Dan's waist, bare, was so unmuscled and slight that Hal wondered if the other man was a waist trainer. Maybe his closets were full of corsets. Dan's face, looking down at him, was kind, and Hal had the swift, frightening thought that he might not be able to get hard, not only not tonight, but ever. He leaned back against the foyer wall. He could still leave right now.

"Hey," said Dan, lifting Hal's chin. He had a light voice. "Are you sure this is for you?"

Hal stood up and pulled Dan toward him and kissed him hard, as if he were fully willing and able to be daddy-something-or-other, stiff-cocked, fast, and laughing. He kissed Dan as if he hadn't told the other man his real name.

In one fluid gesture, Dan stepped neatly out of his clothes, folded them over a chair, turned off the foyer light, and led the way into the bedroom, where it wasn't windy at all. Hal, still standing next to Dan's king-size bed as Dan knelt before him, glanced down at his discarded jeans, where his condoms were, and told himself that it had been a mistake to go out, that this didn't work any better than not really reading or not really watching television. And he was so tired. He should be home, waiting. As the wind whispered through the other rooms of Dan's apartment, Hal pulled back just in time and came all over Dan's orange raw silk bedspread. "Fuck," he said. "Fuck. I'm sorry." He lay back on the mattress.

"It's all right." Dan stood at the edge of the bed with some uncertainty. His body, even naked, was exceptionally poised. Was he a dancer? Did dancers have fine white shirts with onyx buttons? Maybe he was a shirtmaker. Keeping an eye on Hal, Dan opened the dresser drawer, then climbed up onto the bed and moved between Hal's legs. "Shhh," said Dan.

A while later, when they were lying across Dan's bed in the dark, Dan said, "So, are you a married guy or something?"

"No," said Hal. "I'm not married. It's — I have a teenage son. He's missing." A breeze tapped him on his bare chest. He felt drifty, not just spent, but spinning slowly to earth, like a falling leaf. He drew the orange raw silk bedspread over his nakedness and thought he should be going. He should have been gone already.

"I can help you," said Dan. Hal left the apartment with Dan's card in his pocket.

Hal, calculating other people's losses and gains, hesitates to call. He picks up the card, puts it down again. Underneath DAN JONES, it says MEDIATION. At first Hal had thought it said MEDITATION and that Dan was some sort of guru without portfolio. Although MEDIATION isn't any more useful. What is there to mediate? An empty room? Sometimes Hal wonders if he is a brave man. He realizes that as much as he wants to find Christopher, he is also afraid to find him. Any nightmare could have transpired in the last week. It is a shameful thought. But there it is. It circles his mind once, twice, three times, seeming to get bigger with each revolution.

On the tenth morning since Christopher has been gone, Marina stands in line at the bank, shifting her weight from foot to foot, a deposit slip and a check folded in her hand. The check is a large one, for a painting she doesn't think is very good, but the collector doesn't know that. Idly unfolding the deposit slip, Marina sees that she has forgotten to write the total in at the bottom. She forages in her bag, then her pockets, for a pen; she finds half a green pencil. Awkwardly, she holds the deposit slip against one bent, upraised knee and pencils in the total, which barely comes through to the pink carbon below. Marina is something of a hoarder, a trait that she considers to be a vice but that she cannot help. Because of this vice, though, she has had to work far fewer day jobs than any other artist she knows; she once made a $10,000 state grant last for a year. Also because of this vice, she has a reputation for selling quite a lot of her work, though she sells far less than people imagine she does. At the moment, she's surviving on what's left of an NEA, along with a very modest inheritance from her grandmother, and the collector who doesn't know a good painting from a bad one. She's hoping the collector, who has a massive house in Seattle filled with questionable art, won't acquire taste anytime soon. If she's careful, she figures she can hold out for a year without teaching, and then — well, maybe she'll have made a really good tree by then. If she can solve the problem of the tree, having to teach won't be so bad.

Making her way for so many years from project to project has caused Marina to become overly fond of cash. She has had to steel herself to divert some of her money into investments for retirement. She will sometimes write Nan a substantial check without being asked and refuse to take it back, but she doesn't want to combine their incomes into a joint account. Liquidity, to Marina, is a beautiful word and an even more beautiful concept. In liquidity is depth and mystery and possibility; liquidity means India, or art supplies, or a month away somewhere alone, though she's taken such a month only once since being with Nan. Marina hoards her freedom the same way she hoards her cash; she likes to think of her freedom piling up in some anonymous dark.

The bank teller with long red fingernails behind the plexiglass takes Marina's check and deposit slip, turns the check over, glances perfunctorily at Marina, stamps the slip, and says "Have a nice day" with no inflection whatsoever.

"My copy," says Marina.

"Oh, yeah," says the teller, sliding the pink carbon back under the plexiglass.

Marina takes the slip with its fuzzy impression of a sum and puts it in her pocket to file later. Her studio may look like an archaeological dig, but she keeps careful records of sales. The light, as she leaves the bank, is also fuzzy, the sun having not yet dissolved the fog. Marina unlocks her bike. She considers dropping in on Nan at the store, then decides to let her be. Maybe Nan will be able to put in at least one full workday. Maybe they all will, although Marina isn't going to her studio, not yet. She takes her cell phone out of her bag and turns it on, puts it back in her bag, and begins cycling slowly down the street.

The girl is both much too serious, and not serious enough. Her name is Shiloh. She's twenty-three, with a wide mouth, fashionably destroyed orange hair, and a gorgeously wounded, hazel-eyed gaze. As Marina undresses her, Shiloh holds her arms slightly away from her body and inclines her head, like a girl being fitted for a dress. Downstairs, one of Shiloh's roommates is watching the Teletubbies and talking on the phone. Teletubbies music plays. The roommate laughs, exclaims indecipherably. Marina unzips Shiloh's jeans, pulls them down to the floor; Shiloh's hips, in Marina's hands, are silky and wide. Shiloh, retiring to the unmade bed, is herself like an unmade bed, curvy and generous, with large breasts. She sighs happily, unworried. She turns over, showing the labyrinth tattoo she designed herself in the small of her back.

Marina, as always, feels pure, guilty happiness at this moment. She is ravenous for Shiloh, all of her, she wants to fuck her in every opening, she wants to make Shiloh come all day long. That Shiloh yields so easily makes Marina wild, as if she must, at all costs, find the bottom of Shiloh's generosity. But there is no bottom. Marina searches harder.

"What do you want?" whispers Shiloh in Marina's ear, after a while.

"I don't know." Marina opens her eyes to see Shiloh's hazel eyes staring seriously into hers.

There is the sound of a door opening and closing; the house is quiet. Shiloh is even messier than Marina; she's an art student — not one of Marina's, though she was a student of Marina's friend James, in fact his advisee; she seems to be in a band called Wet Mink. Her many-layered room reflects these interests, besides containing her profusely ornamented shrine. A picture of Marina lounges on one of the crowded lower tiers of the shrine. In the snapshot, Marina is sitting, naked, against the headboard in this very room, looking playful. A tiny painting of the Virgin of Guadeloupe is propped up next to the snapshot, along with a skateboard key. At the top of the shrine is a photo of Shiloh smiling astride a sleek brown horse, along with a blue dish with red stones in it, a small round mirror, and a vial full of a purplish liquid. Marina rests her head on Shiloh's stomach, wondering idly what's in the vial; Shiloh strokes her hair. Sitting on end next to the vial, so that Marina would be sure to hear if it rang, is the cell phone.

Marina's guilt — once a Catholic girl, always a Catholic girl — is multifaceted. She feels guilty, first of all, in regard to Shiloh, who strokes Marina's hair as seriously as if it were her job, or a treatment of some kind. Which maybe it is, thinks Marina. She feels guilty, terribly guilty, about how hungry she gets for Shiloh, as if Shiloh minded, which she plainly doesn't. Shiloh fucks as if there's plenty: plenty of time, plenty of flesh, plenty of hours to talk about it all and what it means. Marina is the one who knows that there's not that much time, not really. She feels guilty in regard to Nan, though the betrayal, in Nan's eyes, would not lie so much in the sex itself. Nan prides herself on being modern, well traveled, more or less enlightened, and above all, tough. They had always shared a philosophy regarding things like this: that they were inevitable over the long haul, that they were nothing to wreck your marriage over as long as they were open and known. The thing not to do, they agreed, was to be making calls from a phone booth in the middle of the night in the rain. (They hadn't counted on cell phones.) The true betrayal lies in the fact that Marina is keeping a secret from Nan; worse, Marina is fully aware that it may be the very keeping of this secret that is so attractive to her. To herself, Marina thinks of the relationship with Shiloh in terms of that phrase of hers and Nan's: *things like this*. As in: Don't last. Aren't the point.

Shiloh was the first one. Before Shiloh, Marina had stored up the possibility, like that money in the bank. She could; she didn't have to; she didn't have to not. She and Nan were modern; they

knew about love and all its interesting faces, some of them jokers.
Indeed, there was something wonderfully free about knowing that
she could, and not even doing it: her adventure was still waiting
for her, whole and unspent. When the thing with Shiloh began
last winter, it was clear to Marina that this affair wasn't her real
adventure, this was just a bit off the top. Marina told herself, and
Shiloh, that after seven years with Nan she merely wanted to experience something of her own for a minute or two, a bare room
with a bed in it. She had the vague idea that a little fling might
help her artistically, hone her edge. Anyway, things like this, she
told Shiloh, were what they were, no more. Shiloh said that was
cool with her, because she, like Nan, had principles. But as they
went on, Marina began to wonder what her own principles really
were. Because her lust feels almost predatory. The tree hasn't im-
proved. And she's discovered that what she feels most guilty about
is the fact that she isn't in love with Shiloh, and she really thinks —
no matter Shiloh's twenty-three-year-old principles, or anyone's
— that to be doing what she's doing, she should be. Besides, with
everything else going on, it's obvious that she really needs to break
it off with Shiloh.

Shiloh softly pulls Marina's earlobe. "What's the news?"

Marina shakes her head on Shiloh's belly. "Nothing."

"God. How's Nan?"

"Bad. We're all bad."

"Did you ever want to have kids?"

"Not so much," says Marina. "I don't know."

"I do," says Shiloh. "I want four. And a house in Marin, and a
great studio, and a world tour." Shiloh's stomach is warm and
round, and it rolls slightly as she laughs, stroking Marina's hair. "I
don't want to limit myself."

Marina tries to imagine Shiloh at thirty, at forty. "I used to feel
that way, and then I realized that if I could just do one thing well"
— she doesn't say *one tree*, though that's what she means — "I'd be
lucky."

"No, that's wrong," says Shiloh. "I mean, those installations you used to do were great. James rocked our world with the slides. When was that?"

Marina steps outside the house. She pushes vaguely at her hair, standing at the top of the front steps. After every time they meet, and this time it's just the same, Marina feels satisfied, and lighter, but also curiously vulnerable. She would like to throw a hood over her head and pass into the night, like a woman in an old movie. Instead, because she's modern and real, it's broad daylight and she, a bareheaded woman wearing black jeans and carrying a cell phone in her bag, is standing at the top of the front steps of a ratty group house in San Francisco while her secret lover, a girl with orange hair named Shiloh, makes herself a postcoital smoothie. Marina can hear the blender whirring. They really have to break up.

Marina descends the steps slowly with her bike on her shoulder, thinking maybe she should go back in and do it right now, get it over with. Will she even be able to work today? Midmorning light strikes the street directly from above, illuminating equally the houses and parked cars. It is a moment of almost no shadows; instead, there are blocks of color: beige, white, and green on the cars, pink and white and dull yellow on the houses. A little girl in long, dark braids wearing a red-and-white-striped shirt and brown pants walks by, then turns the corner. At the sight of that momentarily even light and the child with the braids, something squeezes Marina's heart. She feels as if she's being tracked by someone watching her every move. Maybe Nan is thinking of her. Mothers and lovers, she reflects; how quickly they become predators.

Or is that the way she likes it? Just before the party where she and Nan met, Marina had been poking inefficiently at the partly unpacked boxes in the apartment she was housesitting. The glass of iced tea was cold and damp in her hand; with the other, she opened flaps, fished around: a coffee-stained studio cup, a hairbrush. Her bathing suit, with Miami sand still in it. She set them on the floor; grains of sand pattered down lightly. What a mess:

Miami was a mess. It had begun in a mess and definitely ended in a mess. Or, professionally speaking, it had begun very nicely: a semester of teaching at the university, the show, the spring all to herself in the little place on the quiet avenue where elderly Jewish women still sat in folding chairs on the sidewalk, talking away the day. That was when she was making the big installations Shiloh was talking about. Now they seem to Marina tinny and overreaching, but at the time they had begun to acquire a hip cachet. People flew down from New York to see the show, to visit her studio. A curator from the Whitney called. Everyone was interested in her every move, not only what she made, but what she discarded. The light in her studio was clean, unfiltered, and strong. She drank *batidos* as she worked, happy in her aerie, working big, on the verge of something bigger.

But outside that aerie was mess, sheer mess. (Her fault? Only partly. There were circumstances.) Soon they were both calling at all hours, tracking her down, the art-loving husband and the complicated wife, and she couldn't say that she hadn't suggested certain things, and certain things had happened, undeniably; but the further it all went, the more of those crazy all-night dinners (the husband made increasingly elaborate dishes: venison wrapped in grape leaves, white chocolate ravioli filled with raspberry jam for dessert), the more she longed for the peace of the strong light, the *batidos*, her aerie guarded by elderly Jewish ladies in folding chairs. The art-loving husband wanted to drink absinthe with her; the complicated wife wanted to know all about how she made what she made, how she got to be so free and strong. Marina wondered if she needed that, the feeling of being pursued, for the sheer pleasure of getting lost again in her own ambition.

Their fascination became a mess; the mess became a drag; the drag became something worse. The complicated wife had a sojourn in the emergency room. The art-loving husband said, "You were just the catalyst. We should thank you, I guess." The curator didn't call again, but Marina didn't entirely mind because her own hipness had begun to feel thin, and slightly dangerous, to her.

It felt in some way tied up with the officious softness of the art-loving husband. She felt that he wanted to eat her, and not sexually. She needed to think, about everything. Bettina was going to Scotland, did Marina want to housesit? She did. Marina was gone by June. She left no forwarding address. San Francisco was gauzy and blessedly cool at first, but by September it had turned hot and dry. People delighted in telling her that San Francisco had its own special climate, and microclimates from neighborhood to neighborhood. Something about the hills and the air from the ocean.

Marina left her boxes half-open on the floor (where had she put her favorite T-shirts?) and went to the party. Some friend of Bettina's. After Miami, the people at the party seemed almost ludicrously well behaved and nice. She had no idea where the sex was in this city that had such a reputation for sex; she talked for a long time to a gay man who trained guide dogs for the blind. "The trouble is that I just get so attached," he said ruefully.

A small, compact shape with short hair, leaning forward to talk to someone else more or less politely, appeared on the periphery of Marina's vision. She felt something flicker at her outer edge, her ozone layer. Glancing over very briefly, she decided, from the patrician cast of the other woman's features combined with the way her shirttails flapped outside her jeans, that that particular little butch must be rich. Didn't they all have trust funds in San Francisco? The woman looked over at Marina straightforwardly; she grinned. Marina thought, *Oh, definitely rich, a rich butch on the prowl, and she makes . . . what? Films, maybe. Ridiculous films.* Marina approached with confidence, fully in the mood to let this woman think she'd caught her, then slip away. When Marina said she was an artist, the other woman laughed slightly in a way Marina wasn't sure she liked. They talked about politics, how everything was bad, the usual. Marina could see that this woman wasn't quite as nice as Bettina's other friends and she had a southern accent. That was interesting.

A while later, she found herself riding to the house of this woman, whose name was Nan, in her rattling Honda. Maybe she wasn't rich. Marina had no idea where they were — the urban hills went on and on. This Nan didn't fill in any of the space between them with chat; she just looked over now and then. Even in the dark, Marina could see the light in the other woman's eye, the familiar, but always thrilling, little dawn. And why not? Really, why not? She was free, in a city with a reputation for sex. She told herself that she was sleeping with this woman because she was the only one at the party who seemed slightly bad.

Actually, she wasn't sure why she was going home with Nan. Maybe she was just jet-lagged. For a moment, as they left the hills and headed down a broad, flat avenue, Marina wasn't even sure they were really going to have sex, though that was certainly the form that this particular sort of encounter usually took: party, strangers leaving together, the hush of the unspoken pact. Why not? They turned a few more unfamiliar corners, parked, and Nan took her arm as they walked up a flight of wooden steps to a narrow porch. Marina could hear the faint accent as Nan said, "Do you mind waiting while I run the babysitter home? It's a little late for her to walk." The way she said *mind*. Opening the front door, blaze of light, a teenage girl asleep on the sofa.

Marina replaced the girl on the sofa, waiting. Her hands were cold. She decided that a good title for the unwritten story of her life would be *Out of the Frying Pan*. Nan came back in just a few minutes, and Marina was surprised at the preciousness of that sound, the sound of the front door opening and closing, urgency, the miniskirt that was meant to be pushed up was pushed up, two quick flights of stairs, a plain room, Nan reaching behind Marina to tap the door closed.

The next morning Marina woke up very early, simultaneously as sure and as unsure as she had ever been in her life. Nan was lying on her back; in the gray-blue light, her sleeping face looked like the head on a little chess piece. There was hardly anything in her bedroom beyond what absolutely needed to be there. A bed, a wooden dresser, a chair. No mirror. Nan slept soundly, breathing deeply. Her arms were flung over her head, as if, in her dream, she was leaping downward into some nocturnal terrain, parachuting into sleep. Leaning over, Marina kissed Nan in the center of her chest. Nan stirred briefly but remained asleep.

Marina sat up. And this, she wondered, how long before this was a mess? I can't bear it, she thought, I shouldn't have done it. She deftly slid out of the bed, wandering downstairs naked, past the other, half-open bedroom door. She could see a footboard, a dangling blanket, as she went by. Too early even for — him? her? how old? — to be awake, she decided. Or maybe not. Didn't children rise at dawn, clanging and chirping? She grabbed a towel from a Virgin Mary in the bathroom — had she unwittingly bedded another Catholic girl? or a heretic? — and inefficiently wrapped it around herself. The towel was damp in various spots.

Flitting through Nan's house, Marina felt like a bird that had flown in and couldn't find her way out. Nan's house, like her bedroom, was slightly underfurnished, not austere so much as elementary, in the way of someone who would think with satisfaction: well, this is everything we need. The only extravagance was in the living room, where more than a few new, lavish books were stacked on the mantel. A thick biography of Madame Tussaud. An entire set of Proust with silvery covers. Otherwise, the house was like a collection of simple verbs: eating, sitting, watching TV. A red, child-size hooded sweatshirt was crumpled against the arm of the sofa. A few little robot men slept, still locked in combat, on the coffee table. Several plastic trucks were suspended in a convoy into the dining room. Standing half-wrapped in the damp towel, Marina's feet were cool on the cool floor. She stood there looking for something, but she didn't know what. Evidence — though the extravagant books weren't it — of some intractable bitterness, strained rope tethered to rusted stake, some wormhole that would end this thing before it had properly begun. She didn't want another complicated wife. Nan, the night before, had been very quiet and determined, like someone building something. Marina thought warily, *Why?*

The house offered only the most functional explanations: Because I need a table. Because I need a doorway. Because I need a lamp to read by. But how could anyone read Proust in this house? Marina decided the silvery set must be a prop, a girl-catcher: there it was stacked up like firewood, always at the ready. Because I need a girl. She had the sudden, even more dismaying thought that Nan might be a therapist. She tightened her towel.

Nan's kitchen was, in temperament, a barn. It was a large, tilting room with battered cabinets, a long counter covered in scratched Formica, and an incongruously spanking new refrigerator with an icemaker on the door. What appeared to be a feedsack of brown rice rested on the floor next to a toolbox. A pair of thick gloves was stuffed into a pair of mud-flecked work boots carefully set on newspaper. Stools were a popular item; one of the many had a leg wrapped in blue crepe paper, like a horse with an injury. Some papier-mâché creature, a pterodactyl or a bat, was evolving on the kitchen table; nearby, a spoon was welded into a bowl of hardened paste. A shovel leaned against an open pantry door. The pantry was abundantly stocked with cans and boxes and glass jars and brightly colored kid food with smiling animals of indeterminate species on the labels. Marina found the coffee — good coffee, expensive — in the freezer, which puffed out crisply icy air when she opened the door. She could tell that the good coffee was Nan's treat for herself. Nan, she understood, was a woman who would rather spend money on coffee than furniture. The spanking new, wildly efficient refrigerator plainly had a logic behind it. Along with the expensive coffee there was an expensive coffeemaker that Marina wasn't entirely sure how to use. She pushed what she hoped was the right button.

At one end of the kitchen, a sliding glass door opened onto a yard: light, open sky for the restless bird. Marina stood before the door, half tempted to unlock it, open it, and be gone in her borrowed towel. She waited for the coffee. The morning was already lighter than it had been when she left the bedroom; it was that hour when the sky seems to brighten with increasing speed, like a ball rolling downhill. The light that had been gray-blue upstairs was now a clear peach.

Marina looked at Nan's garden in this new light. She didn't

know anything about real gardens or plants. She could tell that it was an ordinary garden: there were no exotically trained vines, no bridges over little ponds, no trellises. Marina's first impression was of grass, and at the back of the garden a bright red bucket with a toy truck butting into it. A plain wooden chair. Then she noticed the bed with the tall stalks of tomatoes, the delicate pansies along the side of the yard near the fence, the languorous orange vine reaching down from the top of the fence to touch the pansies, a scattering of irises, a good-size hydrangea. There were other flowers — something purple, something yellow. If a garden could be said to have intention, then the intention of this one seemed to be dailiness: the sun would rise and set on what Nan dug out of the earth. And standing in the middle of the yard, awaiting planting, was a very skinny tree, not much more than a stick, with a burlap bulb at the end. Its branches were thin and tender.

It wasn't the dream tree Marina had drawn over and over as a child (or, when she was tired or distressed, as an adult), not at all. It was simply a tree, something plain like the plain wooden chair. It was simply a tree that this Nan, now lying asleep on her back upstairs in her unadorned room, was going to put into the ground; she was going to dig a hole and put the roots of the tree in it, cover the roots back over with dirt, and then stand at this very window with a cup of good coffee, watching it grow. Because I need a tree. Because the tree needs a place to take root.

Fuck Proust, Marina thought, holding the dampish towel with one hand. She had a clear belief, as clear as that moment's light (even now beginning to thicken into day): here was a woman who could make a world, table by table and branch by branch, who hunted simply to plant. It felt to Marina embarrassingly maternal, embarrassingly raw in its desire — or perhaps it was her own desire that was so embarrassing. What had Freud said about every bed containing at least four people? Here was a place where a tree could be a tree without irony or sentimentality. If only, Marina thought, she could make art as true as that tree. That was beauty: no trapdoors, no inside jokes. She understood immediately that she was going to have to dismantle the palace of her installations and begin there, with what she drew before she knew anything. Naked, in every sense. As bare as those skinny branches.

How could it be that falling in love felt as if your heart were breaking? Marina didn't understand it. How could she be feeling such a cliché? But it was true. Her heart had broken open. It was a feeling deeper than happiness or sadness, though composed of both, as if the daylight itself had reached in. She turned away from the glass, so badly did she want to stay in this place, with its ordinary garden, its ordinary tree. It occurred to Marina that she didn't know Nan's last name, that at thirty-one she was getting a little old for this, that she couldn't very well bound back up the stairs, shake Nan awake, and shout into her face, *It's you.* Though she wanted to.

It wasn't too long before she learned Nan's last name, that she wasn't Catholic, that she wasn't rich. She was simply Nan Ashby, five foot two with her shoes on. No more, no less. Marina loved her. The gilded shell of Marina's old life fell away behind her. She bent her brush, like a divining rod, to the new tree. The faces that ghosted in the bark were never the faces of anyone she knew. No one from Miami called her. She felt safe behind the brown hills that ringed San Francisco, safe in its many climates. She painted her tree. Over the years, Marina was faithful to both the image and the woman, but she couldn't — she didn't know why — she couldn't tell Nan, not in so many words, that all her own trees could rise and fall, be layered on and scraped off, bloom and vanish, because there was one, in the backyard, that Nan picked up and put into the dirt with a shovel and that has never resulted in a single edible plum or pretty flower.

That morning, she wanted to stay so badly that she left immediately. She got dressed before she found out whether she had pushed the right button on the coffeemaker. And Nan, as Marina kissed her goodbye, seemed relieved that Marina knew it was best to leave before the child woke up. She obviously thought that Marina was being considerate while Marina, standing on Nan's front step in last night's corduroy miniskirt from the Salvation Army, had to lean against the porch rail to catch her breath. She had no idea whatsoever of how she was going to get home. It didn't look like the kind of neighborhood that had taxis.

And later, the child. Did she want to have children? The question seems irrelevant now because once Christopher tumbled into her life he was, simply, there. Marina didn't will him. He wasn't hers to claim or refuse. Nan was fated; that she came trailing a little boy was, at first, only interesting. Also, he didn't like her then. Nan said he did, but Marina knew that he didn't. He answered her questions politely. He made it clear that this house was his, his and Nan's. These trucks were their toy trucks. Marina was careful. She asked to see his room, asked him to point out the interesting things in it. School, he offered listlessly when she asked, was okay. If she stayed over on a night when Christopher was there and not at Hal's, the child would invariably get a stomachache by 11:30. Marina, throwing on a robe, would quietly hand a towel in to Nan, who sat in his room, making soothing noises. The smell of vomit wafted into the hallway.

Then Marina, lying tangled up in her robe in Nan's bed, would listen to the wordless soothing noises that were not so terribly different from the wordless noises of sex, or just after sex. The pillows and sheets smelled of her and Nan. The hallway light slanted harshly onto the floor and fell on a tangent across the foot of the bed. Marina slid her foot into the light, then out. Her father had been a radiology equipment salesman before he died. When she was a child, Marina was terrified by the thought that his profession enabled him to see right through her, to her bones, the way the nuns at Catholic school told her God could. Of course, he couldn't. Her bones remained hers, private and invisible. Yet he was so intense, so intensely interested in her, which was so nice, and not nice as well.

Nan always shut the door behind her when she came back to bed. Sometimes they'd talk for a while. They talked about Christopher, his night terrors. They talked about secrets and bad bargains. Why did Nan's mother stay? Why did Marina's father compulsively chase women? What was the point of misery? they asked each other. They believed in happiness. They wouldn't hide anything.

Nan said one night into the dark, "Everyone always knows everything, anyway."

Marina had agreed, deeply relieved. It was true, of course; her mother was no fool. Nan always said that when the Ashbys' next-door neighbors moved away, everybody knew what they were moving away from. At last, Marina had found a home where everything could be what it seemed to be, including her. She slept well; she found a great studio nearby. She painted the name and number of the Whitney curator on her worktable, which was soon covered with paint and papers and rags and jars of brushes. She avoided New York and Los Angeles — those treeless places — like the plague. She barely glanced at the glossy art magazines; the local coverage of her small gallery was fine. She wishes that people in the art world liked the tree series more, but in a way she can't blame them. There's an essential quality she hasn't managed to produce yet, though at times she's felt that she's come close. Over and over, branch after branch, she's tried to get it. She's pretty sure she's almost there.

Did she want to have children? For years, she felt as if she were on probation as a parent; she was afraid that Christopher might politely ask her to leave. It was only as he was on the brink of becoming a man that Marina felt she might be able to say yes, yes, she wanted him, too. She chose him. That it wasn't only the garden, the plum tree, but the red bucket that he had left on the grass.

Bucket, vomit, garden. One plain wooden chair. Juxtaposed, they both did and didn't seem chosen. This latest turn of events, for example, has been a complete surprise. Equally surprising to Marina at the moment is a spurt of relative equanimity and decisiveness. She won't bother Nan with Shiloh, not now — better simply to end it. Things like this are personal follies, or, in her case, some vestigial, probably childish need to prove to herself that her insides remain under her own sovereignty, out of the reach of all X-ray machines. Also, she suspects Shiloh could be volatile, and she wants to protect Nan, who is nowhere near as tough as she likes to make out. After she bathed Nan the night before, Nan held tightly to Marina in her sleep, as if she were a rescue buoy. Marina was careful not to move.

The cell phone rings as Marina is buying water in a bodega.

"Where are you?" says Nan.

"Near the studio — I came down to get some lunch."

There is a pause that unsettles Marina for a second, but then Nan goes on. "I had lunch with Hal."

"Good, I'm glad you ate," says Marina, paying for the water, hoisting her bag into a slightly better position on her shoulder, checking her watch. The day is half-gone.

"Can you come here?"

"Sure. Okay."

There's a crackling sigh. "No, it's all right. Don't. Go back to work. Christ, I have to work myself."

"Nan, I'll be there if you want me to. I'll help you. I'll sit with you."

Fuzzy silence, then, "It's not that many more hours. I'll see you at home." Nan hangs up.

Marina turns off the cell phone and leaves the bodega, its door jingling goodbye. She squints in the sun, wondering if it can see through her. She has a moment of fleeting homesickness for the golden light of Los Angeles, where she grew up. In Los Angeles, she thinks, she might be transparent now and then, transparent and floating. In this silver city, however, she is solid, and she has work to do. Even now.

Nan hangs up the phone. Is the stupid girl tall or short? Fat or thin? She ejects the questions from her mind. Why Marina would need to have some ratty little secret is beyond her. Nan is too exhausted to deal with it, anyway. But why, in all this open air? Why now, still? She ejects the thought again, more forcibly this time.

Hal punches in the number. He really shouldn't. Let sleeping tricks lie has always been his motto. But then again, what had Dan meant? Why had he offered to do . . . whatever it is that he does? It doesn't matter, Hal thinks as the phone rings. It couldn't hurt. He listens to the outgoing message, but doesn't leave one in return.

The daylight is nearly gone from Marina's studio when she glances at her watch — 6:30. Downstairs, Turner does something that sounds like dumping a bucket of pennies on the floor. Maybe he is: every now and then, he abruptly abandons the fine work of prints only to return, chastened, apologetic. Also, his prints are quite lucrative. At the sound like falling pennies, Marina decides it's time to go. She wants to be there when Nan gets home.

Standing in the kitchen, her jacket still on, one leg of her jeans still tucked into her sock, Marina answers the phone.

"Hello," says Christopher. "Marina? I need my mother to send me some money."

"Where are you?" says Marina.

Silence. Unidentifiable hum: an air conditioner? The clink of cutlery against a plate or cup.

"Christopher? Christopher? Don't hang up, Chris."

He hangs up.

Marina opens the front door and waits there for Nan. Marina wants Nan to see her, first thing, when she pulls up in the car. She wants by her presence in the doorway to say she's sorry that she couldn't keep him on the phone, couldn't bring him back, and that she offers, instead, herself. She leans in the doorway, folding and pressing the loose hem of her shirt against her hip.

Nan pulls up and jumps out of the car. "Marina!" she calls, as if they are far away from each other, her face uplifted and tense. "Marina!"

Marina walks down the steps to meet Nan, who grabs and holds her tightly. "Jesus Christ, where is he?" says Nan.

Marina shakes her head.

"Did he call again?"

"No," says Marina, as Nan releases her and bounds into the house. Marina hears her yell into the emptiness, *Where the fuck are you?* Through the open front door, she can see Nan's small, energetic form heading for the kitchen phone, which is not ringing. Marina follows slowly up the steps, feeling strangely guilty.

Christopher, with a pen that leaks ink onto his hand, begins on the mountains.

Marina, Nan, and Hal eat take-out burritos at the kitchen table. The phone is attached to a brand-new tape recorder with a black-corded gadget Hal found at RadioShack. The tape recorder sits on a tall, yellow, wooden stool, as if it is on display. Tacked onto the bulletin board near the phone are a calendar, photos, the postcard from Marina's last show, a running grocery list, the schedule of Christopher's school holidays, and a picture he liked of a man in a band: his face is painted green and he is sticking out his tongue, which has a bolt in it. Marina holds Nan's hand across the table as they both dutifully fork up their food. Hal gets up to check the wires on the tape recorder, sits back down again.

"Maybe we should just get in the car and start looking for him," he says.

"Which direction?" asks Nan.

Hal shakes his head.

Marina squeezes Nan's hand. Nan is looking vexed, which, even after the seven years they've been together, seems to Marina to refer to a past with Hal that she doesn't entirely get and that makes her feel like an interloper or a child. Though they are nothing alike in physical structure — Nan is small and masculine and patrician, Hal is tall and blond with a western plainness of face —

Marina often thinks they look related. They're both so intentional, as if they can see the next step in front of them at all times and have no qualms about taking it. They both favor jeans and simple shirts. They both have level, practical, American gazes. Nan takes the salsa from Hal's side of the table.

"It's the mango," he cautions.

Like a brother and sister, Marina thinks, they're too related to notice how related they are. She notices it, perhaps because she was an only child: it was always just her, her mother, and her father, one-two-three, one-two-three, like a waltz. Circling, again and again.

"I'll make us tea," says Hal, abandoning the remainder of his burrito, which has taken on a gluey cast. "You two go in and sit down." It's dark in the garden. The sliding glass doors reflect the three of them at the table, the kitchen behind them, the plates of half-eaten burritos and the three Corona beer bottles, a cheap glass vase with a few tiger lilies in it. To someone looking in, the shapes would be domestic, pleasing, except for the discordant note of the tape recorder crouching on the yellow stool, hooked to the phone.

In the living room, Marina sits on the sofa while Nan hovers in the doorway. Her white button-down shirt is tucked into her jeans, which have become looser in the last week or so. Her hands are in her pockets.

"Do you know why he called today?" asks Nan.

Marina shakes her head.

"He had his SATs today. He knows he's really supposed to be here. I wonder if that's what this is all about, maybe —"

"Academic pressure?" asks Marina.

"Don't say it like that. It's awful what they do to kids now. It's very intense." Nan, hands still in her pants pockets, deposits herself in a chair. "I hated the SATs."

Hal appears in the doorway with a carefully arranged tray of cups and milk and loose tea slowly darkening in the perforated column of an expensive glass teapot, which he gave them. He has also fanned out a number of Oreos on a little plate. The entire effect is a sort of cross between irony and Idaho that makes Marina, as she clears a space on the coffee table, want to cry.

"Voilà," says Hal, setting down the tray. "Nan," he continues, still standing, "do you want me to stay tonight?"

Nan reaches for two cookies, then lightly clacks them together in her hand like poker chips. "But he could call over to your place."

"I don't think so," says Hal. "It seems like this is the place he picked." His arms hang awkwardly at his sides. Marina stares at Nan — *say the right thing*— but Nan is studying the Oreos in her hand as if deciding what number to put them on.

"Do whatever you need to," Nan says. "You can stay here if you want."

Hal sits down in the other chair. "All right," he says mildly. He leans forward and pours himself a cup of tea, then holds the cup on his knees, his long legs rising nearly to the chair arms.

"This looks great," says Marina. "I was feeling chilled." She pours herself some tea, takes a cookie. The combination is surprisingly comforting. Marina takes off her shoes and tucks one leg under her on the sofa.

"I don't know what to do with myself," says Hal. "Everything seems so beside the point, or more important than it is."

"Our entire lives," says Nan. Marina is startled for a moment by her reply. So is Hal, who raises an eyebrow.

A small wooden lamp sits on each table next to Nan and Hal's chairs. Their even-featured faces harmonize in the lamplight. Marina rubs her toes, which are cold, through her socks. They will go on, she thinks, like my parents. They will go on without me. She pulls back from the thought.

"At least you two have each other," says Hal.

Nan looks at Marina with both hunger and sadness. "You know what I keep thinking? How a family becomes a family when it falls apart. I feel like I know who we all are to one another now."

Hal seems about to say something, then shakes his head. "I'm just so very worried."

"Listen," says Marina. "He called. The police said that he'd call when he needed money, and he has." She doesn't say how strange the tone in his voice was: flat, formal, faintly aggressive. For a minute, she had almost wondered if it was really Christopher.

Hal and Nan both nod.

Marina checks her watch. It is 7:35.

Hal sips his tea. Nan lightly clacks her cookies together, not eating them. Marina thinks about the moment on the street earlier that day, the perpendicular light, the colors of the houses and cars, the little girl with the long, dark braids turning the corner.

"I had a cousin who ran away," says Hal. "Really smart girl. They found her in Oklahoma City living with a black man. I think they tried to arrest him."

"I wish he'd liked that therapist more," says Nan. "I thought that guy was pretty good. If he'd gone even one more time —"

"When he comes back," says Hal. "We'll find out everything then."

"See, I knew we shouldn't call a detective," says Nan.

"Mmmm," replies Hal. He crosses his legs. "This house. My God, Nannie, did you ever think we'd still be here all these years later?"

"You know," says Nan, "I did. As soon as I got here, I had the feeling that this was where I was meant to be. Kismet."

"Chris is such a California kid," says Hal. "Remember when I took him to New York? He hated it."

"I know," says Nan. "He's like you." She nods at Marina. "A child of the left coast."

"Isn't it funny," says Hal, "that he would feel so deeply at home in a place that isn't home to either of us? You see," he says to Marina, "we need you. We're strangers here."

Marina knows he's trying to be kind because he's always kind, though she finds him somewhat distant. Hal likes everyone, but truly loves very few. He and Nan have that in common as well. Their circle is essentially small, in the way of people who have come from small places. "I don't know that I've ever felt at home anywhere," says Marina.

"Except with me," says Nan, and Marina loves her for her mat-

ter-of-fact tone, as if Marina has simply forgotten something ba-
sic, such as gravity. She loves Nan's certainty. Like the light on the
street earlier today, Nan's love, once obtained, falls directly on the
perpendicular. No mystery, no plot, no tendrils of possibility.

"Right," says Marina. "Before you, I always felt sort of like a
runaway — a runaway manqué. Maybe it was all that Catholic
school. Running to art school. Running from city to city."

"Me, too. On the lam. We're all runaways of some kind, aren't
we?" says Hal, setting his empty teacup on the side table. "This entire town is runaways. Built by runaways."

"No," says Nan. "He's not a runaway."

"Nan," says Marina.

"Nan," says Hal.

"I understand that he's not here now," says Nan tightly, "but he
was *happy* before. He had Tamara, he had us, he had his fish, he
didn't do drugs, he didn't even like New York. Why would he
leave? It's almost like he was forced out, like there was something
here he couldn't stand, suddenly. Something went wrong. And
that knife. I just don't get that. He wasn't like that."

Hal glances at Marina in a way she can't quite decipher. He is
asking her either to say or not say something, but she can't tell
which. And she doesn't know what it is, anyway. He blushes,
stands up. "I should go on home. You're right, he could call there.
I'll come back in the morning, and we'll figure out what to do
next."

Hal kisses them both goodbye. His fair, drawn face, near Marina's, looks almost translucent to her, as if there are dark shapes
moving around underneath. She wants to close her eyes and
touch it; she has the idea that she could identify the shapes with
her fingers. He's so private, in his way. Instead, she reaches up
awkwardly to hug him.

"We'll be up early," she says.

Nan and Marina wash up, sit in sweaters on the back steps holding the portable phone, go inside and look at the paper together
in silence, and finally turn off the lights downstairs, Nan peering

outside before closing the curtains. She hesitates before locking the front door, then locks it. Marina picks up Nan's reading glasses from the table where she left them and carries them upstairs. As they round the corner past Christopher's room, Nan shuts his door, but it swings back open, revealing the bed, the sketches on the wall, his desk with his computer on it, his neat bookshelves, all blurry in the dark, like things that are in the process of melting away. Nan walks on; Marina pulls the door to and makes sure that it catches this time.

Marina sees that their bedroom is a mess again, mostly hers — hairpins, magazines, single socks, the four books she's reading simultaneously all face-down in various spots on the floor, a letter from a friend lying among the tossed bedding. She folds the letter, closes one of the books. She studies the other three, trying to decide which one she wants to read. Nan, sitting against the headboard, says, "Don't pick up. I like to feel you around me."

Marina sits down next to her and Nan gathers Marina up in her arms, holding her tight.

"It's going to be okay," says Marina into Nan's ear. "He loves you so much."

Nan shakes her head wearily. "I don't know. Did you think Hal seemed off tonight?"

Marina shifts so that they are curled together on the bed, still in their clothes. "I can't really see past this — crisis — you know? More tired, maybe. But we're all tired."

"It's a lot for him," says Nan. She rests her head on Marina's shoulder.

"For you, too."

"Yeah, but he's a swan. He can get ruffled on a good day. I worry about him."

Marina kisses Nan's forehead. Nan's head feels heavy on Marina's shoulder; her forehead is warm, as if she has a fever, but Marina knows it's not a fever. It's the fierce, vigilant energy that constantly courses through Nan these days. "You know," says Marina, "you're more like a mother wolf. Maybe you should howl."

"Maybe we all should," says Nan.

They lay quietly in the bedclothes together for a while, then un-
dress and shut off the bedroom light. Marina feels Nan trying,
hard, to sleep beside her. Marina, though she feels guilty about it,
does begin to drop off, Shiloh and Teletubbies music and the
light, all jumbled together.

Around 4:00 A.M., Nan picks up the phone before it has finished
ringing its first ring. "Yes," she says. "Yes. Yes. It's all right. Tell
me —" Nan turns on the bedside lamp, writes something on a
back page of one of Marina's books. Marina shades her eyes,
squinting.

"Is it him?" says Marina.

Nan holds out one hand — *wait.* "We love you. We all miss you.
Yes. Now." She hangs up and pulls on her pants, shoves her bare
feet into her sneakers, tears out the book page, and stuffs it in her
pocket.

"I'm going to Phoenix. Call Hal. I'll be back tomorrow."

Nan is down the stairs and out the door before Marina's eyes
have even adjusted to the light. She hears the rattling sound of
Nan's old car starting for the airport. Marina sits up in bed and
begins dialing Hal. The messy room looks surreal to her, suddenly
awakened and glaring. It looks like a room that's been robbed.

The rental car is hot and padded and meticulously, anonymously
clean. Nan gets in and pulls the seat forward. She puts her coffee
in the plastic cup holder, chews off a bite of bad, greasy muffin.
Everything tastes as if the car produced it, metallic and chemical.
She unfolds the city map she got at the rent-a-car desk. The map
has big red arrows pointing to important local landmarks like
Denny's and the other rent-a-car company locations. Nan has
never been to Phoenix before, but she can tell already that it's
hateful. Landlocked, dry, flat, with a stultifying dead summer
heat. Exactly the opposite of everything Christopher, a fair and
dreamy and aquatic-minded boy, likes. He would never have come
here on his own. Nan finds the road she needs and traces it along
with her finger, but the road leaves town without crossing the

road where Christopher said he would be waiting. He dictated an address to her; he said it twice.

Rolling down the car window, Nan traces the road again, past two Denny's restaurants, holding the map out nearly to the windshield. She should have remembered her reading glasses, but even without them she can tell that Christopher's road is not there. Whoever made the map thought it was more important to mark the two identical Denny's than to include the road where Christopher is waiting for her. It occurs to her that perhaps he's not in Phoenix at all, perhaps he got it wrong, but that possibility is so agonizing that she can only, mentally, nod in its direction. *Now* is the only thing she can do, though it tastes as metallic and chemical as the bad coffee and muffin she forces herself to finish. Marina said she was a wolf, so Nan tries to concentrate on the wolf, to ask the wolf, Where is he? She tries to tell the time by the sun, just for practice, and she's not so far off; she considers taking off her watch to strengthen her instincts. In the old days, she never wore a watch. Inside the awful rented car, she thinks she feels the sharpening of the wolf's nose, the wolf's eyes.

Nan turns on the ignition and follows the wolf out of the parking lot. Phoenix is placid and horrible, stretching out before her. A desert with a desert's deceptive, wide vista. But under the sand, somewhere, is Christopher.

Outside the first Denny's, a few teenagers are draped over the hood of a car in the parking lot, but none of them has Christopher's bright hair. The road, he said extremely calmly, was called Old Trail Road. He would be waiting at a house with pink shutters, number 258. Then he hung up. The main road that Nan is on is full of strip malls and fast-food places; she watches intently for the smaller street, though nothing here looks as if it could possibly be connected to anything named Old Trail. The papery mountains in the distance look like enormous wasps' nests. Nan passes the second Denny's. From here, she can see, the main road turns into a four-lane highway. She makes an illegal U-turn at the light.

Coming down the other side of the strip, it all looks just the same: hot, baked, plastic. Nothing to smell or touch, no trail to follow, old or new. As empty as Texas. Nan tries not to despair, driving slowly. When she reaches the first Denny's again, she pulls in and stops next to the teenagers, who are still there. It's a Tuesday morning; she refrains from asking them why they're not in school.

The two girls are both wearing tight, cropped tops and low-cut jeans that show off their bellybuttons; they're sitting together on the hood of a Geo. The three boys, lounging against the outside of the car, have wide shoulders and smug, pimpled faces. All the kids are white and fleshy and they slide their eyes at one another as Nan gets out of her car. "Hi," she says.

"Hey," answers one of the boys politely, but with an expression that clearly says, You're a freak.

"I'm trying to find a road —" she begins.

"Are you from the base?" asks one of the girls, a brunette with bangs.

"No. I'm looking for Old Trail Road. Do you know it?"

"Old Trail," says a boy wearing a backward baseball cap. "Old Trail?" He scratches his chin, goofing on being asked a question. Nan would like to shoot him, but instead she cocks her head, listening.

"Why do you want to go over there?" asks the boy. "It's all trash down there."

"Where you live," says the brunette. The other girl laughs.

"Do you know it?" repeats Nan, more firmly this time, like a teacher expecting an answer.

"How much is it worth to you?" asks the boy, adjusting his cap.

"See you," says Nan, getting back into her car.

"I'll tell you," says the brunette, hopping off the hood and walking slowly away from the boys in her tight jeans. She leans into Nan's window, smelling like sweet lipstick. "Assholes," she says over her shoulder. To Nan, she says, "You go down three blocks, make a right at the Midas, cross the little bridge, make a left. It's off there, maybe half a mile."

"Thank you," says Nan, rolling up her window.

"Aye, aye, sir," says the cap boy, saluting as Nan drives away. The brunette slaps him on the arm.

Nan makes another illegal U-turn and follows the girl's directions, past the boarded-up Midas, over the bridge. The neighborhood is worn, even more worn in the heat. No one is outside on any of the parched lawns. Then the houses end, but the road continues. A ways down, she discovers a small street sign for Old Trail Road. She turns left, the only direction available. There are a few little, scrappy houses on Old Trail. One, with pink shutters, is dwarfed by an enormous truck cab with an empty flatbed parked in its driveway. Nan pulls onto the dirt on the side of the road opposite the house and turns off the car. Anything could have happened already inside that house; she knows that houses hide everything. She studies number 258 for back doors, side doors, in case she has to grab him fast and run. She wraps the car keys around her knuckles.

Number 258 is as silent as every other house in the neighborhood. The wasps'-nest mountains rise up in the distance. The heat shimmers. The side of the truck says SANTA FE BEEF; the house looks as if it could fit inside the truck. The pink shutters are peeling, but the little scruffy yard has an assortment of desert plants. The back of an air conditioner protrudes from one side window. A tire, painted white, has been laid on its side in the center of the front yard; inside the tire are several cacti. Why anyone would ever cultivate a cactus is beyond Nan. She's always thought of them as glorified weeds. The wolf wants to leap out of the car, but now that she's here, Nan is suddenly afraid, paralyzed. This fear embarrasses her, shames her even. *Go inside,* she thinks. *Go get him.*

But instead she sits in the anonymous, superpadded rented car, holding back the wolf, studying the silent house. The bad map rests lightly on the passenger seat, its red arrows pointing to nothing important. Nan's hip hurts, as if she's been running all night. She wants to know about that failing grade. No, the first thing is to ask him how he ended up here and to get him out as soon as possible. No. It's as hot as hell, but Nan feels cold. She could fail herself: that's clear. Her son could be buried under those sad cacti. She could end up buried there, too, for all she knows.

Nan lets slip the leash, and the wolf bounds out of the car. She knocks on the door of 258.

A round-faced, bearded man with a potbelly answers. He is wearing a blue-and-white-striped engineer's cap, jeans, and a black denim shirt with embroidery on the points of the collars. "Hello," he says in a friendly way, "you Nan? Chris's mom?" She nods. "Come on in. We're just having breakfast." He opens the door wide for her, shakes her hand. "I'm Johnny."

Inside, it is cool and dim. The furniture is also rounded, well stuffed. Mahogany legs on thick carpet. Hanging over the sofa, which has a rumpled sleeping bag and pillow on it, is an oil painting of a truck. Painted on its side is SANTA FE BEEF. Sitting at the round, mahogany dining room table is Christopher, barefoot, busily drawing on a large sheet of paper. He doesn't look up when Nan enters.

"Chris," says Johnny, "your mom is here." Johnny stands respectfully to one side. "Coffee?"

"Sure," says Nan. Some instinct makes her hang back, not run toward Christopher and embrace him the way she longs to do. He is drawing intently, shoulders hunched. He is wearing a pair of tan pants she recognizes, but with a T-shirt she hasn't seen before. The T-shirt, which is torn around the collar and too big for Christopher, is imprinted with the faded iron-on of a football helmet. Christopher doesn't even like football. His blond hair, which is cut in the fashionably half-shaved, half-floppy way of his peers, is dirty. His feet are dirty, too. Around his neck is the leather cord with the bright blue bead on it he always wears; he hung onto that, at least. He is drawing very quickly, but she can't make out what the picture is. Something with a squiggly green line. He glances up, nods at her, then returns to drawing. His blue eyes, in the instant that Nan sees them, seem larger, their gaze stronger. There is something underneath his gaze she doesn't like in the way one doesn't like a certain stranger, a certain dog, on a playground and tightens one's grip on a child's hand. Nan's fingers grow tense. Her shoulder aches. "Christopher," she says softly.

He looks up at her again, seeming annoyed, as if she has interrupted him at some important task, or woken him from a sound sleep. "What?" His eyes are dark and hard.

"I'm here," she says.

"I know. *I* called *you.*"

Johnny hands Nan a cup of coffee. "Come on and sit down," he says, pulling out a chair from the dining room table for her. "Chris and I came all the way through New Mexico yesterday. He called as soon as we got in." Johnny sits down at the table. "Make some room for your mom there, Chris." Christopher, frowning, moves the large sheet of paper so that half of it furls in his lap. Nan, seated at the table, can see now that the squiggly green line is a border, like the border of a country. The back of her neck prickles. With or without the coffee, she is wide awake.

Johnny, despite the potbelly and his slow way of moving, has very sharp brown eyes. "Quite a talent your boy's got there," he says, casually sipping his coffee. "I told him he should develop that."

"Did you paint the one of the truck over the sofa?" says Nan to Johnny while maintaining an eye on Christopher, who is plainly listening carefully, though his head is bent over the paper.

"Sure did," says Johnny. "Had to wait till it wasn't moving, though." He laughs.

"So, listen, Chris," says Nan evenly, "Marina and Hal really miss you a lot. They can't wait to see you."

Christopher shrugs, winces. "I want to stay here," he says.

Nan glances at Johnny, sipping his coffee. "The thing is, Chris," she says, "I bet Johnny has to go back out on the road again soon." Johnny nods. "We can't just leave you here alone."

"I can go with him." Christopher's tone is plaintive, but also exasperated, as if he is the adult at the table and they are being ridiculous.

Johnny says easily, "No, see, Chris, I'm not really allowed to take passengers. You know that. I could lose my license."

Christopher, lapsing into a morose silence, says nothing.

Nan breathes in and out a few times, regarding Christopher, thinking. She is careful not to look at Johnny. Inside, she paces restlessly, searching. "Tamara misses you, too," she says.

There is a flicker of emotion over Christopher's face, then he tightens his lips. He shakes his head. Nan thinks she sees him tear up, but she can't be sure. Very gently, tentatively, she reaches over and takes his hand. Covering his eyes with his other hand, he lets her. His hand in hers is warm and electric and large. His drawing slides to the carpet.

Not too long after, Nan leads him, in flip-flops, out of Johnny's house and to the rented car.

Johnny hands Christopher's neatly rolled-up and rubber-banded drawing through the window to him. "You take care, Chris," he says.

Nan feels as if she is driving a bomb through Phoenix, as if she is carrying a bomb through the Phoenix airport, as if she is smuggling a bomb onto the airplane, as if she is sitting next to a bomb on the flight to San Francisco. The dry mountains like wasps' nests grow small on the ground beneath them; they are flying out of summer. It's clear to Nan that she cannot tinker with or ask the bomb any questions until she has him home. Christopher is strangely quiet. Once on the plane, he closes his eyes, but not in the way of someone who is sleeping. He closes his eyes in the way of someone who doesn't want to see, or perhaps be seen. Nan has the sense that if he had a pair of sunglasses he would put them on. He keeps his drawing next to him and doesn't eat or drink during the flight. The engines drone. The wolf is quiet. On her wrist, Nan's large man's watch ticks, but even without looking at it she always knows what time it is to within five minutes.

Hal and Marina sit in folding chairs in the garden, waiting. Marina's legs are white in shorts. Her white toes are braced against the aluminum legs of the chair; one toenail is painted red. Her silver hair is messy, as usual. Hal wishes that he liked her more. He doesn't mind her art, the tree thing is okay, he even bought one, but the woman herself he finds annoyingly elusive. That she's sleeping with some other woman and doesn't know that everyone knows doesn't help. Nan has told him to leave it alone; he does try. He knows Marina loves Nan; he knows long-term things are complicated. Especially with women.

Still, Marina reminds him of the album cover of *Sergeant Pepper's Lonely Hearts Club Band:* a jumble of images with a secret message hidden inside, or was that if you played it backward? He can't remember anymore. He remembers only that he used to play it over and over on the portable record player in his bedroom, hoping to go into a trance. Marina, by contrast, seems as if she's always half in a trance or half out of one, a quality Nan never fails to find massively alluring. Nan likes to get lost in these elusive women even while pretending that she's marching straight ahead.

That elusive kind of woman, Hal reflects, shivering even in a sweatshirt — Marina never dresses appropriately for the weather, he guesses it's part of her mystique — is exactly what they don't need at the moment. He wishes Nan's lover were a big, warm, gal kind of person, like Fannie Flagg. If he were sitting in the garden with Fannie Flagg, he'd feel much safer. As it is, he's sitting in the garden waiting for his runaway son with a silver-haired riddle.

"Are you hungry?" asks Marina.

"I ate," says Hal.

"I am," she says, getting up from the chair. Her white legs take the back stairs two at a time. Hal, in the garden, rubs his hands together. It was her idea to sit outside. They agreed that it seemed better than waiting in the house, more optimistic. A cool breeze ruffles what's left of his hair.

Marina comes back with three toasted waffles on a plate. She picks up one waffle and begins eating it as if it were a slice of bread. "Do you think she found him?"

"Dear God, I hope so," says Hal. "I'm losing my mind."

"I don't know why she won't get a cell phone."

"I've told her. Especially now."

She squints at him in the sun. "Was that the phone?"
"No — is it?" He hops up.

It wasn't the phone. Standing in Nan's bathroom, Hal looks at his face in the bathroom mirror. He has never been handsome, not even when he was young and semifamous and everyone in San Francisco wanted to fuck him. Now that he's balding, he looks, he thinks, like a contestant on a game show: *Hal Cooper! Idaho!* He has a nametag kind of face. Christopher has Hal's height and coloring but Nan's more classic features. Christopher is a good-looking boy because Nan strained the heavy Cooper-ness out. Hal rinses his hands and dries them on the old, damp, navy blue towel tossed over the shower curtain rod. On the floor is an open box of tampons; on the bathroom wall is a framed glamour shot of Betty Grable looking back over her shoulder, her long legs in seamed stockings. A book about the collapse of the Soviet Union that someone is reading — Nan, he bets — rests on the toilet tank cover. Hal wonders if he, not Marina, is the odd one out in this house. He sits down on the edge of the tub.

In the corner of the bathroom where the rusted Virgin Mary used to be, there is now a laminated, multishelved, plastic and metal contraption, with myriad domestic things tumbled among its open shelves: more tampons, cotton balls, soap, razors, a blow dryer, hairbrushes, Tinactin, Monistat, the sleek electric razor Hal gave Christopher last Christmas, bath oil, shaving cream and aftershave, a sprung smoke detector with no battery inside, moisturizer of all kinds, a length of twine, an open package of the batteries that should be in the smoke detector. Hal's bathroom has one glass trolley on which items are arranged nicely. Christopher, of course, has a sleek razor there, too, on his own sparse trolley shelf. The *Star Trek* toothbrush that used to be there has long since — but when exactly? — been replaced by a more knockabout one with flattened bristles. When Christopher is at his house, Hal is so happy. He has always been proud of that, but today he wonders if such pure happiness is in and of itself a sign of inauthenticity, or neglect. Isn't that what clueless parents say after their kids hold up a bank, or worse? "I thought he was fine." He and Christopher, for instance, almost never fight. Until recently, when everything seemed to irritate Christopher, they could go for hours in easy silence, cleaning out the fish tank, or hiking, or watching television, an aptitude Hal thought of as Cooper-like, as opposed to Ashby-like. The Ashbys are always in motion; Nan and her brothers can't leave any field unplanted, any soil untilled, any baby unsmiled at, any fight unfought. Everything is an opportunity for turning over, tilling, as if the world were a vast garden of helpful or possibly injurious, but still interesting, plants.

The Coopers, say what you like about them, are a pretty judicious bunch. They see no need to dig everything up all the time; they calmly roll the world, like a hoop, alongside them; they tend to be very long-lived. Hal was the one who took Christopher to get his haircuts. When they walked back from the barber together, Hal always felt a simple, masculine joy: this is my son. Chris would tell him things, ask him things. It was easy.

Now he wonders if it was too easy. José, when he was mad at Hal, which was often, would always begin, *Mira*. Most of the time, Hal had no idea what it was exactly that José wanted him to see or why José was so angry. For his part, Hal felt grateful to have been airlifted out of the Midwest and into this foggy land of plenty. He felt grateful to have changed. Christopher, to Hal, was an unexpected gift, that much more wonderful because Hal had never even dreamed of him. *Mira*. Look: a son. But he was no Geppetto. He labored only after the child had appeared. You could almost say it was sexist: gee, thanks for the baby. Callow, at least.

Sitting on the edge of the tub, Hal imagines himself a ghost in this house, with a ghost's diffuse restlessness and pain. Don't ghosts hang around places they left too soon? Maybe he should have stayed on that night so long ago. After he gently squeezed the syringe ("Give it a good whack," said Nan), he sat down and leaned against the headboard. Nan was lying on the bed with pillows under her bare hips and that towel discreetly covering them, but it was only a hand towel and it revealed the thick muscles of her short thighs. Not that she cared. She had such a wild streak in her, especially then. She'd ride any pony going. She never even asked him if he'd been tested, probably because she thought her egg could beat his sperm blindfolded, or whatever her dusty terms were. She obviously assumed that this method would work because that's what she wanted. They spoke fondly of Adam; they talked about boys' names and girls' names with increasing silliness; they had no idea what they were doing, just like most people. They were idiots, really. He didn't feel at all in a trance then, either, mostly because it all seemed so tenuous and unscientific, so unlikely. Nan was always slamming in and out of the swinging saloon doors of some big idea or other. He didn't stop to think that there was quite a bit in his life those days that was unlikely, yet real. And as for Nan: he had obviously underestimated her. She reached over and slapped him on the butt when he got up to leave, waving goodbye from her position under the ratty hand towel. "See you, Pa," she said.

Maybe he should have stayed. Maybe they should have actually had sex. Maybe he should have held her and tried to understand whatever it is that she seems to know almost bodily, that thing in her that never hesitates to plant the field, till the soil, pick up the baby, brood, plunge into the mystery with silver hair. But he didn't, and now it's all moving so fast.

Christopher walks into the house without speaking, brushes past Hal on the landing, goes upstairs and into his room, and shuts the door. Nan stands in the hall, holding what looks to Hal like a rolled-up poster. She is haggard, shirttails flapping over her jeans, in sneakers with no socks. Marina rushes in from the garden.

"Where is he?" Marina says, embracing Nan. "Are you all right? What happened?"

"I don't know," says Nan.

From upstairs comes the muffled sound of a CD playing: a woman, or maybe a girl, is singing in a high, atonal, ethereal voice. She sounds like a witch.

The three adults pause in their positions, as if playing freeze tag.

Hal frowns. "What is he doing?"

Marina wonders if Hal feels the same, almost electric quality of Nan's agitated fatigue that she does. It's as if Nan were a battery, and the two of them grounding wires.

"We have to go up and talk to him," Hal says.

Marina remains where she is. "I'll put coffee on."

Hal and Nan ascend the stairs. The atonal sound of the witch girl gets stronger and clearer: she is singing something about a perfect day. Hal has the momentary fantasy that they will open the door to find Christopher at his desk and smiling. *It's a perfect day,* sings the witch, *a perfect day.*

Hal, ahead of Nan, who is stolid and silent, opens Christopher's door. It is sunny and warm in Christopher's room; the witch is singing loudly. Christopher is in his bed, curled up under the covers with a bit of blond hair sticking out. The sun touches his hair in an absurdly lovely way. His flip-flops are lying on the floor, not far from the knife gash, which is still there. A colorful mandala sticker, a gift from Tamara, ornaments Christopher's window, and the shape of it is cast on the floor as well, distended by the angle of the sun. Nan looks at the shadow in a way that is almost angry. Hal hesitates. There is something wrong in the room, something besides the gash in the floor. It smells wrong somehow. The atmosphere is wrong. The atonal girl sings on. She begins to screech.

"Christopher," says Hal. "Christopher."

The heap under the covers is motionless. It is impossible, Hal thinks, that Christopher is asleep, considering the volume of the CD.

"That's enough, Chris," insists Hal. "It's time to get up and talk to us now." Hal sits down on the edge of the bed.

Christopher erupts, covers falling from him, feet kicking under the blankets. His face is red and distorted. "Don't touch me!" he screams. "Don't anyone fucking touch me!" Then he begins to cry, to sob, like a lost boy. His face is crumpled in his hands, tears leaking out through his fingers. He is fully dressed under the covers.

Hal gets off the bed but doesn't move away from it. Nan, stationed in the doorway, nods toward the CD player. Hal turns it off.

"Chris," says Nan, "did you take something?"

Christopher laughs in a throttled way, shaking his head in his hands. His hair is dark with grease and dirt. Nan, thinks Hal, looks frightened; he knows that he must look frightened, too, and despairs for a moment: they're losing, already.

"Why were you asleep, Christopher?" says Hal. "It's the middle of the day."

"Be*cause*," says Christopher, almost whining, "because." He sits up straight, pushes his hair back, stops crying. "I can't tell you here," he says in a very low tone.

"Christopher, what are you talking about?" says Nan from the doorway, a little testily.

Christopher looks at them both levelly, but distantly, as if he knows something, like a language, that they couldn't possibly understand. "If I could tell you," he says in the same barely audible tone, but with increased tension, "I would. Don't you think I would?" He glares righteously from the bed. "I'm not going to be able to stay very long, by the way."

Nan braces herself in the doorway as if to keep him from leaving that minute. Hal, standing awkwardly in the middle of the room, says, "Chris, what's wrong?"

Christopher shakes his head slowly, with great sadness. The silence in the room is oppressive. Hal almost wants to turn the CD back on, but Nan's presence in the doorway warns him against that.

"Jesus Christ," says Nan.

"Listen," says Christopher, quite softly but also annoyed, "if you're going to turn the music off, you really have to keep your voices down."

"Why?" says Hal.

Christopher shakes his head again. The shadow of the mandala on the floor elongates. Nan hangs her head, rubs her eyes. Hal feels that he is falling from a great height. Christopher crosses his arms, impatient, done with them.

Nan, Marina, and Hal sit in the living room, speaking in low voices.

"We have to get this kid to a doctor," says Marina.

"He looks like a refugee," says Nan. "He doesn't look like himself."

Hal says, "He's not." The women look at him questioningly. It's on the tip of Hal's tongue to say, He is mad, he's gone mad, can't you see it? Maybe he truly is a ghost, Hal thinks, because he has the awful sensation that he can see things that aren't there, or aren't there yet. He drops his eyes, makes a vague gesture with his hands.

Nan unrolls Christopher's drawing on the kitchen table.

"What is it?" says Marina. Next to her at the table, like a sleeping spider, is the unhitched phone recording contraption, and, next to that, her small, daily sketchbook. She idly riffles through the pages with one hand.

"I think it's a place."

"Where?"

"I don't know. I can't tell yet." Nan cocks her head. "Did he say something?"

"I can't hear anything up there but that awful music." It's evening, and the witch is still droning on. Every once in a while, there is a small thump.

"Jesus," says Nan. "This thing is intense." The size of an opened newspaper, Chris's drawing is creased and spotted from its travels. One corner is torn. What Nan notices first about it, however, is that it isn't finished: at about the halfway point, it trails off into tentative pen and pencil marks and semi-erased contours of things that might be countries or oceans or valleys. She's encouraged somehow by the fact that she has in her possession something that Christopher is actively working on and that he clearly values. Something he'd want to stick around to finish.

The rest of the drawing is more troubling. Nan would like to love it the way she loves everything about her son, but it's too vibrant, too intricately worked, to love. It resists simple affection. It resists simple reading. It's so dense and complex that it resists, in a way, being viewed at all. It looks medieval to Nan, the proportion and perspective so flat, everything at peculiar angles. She has a sense of déjà vu, peering down, and remembers the atlases she used to bring home from the store. She remembers turning their pages with Christopher as if they were fairy tales: Nairobi, Saskatchewan, the Bering Strait. He put his small, grubby hands on the pages, laughed, tore more than one. But what he has made now is less atlas than realm, some kingdom or frontier. Maybe it's one of those planets from the Sci-Fi Channel.

"Crayon," says Marina, peering. "Ink. Charcoal. Cray-Pas. Magic Marker. Gold felt tip, I think. And — oh. Wow."

"Yeah," says Nan. She holds her hand over the three uneven spots of blood, suspended in a circular structure into which many roads twine and crisscross. There are several of these circular structures on the map, like cloverleafs or maybe cities, it's hard to tell. Only one has blood in it. Inside another, at the center, sits a crow. Inside another is a rocket. The drawing as a whole has a cutaway feeling to it, as if Christopher were drawing not only this landscape, but all the landscapes beneath it as well.

It's undeniably good, but there's just too *much* of it. Too many roads, too many mountains, and what look like several deserts, their sands filled in with the gold felt tip. While some of the drawing materials are childish — the crayons, the Magic Markers — the drawing itself is almost brutally sharp and decisive, simultaneously architectural and visionary. Nan sees that Christopher obviously has a very specific plan in mind. The strength of his will is apparent in every line. How long was he working on it? And when? Maybe this project is what preempted his English homework. It worries her deeply that he would not only make this thing, but drag it around with him on the open road. On the road, you take only necessities.

"It's a kind of dream," says Marina. "It's incredible."

Nan rolls the map back up. "If I had any balls," she says, "I'd burn it right now."

As Nan goes upstairs, Marina unrolls Christopher's landscape again. It is astonishing, and frightening. An unknowable, unlivable place. Wild rooms within rooms. She opens her sketchbook to make a hasty copy — just to remember it, she thinks, just to contemplate it, there's such a peculiar perspective thing happening — then immediately closes it, abashed. She wants to stay in the country Nan tills. Where trees are trees, and not painted in blood.

Outside Christopher's bedroom, Nan thinks, he's forfeited his knocking rights, but she hesitates at the door. She's terrified but she wants to open the door to stare down her terror, unwarned. She knocks. There is a vague assenting sound from inside.

When Nan opens the door, she sees Christopher sitting quietly in the middle of the floor near the knife gash, staring at the palms of his hands. The CD has ended.

He holds up one palm to her. His eyes seem somehow uneven, and much darker. He is showing her something in his hand, but she can't read it.

Nan closes the door. She goes downstairs, gets a kitchen chair, carries it back up, sets it outside Christopher's door, and sits in it. She's glad for all the nights recently that she didn't sleep. She sees now that they were training.

Marina wakes up alone. For a moment, she doesn't remember their situation, she feels only the sweet blur of linen and morning, but where is Nan? Then she remembers and feels sleepy. She looks at the bedside clock: 8:10, 8:11. Marina drifts, cheating: 8:13. She closes her eyes as if she's going to go back to sleep, opens them again: 8:19. She's certain that Nan is still sitting upright in that kitchen chair, posted outside Christopher's door as if she were a sentry. She's certain that Nan is awake, maybe tilting back in the chair, staring up at the ceiling. Perhaps Hal is there already, standing outside in the garden. Perhaps he's calling the doctor on his cell phone, or he's already called the doctor, and the doctor is on his way. Except that doctors don't do that anymore, of course. The three of them will have to take Christopher, in Nan's rattling car. Nan will insist on driving. But where, exactly, will they be going? What will the doctor say?

Marina takes her daily sketchbook off the bedside table, finds a pen on the floor, and begins making a little sketch of some things she dreamed, a tree waving in the wind, some circles, a man in a hat. She writes out a few phrases in loose, indecipherable letters — *the wind was strong* — as the clock turns over to 8:22, 8:27. She sketches Shiloh's face, her arm: Shiloh asleep, her cheek resting on the full interior curve of her elbow. All the girls in Wet Mink love the way Shiloh plays the bass, but with them Shiloh is aloof. She often skips rehearsals to paint. Only with Marina is Shiloh so open, so generous. Shiloh's friends think she's hard to know.

It's 8:32. Marina knows she's being a bad person. An avoider, which is the thing she hates most about herself. She hates it that she's the sort of person who sees a small hole in one of her best sweaters, and then lets the hole grow and grow until it's unmendable and the sweater is ruined. She hates it that at any given moment she never knows where her keys are, such as now: where are they? She can't remember, but, she thinks defensively, they're somewhere. She did come home, after all. She came straight home. Marina hears a murmur downstairs, just one voice. Nan is on the phone. The low, even tenor of her voice is such that Marina believes, for a moment, that it could be an ordinary day. She and Nan could be ordinary, doing ordinary things, having a random, ordinary conversation with Nan's son, Christopher, who is ungainly and sixteen but already showing signs of adult grace. She and Nan could be feeling, in the most ordinary of ways, old by comparison. When he leaves to go to school, they could go back to bed for a little while. Nan could be late for work.

Instead, Marina is alone on her throne of pillows, an uneasy queen. Nan is murmuring to someone, about Christopher no doubt. And Christopher, where is he? At 8:46, Shiloh's question of a few days before lingers in Marina's mind; looking at the sketch of Shiloh asleep, Marina realizes that, if she wanted a child of her own at all, she would want a daughter. They could share everything, and hide everything from each other.

Marina, in her bathrobe, walks down the stairs. The door to Christopher's room, as she passes it, is innocuously open. A discarded brown sock is balled up on the floor, near his desk. His window is open. Marina walks past quickly, superstitiously. As she rounds the last step and enters the kitchen, she sees Nan, phone cradled between shoulder and ear, staring out the sliding glass doors to the garden. Christopher is sitting on the grass, legs splayed, head bent, drawing. Then Marina sees that he is wearing a Walkman; his head is bobbing in time to some tune. Marina rummages through the breadbox on the counter, puts a piece of whole-wheat toast in the toaster.

"I asked him that," Nan is saying. Then, "But what if he doesn't — right. But — sure. Sure. Okay, thanks." She hangs up. Without turning from the glass doors, she says, "I'm supposed to persuade him that he wants to see a doctor."

"Doesn't he?" Marina butters the toast.

"Well. I don't know. He was up all night, I'm pretty sure. I may have fallen asleep once."

"You should have asked me. I would have relieved you."

Nan shrugs. Christopher, through the glass, looks ridiculously happy. Even from this distance, Marina can see that his hair is filthy, that the soles of his feet are black with dirt.

"Where's Hal?"

"He's on his way," says Nan.

"Why didn't you ask?" Marina says again. "You must be completely worn out."

"I don't know," says Nan. "It's like I can't stop. If I had woken you up, then we both just would have been up."

Marina hands the toast to Nan, and she bites at it, chewing slowly.

"I liked to think of you asleep, actually," Nan says. "I liked to think that you were sleeping, and that I would come to bed after a while and get in next to you, and we would sleep. But then he kept on staying up, and I didn't think it was —" Nan hesitates.

"Safe."

Nan turns briefly from the glass. "Right."

Hal arrives with an elegant box of puffy, expensive doughnuts frosted with tiny sugar lilacs, sugar roses, and other whimsical sugar things. He's wearing a fuzzy fleece top, zipped up to his chin in a businesslike way, as if he is going on some sort of expedition requiring polar fleece and flowered doughnuts. His expression is uncharacteristically impatient and brusque. He looks to Marina like a man playing a part, but uncertainly. He makes his entrance.

Opening the glass doors, Hal calls out sternly, "Christopher! Chris! Come in here!" The boy remains transfixed by his drawing. Markers are scattered around him in the grass.

"What the hell is he doing now?" says Hal.

"I talked to this psychiatrist," says Nan, "and she says we need to get him in to be evaluated, they have to work him up —"

"He seems pretty worked up already," says Hal, biting into a chocolate doughnut with orange roses. "He's ignoring me." He closes the glass door, annoyed.

"I don't think he can even hear you," says Marina.

"Blood work," continues Nan. "Talk to him. Certain kinds of tests. She said that behavioral changes can be symptoms of lots of different things, that we should just try to gently talk him into seeing her —"

"He's pissing me off now," says Hal. He frowns, his blond eyebrows drawing together as he glares through the glass at Christopher. "My father would have tanned my hide if I had done what Chris is doing." He adds morosely, "The bastard."

"She said she'll see him anytime," says Nan. "We just have to get him there."

Hal pounds on the glass with one hand, holding the orange-flowered chocolate doughnut in the other. "Chris!" he yells. "Christopher!"

"Hal," says Nan, "have you lost your mind?"

Marina picks up the box of pretty doughnuts and, still in her bathrobe, walks out and across the grass to where Christopher is sitting and drawing, his head moving up and down as if he were a very large, unkempt, exotic flower. He flips his pad over as she approaches, turning his head to stare intently through the gap in the fence to the yard next door, where a picnic table sits on a patch of concrete. Its umbrella is folded and tied; the yard is otherwise empty.

Marina puts the box of doughnuts down on the grass, chooses a coconut one with little inlaid green sailboats made out of Jujube pieces and holds it out to him. "Hey, honey," she says softly.

Christopher takes off his headphones, reaches for the doughnut, eats it quickly, and reaches into the box for another. This one is white with little red icing lips traced on it, as if it has been kissed all over. "I like these," he says in his new, extremely low tone of voice. Marina has to bend forward to hear him.

"I thought you must be hungry, you didn't have any dinner."

He slides his gaze toward her, smiles a half smile. The expression on his face is uncharacteristically sly, almost arrogant, and knowing. Marina doesn't like it, but she doesn't move. Out of the corner of her eye, she can see Hal and Nan standing at the sliding glass doors, watching. Hal's arms are folded. Why did she think she could do this? She doesn't know her lines any better than Hal does.

"Can I have some paper?" she says, picking up a green Magic Marker from the lawn.

Christopher carefully pulls off a sheet from inside the pad without turning it over and hands it to her. From his headphones, the tiny jangle of some assertive youth music plays on. It would be quite loud, Marina can tell, if you were wearing the headphones. Marina folds the sheet of paper a few times, uncaps the

Magic Marker, and begins to sketch the back of the house. "So, what's up?" she says, turning the marker on its side to get the slope of the roof.

Christopher sucks the sugar off his dirty fingers, picks up another doughnut, with zebra frosting. "It's in my back," he says in his determined mumble, "and it's spreading. Don't tell Mom, but it's definitely in my spine, and at night if I stop moving it travels, and you know I can't let that happen, I couldn't do that to her. I have to keep moving, even if it's just one finger, like this." He taps one finger in the grass, like the ticking hand of a clock. "It can get very tiring. But I'm not tired yet. Because I'm still young, you know."

"Does it hurt?"

He regards her with something like pity, but also desperation. "Of course it hurts. I'm in constant pain."

"Sounds like you might need a doctor, Chris —"

"I'm not going to any fucking doctor." He balls up the hand that was ticking and pounds it on the grass: a fleshy gong now, striking the hour. "Don't ever say that to me." His eyes tear up. Black and white frosting flecks his chapped lips.

Marina draws the drainpipe, dots bits of green for tree leaves. The dots look a little like faces to her, plaintive and small. Faces at a window. She doesn't glance in Hal and Nan's direction; Christopher seems unaware that they are there. She breaks off a piece from the only plain doughnut in the box, though she doesn't like doughnuts. She feels suddenly, uncomfortably self-conscious about the thinness of her robe and her nakedness underneath it. Not that he's looking at her body; on the contrary, he's chewing a mouthful of zebra-frosted doughnut, frowning down at the pad on his knees, with tears in his eyes. He has never seemed more childlike. At the same time, he has never seemed larger, to such an extent that Marina wonders if he could possibly have had a growth spurt in the days that he was missing. His hands and feet, his face, even his hair, seem bigger. There is much more of him than there used to be, leaking into the air between them. He seems to exert a dark, off-center gravitational pull.

Marina crosses her legs, stretched straight out in front of her, on the grass. The marker is turning the side of her fist green. It is, surprisingly, almost pleasant to be sitting here with him, sketching in the morning light. As if he feels the same way, he smiles, but not a sly half smile this time. He smiles with innocent abandon, the sun bursting out from behind his teary clouds of just a moment ago.

"Fuck!" he yells up at the sky, exuberantly. "Fuck!" He gives Marina a quick, boyish hug that almost pulls her over. His smell is rank, on the way to being ranker, mixed with the hypersweetness of the doughnuts and the etherlike scent of the markers. As she rights herself, Marina manages to sneak a glimpse of Nan at the glass door. She's leaning against one arm on the glass, her other arm upraised. Hal is at the table, on the phone. It seems to Marina as if they are on land while she is tilting at sea in a small boat with one oar. Though she knows she has only to get up and go back inside the house, she is momentarily unsure that she can and she nearly panics, clutching the green Magic Marker, which squeaks.

"What are you doing?" he says, mumbling urgently again. "What's going on?"

"I was just — nothing. Don't worry about it, Chris."

"About what?" He looks frightened, wary.

Green line of window frame. Faint green dots of mandala. Marina wiggles her toes in a casual way. In the open box, the remaining doughnuts are weeping sugar in the weak sun, their flowers and trinkets softening and shining. "What are you working on?"

The half smile creeps back over Christopher's face. He shrugs, turns the pad over, props his drawing on his knees, facing Marina. His picture, in brown and black and red Magic Marker, is of a head with a flock of crows picking at it. The head fills just one lower quarter of the paper, the eyes rising about an inch above the lower edge, like eyes appearing over a wall. The crows are feasting on the head's open brain; one crow is flying away with a tendril of brain in its large beak. The head is brown; the brains are red; the crows are black. Christopher's large, boyish fingers on the top edge of the paper are grimy, with broken nails.

"We don't need his fucking permission," says Hal, leaning against a kitchen wall. "He's still a minor."

Nan nods.

Marina, at the table, watches as Christopher, still in the garden, covers his face with a blank piece of paper and lies down on his back. He keeps hold of the paper with one hand; the other is open in the grass. His dirty feet slowly fall sideways, in the manner of someone asleep. The doughnut box rests beside him. The tip of the upraised sugar beak of a singing sugar bird is just visible above the edge of the box. It occurs to Marina that the boy with the white paper face, the tiny singing sugar bird, and the placid, ordinary garden all look equally unreal and vulnerable. She is afraid of Christopher, but she also wants to rush out and gather him up in her arms, and take him to Sugar Mountain. She is afraid of Christopher, who has never entirely warmed to her, but she has never felt more tender toward him. It is a tenderness, she knows, that is probably wrong, emanating as it does from the fact that she has, after all, just failed him.

"Could we wrestle him into the car?" asks Nan.

"I don't know," says Hal, going pale. "Though if we have to, we will."

A breeze flutters at the piece of paper over Christopher's face. Otherwise, he is quite still. Marina feels, perversely, that the three of them in the kitchen are nothing but a flock of crows themselves, picking at the downed boy. She is momentarily disgusted, then disgusted by her disgust. They are the adults, after all.

"I can't stand this," says Marina, and the other two look at her with surprise.

"So what?" says Hal miserably. "Do you think we're happy?"

"I'm not really concerned about whether or not you're *happy*, Hal. Or if I'm *happy*. I mean that this is unbearable. I mean that it's like we're in hell with him. I mean that I'm exhausted."

"So what?" says Hal again, unforgivingly, his long form leaning against the kitchen wall like a length of rope, tightly wound. No one says anything for a minute.

Outside, Christopher slowly, methodically, replaces one hand with the other on the piece of drawing paper.

Hal sits on the sofa at Nan's house, reading *Memoirs of a Geisha*. He has tucked his feet, in woolen socks, under one of the sofa cushions. His eyes are tired — they always seem to be tired these days — but he reads on, compelled. Nan and Marina are out; he said, *Go out to dinner. See a movie. I'll stay here. Look, I've brought my book*. Marked with a good leather bookmark, though the book itself is a paperback. He thinks about how he would play Sayuri in the movie. Upstairs, Christopher is quiet. There's a rule about CD hours now. He has an appointment with a doctor tomorrow, though he's already said he won't go, he totally won't. To Hal, the quiet is the sound of a stalemate that might almost be ordinary: a teenager fighting with his parents.

Hal turns a page. He could nearly doze, lulled by story. He thinks, Nan really needs to fix that window. She tends to neglect her interior work.

Instead, he looks up. He lifts his head, then drops the book and climbs the stairs two at a time with his long legs, trying not to make a lot of noise, making sure not to slip in his thick socks. He opens the door of Christopher's room.

His first reaction is to think how slow on the uptake they've been, how unutterably, irresponsibly slow. His second is astonishment. His third is terror, a terror deeper than his immediate fear for Christopher's life.

The bloody handprints seem to cover every square inch of the room, floor to ceiling. They are light in some places, but then much heavier and darker in others. Christopher is sitting on his bed, hunched over with the knife, poking at the side of one hand that appears to be covered in sharp, deep cuts. The hand holding the knife is bloody as well, but still efficient. There is blood in his hair, where he has pushed his hair out of his eyes. There is blood on the sheets.

What terrifies Hal as he tumbles into Nan and Marina's room to call 911 (how much blood? how much time?) is not only the violence to the flesh in the handprints running red on Christopher's walls. It is the fact, as Hal could tell even in the two seconds of his apprehension of the scene from the doorway, that there was so clearly an order to it.

SONOMA

IT'S HOT IN SONOMA, and Christopher is fat. The corridors of
the Pacific Institute are wide and graceful, but he drifts down
them without looking. His head feels heavy on his shoulders; he
has the constant feeling that one of his vital senses has gone missing, though everyone seems to think that the standard five are
enough, and that he should be happy to have them. He might be
happy. He isn't sure. He holds out his arms, touching the hot air.
Because the corridors are pierced with arched doorways leading
to courtyards, only the rooms are air-conditioned. Even in shorts,
Christopher is sweating. He can taste a metallic sweat on his upper lip and feel it as it collects in his armpits. His shirt clings
lightly to his back. The only parts of him that feel cool are the bottoms of his feet as he steps and his flip-flops stir a small, personal-
ized portion of the air. The stirring whispers to him, but too
faintly to hear. This is disappointing. He feels like a loose string.
The gauze on one pinky is unraveling.

Christopher turns left through an archway and passes into a
courtyard. He sees Candy sitting on a shady bench, eating a melting chocolate bar. Her hair is streaked red and purple, her breasts
are heavy in a halter top, and her face is crumpled with the sort of
lines a person gets from being out in the sun day after day, year after year.

"Hi, Chris," says Candy hopefully. Her tone is bright, but her eyes are flat, wide, and suspicious.

Christopher nods curtly.

"Where are you going?"

"Around." He makes it through the courtyard's pressing heat, as if jumping through a ring of fire, and out an arch on the other side. He flip-flops along a brick path past a series of sleeping flower beds, dirt crumbling and dry in the sun. Now the soles of his feet are hot, too. The air smells of dry brown grasses; somewhere nearby something is burning, or already burnt, maybe the air itself. Christopher reaches the pergola on the far side of the flower beds, and sits down. There are no vines or grapes draping over the pergola just now, only curving brown sticks twining around its wooden pillars. A single doll arm is stuffed in a crook where several sticks meet. From where Christopher sits, he can see the western end of the grounds. An old stone wall marks the boundary. On top of the wall is a green chainlink fence. Wall and fence corner together, running into the trees.

"Fucker," says Christopher, shaking one bare, white foot.

There is no breeze. A man in khakis and sandals flickers briskly along the exterior walkway, his white shirt like a crisp sail in a good wind. Candy, in her courtyard, is turning in slow circles in the sun. The man pauses, calls to her. They chat.

"Too hot," says Christopher softly. "Too, too hot." He feels suspended in the burning air. He pulls the grubby doll arm from its sticks and pats his cheek with it. His cheek feels the same way it always has. Christopher sighs. This hot world is so flat that he can't believe he doesn't fall right off the edge, though everyone tells him that this is it, this is the world. He isn't sure what he believes.

In the doctor's office of the Pacific Institute, Nan crosses an ankle over a knee and taps her empty plastic water bottle against the splitting sole of her sneaker. The bottle makes a hollow sound.

"I don't like it," she says.

The doctor is young, with a sprouting mustache. His name is

Dr. Friend, and he often indicates that he knows this is funny by raising an eyebrow or gesturing ironically at the nameplate on his desk. Nevertheless, he seems to be a confident young man, with clean, strong hands and neat rows of current psychiatric journals lining his bookshelves. The only hint that he might be less than confident is his tendency to blush, which he is doing now, though it is also warm in his office. Dr. Friend apparently prefers breezes to air conditioning; a gleaming, retro-modern fan stands tall and silver in the corner, blowing the heat around. "Should I explain it again?" asks Dr. Friend.

"No," says Nan curtly, tapping. "I said I didn't like it, not that I didn't understand it."

Hal appears in the doorway, and Dr. Friend looks up gratefully. "Find him?" says the doctor.

"He wasn't in his room. His roommate said he went for a walk." Hal lowers himself into the chair next to Nan.

"I bet I know where he is," says Dr. Friend. "There's a place he likes to sit. I'll show you."

Nan taps faster.

Dr. Friend sits up straight in his chair. A growing wave is furling his dark hair. "Schizophrenia," he says, "is not just one thing, and that's what this new drug is trying to address, but because it does several things at the same time, it takes longer for it all to be integrated. That's why Christopher seems uncoordinated as a personality right now. He is. The old drugs — the old new drugs, I should say — were very good at targeting certain symptoms, but then we had to balance out the other problems with other drugs, plus neutralize the side effects of the primary drugs, and frequently the recipe was never quite right. But Serenepan" — he gestures at the square notepad on his desk with *Serenepan* scrolling in script on the collective edges of its sheets — "is incredibly responsive to every subtle imbalance. It's very fine. But because of that it takes longer to . . . how shall I put it? Set. We have to be patient." He adds, earnestly but also firmly, "He's really doing very well."

"But it's still *experimental*," begins Nan.

"That's what we do here," says Dr. Friend evenly. "You know that."

"Nannie," says Hal, "this is the best, most advanced —"

"He's still a guinea pig," says Nan, frowning. "We all know that, too."

Dr. Friend shakes his head. "No. I really have to stop you there, Nan. Serenepan is very far along. We didn't mix it up out back yesterday." He smiles at his small joke. "Sorry. It's hot." He glances at the fan, which is set to high. "I think you're asking me something else, Nan."

"Don't patronize me."

He presses on. "I think you're asking me if this diagnosis is really true."

The doctor points the way from a courtyard arch, and Nan and Hal trudge up the brick path toward the pergola. Christopher, with his gauzy white hands, stands up, watching them approach. Candy follows them until Hal turns around and says, "We need to hang with Chris alone for a while, Can. We'll find you later on."

"No, we won't," mutters Nan as Candy stands alone on the path, waving her chocolate bar wrapper.

Hal laughs. "What's her diagnosis again?" he says in a low voice.

"I don't know. Burnout or serial killer or something. Chris doesn't like her."

"Well, she sure likes him. Guess he's got a way with the ladies."

"For God's sake, Hal."

Hal turns, waves back at Candy. "She's got a certain blowsy charm."

"Please shut the fuck up."

"Nan," says Hal, "I do believe that they know what they're doing." His forehead is covered in sweat. His ears are red. Standing on the hot brick path in the sun, he looks like a wandering column in search of a building to support. His hands are turned up awkwardly at his sides.

Nan pushes at a loose brick with her foot. She has always halfway hated Sonoma. In the dry season, it reminds her too much of Texas. "They're just playing with his brain," she says quietly.

Hal's ears redden further. He turns his back so that Christopher, in the pergola, can't see his face. "God*damn*it, Nan, do you know what this place would cost if he wasn't on the protocol? Were you listening? Since I'd be the one who —"

"Don't you dare bring up money to me. This is a child. Our child."

"Nan, he is my child, so I *have* to think about it. You know that. Someone does." Hal feels desperate but also determined. In his mind's eye, he sees money and Christopher's sanity washing out together and staining the dry, hot earth.

Nan's gaze shifts to Christopher, still standing patiently in the pergola. "He's waiting," she says. "What's that in his hand?"

Christopher, watching Nan and Hal argue on the path, thinks that the two of them look soft, like wax figures melting in the sun. Dr. Friend, in one of their sessions, asked him, "What is it about them that worries you so much?" Christopher didn't have an answer, but now he sees that it's the way they're always coming after him, following him, the way they unite in his presence. Like the angelfish looking for food.

They embrace him, they kiss him.

"You're flushed," says Hal. "Are you all right? Too hot up here?"

"No," says Christopher. "I'm always hot. It's the blubber." He grabs a handful of his belly, shakes it. "I'm an Eskimo."

"No, you're not," says Nan, sitting down on the bench. "You're an Ashby-Cooper. Christ, it's hot."

Christopher puts the doll arm in his back pocket, remains standing.

Hal stands next to him. "The doctor says you're doing well."

"Are you?" says Nan.

Christopher shrugs again. "When can I go home?"

There is a silence.

"Soon," says Hal.

"How soon?" The alternating light and shadow of the pergola slats fall across Christopher's face and body. Though he is fat, with sweat on his upper lip, his paleness and roundness make him look buoyant, as if he is floating, striped, inside the structure. His white hands seem webbed. Nan, looking up at him, has the impulse to grab his ankle, as if he's a balloon.

Instead, she says, "Baby, you need to let the doctor do his work. You'll be home before you know it."

Christopher nods. "When is Tamara coming?"

Marina goes with Nan to the Pacific Institute. Hal isn't making this visit; this is how they do it now, switching off, taking turns, spelling each other. As if any decisions are made by her, or when she's there. She and Nan are going to have to talk about that, later. Marina drives. At least I'm doing that, she thinks. Nan broods on her side of the car, smoking. She has begun to smoke again from time to time, a development about which Marina says nothing. Nan, brooding, smoking, keeps her window open, tapping ash out now and then.

"Shit," says Nan.

Marina adjusts her sunglasses.

"Fuck. Motherfucker. Cocksucker." The hot air blows in.

"Do you want to stop?"

"No. Fuck. Goddamn."

Marina watches the road, which snakes and swerves between the dry, brown hills.

While Nan talks to the doctor, Marina sits with Christopher in his room. He shares it with an obsequious, fiftyish man named Mel whose wrists are crisscrossed with thick scars, but Mel is apparently out. The television in the room is inset into the wall, its screen covered with a thick sheet of scratched plexiglass. The remote is permanently affixed to a spot on the nightstand that can't be reached either lying down in bed or sitting in the one chair. A person would have to stand up to change the channel or the volume. You'd have to stand up and be reminded that everything in the room was bolted down, including the chair you sat in or the bed you lay in, watching the untouchable television through scratched plexiglass. Marina thinks that scratched piece of plexiglass would be art to some people, but she finds it awful. It seems to her that something in her would be truly dead if she gave in to the impulse to think about that scratched piece of plexiglass as art.

Christopher looks at her with clear eyes. He is, undeniably, much better. "So, how are you?" he says, crossing his legs on the bed.

Marina, in the chair, says, "Well, I'm okay, Chris. I'm glad to see you."

"Do you want to watch TV?" He is wearing a white T-shirt and a pair of loose, blue drawstring pants. Someone has cut his hair into a neat, classic boy's cut with a side part, short at the neck and ears. This cut, along with his newly round face and almost excessively straightforward expression, makes him look like a young Mormon, like the purely American boy he is, the only son of Nan Ashby and Hal Cooper. He looks like the kind of boy who could sell you a car, or a religion.

"No, I'd rather talk to you."

"All right." Christopher reaches over to scratch his toe. As he slightly inclines his forehead, his face goes blank for an instant. It's the drugs, thinks Marina, and she is embarrassed to admit to herself how grateful she is for the chemical wall interposed between them. She thought she had succeeded in loving him, finally, before all this started. She hates him for that, in a way: he has deprived her of her confidence in her own affection, her empathy. He has cast her back into that lonely orbit where she always used to spin before Nan, convinced, secretly, that she didn't love, not really. *La belle dame sans merci.* There had been so much comfort in being caught, and no matter how modern they were, how evenly matched, how intricate their conversation and their principles, Marina knew that she cleaved to Nan, helplessly, and she was glad to know she could be that helpless, thankful to be X-rayed at last.

Christopher regards Marina politely, and far underneath his good manners Marina wonders if she glimpses something smug. He has finally unmasked her for the impenetrable creature she is. She has the disquieting thought that he knows about Shiloh, that his illness has given him special powers. A bird cries outside the window; Christopher turns his head slowly, and Marina decides that she is being too hard on both of them. This is a boy in trouble on a hot day. Kin to her now, though unchosen, as all kin are.

"Have you started to draw again?" She gestures at her bag, resting on the floor. "I brought some things."

"I haven't really felt like it," he says. The skin on his palms is new but plainly intact.

Christopher's drawing, Marina knows, is rolled up and resting on a top shelf of Nan's and her bedroom closet. She was the one who wouldn't let Nan throw it away, but they didn't bring it to him at the Institute, either, and Marina wonders guiltily if he remembers that it exists. She wonders if he remembers why he acquiesced, because it was a mystery to them, a miracle, as the fan in Dr. Friend's office whirred on and Christopher stared at the floor as if he were a spy being interrogated. It was the one decision at which she was present. *Okay*, he finally said. *Okay, all right.* Hal cried. Nan looked stubborn and sad. Marina was exhausted. *Okay,* Nan had echoed. *That's it, then.* Dr. Friend seemed unsurprised, leading Christopher away from them and down the Spanish Revival hallway, one hand resting gently, precisely, on Christopher's shoulder: a trick accomplished without visible strings or pulleys or winches, just words. Drugs to patter softly, unobtrusively behind. This, they all knew, was why the Pacific was so expensive, and why they, too, acquiesced quietly, signing the papers, agreeing to the terms, accepting the risks. It was clear that Dr. Friend was very smart. It was also clear that he wasn't telling them everything. Silently, they agreed that they'd rather not know. They were all tired, silent, listening to the gleaming silver fan whir. They'd been there for hours. It was dark outside. When Marina stopped for gas on the way home, Nan bought a pack of cigarettes. Marina watched Nan's small, grainy replica on the security TV through the convenience store window, hands balled up and stuffed in her jacket pockets, head lowered. If she weren't a forty-five-year-old woman, she'd seem like a boy looking for trouble. But the man behind the counter barely glanced at her as he handed her the pack and her change.

Marina reminds herself that Christopher knows nothing of the distress back home, nor should he. He fluffs a pillow behind his back with clean, plump, new hands. His fingernails are whole and pink, though his right hand has a faint tremor, ticking against the pinkish bedspread. He doesn't appear to be particularly self-conscious about it. "What about you?" he asks. "What are you working on these days?"

"Me?" Marina isn't sure how or if to answer, then thinks, Well, all right. "You know, I haven't gotten so much done recently."

"Why?" he inquires.

"Because." She stops, brought up short by all she can't say; she should have lied to protect him. "Because. It can be like that."

He nods. "I know what you mean." He adds reassuringly, "But you'll get back into it."

"Absolutely." She reaches over and gives his pale toe a little pull. She wants so much to love him again.

"Absolutely," he agrees. "Trees are a classic."

Hal agrees to take Tamara to see Christopher. Tamara's father, a big man with a soft voice who works for Wells Fargo, and her mother, a psychotherapist, tell Hal that they have a lot of faith in their only child. "Tamara really has terrific boundaries," says her mother. "She'll let you know if she's getting overwhelmed." In the car on the way to Sonoma, Tamara dips artichoke leaves into a jar of pungent, greenish sauce while listening to her CD-man. Hal is surprised to discern the miniature, tinny rattle of Bob Dylan leaking from Tamara's earbuds. Somehow, it makes him feel even older. As they drive through the gate of the Pacific Institute, Tamara pulls out the earbuds and sits forward. "It's like college," she says with some admiration. Hal, absurdly, has a moment of pride at having impressed her. She's a difficult girl to impress.

Despite the averred faith of Tamara's parents, Hal doesn't leave the two teenagers alone. Christopher leads them all to a day room that could, indeed, be a day room in some college somewhere. There are several couches and many deep chairs covered in a vaguely Native American print; there are old magazines scattered on wooden tables; there is a soda machine against the wall. Residents mill around with their guests; the difference between the two is mostly a matter of bundles: guests arriving with them, residents accepting. A few orderlies hover, discreetly checking that nothing has been brought in that's sharp, or potentially poisonous. A young woman with a melancholy face and cornrows begins unfurling a red and yellow kite for an extremely dour, elderly white man, but the kite, trailing string, is quietly confiscated. One yellow bow sticks up from the canvas bag the orderly carries. Hal, as usual, would like to know how the man and woman are related to each other, by blood or affinity. The only thing they appear to have in common is their sadness.

Tamara drops comfortably into a chair as if she's a regular visitor. Christopher drops into the deep chair next to hers. Hal takes the sofa, trying to relax. As a group, the residents make him nervous. He has just begun to understand Christopher's condition — there is a stack of books on his bedside table — but he doesn't understand what's wrong with all these other people, and their accumulated misery and disarray weigh on him. It feels to him almost impolite to be so ignorant, like not knowing the last name of someone's lover or thinking that every Hispanic person is Mexican. Hal wants to go around the room and ask everyone's diagnosis; then he could separate them into uniformed squads: manic-depressives in red, schizophrenics in blue, multiple personalities in parti-color, and so on. That would be more organized, but also somewhat festive. Instead, however, the day room is jumbly and filled with banal small talk. The emotional atmosphere, to Hal, is cubist. "Is your stomach still hurting you?" says the melancholy woman to the dour man.

"Yo, C," says Tamara. "What's up?"

"I live in an insane asylum," says Christopher roguishly, and they both laugh so hard that Tamara starts hiccupping.

Hal, holding an ancient, battered issue of *Martha Stewart Living* on his knee, isn't sure whether to be happy or alarmed that Christopher has regained his ability to flirt.

"Yeah, right," says Tamara. She pulls an ottoman from a neighboring chair and props her feet on it, one sandal dangling from a toe. "When do you get out?"

"I don't know." His right hand trembles against the chair arm. Were they lovers? No one knew before, and now no one asks for fear of alienating Tamara, their living link to the Christopher who talked on the phone for hours and ate red Twizzlers.

"You've missed a ton of school," says Tamara in an approving way. "I told everyone you went to Fiji."

Christopher smiles. Hal has the sense that *Fiji* is code for something, an inside joke; he turns the slick magazine pages, thinking, Tamara, help us.

"Yeah," says Christopher. "That would be cool."

"We could," says Tamara brightly, casually. This encouragement amuses Hal somewhat less than it makes him want to throttle her. She is too young to understand the nature of a true emergency. He shifts on the sofa, then gets up and buys himself a ginger ale out of the soda machine. The simple sound of the coins dropping, the thud of the soda can tumbling down, calms him. One of the orderlies, Raúl, passes by. "How you doin' today, Hal?" he says, then answers the question himself: "All right." He continues down the hall.

When Hal gets back, Tamara and Christopher have turned in their chairs to face each other, speaking in low voices. Tamara is curled in her chair, both sandals fully discarded on the floor, bare feet on the cushions. She is touching Christopher's arm with one finger, emphasizing some point.

" . . . like you," she is saying.

"No, no." He has the new naked look on his face, a single emotion: *No.*

"Chris," says Tamara in a cajoling tone. "Come on."

"What?" says Hal, standing over them with his soda.

The teenagers exchange a glance. "Nothing," says Tamara. "It's cool."

Christopher, in his chair, is pouting and shrugging at the same time. He shakes his hair out of his eyes boyishly, shrugs again. "Yeah," he says. "It's cool."

"Let's take a walk," says Tamara. "Over that way." She nods in the direction of the French doors that lead to the shady side of the grounds. She slips on her sandals.

Christopher stands up. With an almost visible shifting of gears, his expression changes from annoyed to pleased. Hal musters the courage to say, "You two go. It's too hot for me. I'll stay here and read about how to make bleach out of raisins." He forces himself to laugh, sit down on the sofa, and pick up the magazine he's just leafed through.

Hal watches as Tamara and Christopher exit the room, then re-appear on the other side of the French doors, in the sun. Tamara firmly takes Christopher's hand, and he picks up their joined hands, making a single, wavelike arm. Tamara laughs, looking up at him. They disappear around the side of the building. A few minutes later Hal sees them, smaller now, walking between the neat rows of trees.

Tamara, holding Christopher's hand, thinks that his hand feels dry. Maybe that's because this is the one that shakes; she can feel that they already have a joke about it. He kicks off his hospital sandals as soon as they enter the little grove of trees, a gesture that reassures her. Christopher always liked to be barefoot. Tamara kicks off her shoes as well. Their two scuffed pairs of shoes lie be-hind them on the grass in hugely distended steps, as if giants dropped them there. He sniffs the air like an animal, and this ges-ture, too, Tamara finds reassuring. Christopher is that rare boy who's earthy without being revolting; Tamara knows that he thinks she is that rare girl who's feminine without being cunty.

There are a lot of cunty girls and revolting boys in their school, in fact, practically all of them.

"Way to get committed," says Tamara. "It's nice here."

"It's okay." Christopher sits down heavily beside a tree, his back to the red-roofed institute. Tamara kneels next to him, looking into his face. If his face were a clock, she thinks, it would be slow. Not by hours maybe, but by enough minutes that you wouldn't be able to rely on it to get anywhere on time. His right hand flutters in the grass beside them, like their child or their pet. She puts a hand on his thigh — *it's me* — and he puts his hand with its soft new skin on hers. Tamara's heart turns over.

"Looks like someone's been hitting the minibar," she says.

He laughs, but doesn't remove his hand. "It's the drugs, Tam. I have to take them every day." His gaze, for a moment, is vulnerable. Tamara, as usual, tries to dodge quickly through the opening in their two sets of eyes: his blue ones, her green ones, locked, appraising. But Christopher, as usual, drops his gaze before she can quite get all the way in, leaving half her expectations blowing in the breeze like someone's ass and legs hanging out a window, the ladder kicked away. I'm an idiot, she thinks.

"So tell them you've been faking," she jokes. "Tell them what a good actor you are. Not."

"Yeah," he says, but in a cloudy way. "I wish."

Tamara, resting on her heels, tries to hate him, or at the very least dislike him (she know it's bad for her self-esteem to feel rejected all the time), but she just can't. She knows how shy he is, basically. "What do you do all day?"

"Stuff — therapy, group, art time. I get bored. It's dumb a lot. They have rules for everything." He shrugs, pulling at a blade of grass. "I've missed you sometimes."

Tamara remains still. "Oh, yeah?"

He smiles at the grass. "Yeah, sure. Why not?"

"Fuck you."

He reaches over and pulls her into his arms awkwardly, and she rests her head against his chest. He's wearing a kind of preppy,

white shirt with a collar which he would never have chosen himself over some loose blue pants that make him look, Tamara
knows, like a crazy person. But his scent and his skin are all Christopher. His neck is Christopher. He's wearing the cord and blue
bead she gave him. The flutter of his hand is already familiar. It's
hard for her to believe, even now, that he could have done to himself what they said he did. Her mother had explained it to her —
bipolar, schizoaffective, schizophrenic, decompensated — adding, because she could still be pretty great sometimes, the names of all
the famous people who had had things like that, how it could
have a positive side, and new drugs, and nothing so scary, in a
way. Like diabetes. But her mother also said, He's ill, Tam. Christopher has a serious illness. Tamara nodded. She got it. Though
when she brought up the famous people to him in the day room,
he said so strongly, *No, no.* As if she were missing an important
piece of information, either about him or the famous crazy people, she wasn't sure. And no one had told her how quiet it would
be, how peaceful, resting under the trees in the heat of the day
with Christopher. She is so glad to see him.

"You were stupid not to sleep with me that time," says Tamara,
touching his foot with hers. His foot feels dry, too, and this trou-
bles her. Why is he so dry? Sonoma is dry, but he's drier. It's as if
he's in a constant wind that doesn't affect anyone else. His eyes,
she's noticed, are of a darker blue now. An older, more condensed
blue. She tries to imagine what he sees with them, his world
through this blue filter.

"Yeah, I don't know." He strokes her back.

"I just meant that then we could have gotten it out of the
way." Remembering her self-esteem, Tamara sits up. "So, come on,
tell me."

"What?"

"What it's like." It's always this way with Christopher: Tamara
asks, and he answers, slowly, sometimes only in a note or an e-
mail. He didn't even tell her about his whole parent thing for the
longest time, until she finally asked him point-blank, and then it
was like, Yeah, it's cool. She still doesn't know if it's cool or not. He

draws her on with his silence, but, anyway, today is different. They have fallen beside this tree together, barefoot, alone, and no one at school except Tamara knows where he is or what's really happened to him. It's more Fiji than Fiji. Where they planned to live in the trees, with their sixteen longhaired children, who speak their own language that sounds like a cross between Chinese and French, and make perfect little ships out of bark that they sell for tons of money in the market. Christopher likes to make things up more than he likes to talk about what's happening at any given moment. Though the things he makes up are usually great.

"What it's like." He seems almost confused by the question. He frowns. "What it's like." He glances around them at the orderly, silent trees. The sun glares just beyond where they sit, loud in its intensity, but they are in the hushed shade. Tamara waits patiently, not touching Christopher. With his steady hand, he tucks a lock of blond hair behind his ear. Tamara has always thought that Christopher would make a good rock star. In a bloated phase, these days, but that could be part of it.

He pulls up his knees; his bare toes on the grass look sincere. "It's hard to explain," he says. He puts a hand to his head. "And then this stuff, fuck." He sighs. "Okay. I met people, and some of them were really cool. People will help you more than you think, like this guy Johnny, he was so cool. We got to know each other so well." Tamara smiles, trying not to feel hurt. "Other people were fucked up. They did fucked-up things and then tried to pretend they hadn't. I had to watch out." He makes karate arms somewhat slowly, looks at them, or maybe at his sleeves, Tamara can't quite tell. "Anyway. It was an experience."

"But what was it *like?*" asks Tamara. "Inside."

"Um. Kind of stressful. I worried — about you, too, Tam. I worried about you a lot."

"Me? Why?"

He shakes his head. "I can't tell you."

"Like that thing with the knife?" She carefully does not look at either of his hands.

He stretches out his legs, folds his arms. The fluttering hand disappears, like a bird that has flown into a tree. His face closes up, leaving just his blue eyes, clear and dark and hard, to focus on Tamara. "That had a reason, Tam. *Everything* was for a reason. Every single thing. It would take too long to explain. But, you know, let's just say, okay, if you knew that you were always being *overheard,* that there was a record and there were dates and you were in constant pain — it's like an extreme emergency situation. You wouldn't ask a doctor or a fireman why they did a certain thing at a certain moment. It was like that. That's all I can say."

Tamara nods. She isn't sure she understands, but in a way she thinks she does. It's an imaginary emergency, but it isn't imaginary to him. Most important, it's a confidence. He obviously trusts her or he wouldn't be telling her all this. She resolves to write it down later, then moves to be next to him, leaning against the same, slender tree. It's rough against both their backs. He has been breathing hard, but after a few minutes he breathes more quietly, and in the quietness Tamara plunges ahead, stepping out of her irony the way she had stepped out of her shoes. "Why didn't you call me?"

Lying in bed listening to the night sounds in the corridor, Christopher pulls the cotton sheet up to his shoulders, and waits. In the other bed, Mel turns over and gently begins to rock in his sleep. Christopher closes his eyes, but he's not sleepy yet. He often doesn't sleep at night, and he knows he's supposed to tell Dr. Friend this, but he doesn't. He conjures Tamara — her straight brown hair, her palm on his thigh — then slides his hand into his pajama bottoms. He's half-hard. The tender skin on his palm tingles. Yes/no. He now often thinks just those two words. He puts the time before he got here sometimes into the yes category, at other times into the no category. There was so much to see and hear then, so much to figure out. Some of it would scare Tamara if she knew about it, the way dark things leaned toward her, the words in the songs about her, the cars outside the school. Who was really in those cars, waiting for Tamara? He'd still like to know. It's like a math problem he can't quite solve, though he tries, all day long. He worries that the pills have made him less smart. It's all so frustrating. When Christopher thinks of his own mind, it's like standing in an empty room looking at a locked door. Yes. No. Yes. No.

Nan stops for gas on the way to Sonoma. It's a Tuesday, and she's alone. She pumps the gas, staring idly at the road, the hills, the electrical towers that line the hills, made delicate by distance. She reracks the gas nozzle, walks inside to pay. A boy who seems to be about Christopher's age, wearing a silver ring in the shape of a skull, rings her up.

"And a pack of Merits."

"That shit will kill you," says the skull-ring boy. His dark hair is cut every which way. Above his head, the television is tuned to a baseball game. A bat cracks against a ball.

"Did I ask for your opinion?"

He smirks, charmed by his own ability to annoy people, and hands her the cigarettes.

"Are you watching that game?" says Nan.

"Yes," he replies, "I certainly am."

"So who's winning?"

He makes a face and laughs. "No fucking idea."

A few minutes later, Nan pulls onto the hot shoulder of the hot road to cry. She blows smoke out the window, crying helplessly, angry beyond angry. Angry, she now realizes, forever. She will be angry forever. She slams her fist into the dashboard over and over, until it hurts. She and her brothers used to have a deal in the old days that whoever got hit by their father that evening, or morning, or middle of the night, was allowed to pick one of the other siblings and hit that person as hard as possible. They got goose bumps from the wild justice of it, standing in the culvert as Jonathan (most often) or Henry or Robert or, not as often, and this was a kind of shame to her, Nan, pointed at one of the others, said, "*You*," and slammed a fist or a head into some soft part of the body where bruises weren't immediately visible. No face shots, ever, and if they were in the car and someone had just gotten smacked, that one, hunched up and not crying, would secretly point, and at the first opportunity they'd all skulk off. Come back feeling better, cleansed. *You. J'accuse.* It's a dark joke among the four of them now. Sometimes, as Henry and Robert's kids run shrieking and innocent through various rooms and yards, one of the adults will point at another, *You,* make a fist, and they'll laugh. Refuse to explain, should a child pause in midflight to ask. Jonathan will pick the child up, kiss him or her. "C'mere, darlin'. Tell me a story." Jonathan is magical with children, a pied piper.

Nan leans her head back against the molting headrest and enjoys the throb of her hand in the hot car. *You. You. You.* Even though she was the oldest, it was so rarely her turn.

Marina paints Christopher's room. She offered to do it while Nan went up to Sonoma, making a joke about painting, her finest work, though there is truly something pleasurable about even this mundane task. She never tires of the way paint moves and changes. She decided to paint his room a soft yellow with an even softer blue ceiling. His favorite shirt was striped in just those colors. First she bleached the blood off the walls, then she primed them. It wasn't grisly to her so much as poignant, like washing the body of someone who is ill. As she drapes his furniture in plastic, mixes the acrid, creamy paint, she feels that this act is her gift to him, to his getting better. It occurs to her, as she brushes a streak of tender blue along his ceiling, that her role in all this would seem small only to someone who didn't understand the importance of the intimate outsider: the interesting aunt, the traveling uncle, the parent's lover. A few drops of blue paint spatter her face. Isn't voluntary love as important as involuntary love? Doesn't it paint the walls just as well? Better, maybe. She takes her time with the edges, making them as perfect as possible.

Dr. Friend turns off the fan. The gleaming silver blades slow, then still. On Wednesday afternoons, Dr. Friend, whose first name is Jacob, leaves work early and meets his bike club in Napa. Dr. Somers, a busty woman with enormous lilac eyes, will be hurrying in, late, in a few minutes. Jacob finds her irritating, a Busy Little Thing, but knows that that's not the point, and, besides, it's misogynistic of him to be irritated. He leans out the window to see who's sitting in the courtyard: Drew, Cassandra, Candy, Christopher leaning against an archway. Jacob wishes they all weren't quite so fat; they're all on Serenepan — the group that clearly didn't get the placebo, standing together and laughing, as if on the cover of a drug brochure — and they're all, quantitatively, quite a bit better, except Candy, who can't get it right no matter what she does. Her body continually betrays her. Jacob dreams about Candy at night, often that she's gasping for air, or that she's extraordinarily tiny, like a mouse. Just now she's chatting to the others, laughing, throwing up her hands. Jacob ducks back in the window before she can see him and call out to him. It's his Wednesday afternoon; it's time for him to leave. Having seen Christopher reminds Jacob to fold the boy's file and put it away. At the bottom of Christopher's chart, he has written "Stable," and the date, and signed it. A good note on which to end a Wednesday.

In truth, the fact that he's living at a moment when real hope is available to patients like Christopher makes Jacob both happy and nervous; he doesn't relish the role of drug jockey. He believes there is still much work to be done in diagnosis. They still don't even know, really, exactly what these people have; the pills are getting so good that they're extinguishing all the symptoms in one fell swoop, like the fires burning down the rainforest. Jacob sometimes mourns these lost ecosystems of insanity; in Christopher Ashby-Cooper, for instance, he thought he spotted a kind of intriguing magenta feather, but it's since disappeared. He could leave the file out for Dr. Somers with a note, she could make the call to the family as well as he, but Jacob saves the task for himself. It is, he knows, a bit of a petty, self-aggrandizing gesture. He is aware that he is not by nature a kind man, only a curious one.

Nan and Marina eat breakfast. The sliding door to the garden is open. A breeze blows in. Nan turns a page of the *San Francisco Chronicle,* looking for news she can bear. Marina eats granola and yogurt, wearing a long, white, destroyed T-shirt that is more like the idea of a T-shirt. Her hair is dirty. Nan eats toast with butter; the Trader Joe's wrapper is open on the table, a ragged, sloping tablespoon or so of butter left at the end. A butter knife lies on the wrapper, its handle greasy. Near the butter knife is a cigarette pack with two cigarettes left inside and a pack of matches wedged under the cellophane. The house still smells faintly of the new paint upstairs. Outside, a few tendrils of trumpet vine are being tugged by the breeze. The neighbors' cat looks into their yard from the gap in the fence, but doesn't enter. Instead, she sits down and stares.

"Going to be a hundred and two up there today," says Nan.

"It's hot here, too."

The phone rings.

On the drive to Sonoma with Nan and Marina to bring his mad son home, Hal realizes the purpose of his life. Hal is driving, because they're in his car, a black Audi wagon. The Internet boom bought him this car, so Hal refers to it as his virtual Audi. Nan, buckled in beside him in the front seat, calls it the globalizationmobile. She slants all the air-conditioning vents so they blow on him.

"Can I smoke?"

"No," says Marina from the back seat. "What are you doing up there?"

"Helping Hal drive."

"Why don't you put on a CD?" says Hal. "Something festive. For a good day."

"Look at the hills," says Marina. "They're so dry. It's great, in its way."

Nan sighs, clacking through CD jewel boxes. "This is the music our parents listened to. Isn't Barbara Cook dead?"

"Do you even know who she is?" asks Hal.

Nan eyes the CD. "A fat lady?"

In the rearview mirror, Marina laughs, shadowed by a flowing filmstrip of desiccated hillsides, as if it is the hills that are moving, not the car. She rubs the line between her eyebrows.

"Okay, I give up. It doesn't matter, anyway." Nan slips in a CD.

"That's nice," says Hal.

"Can I smoke now?" asks Nan rhetorically. "I should quit. Chris isn't going to like it that I've become a smoker again."

Hal, strapped in to the virtual Audi, realizes that he has never been happier in his life, and that this drive is the purpose of his life. This exact drive, on this exact day, at this exact moment, 7:43 A.M., going sixty-eight miles an hour, the internal temperature seventy-two, the external temperature ninety-one. He is carrying them, Nan and Marina and, soon, his mad son, Christopher, whom he does not believe to be cured, not at all. It doesn't matter. He knows they are going to lose. He will carry them on his back, in this expensive black snail shell of an Audi. He is a fatally steady man; he would happily drive them all to hell. The car is still, the desiccated hills are moving. Even Marina's faintly eerie silver glamour, her off-putting distance and lying, he understands, is part of it. When Christopher was first speaking, he referred to both Hal and Nan for a while as Mommy. "Mommy," he'd squeal to Hal, holding out his arms to be picked up. Everyone was a mother — everyone in the world. That's how it should be.

The stucco buildings of the Pacific Institute, graceful in the sun, look like a winery that's closed to tourists for the day. They get out of the car. Marina turns around, waiting for Hal. Nan glances up at the sky. Her shirt is tucked in, her hair freshly cut. Her pants, belted, are slightly too baggy in a way that makes her look older. Her reading glasses — perilously, recklessly — poke up from a back pocket. Hal resolves to buy her a glasses string.

When Hal reaches the two women, Marina says, "I can't stand this place. I'm so glad we're getting him out of here." Willowy, one arm crooked, her hair a silver mess, Marina seems to Hal to have a faintly immigrant quality, like a Slav. When she speaks, it's almost as if English is her second language: she picks up each word and sets it down carefully. Hal suddenly understands that this slightly alienated, immigrant air is what Nan loves so deeply. Nan, who is slowly retucking her shirt, loves it when beauty slips on the gap; she flings herself to its rescue, over and over, heroically. On this hot morning, Hal loves Nan for that: my beautiful loser, he thinks. She tucks her shirt in again. Their eyes meet.

"It's okay," he tells her. "Let's go in."

The three of them pass into the institution without speaking, as if they are a team of burglars committing a heist. The orderly at the discreet wicker desk nods them inside. The hallway is underpopulated and quiet, because visiting hours haven't started yet. One of the doctors, a balding man with a solemn expression, is sitting in a wicker chair reading a book. As they pass by, his highlighting marker squeaks. He smiles at them. When they reach Dr. Friend's office, Hal and Marina wordlessly hang back. Nan goes in but immediately reappears.

"He's not there," she says.

They proceed with soft criminal steps. The halls are all as quiet as a school in summer, and they have a school's fleshy, antiseptic air. The dust motes might be chalk, instead of dry Sonoma dirt. Marina subtly peers into rooms as they pass, as if Christopher might be hiding in one. They turn a corner — Nan first, then Hal, then Marina, glancing over her shoulder at a painting of some California grandee — and come upon Candy, in a baseball cap. Her eyes appear to be slanting in different directions, though that isn't true: it's something about the way she's holding her face. Her body, under the fat, is tense.

"Where are you going?" she says plaintively, and loudly.

Hal steps forward. "Hey, Candy. That's a great hat. We've come to get Chris. He's going home today."

Nan begins walking.

"Do you want to come along and say goodbye?" asks Hal.

Candy turns to follow Nan.

The four of them continue down the hall, Candy in her baseball cap close on Nan's heels. On the back of the cap is a blank

Post-it that remains affixed all the way to Christopher's room, where it drops off and twirls gently to the floor.

"Chris!" hisses Candy from the doorway. "Christopher!"

Nan pushes past her. "Chris, we're here."

Christopher is sitting on his stripped bed, next to a zipped, nylon, navy blue duffel bag. His face is round and clear. His blond hair is combed. He is wearing new blue sneakers. His right hand, the shaky one, is holding fast to the handle at one end of the duffel. That he's wearing the leather cord with the bright blue bead on it is reassuring to Hal: it's so ordinary and young. Mel's bed is neatly made.

"Hi," says Christopher.

The orderly lets Candy go all the way out through the doors to the front landing, where she stands in silent agitation as they put Christopher's navy blue duffel bag into the trunk. The last they see of the Pacific Institute is Candy in her baseball cap, waving, in the rearview mirror.

BREATH

NAN NOTICES that she has begun to breathe in time with Christopher. He breathes more heavily — something about the medication — and often through his mouth. He seems to be concentrating when he breathes, creating each breath anew. Nan finds that she inhales and exhales with him in his presence, though she suspects she breathes with him even when they're not in the same room. She's back in synch with him, breath to breath, pulse to pulse. Her heart pumps for him, too, now, reminding him: live, live, live. Paradoxically, she finds that this exercise does not make her feel drained. On the contrary. She can tell that she's getting stronger. Her lungs are expanding. Her arms are tightening. Her reflexes are quickening. Her nocturnal vision is improving.

Driving to work or ordering books or squinting at a hairline leak in one corner of the living room ceiling — the leak is delicate, organic-looking, tentative — Nan thinks about how her nature has always been divided between the Sleeper and the Hunter. Complementary forces. At thirteen, for instance, she kept her favorite, and only, pair of pants, stolen from Jonathan, hidden in a tree a little ways past their house. Her brothers were alternately sworn to silence or blackmailed. Every morning before school, her mother would zip Nan into her school uniform, which had a horrible knee-length skirt. Nan's mother's warm, manicured hands brushed Nan's shoulders, smoothing the fabric. In the mirror together, Nan and her mother looked to Nan like a prince and a delicate tall queen, the prince straight-bodied in tights. The prince young, strong, and victorious. Her mother would often say distractedly, brushing Nan's hair from her eyes while listening for any sudden loud noises from downstairs, "You're my pretty girl."

Every afternoon, on the way home from school, or sometimes midmorning when she cut school, Nan would reach up into the tree and tug at the dangling, dirty hem of the pants until they fell down on her, forbidden fruit. The beskirted uniform was tossed up into the tree, where it billowed, empty. She was entirely loyal to those pants, which were brown and buttoned. Then she'd sit and lean against the tree for a while, lingering, calculating, working on her map route of riding her bicycle to Canada, where the draft dodgers lived.

When she got to Canada, she'd probably have to learn to survive on what grows in the woods until everyone stopped looking for her. It would be her and a few draft dodgers, smoking, spitting, taking turns sleeping at night. During the day, they'd fish with hooks on strings and occasionally shoot something, one shot, clean. There, she knew, she'd finally be in balance, the Sleeper and the Hunter working perfectly together, like brothers. Each looking out for the other, sleeping with one eye open, hunting with long, loose limbs. *Old man, take a look at my life* was the song she sang under her breath, but it really meant the opposite: *You can't see me. I'm not there.* She'd never come back, except maybe once, for her mother. She'd give her one chance. She toughened her mind the way she toughened the bottoms of her feet as the skirt floated above her, twined in the branches, billowing with a destiny of its own. The skirt wasn't the Hunter, but it wasn't exactly the Sleeper either. Rustling against the branch, it was a disguise, a double agent, someone else's pretty daughter. Nan eyed it from time to time, then returned to plotting her bicycle route; it was frustrating that she didn't know the elevation of the Rockies for her map. The skirt, way up in the branches, snapped in the breeze. When she was done with her work, she'd fork the skirt down with a stick —

every day, it seemed, she tossed it higher — kiss the pants, and loft them back into their secret lair.

Of course, Nan thinks now, she didn't have the terms Sleeper and Hunter at that age, but that was what she meant. As she tracks the dichotomy through her life, she sees that it applies again and again. Her work, actually, is done by the Sleeper, shuffling papers and carting around books and locking up the store at night. But the Hunter is what matters. For a long time, she had thought the Hunter had to do with sex. Once she found Marina, for instance, she thought that she had been hunting for her all along. Now she doesn't know. Now she suspects that the Hunter — when he was born, of course, but even more these days — is there for Christopher.

The Hunter is the mother.

In Christopher's first days home, he is rather quiet and orderly, like a newly released prisoner. Nan hates what they did to his hair. But, she knows, it doesn't matter about the hair, it doesn't matter about the weight, or the tremor in his hand. All that matters is the breath, moving in and out. She can hear it.

Hal hands Christopher the small, delicate fishnet. Christopher squints, drawing it through the water; several of the fish follow the net, as if curious. Christopher scoops up a wayward clump of algae and deposits it on the newspaper that Hal has spread on the floor. He scoops carefully, slowly, using his left hand. Hal has tilted the desk light on its rubber gooseneck so that it shines directly into the tank, like a searchlight. The fish look alarmed in its glare, though they're not actually alarmed at all. It's one of the things Hal can't quite understand — that fish are so impervious to certain stimuli — but that Christopher seems to accept without even thinking about it.

"Hand me the drops?" says Christopher, setting the net down on the newspaper next to the algae.

Hal hands him the little violet bottle. "It's getting late."

"I know. But we just have to finish." By the light of the gooseneck lamp and the watery tank light, Christopher's face is impossibly serious. To the fish, Hal thinks, the boy is a god. The biggest angelfish, bright yellow with a blue face, shimmies along the length of the tank, hurrying somewhere. The bamboo cat shark flaps its tail languidly. Christopher looms above, dropping violet on his charges.

"I tried to keep it down while you were gone," says Hal, "but I don't think I have the touch, or something. And the shark won't eat."

"We have to get more glass shrimp." Christopher sets the violet bottle next to the tank. "Do you remember when we went to Mexico with Mickey?"

Mickey, Hal recalls, the short dancer with the tilted blue eyes of a Siberian husky. It was a failure of a trip. Christopher was seven, had diarrhea the entire time, and said he was bored about every three seconds. He yelled it, running to the toilet. Mickey didn't like Mexico, either. "Yes, sure," says Hal. "You hated it there."

"I know, but do you remember what Mickey said? About the curse?" The tank burbles.

Mickey, thinks Hal, was insane, though he's not sure what he means by that now. Mickey, he corrects himself, was awfully *energetic.* "What curse? Mickey wasn't really —"

"He said his family was cursed. By a Gypsy. In the old country."

Hal stares at the impervious fish, so exquisite and useless. "Chris, Mickey was from the suburbs of Cleveland. That was just his way of telling you a story." Telling himself a story was more like it; Mickey was a fanciful creature. Hal remembers a moment from that trip when he had to hit the brakes suddenly on that rented van with no seat belts. Mickey put his arm back, to hold Christopher in. Hal doesn't remember anymore why he hit the brakes, only that instinctive swing of Mickey's arm toward his child, and, on the arc of it, some hope he had. But Mickey was just too energetic. And telling his son lies for entertainment, obviously.

"Okay, but it still happens."

"What?"

"Curses." Christopher's blue eyes are bright, almost happy. "They're part of nature, too."

"Oh." Hal sits down in the curvilinear modern chair that Christopher, in the past, usually heaped with books and clothes and Rollerblades. But now only one button-down shirt, two sizes larger than Christopher used to wear, is draped over the back. "Chris, listen. Your problem is chemical, it's physical, maybe even genetic. Dr. Friend explained that to you, I know he did."

"But he's just a doctor. He doesn't know about this. He told me."

"Told you he doesn't know what?"

"He told me that he doesn't really know, not ultimately. No one knows, you know, ultimately." Christopher's expression borders on the exultant, even, the liberated. "It's a curse."

"But why would you be cursed?" Hal pulls one of Christopher's sleeves toward him from the back of the chair and smoothes the cloth on his knee. The shirt is made of a not particularly fine blue cotton. One of the buttons is already missing from the cuff. Hal resolves to find the right button and sew it on. The fabric feels rough to him, ungainly; he doesn't like it that Christopher is wearing this coarse fiber. A graceful white shirt with onyx buttons appears in Hal's mind's eye. No time, he thinks, mentally replacing the white shirt on the rack.

Christopher, meanwhile, has a stumped expression. "Well. I don't know. Maybe it was something you did. Or Mom." Christopher clicks off the tank light. The fish glide by in their dusk, sedately.

Hal laughs, though he doesn't find the suggestion all that funny. "Chris, I wish it were that simple."

Christopher shrugs.

Later, before turning out his own light, Hal walks down the hall to check on Christopher. The boy lies on his side in the bed, mouth open in sleep. He is wearing white boxer shorts, the different white of his heavy belly curving over the waistband. His gently outstretched arms and curled hands are thick, pale at the shoulders, reddened on the forearms. He looks like a baby trucker lying there, or like a middle-aged right fielder poised in mid-flight for the ball. His feet tilt at a downward angle. His right hand shakes slowly in a rhythm that seems to be the rhythm of his pulse. Across from him, the eccentric fish proceed, syncopated shadows in ritual orbits, marking some strange kind of time. They make Hal uneasy. Maybe the fish, he thinks irrationally, are what made Christopher sick. Maybe it was indeed Hal's fault, somehow, for giving Christopher those exotic fish. Curses, bad karma, all that: such beliefs, Hal realizes, are a luxury now. Like Mickey, who was always throwing the I Ching. Still, Hal feels that he should do something about the fish, interrogate or dissect them, but instead he steps quietly into the room and picks up the shirt with the missing button on the cuff. He closes the door behind him.

The bed is a boat. They float down the night. Marina turns Nan over and spreads her legs. There is a scar on Nan's right hip; one of her toes has a bad, wavy nail, like a yellow tooth. Marina isn't touching the scar, or the toothlike nail, but she knows they're there as she hovers over Nan: familiar landmarks. Nan is breathing in short bursts, as if she were running uphill. The bedclothes are tumbled at the bottom of the bed, socks and T-shirts and the A section of the *Chronicle* tumbled in with them. Marina's hand is slick. *There,* says Marina. *I have you. I have you, Nan.* Marina's knee rests against Nan's knee, bone to bone. The bed seems to rock, gently.

Nan digs, working in what's left of late fall's heat. She pushes the shovel into the dry dirt with the heel of her sneaker, drives it down, pulls up a chunk of earth. She drops the chunk of earth next to the forsythia that's going to be unseated and transported across the yard.

Christopher sits in a chair reading *Cry, the Beloved Country,* one bare foot propped up on the head of Sor Juana, a glass of iced tea beside him on the grass. He is wearing a sun hat; Serenepan causes, among other things, photosensitivity. His right hand, trembling gently, hangs down toward the grass as he holds the book with his left. His profile is thicker, yet still classic, like Nan's. Nan, pushing the shovel, wonders if he's really reading, but when she covertly glances at Christopher she can see his eyes moving slowly, steadily, over the printed lines. She would like to pick him up by the nape of his neck with her teeth but refrains. Instead, she digs at the forsythia. The ball of her foot is sore from the shovel edge.

"How do you like that, Chris?"

"It's for school. I have to read it to make up."

"Right, but how do you like it?"

"I don't know," he says with complete sincerity, turning a page. He picks up the glass of iced tea, drinks from it, and sets it down. His right hand resumes its silent accompaniment to his reading.

"It's about politics," says Nan, leaning on the shovel. On the cover of Christopher's paperback edition of the book is a black-and-white photograph of a melancholy African landscape, devoid of people. "That's a silly cover. It's not right at all."

"I have to read it for English class." Christopher's toes curl cozily over Sor Juana's stone wimple; one of Sor Juana's eyebrows is chipped. "I'd like to go to Africa sometime."

"Hot there," says Nan. "Very sunny. You'd have to wear your hat all the time."

"You're being very pessimistic, Mom. Ever since I got back, you're so pessimistic about everything. I mean, are you ever going to forget about this, or are you going to remind me every day?" He crosses one leg over the other and puts down the book. "You're my mother, you know? You're supposed to forget."

Christopher's face, to Nan, has never been more lovely or exasperating. Her history, her future, and her terror are all there just under his skin, a palimpsest. She wants to kiss him for having the luxury of being so cavalier; she also wants to hit him with the shovel, really hit him, until he is lying on the ground, bleeding. If she were to kill him, she thinks as she leans on the old shovel, and then herself, they could dwell forever in the underworld together. It takes two beats before she realizes what she has just thought. Lord, she says to herself and shivers. "I'm looking out for you," she says evenly. "That's my job."

"Still." He pouts. "You should be a little nicer. I want to go places. You went places." The melancholy African landscape rests, like a window onto another reality, on the grass.

It is all Nan can do to turn back to the half-unearthed forsythia. It is all she can do not to run into the basement, get a rope, and lash Christopher to the head of Sor Juana. "Read your book," she says. "You have a lot of catching up to do."

Nan slices tomatoes at the kitchen table, watching Christopher read, remembering Quince, whom she actually did tie up from time to time out of something a little like love. Christopher was right — she did travel, and Quince was one of the last places she went. Quince was a pale woman with frizzy black hair who worked at the free clinic in Kansas City, couldn't come, and never said a word in bed, but would never leave, either. She was a few years older than Nan. She always stayed the night whether invited to do so or not. Nan's mattress was on the floor; after sex, Quince would roll over, curl up, and run her fingers over the lime green wall-to-wall carpet in Nan's rented room. The action was compulsive, self-soothing, catlike. Hash did the same thing with his claws, purring. Quince never purred; Nan was frantic to know what made her tick. Sometimes their sex bordered on the mean. Nan often dropped by the free clinic on her way home from school; she was kind of enrolled at the community college, studying political science. She'd wait for Quince in one of the waiting room's orange plastic bucket chairs, underlining in some secondhand text. At 8:30, Quince would lock the files, put the medical waste in its special red box on the stoop for the evening pickup, and lock the front door.

Nan didn't understand Quince; she admired her conviction; in bed, she lashed Quince's hands behind her back with a bathrobe tie, trying to get to the heart of her. There were lines of sadness in Quince's face already, though she was only twenty-nine. They ate eggs together a lot; Quince liked to put cilantro in them. Together, Nan and Quince watched Ronald Reagan on Nan's bad little television.

"In the future," said Quince one night, lying on the lime green wall-to-wall carpet, "people will look back on this time and ask what you did, you know? They'll say, Who did you stand with?"

Hash delicately began eating Quince's untouched scrambled eggs off the plate on the floor. Nan, sitting on the carpet next to Quince, felt a rush of tenderness for the three of them. They were all half-wild creatures, on the run, like outlaws with horses hidden around the back of the building. Reaching over, she began to braid Quince's black hair. Because it was long, with shattered ends, it wouldn't braid smoothly; strands leapt out everywhere. Nan persevered, combing through Quince's electric hair with her fingers. "Sit still."

Quince, stretched out on the carpet, bent her head along her arm. On the television, Reagan stood tall. "You won't be here next year," said Quince.

"I guess," said Nan. "I don't know." She began looping a length of hair around the end of the braid, tying it to itself. "We could all be blown to shit next year. There."

Quince idly ran her pale hand through the green carpet. "You don't really know anything about me," she said softly. Nan, deeply offended and frustrated, dumped her on the spot.

Now Nan, slicing tomatoes, wonders if she ever really went anywhere and what the point of all that motion was. She's been off the road for a long, long time. After Quince and Kansas, she went to Portugal, met the skinny woman, and moved to San Francisco. She couldn't see it then, but in reality Quince was just one turn before the end, the last house on the plains before reaching the city — though they always went to Nan's house, actually, because Quince lived with her acid mother. Nan reflects that she must have been kind of an asshole then, because she never went to Quince's sad house, not once. She never even took the phone number. For her, Quince existed only as that pale woman in the clinic, pushing back her shattered hair to listen to some poor person's poor heart. That attitude was worse, Nan thinks, than any of the mean sex. She probably *didn't* know anything about Quince.

But she's a mother now, not a drifter. She was still running in the Quince days, and for good reason. In answer to the question

Who did you stand with?, Nan would have to admit that, despite the crowded canvas of people and events and convictions, the true answer was *no one*. She wasn't tied to a soul, not really, until Christopher. Well, maybe Adam. She understood that she loved him when he died. But only after Christopher was she able to admit that she loved Hal, loved Marina: her two perfectionists with the even voices. She knows that Marina thinks of her as the one who can love, the one who made Marina love. But if Marina only knew how recent this all was, how small a dot relative to the rest of the road, that she was the first woman Nan wanted to hold onto as firmly as she held her son, though now they're both slipping from her grasp. She hasn't even been able to help that much. Nan thinks of her father, her mother, her brothers. Looking at the pulpy, red heap of tomatoes on the worn cutting board, she begins to shake.

Marina breaks up with Shiloh on a hot Wednesday morning. "Listen," she says. They are in a pleasantly disheveled coffeehouse not far from Shiloh's place. Because a friend of Shiloh's, a woman with a sketchy mustache, works there, Marina tries to keep her voice as low as possible. "It's not you. It's me. I can't really be with you, there's too much going on. It's wrong — I think it's wrong for you."

"Don't tell me what's wrong for me. You're the one who wants to bounce." Shiloh does not try to keep her voice down. The woman Shiloh knows glances over the espresso machine in their direction.

"Okay, it's wrong for me, then. All right? It doesn't matter —"

"Yes, it does, Marina." Shiloh taps a spoon on the table. "Things matter."

"Shiloh." Marina fights the urge to jump up and run out of the coffeehouse altogether. She has to explain, even if Shiloh doesn't want to listen. She speaks softly, but firmly. "I know that *things matter*. That's the point. That's why I have to stop this. I matter, and you matter, and Nan matters, and — the other people I love.

To keep on, now, it isn't right. I am living in the middle of a tornado. You're only going to get hurt. My family —"

"Like now."

"What?"

"I'm hurt now. Marina. Look at me. Right now. Do you get it?"

Marina holds Shiloh's hazel gaze. Shiloh has the expression of someone who is not crying, who is pointedly refusing to cry right to Marina's face; she'll cry without Marina, listening to a song Marina's never heard while talking on her cell phone and using words like *bounce*. Beneath the pleasing curves and softnesses of Shiloh's youth, Marina can see, there is an unswerving stubbornness. Why, she wonders, does she always choose such willful people? Is she so lacking in will herself that she must desire it? The whole affair seems parasitic on her part; she's embarrassed that the sketchy-mustache woman is witnessing their tawdry scene. She can imagine the two younger women talking about her ruefully later, over iced lattes, on one of the coffeehouse's lumpy fringed sofas.

"Sweetheart," says Marina gently, "you might have to hate me for a while." She's sorry for the sacrifice, but she knows where her allegiance lies. The experiment is over.

"You wish," says Shiloh with a bitterness Marina would have thought was beyond her years. "You like it easy."

Nan, standing in the Husky Bill Store for Men with Christopher, feels the tug of cramps like a small fist in her uterus and an accompanying wave of haziness. Her periods, she's noticed, are definitely getting less predictable. She bleeds more some months; others much less. And every month, she feels it a little more, as if she's missing a layer of skin, or perhaps fat. Her cycle, which used to tick along fairly pleasantly, now clangs, or beeps, or roars. It's loud; she's aware of it. The doctor said these symptoms could go on for some time, that's the way of it, her body's own timing. This attitude annoys her.

"Chris," she says, "come on. Just choose three." She has much more important things to think about, such as why everything in the Husky Bill store costs three times as much as non–Husky Bill clothing. It's as if an extra tax is being levied on fat people, like the rapacious markups in ghetto supermarkets. Nan thinks crabbily about the fact that she's spent her entire life in one expensive ghetto after another.

Meanwhile, Christopher is staring as if hypnotized at a rack of brightly colored shortish pants that seem to be made out of parachute silk, or perhaps wax paper. A cardboard cutout of a burly surfer rides atop the rack and, above that, on the wall behind the rack, is a neon sign that reads HANG TEN!

"I like these," says Christopher, holding up a pair of orange knee-length pants with hot green stripes down the sides.

"For school?"

He regards the orange pants. "Maybe."

"How about *actually*? Yes or no." She's sweating; she feels weary and headachy and her left foot is cramping, as if in sympathy with her uterus. "Shit," she says softly.

A solid, well-dressed man appears in the Hang Ten! section. "You folks need some help?" he says jovially.

Got a tampon? Nan wants to ask but doesn't. "Pants," she says. "School clothes."

"You into that surfer chic?" says the jovial man, holding out his arms as if surfing. "Catching the waves?"

"No," says Christopher. "I just like these colors." He hangs the pants back up and gives Nan the old look, the one that means *retard*. Nan knows that he liked the pants because they were orange, aquatic, and strange, like pants in a dream, but now the jovial man has ruined them with his fat, outstretched arms and surfer chic sales talk.

"Chris," she says, betraying him, "we have to find you something." Worse, she turns to the jovial man. "Can you take him over to, wherever, while I find the ladies' room?"

"Wherever?" says the man with a laugh. "I think we can find wherever." He claps a hand onto Christopher's shoulder. "The bathroom's that way. Meet us upstairs."

Nan bolts through the fabric corridors of bad Husky Bill clothes. A slightly grimy door appears at the back with a restroom sign on it. It's unisex, and once inside she sees that, of course, there is nothing like a tampon machine because this is the Husky Bill Store for Men, after all, and she is profoundly annoyed in some way that seems to relate to the sum total of all the gender trouble in her entire life. She sticks her head out of the restroom door and spies, just to the left of the door, a rack of ties. They are ugly, expensive, polyester Husky Bill ties. She grabs a somber pin-stripe and ducks back inside the grimy bathroom. She folds the tie over several times and stuffs it into her underwear, whereupon she immediately begins to bleed on it, heavily.

Feeling much better, she zips up her jeans and sets off to find Christopher.

Upstairs, the jovial salesman and Christopher are standing in front of a wide mirror, which shows Christopher in a pair of jeans, a black leather belt, and a dark green cotton crewneck sweater. The salesman is smiling; Christopher is standing straight and square, with a doubtful expression. His eyes meet Nan's in the mirror.

"What do you think?" he says, as if he truly wants to know, a vulnerability that fills Nan with apprehension. The last time they went shopping for clothes, the only thing they could agree on was a plastic package of plain white T-shirts, which he and Tamara promptly tie-dyed. Was that when he started listening to the witch girl? Nan tries to remember.

Feeling her blood pulse onto the tie, Nan hazards a guess. "It's too conservative. I don't think it's what they're wearing, is it, Chris?"

He shrugs. He has clearly forgotten about, or given up on, the orange pants.

"It's casual," says the salesman, frowning. "It's a great color on him."

Nan wants to elbow him out of the way; she can tell that his eagerness is crowding Christopher, making it difficult for him to say what he really wants. The salesman takes up half the mirror all by himself, leaving Nan and Christopher hunched up in the other half together, like refugees. Nan can see that her own jeans are baggy-assed and old and her hair is flat on top. Her face looks flat to her, too, flat and wan. Christopher is wan as well, but in a dense, moony way; his wanness seems to indicate extra gravity, whereas Nan's seems to indicate less. He is so much taller than she is that it seems that she must be shrinking an inch for each one that he grows. But this is right, she thinks, this is natural: the son is supposed to empty the mother. Despite her annoyance, Nan does believe, quietly, in the natural order of things. Children are meant to make husks of their parents; she has no intention of taking estrogen.

And yet. Christopher, in the mirror, is not fidgeting at all. He's quite silent. His reflection is silent, practically motionless, except for the faint tremor of his right hand.

"Really, Mom," he says. "What do you think?"

Nan wants to tell Hal . . . something: something about Christopher not fidgeting in the mirror, and the paleness of his face, and the loud, happy salesman. She knows she could call Marina, but who knows where Marina even is, and she doesn't have time for all that hide-and-seek when Christopher stood so still in the mirror. She also knows that Marina will find out that Nan called Hal first and be silently angry. Last, worst, Nan knows that she doesn't care. That's the stupid girl's legacy. Nan runs into the house and finds a tampon as Christopher waits in the car, then drops him off at Tamara's house, a white Victorian with purple trim. He stands politely at the door, turns and tries to wave Nan away, but she stays until the door opens and she sees the gently ironic sweep of Tamara's hair, sees Christopher step inside, carrying his bag from the Husky Bill store. He said he wanted to show Tamara what they got. How can it be, she wonders, that he isn't embarrassed by it? Wouldn't he have been embarrassed before? She turns onto Mission. Even after his shoulders broadened, he was always gentle, faintly geeky, a sincere boy, but not quite this innocent. She had thought, until now, that he had his ordinary boy's secrets. She counts the SUVs as she drives down Mission: ten today. A Jaguar the color of sand goes by, passing the check-cashing store, the little supermarket with the swaybacked aisles. Nan attempts to loathe the Jaguar; instead, she finds herself wishing that it was Christopher's and that she was standing on the curb watching it go by, full of proud ambivalence about her dot-com son. Of course, she reminds herself, he's too young for that, anyway. This would be in the future: Nan on the curb, Christopher driving his new Jaguar. And dot-coms aren't what they used to be. It will have to be something else.

The Honda rattles. Nan rolls down the window on the driver's side and lets the noise of the street fill the car. She has always liked the sound of local transactions, goods passing from hand to hand, legit or black market, it doesn't matter. An elderly Chinese woman, peering ahead cautiously, perhaps for rogue SUVs, crosses the street, carrying a stick along her back with stalks of silk slippers weighting down each end. Seeing her, Nan is buoyed: the elderly woman is carrying something from someone to someone, someone she probably knows and has dealt with before. They will bargain. They will gossip. Then the woman will take the cash home and tuck it into the back of a drawer, behind some black socks, because she doesn't trust banks. It is a relief to Nan that there are still people in the world who don't trust banks, who like to hold what they can feel, not a fantasy or a possibility. She herself has bonds, a concession she made only after Hal explained to her, several times, Christopher's likely higher-education scenarios. "But we live in California," she said. "The state school system —"

"What if he wants to go somewhere else?" said Hal, reasonably, holding her gaze. For a former orchid in a torn dirndl, he was awfully pragmatic.

Nan leaves the Mission, rattles along to Noe Valley, and parks on the shady, quiet street where Hal has his office in a tall blue house. He shares the house with a dentist, a grave woman who does Hal's teeth in exchange for his doing her taxes every year. Recently, they built a deck on the back which in good weather functions as a common waiting room for the dentally and financially anxious. Hal likes to leave dishes of candy, as a corny joke, on the tiled table, next to the little silver open hand that offers his cards on its palm. Outside the tall blue house, a discreet black and white sign hangs from the lantern post: HAL COOPER, ACCOUNTING.

When Nan goes inside, she finds Hal clicking away at his new computer, a slender, flat-screened machine on a stand that looks like a happy little animal. They kiss; Hal hits a button and all the numbers on the screen change.

"I am so into this," he says. "It's like magic." He looks up and smiles with exactly Christopher's innocent smile, though on Hal the innocence isn't eclipsing anything behind it. Hal, as he would be the first to admit, has never been particularly sleek, though his office is. Everything in it is sleek and small and either rolls or slides into something sleeker or smaller — Nan would not be surprised to learn that the computer folds itself up into an envelope, or a button. But she's always wondered why it is that Hal has been so dogged in this aesthetic when it only has the effect of making him seem large and abashed in his own space. It's the newness in him; everything in the office says NOT IN IDAHO ANYMORE, and for that she loves him. Behind him, through the window, the deck with its open silver hand juts out into the jungly foliage of the backyard.

"You know," says Nan, choosing just one of the many overgrown shrubs, "if you prune that hibiscus, it'll flower all the way around. You should do it before it starts raining."

He glances over his shoulder. "Which one? The plant?" They laugh. "How's the boy today?"

Nan sits down and braces her feet against the front of Hal's translucent desk. "I'm not sure. This stuff they have him on — I don't know, Hal. I mean, I guess he's a little better —"

"Nan."

"All right. But we still don't even know what this shit *is*, and when I took him shopping today, he was so damn compliant. I feel like I don't know who he is, and I'll tell you something else: I don't think he knows who we are, either."

Hal slightly furrows his brow. "What are you talking about?" He glances at the flat screen, which appears to be recalculating numbers on its own.

"Of course he knows, nominally: you, me, Marina, the day, who the president is. It's not that kind of knowing. It's the deeper knowing. When he looks at me, I don't think he sees me. I don't think he really thinks I see him." Nan pushes at the desk front; on the other side, hazily, she can see Hal's feet fidget on the carpet. She knows that she is exasperating him; she sits more squarely in her chair.

"That's selfish, Nan." Hal puts the computer into an indigo sleep. "Don't you see how selfish that is? Do you think he can do any more than he's doing, or that Dr. Friend can, or I can, or anyone? The Pacific is one of the best facilities *in the country* — the whole fucking country. We don't — Nan — we started at the top. It only goes down after that. Down. Do you not understand that?"

Nan flushes. "Don't *patronize* me, Hal, and I'm not talking about the ranking of some institution. I'm talking about what I see in his eyes. I'm talking about his life." If only she hadn't been so rash, Nan thinks meanly, if she had gone for a numbered vial — but then she reflects that Hal is a kind of numbered vial, and that's why it gets like this. He's always counting when she's trying to hold on to what actually matters. She's local, like twisting local streets; he's global, a creature of the invisible grid, like his new computer.

Hal leans forward. "This *is* his life now, Nan. Which was not easy to set up — I practically had to blow fifty people to get him in there. You can't put these insane expectations on him. He'll fail. He can't do it. No one can."

Nan, feet still braced, says, "Fine, Hal, but you look me in the eye and tell me you don't know what I'm talking about."

Hal shakes his head. Outside, a woman in a white lab coat walks onto the deck and stretches, then stands for a minute, gazing into the overgrown foliage. Nan feels suddenly, acutely, jealous of her, as if this dentist is Hal's second wife. The more reasonable wife. The not-angry wife. How, she thinks, could Hal have chosen her?

But then Nan remembers that the woman, whose name is Mary, only does his teeth in exchange for tax returns, that they have a business arrangement, she and Hal. They are business partners. Nan takes her feet off the front of Hal's translucent desk and crosses her legs, ankle to knee.

"We found some clothes he liked," she says. "But I think he needs some man stuff, too, you know, underwear, jock straps."

"I'll take him tomorrow," says Hal. "Today, even. No, he's probably had enough for today — tomorrow." On the deck, Mary turns and walks back inside.

Marina buys Christopher a set of colored pencils to celebrate his first day back at school. There are eight pencils in the set: white, black, red, blue, yellow, green, brown, and an indeterminate cantaloupe-ish hue. Alone in her studio, as the afternoon sun illuminates the old, porous floor, she takes out a large sheet of drawing paper and sketches with the green pencil, holding the other seven in her left hand. She finds that she is drawing a tree. Little child-like leaves twine. She sketches very lightly, not wanting to blunt the pencil — it's a gift, after all. But she loves the green, the green entrances her, and she feels an unexpected pleasure in drawing. As if her hand had been cramped without her knowing it until now: she is making a tree. She sets the other seven pencils on the table and rolls her palm over them as she makes the tree with her right hand.

Nan sits in Adam's old wooden chair in the garden. The sky is gray. It's going to start raining soon. Every year, when the rains start, Nan feels greatly relieved, as if she's escaped Texas once more. The rains are like a moat. Her father can't swim, never could; he'd stand shin-deep in water in Bermuda shorts, squinting. She and her brothers would swim far out, away from him, screaming at him that he could go fuck himself as the waves erased their words. But they could still see him standing there, a wiry little switchblade of a man with knobby knees. He had that way of standing; you'd think he was royalty, how he looked out to sea. Nan taught Christopher to swim first thing, setting him gently in the Y pool in water wings, enrolling him in class the second he was old enough.

Nan takes off one boot and sock and rubs her foot against the cool grass. Putting the world between herself and her father was the only choice she had. The distance made him smaller but couldn't make him disappear. Adam talked to his mother in the Bronx so often, and she stayed in his house for months when Adam got sick. Nan found that astonishing. She could never relax around the woman, the whole thing was so peculiar to her then.

"What do you talk to her about?" she asked Adam once.

"Oh, we laugh. We laugh and laugh."

Nan dropped it. Adam's mother still sends Nan and Hal holiday cards, and Nan carefully sends a card back, checking the calendar to see when Hanukkah starts. She still wonders what they laughed about every day.

Adam wasn't much of a swimmer. He claimed that no one in the Bronx could swim and would lie on shore with his hair in a scarf, arranging pebbles in artful designs. He claimed a lot of things — he claimed he could speak Greek, though she never heard him do it. He said he had been in the army. Nan understood that it was his way of being fancy. He was slightly strange to her, always; like Jonathan, he was a creature of the night. He was constantly at the center of everything, making it all happen, knowing everyone's secrets, but holding some delicate crescent of himself in reserve. Nan thought of that crescent as the Bronx, where she'd never been. The only thing she knew about the Bronx was that it had a zoo. She imagined Adam growing up next to lions. No, he said, the expressway. She never did quite get it.

Adam was a show — the biggest show in town for a while. She couldn't believe what he got those boys to do. Goofy Hal with his ass hanging out. She liked to watch, smoking. It was like watching cartoons. She thought it was fun that he was sort of famous, and it did help her get a few dates. But she was always surprised at the fuss everyone made about the Flytrap. You'd think Adam had invented penicillin instead of getting four guys to act the fool and bend over in taffeta or leather or aluminum foil (that one came off before they even got on stage). The music was unlistenable. He was always engaged in big, shaggy projects with everyone else, hanging the moon or whatever, but all the two of them ever really did was sit in his yard or Nan's and shoot the shit. He'd sit in the chair she's sitting in now, turning his face to the sun to work on his tan, and she'd lie in the grass, complaining about women.

"Your expectations are too high," he often said, determinedly not crinkling any part of his face.

"No," she'd insist. "No. She *lied.*"

He didn't have the same problem with liars that she did. He had his own particular morality. She supposes that she misses the show; lots of people still do, they still talk about it. When Adam died, though, she gave her cache of Flytrap pictures and junk to Hal for his scrapbook and she went into Adam's yard and re-trieved this chair. It was old even then. She's renailed it, reinforced the seat several times. It wasn't that he gave her great advice. He gave her bad advice, and she never followed it, anyway. She gave him pretty bad advice, too, now that she thinks of it.

Nan idly pushes at the grass with her heel. She just misses sit-ting with him. You could talk to Adam about anything, he could talk trash for hours. Sometimes, as she lay there on the ground, complaining and smoking, she'd reach over and hold his big bare foot with her hand, pulling at his toes as she ticked off various points about the importance of complete openness. He didn't mind. He cast a large, benevolent shadow over her. It was easy, how they were together. It was a good time. Are she and Hal, she wonders, as open with each other? Do they want to be?

Hal, having ironed Christopher's shirt and packed his lunch and put him to bed, calls his mother in Idaho. The first thing he learns is that it's snowing there already, as usual; and, as usual, there is no little amazement over the fact that it won't ever be snowing where he is. Hal has explained San Francisco's terrarium seasons to his mother many times, but she can never keep them straight.

He used to think this lapse was an oblique expression of homophobia, but now he suspects it may be her way of telling him he should come home, where he can sled.

"Oh, my," says Hal's mother finally in a way that refers to nothing in particular, just life in general. She waits for Hal to help her up over the high step of it.

Hal does. "I miss you, Ma. When are you coming to visit?" This gesture is purely formal: she came to visit for two days once, with Hal's father. They rode a streetcar and went to the Top of the Mark for cocktails. They got lost in Chinatown, from which his mother boldly extricated them. Hal had no doubt that it was his mother who had propelled them both to come, but now that his father is gone his mother seems to have no desire to visit. Hal has attempted to talk her into a trip, even thrown in Napa, but to no avail. He would truly like for her to stay with him for a while, particularly these days, when she is so much smaller, with such fine hair. To Hal, she has begun to look like an elf.

"Oh, I don't know, honey. Maybe in the spring. When the weather clears up."

"How's Margaret?" Margaret is Hal's sister, whom he has refused to call Meg since grade school. She has three boys and a husband with a twitchy eye who loves her.

"Oh, she's busy. You know. Dave got a job over at Blue Mountain — they let him take the truck after school. It makes Meg a little nervous, but that road is very well maintained now. Not like when you were here." She sighs as if, had the Blue Mountain road been well maintained thirty years ago, Hal never would have left.

"Yes," says Hal. He remembers the Blue Mountain road very well. It was the road the bus took out of town. He doubts he had even seen an orchid then; he's certain he didn't know the word *candelabrum* because he spotted it in a dictionary, next to its illustration, after he got to San Francisco. Through the kitchen doorway, he can see the parallel glass disks that compose the light that hangs over his steel and wenge wood dining room table. *Candelabrum* was a joke, even then; the glass disks are hushed and quite serious, though extremely light. Hal loves his house. He thinks of it as a setting that amplifies and frames, kindly, the events that take place there, like a tender little theater.

"And how are . . . all of you?" asks his mother in her usual code. She has a horror of appearing rude.

"Well." Hal hesitates. He didn't tell his family when Christopher was missing because he kept thinking, *Give it one more day;* then, when Christopher did come back, he didn't say anything because who knew what was really going on; when Christopher went to Sonoma, Hal let on that the boy was having some problems in school and they were getting help for him. Now, of course, it has become impossible to say anything without unraveling the entire cloth. Also, his mother is seventy-six, and Christopher, her beloved first grandchild, was proof to her that Hal, no matter what he might think, was inevitably a Cooper after all: his mother, in her ladylike way, believes in blood with the same fervor that his father believed in numbers. Blood tells the real story. "Well. Ma. Christopher is still having some trouble." He rushes to reassure her: "Not as bad as before. He's making great progress. It's just —"

"That much more for him to make up."

Hal can never be sure if she understands much less, or much more, than what she lets on. He knows he should explain, forthrightly, but he simply can't. He doesn't want to. And who is to say that she would even welcome it? She has never been back to San Francisco; they always visit her in Idaho, three planes and a long car ride away, over Blue Mountain. "Yes," he says.

"Maybe you should send him out here for the summer. Dave could get him a job."

"You never know," says Hal. "Summer's a ways off still."

"Oh, don't I know it," says his mother, and they speak of other things for a while.

Just before they hang up, his mother says, "Boys are hard. Meg and I were talking about that the other day, the way boys are so different to girls. Girls you know you don't know, but boys you think you do and then you're wrong."

"I guess that's true," says Hal.

Watching a bit of glossy television later — something with a laugh track, and pretty people in tight clothes — Hal marvels at his mother. If you never know boys, what does she think about him? And, anyway, she's wrong. For instance, how well he knew Adam. With his big feet curled under him, Adam would lean over and say, "Tell me about it" in his exceptionally deep Adam voice. It was the sexiest thing Hal had ever experienced in his life. He told Adam everything, every last thing, and then he might have made a few things up, just to keep the conversation going. Adam didn't care. He never seemed less than fascinated. It was one of the ways he got everybody in bed. Although, in a way, Hal always had the feeling that Adam didn't care that much about the sex itself, maybe not even about the particular people. He was somewhat detached in his sluttery. More than once Hal caught Adam writing down various details immediately after whatever adventure at one of their famous parties, naked with a pencil and the back of an envelope: "the dark hairs around his navel," "feet like lilies." Flipping his curls behind one shoulder, crouched down, rangy as he was, he could still sit forever, butt to heels, like an Indonesian, oblivious to the noise around him.

What was Adam's novel even about? Hal can't remember, it was always changing, spiraling new story lines and characters endlessly running away with the plot. Adam would have to stay up all night on speed to chase after them. Hal has no idea what happened to *War*'s many pages. It gives him a bit of a lonely feeling to remember that now; maybe he didn't know Adam as well as he thought, after all. The really funny part was Adam's idea that the Flytrap could be a big moneymaker, a sort of novelty act, like the Pointer Sisters, that would support his writing. What in God's name could any of them have been thinking?

As the pretty people swan around making jokes, Hal considers the possibility that his mother, the Idaho elf, is right about boys: Christopher is not so clear to him, either, not so clear as he once was. Not so clear as he has always been to Nan. This evening, he seemed, for instance, neither nervous nor not nervous about going back to school. Dinner was quiet. Hal thought it must be the medication, but he really doesn't know. Christopher methodically forked up the salmon and eggplant. They had rhubarb pie for dessert; Hal cut Christopher a large slice, and the boy ate it all. Hal took that as a good sign.

"How are you feeling?" Hal asked.

"Tired," said Christopher. "I think I need to go to bed." He put his plates in the dishwasher and ambled off to his room, walking in the new way: head very slightly tilted up, as if listening to something above. Hal hoped that that was all right; he made a mental note to ask the doctor about it. Down the hall, Christopher's light went out.

Hal turns off the television and listens to the silence, which, like everything else, has a different quality now. It can be fickle, a mask. A quiet house, a quiet child, no longer mean what they once did.

It isn't too long before Nan finds that she hates the sound of the atonal girl, the witch girl; the sound makes the hair on the back of her neck stand up. As if he senses this, when Christopher is at Nan's house he plays the atonal girl's CDs practically every minute of the day. Sometimes the girl seems almost merry; at others, she is quite sad. Nan likes her name — PJ Harvey — but how does that eerie hyperfeminine sound go with her music? Obviously, it doesn't, another aspect of the witch girl that Nan dislikes: she's a poser. At work, Nan asks Peta about her, and Peta says, "Yeah, she's so cool. You like her?"

Nan, exasperated, doesn't reply.

Rapping on Christopher's door, she tells him, *Turn that down. I'm too old.* Making a joke out of it. Though in reality she thinks the witch girl is evil, a temptress. Atonal or not. Maybe that stupid girl who Marina is sleeping with is witchy; Nan hates the stupid girl, too.

Recently, Nan has begun to wonder if she's not that modern, after all.

Marina bicycles from her studio all the way downtown. She doesn't even think out loud to herself about what she is doing.

She doesn't tell anyone where she's going. She thinks, I'm just riding my bike a little bit, because it's a nice day. It isn't a nice day. It's gray, about to spatter rain. But Marina, on her bicycle, feels grateful for it, because the fall was so dry. There were tons of fires. Rain is necessary, soothing. Recently, she has been trying to focus on the small gifts of seemingly unpleasant things. How long has it been since all this started? When she tries to cast her mind backward, she loses track. Everything seems to fray, fading out into the most ordinary scenes that now seem bizarrely portentous: Christopher buying sneakers, she and Nan talking in the sun by the water somewhere.

Marina arrives at Union Square. Wheeling her bike down the sidewalk, she's surprised at how busy it is at this midmorning hour. She's usually working now, and she had always assumed that most other people were, too, but the stores here are full of people flowing in and out. They can't all be tourists. She feels like a bit of a tourist herself, an unaccustomed visitor at least. Her fingernails, she realizes, are a disaster; her hands are grimy with studio dust; her hair is barretted at a wayward angle that was fine in her studio, but here, she suddenly fears, seems either faintly insane or part of a strained attempt to look younger than she is. She avoids catching her reflection in any windows.

Nevertheless. She chains her bike illegally to a parking meter and enters the cool, vaulted interior of the Armani building like a penitent, head down, carrying her helmet. She empties her mind of thoughts, the better to drift through the racks, touching the perfection lightly hanging there. She should not be here; she should not even be thinking of here. It still looks like the bank it used to be, though the wealth is counted in silk instead of dollars.

Nevertheless.

She has an espresso at the espresso bar, looking up at the marble columns with leaves carved into the top, like her trees carved in stone. She sets down her cup and ventures in to the racks. She sees a luminous shade of wool that would ennoble her.

Marina simultaneously resents all the beauty on display and feels entirely at home. She understands it, she understands all of it, every line, every buttonhole, and she can even see where he made a few mistakes in his choices, but not too many. She knows exactly where she is in this visual field just as if she is drawing it, tracing a course through the racks. It's a very comfortable sensation, though she also knows — well, she can read the price tags, tucked up all the exquisite, empty sleeves.

Nevertheless.

It seems to Marina that something about this experience is extraordinarily important, though she couldn't say quite what it is. Words come to her mind — *beauty, freedom* — but they are only approximations. She wants to say, to someone — someone who would believe her — *This reckless, private beauty is as necessary as the rain.*

She sees the dress. There is only one, hanging in its own alcove. A discreet sign underneath it reads ARMANI COUTURE, then an address nearby, as if the dress is an ambassador from an even more gorgeous kingdom just over the next hill. The dress is the color of old gold, and it's made in such a way that it appears to be several possible dresses simultaneously, one dress layered on another, as if it is not only this dress but previous incarnations of the dress that it was before it settled, inevitably, on being this one. It is cut to lie close to the body; it is strapless; it trails off onto the floor in an extravagant swirl of folly. It is exactly as it should be in every respect, and it seems to know this. If a dress can be said to be self-possessed, this dress is the most self-possessed on earth, and — Marina slides out the little ivory-colored price tag — it costs the earth as well, which seems just. Feeling as if she's desecrating a shrine, she reaches into the alcove, picks up the hanger, and carries off the dress, slung recklessly over her shoulder like the spoils of war, to a fitting room.

The fitting room is oak and chrome, with a low suede footstool, several chrome hooks, and a padded oak bench. The lighting is warm. The large mirror is as clear as wind, neither flattering nor unflattering; it is only correct. Marina tosses her helmet onto the oak bench. She generally avoids mirrors, but she looks carefully at herself in this one. She sees a woman who is certainly not old, but is not young, either, in some way that isn't attributable to the very few lines at her eyes and mouth. Her silver hair, caught up in the random barrette, is lush; it is excessive, such silver on one her age; it alludes to sex somehow. Her skin is clear and lush as well — lush in tone, not quite olive. Her gaze is perceptive. She is medium-tall, slender. She is wearing a rumpled jacket over rumpled pants with gear grease on one leg, a rumpled shirt, and boots that lace (her studio clothes), but even she can see that the overall effect emphasizes her femininity rather than diminishes it. She tosses her jacket onto the floor. The rumpled pants and shirt indicate the lithe shape beneath; they shadow it. Hanging behind her, like a different sort of shadow, is the dress with its archaeological layers of gold, its self-possession.

Marina undresses. She finds that she isn't embarrassed by her rough, dusty hands, her disastrous fingernails; she's earned them. Whenever, in the past, anyone told her she was beautiful, it embarrassed her, because it was unearned. Her parents were both quite beautiful, a pair of depressed Los Angeles gazelles; she desired equally to be like and not at all like them. At twelve, she refused to let them fix her teeth. Later, her mother particularly despaired of Marina's hair. The gray started to show up in her twenties. Marina dug in her heels; to be pretty, she feared, would be to disappear. Her rough hands, her grays increased the surface area of what rooted her to the earth, to her work. But today — for however long she is in this room no one knows she's in, holding a dress she can in no way afford, on a Tuesday morning when she should be working — she thinks she might be able to stand to release her grip on the earth for a moment.

The dress slips on like water. It's that light, that close. Marina feels naked beneath it, though she isn't. It's more that she feels psychically revealed: the dress knows what she wants. But it is revealing in a more literal way, too, as the invisibly but perfectly structured thing gives her silver and gold body to the world. Her shoulders are bare. In the mirror, she sees herself not in costume, but in beauty, as a beauty, that was always waiting to be revealed. She sees that she was always going to be exactly here, and it frightens her a little. The dress doesn't care about consequences; it is the soul of ambition, like Shiloh. What other color could it be but gold? The bodice holds her tight without seeming to touch her at all. Marina knows already that she is going to buy this dress. She has always known that she would buy it, long before it was even made. She will never be able to pay it off.

The lissome salesman, seeing the empty alcove, makes a face, makes a phone call. Then he wants to send the dress home with Marina on a padded hanger inside a long vinyl bag, but Marina insists on a plain black paper bag, no hanger. The salesman makes a more severe face, but the dress, being mostly gold thread and air, folds right in, as light as whipped egg whites. Outside the store, Marina zips the bag inside her jacket and rides back to her studio, the tissue paper swishing as she pedals. It begins to rain in earnest by the time she gets there; Marina turns her collar up. The bag miraculously stays dry. Marina slides her treasure into a tumbling heap of old issues of *National Geographic* and blueprints for a rec room that she found at a yard sale. She thinks of the dress like that for the moment: as a kind of found object awaiting placement on some future canvas. A blueprint of somewhere. She feels grateful for it, gleaming under the tissue like a light under ice, as well as apprehensive.

Hal closes his umbrella as he steps into the lunchtime café and deposits it, half-furled and damp, into the glass umbrella stand ornamented with multicolored glass polka dots. The café, which was Dan's choice, has a sweeping, umber, modern air; it seems to be made of air, in fact, or hovering on it, like an exotic flying machine. Hal, feeling too tall, tries to step lightly, as if doing so will bring him luck. Though if he had to answer the question *What sort of luck?*, he couldn't. Nevertheless, he tries to surrender to it. His horoscope this morning said, "Emphasis on social activities. Capricorn figures prominently. You're out in front!"

He crosses the room, which is a gallery of haircuts. The rain patters on a glass section of the roof.

Dan Jones not only smiles, he stands up, holding his menu in one hand. He kisses Hal on the lips in a way that might be an acknowledgment of their one evening, or might be simply brotherly. Hal wonders if this kiss is the beginning of his luck, or the end of it. He wonders if Dan is a Capricorn. Does Capricorn get along with Aquarius?

"Hello," says Dan, still standing. "How are you?"

"Fine, I suppose." Hal sits down and motions at the table, which is probably silly, he thinks, as if he's saying that this is his table, he chose this restaurant. He tries to indicate by his facial expression that of course Dan was the one who chose, he knows that. And would he worry about it if Dan were white? He tries to keep that question out of his facial expression.

Dan sits down lightly, glancing around the airy room. "I never do this."

"What?" Hal keeps his eyes on the olive-colored menu, trying to let the luck flow in. He doesn't think Dan looks like a Capricorn, but it's hard to tell.

"Do lunch." Dan laughs at the phrase, which he enunciates. "I'm usually eating a sandwich in some company cafeteria. Okay, an expensive sandwich. I admit it." Dan laughs again, loudly, and Hal realizes that Dan is nervous, too. Today, Dan is wearing another fine white shirt, but this one has small buttons of silver. In the center of each button, a rose is engraved.

"That's a beautiful shirt," says Hal.

"Thank you. I had it made."

"Do you do that?"

"What?"

"Have clothes made?"

"Oh, yes," says Dan seriously. "All of them."

Hal remembers Dan's strange and handsome waist, his poised way of standing naked, and hardens discreetly under the table. This date might well be a mistake, yet — he's curious. As with *luck*, he isn't quite sure what *curious* refers to, and he purposely keeps it vague to himself, letting it float in the floating room.

The rain beats down on the roof, then eases, as if it's about to end. But early winter is the rainy season.

"Oh," says Hal.

"Hard to go back to the rack after bespoke." Dan subtly dips his eyelashes.

Hal crosses his legs. "I guess so." In his khakis, he feels suddenly underdressed, if not undressed completely. But perhaps Dan is also thinking of this meeting in terms of curiosity, or luck, or some other phrase Hal couldn't possibly know. Perhaps Dan wore that shirt to have lunch with him, to draw Hal's attention with engraved rose buttons that in their shining, intricate perfection would suggest unbuttoning.

Bread and oil arrive, orders are placed, the rain taps on.

"Your card," says Hal. "I was wondering —"

"Didn't you say you'd found him?"

"Right. We did. That isn't why I called."

"Ah," says Dan, neatly tearing bread. His fingers are delicate. "So you don't need a mediator."

"I don't exactly understand what that is. Are you a lawyer?" Hal feels that he is fumbling. He's probably offending Dan in ten thousand different ways. Why did he even call?

"I have a law degree, but I don't practice anymore. Companies hire me to make things" — he interlaces his fingers — "work better. Often the occasion is a dispute, obviously. But these days what they all want is to create a better environment, they want the wheels to turn silently." He laughs. "Silence is golden. Silence is no lawsuits. So when it looks like there's a problem brewing, they call me and I go in and talk to folks and try to help them get along a little better." Dan dips one corner of a piece of bread in olive oil.

Hal suspects that "folks" is a word Dan uses when he's on the job, that it's part of his professional persona. He can see it: Dan in his white bespoke shirts, with his airy voice, talking about folks. They would believe him, all those overpaid, badly dressed folks in the technology corporations that line the 101 like cattle at a trough. They would sense that he knew something they didn't about the world. And maybe he does. "How did you get into that?"

Dan gracefully waves a hand. "Long story." He makes a face. "Florida." Then, unexpectedly, he offers something to Hal. "Let's just say that when you grow up in a trailer park, you understand the need for mediation."

It's as if Dan has dropped a glove. Hal studies the roses engraved on Dan's buttons: did he have those made as well? "I'm from Idaho," says Hal. Fumbling again. Holding the glove in a big sweaty palm.

But Dan smiles. "Don't they shoot people like us there?"

Hal shrugs. "Probably. I left a long time ago."

"How is your son?"

"Um, better, in a way. But he, Christopher —" Hal pauses. "He's ill. He will always be ill."

"Is that what they told you?"

"No." Hal attempts a smile. "It's what I know."

Dan nods, unsurprised. Hal chews on a piece of bread, imagining Florida.

"My sister has a kid who lines up all the gum packs by color in the supermarket. But he's very smart. Listens to opera," Dan offers.

"Christopher isn't like that," says Hal, and he can hear the defensiveness creeping into his voice, though he isn't sure what he's defending. "He doesn't have a compensating gift." He makes an effort to rein himself in; this is, after all, a sort of date. "What I mean is, it's just bad luck. Like falling through the ice."

"Does anyone actually fall through ice anymore?" says Dan. "I think that's only in books." He reaches across the table and touches Hal's arm. "I don't mean to be flip. I just think all families have a strange streak, you know? Something wild."

"I always thought that streak was me," says Hal as the splendid miniature architecture of their food arrives. It looks as if it could fly, too.

"Us?" Dan laughs. "We're nothing on the scale of things. Trust me." His delicate hand remains on Hal's arm for a moment longer, his fingertips as light as raindrops.

It's raining hard outside, but inside the house Nan and Marina are as dry as toast. Marina sets down her book. "I think we should talk."

Nan seems edgy, on her feet and peering up toward one corner of the living room ceiling. "Why?"

"So much has happened. I feel as if we're just hopping from crisis to crisis, but while we have a little breathing room —"

"We don't have any breathing room. Does that look damp right there?"

Marina glances. "No."

"Look again."

"Nan." She tries the softer tone that sometimes unlocks the gate. "I think you've been extraordinary. I think we've all done a lot, under really tough circumstances."

"Because we're family," says Nan, with a significant look at Marina. "Right? That's what happens in family, you just cope. Remember when Georgia's father got Alzheimer's and Andy had to clean him up every day, plus those twins. . . . That is damp right there."

Marina doesn't mention what they both know, which is that Andy, in between changing Georgia's father's diapers and feeding the twins, started sleeping with the next-door neighbor, a redhead with a borderline personality. Andy, they had all agreed at the time, obviously had issues. He's been working on them ever since. Anyway, Marina thinks she sees where this conversation is going, or from whence it's proceeding. "I'm not saying this is too hard. It's just like the way we had to figure it out in the beginning with Chris. Kind of."

"Because I would never leave you. No matter what stupid thing either of us did." Nan appears to be talking to the corner of the living room ceiling.

Oh, no, thinks Marina. "Honey, I'm not leaving you." How could she leave Nan? It would be impossible, like falling up. "What I mean is more the way we've always had to make it up, from the beginning. Negotiate our roles, how we're going to do things."

Nan looks at Marina as if she's suddenly begun speaking Turkish. " 'Negotiate our roles'? Marina, we don't have time to negotiate anything right now. This isn't about us. Maybe later. We just all have to pitch in and do whatever's necessary at the moment."

The back of Marina's neck prickles, her voice rises. "Listen to me. I am trying to stay. I *want* to stay. I guess I'm just asking if you even care that it's all different now, that we're constantly looking over our shoulders —"

Nan shakes her head. "But I always have been anyway. The whole time we've been together. That's what being a mother is about. You just didn't notice, or didn't want to know. Maybe you were thinking about something else."

Nan sits down in a chair and crosses her legs neatly. From that neat, sharp cross, Marina sees that they are actually about two inches from a major conflagration they can ill afford. She feels weepy suddenly; they're all tired, she knows that. The corner of the living room ceiling does seem damp. What would a new roof cost? As much as the dress?

Nan blinks. "What do you want to tell me?"

"Never mind. We can do this later. I'm going to go try to work for a while." Maybe Nan brought up Georgia and Andy because that's exactly what she fears. Marina stands up. "I'll call you before dinner. I'll order us a pizza."

"Sure," replies Nan in an undeniably nasty tone. "You do that."

She's just one small, quasi-menopausal person with a bad hip, Marina reminds herself, and this is her son. Taking a deep breath, Marina resists the fight. It would be heartless to pick up the gauntlet. She crosses the room and kisses Nan on the forehead. "You know where I'll be."

Nan apparently can't resist taking one last jab. "You'll be on your cell phone."

After the door closes, Nan relents a fraction. If she were her father, she'd tear the house apart. Marina of all people should know that by now: how hard she's working to stay in one piece, how putting up with Marina's idiotic behavior is the ultimate test of a lifelong effort. Isn't that grace?

Marina rides her bicycle to her studio through the drenched streets, her yellow poncho flapping behind her, making its dull, faintly ominous popping sound. It's foolish to ride your bike in this weather, she knows that, and yet she wants to; she wants to feel herself outside, in motion, wet hair, cold nose; she wants to grip the handlebars. She needed not only to get out of the house, but to *feel*, definitively, that she was out of the house. Which made it better that it was raining, in a way.

Marina's front wheel pulls to the right, and she corrects it with some effort. She may be foolish, but she doesn't actually want to have an accident. Not in homely San Francisco rain, anyway, encased in a yellow poncho. Marina is generally ambivalent about rain. Sometimes there was so little of it in Los Angeles, sometimes far too much; it was a star, rain. Unpredictable. Grand. Here in the north, rain is more ordinary, like a complaining aunt come for the holidays. You still love her, but you sigh a little as she drizzles on the Christmas carolers. People here don't comment on the rain the way they do in L.A. They expect it, as if it's their due. Which is part of the whole thing, to Marina's way of thinking, the whole arrogant Bay Area Valhalla myth. The Bay Area — Marina has made this point to Nan — has a smug arrogance in relation to L.A., because it feels that it is the *real* Valhalla, as opposed to the silicone and imported palm Valhalla of its southern neighbor. San Francisco has the snobbery of cotton, or really, Polartec, which is made out of old plastic six-pack carriers, a fact she has also pointed out to Nan, but it doesn't matter because Nan, she

knows, will live and die in that house. They will never live anywhere else.

No. That's not it. It's not about geography. She has to be honest,
at least to herself. What she wants is to prevail over a force she can
see; she wants to reach her studio safe and sound, toss the cold,
wet poncho to the floor, shake the rain from her hair, and enjoy
the victory of having reached her destination in one piece. What
she wanted to say to Nan was: I don't want to disappear. I can't.
Then somewhere on her person, her phone rings. The baleful
poncho flaps, heavy and anxious, behind her, like Juliet's nurse.
The poncho is wrong. She's not going that far, or that fast. She just
wants to brandish a bit of foolishness between her teeth, small pi-
racy, a little taunting of the gods. Because — the wheel pulls again
on the water, but she holds firm — what is she, really? The phone
stops ringing. Nothing that dramatic: a woman riding her bicycle
through the rain.

Marina and Nan sit on folding chairs in a smallish room at the
YMCA. They are early. Across from them, there is a middle-aged,
straight couple in tracksuits. Hers is baby blue; his is forest green;
they are holding hands.

Nan looks over at them and takes Marina's hand. The tracksuit
couple drop their eyes to the pamphlet the man is holding; it says
"Mental Illness and You." They begin reading it together.

"This is bullshit," says Nan.

"No," says Marina, putting her other hand over their two joined
ones. "This is good." She can feel the thrum of anxiety in Nan's
grasp, like a spooked horse about to bolt. Marina gently loosens
her grip, playing out the rein: see, there's nothing there.

Nan sits back, then forward again. "What time does this thing
start?" she mutters.

The man in the tracksuit couple flicks his gaze at Nan. "First
time?"

"Yeah," says Nan.

"Us, too." He hands the pamphlet to his wife. "Her idea."

"Right," says Nan, and she and the tracksuit man both laugh, complicit.

"Excuse me?" says Marina in a low tone, removing her hand from Nan's.

The tracksuit man returns to the pamphlet.

"Nothing," says Nan. "Forget about it."

A few minutes pass. A black woman in office clothes comes in; she sits down and folds her coat over her lap. Another middle-aged, straight couple, who look like the cousins or next-door neighbors of the first, also enter; the woman has a limp. Marina thinks that not only is the adage true about people in couples coming to resemble each other, but they also, she sees, come to resemble other couples: a little soft, a little casual, like people made out of gingerbread. She and Nan, for instance, are both wearing cotton turtleneck jerseys. And do the two of them, she wonders, give off that same air of barely controlled hysteria? Do all couples, in crisis or not?

The tracksuit woman closes her pamphlet. She's finished it.

A tall, sloping man with a beard and mustache comes in and takes his place in the circle of folding chairs. Carrying a sheaf of papers and a book, he is clearly the leader; though only perhaps fifty, his eyes are old, heavy-lidded, like turtle eyes. Nan, alert, sits up straighter.

"Hi," he says, "I'm Bob." He looks promptingly to his right.

"Hello," says the tracksuit woman. "I'm Cherry."

"Bob," says the tracksuit man and laughs uncomfortably.

"Barbara."

"Marina."

"Nan."

"Shirley," says the woman with the limp.

"Dave."

"Good," says Bob the leader. "Glad to see you all." He glances approvingly around the circle, as if it is not small and motley, but capacious and optimistic. Marina can tell that Bob is the sort of man who sees potential movements in gatherings as small as two, which gives her hope that Nan will like him, like the group. *We need this,* she had told Nan, though she wasn't sure what they needed, just that they needed something other than a fight. The relative quiet was almost worse, a continual waiting for the other shoe to drop, though Marina knew that in this situation it could never drop, or maybe it was constantly dropping, or maybe one day they would wake up to find that it was raining shoes, pouring shoes, shoes battering the roof and thudding into the garden. Or maybe she wished for that. Nan had shrugged, consented. *We can try it,* she said. *Is he playing that record again?*

Bob smiles. "Lots of new faces tonight. Let's go around the room and talk about why we're here, and then we can discuss some strategies for helping our mentally ill relatives. Cherry?"

Cherry brightens, while her Bob shifts in his seat in the way of a man who fears what his wife is going to say next. "Well," Cherry begins, "Bob and I are here because our daughter, Denise, hasn't left her room in five years. She keeps quite a bit of newspaper and old junk in there, and we've had her on different medications, but they just don't seem to stick, and then the newspaper piles up again, and —"

"She pulls out her hair," adds Bob. "We can't keep her from pulling out her hair."

Bob the leader nods. "Trichotillomania."

"Exactly," says Cherry. "We know. But Bob and I — well, I think we've reached the end of our rope, and we were hoping we might meet some people here who maybe have experienced something similar, maybe they've tried some other course, something with diet, or —" She looks at her husband, who is staring at the floor. "He thinks it's hopeless." She pats his knee. "Our family doctor told us about this group."

Bob the leader addresses the other, hopeless Bob in forest green. "You'd be surprised what you can do," he says. "My son was institutionalized ten times in twelve years before olanzapine came on the market. Now he's doing great. Barbara?"

"I'm a nurse," Barbara responds, folding her hands over her

folded coat. She is the calmest person in the room. "I'm working on my master's in social work, so I'm sitting in, just trying to listen and absorb. Thank you for letting me be here."

Hopeless Bob eyes Barbara suspiciously, and Marina is surprised to find herself in sympathy with him: she didn't agree to be observed. And yet here she is, an example, a case, like Christopher himself. It shames her to realize that she doesn't like it, that one of her impulses is to say, *He's not really my son.* Cherry, having finished her speech, crosses her baby blue tracksuited legs at the ankles and smiles wearily at Marina. It is all Marina can do not to run from the room, though she would like, for once in her life, not to have to run.

"I don't know how to do this," says Marina. "I don't know how to live like this. Christopher — Nan's son, Christopher — is sixteen. He went at his hands with a knife." She finds that she is beginning to cry, and makes an attempt to stop. "It's awful."

"It's not that bad," Nan interjects. "I mean, yeah, we had an incident, but he went to the Pacific Institute —"

"The Pacific is very good," says Bob the leader.

"The best," continues Nan. "And he did really well, and he's home now, and he's going to school, and this diagnosis —"

"What is his diagnosis?" asks Bob pragmatically.

Nan hesitates. "Schizophrenic. That's what the doctor told us. They put him on something experimental, so what I really want to know is about *that,* because his hand shakes and he's gained weight and he's not himself. His eyes," she says, then falls silent. Marina, pitying her, lets slip the opportunity to correct or add anything; instead, she fishes in her pocket for a crumpled napkin and blows her nose.

"I know those eyes," says Bob the leader. "My son is schizophrenic, too. It's a condition. An illness." He looks around their small circle. "That's one of the things we all have to remember." Everyone, except tracksuit Bob and Marina, nods. "If we're going to help them get well."

"He *is* well," insists Nan. "It didn't take twelve years. He's well now. I just have some concerns —"

Bob holds up his hand. Marina sees that there is a wedding ring on it and wonders where his wife is. She puts the napkin back in her pocket.

"We'll get to that," Bob says. "Shirley?"

The woman with the limp is wearing lipstick of an unflattering purple hue. Her clothes fall about her in disordered layers, with gaps and puckers. She is large. Her husband is also large, but quieter in his arrangement of self. He's wearing glasses and Rockports; his hair is nicely combed.

"I think our daughter is either a nymphomaniac or a kleptomaniac, or maybe both," begins Shirley. Her voice has a thickness, like an accent, but it's the accent of a speech impediment. "She denies it, but I've seen very clear signs." Shirley stops speaking and smoothes her hair. Dave sighs.

"Dave?" says Bob.

He shakes his head.

Next to Marina, Nan pushes on the balls of her feet, making the folding chair rear up on its back legs. She stares at Shirley as Bob welcomes them again, then whispers into Marina's ear, *"She's fucking crazy."*

"Shhh," says Marina. She is surprised to find how much she wants it to work, as Dostoyevskian as the gathering may be. She's never been a joiner, not even a Girl Scout, but this: this is important. And where else do they have to go?

Shirley, with narrowed eyes, is listening intently as Bob says, "We have to try to think the way they do. For many people with these sorts of chemical disorders, their primary motivation is *protection*. It's like that joke — just because you're paranoid doesn't mean they're not out to get you. For them, there are things that are out to get them. They're bedeviled."

The other Bob raises his hand. "How would that apply to pulling out your hair?"

Bob easily lobs this one back over the net. "She pulls to relieve her anxiety. When she pulls, she actually feels better. For a minute." He meets each pair of eyes without hesitation. "You have to begin to have a different understanding of pain. Some schizophrenics, for instance, simply do not seem to feel the cold. Nobody knows why. My own son could stand outside in the snow for hours, in a T-shirt, if we didn't physically force him back inside the house. He felt safer outside, where there were no tape recorders."

Bob says this last in such a matter of fact way that for a minute Marina thinks he means that there really were tape recorders in that house, wherever it was, where it was winter and his son was outside in a T-shirt, refusing to come in.

"Jesus," says Nan. "I'm glad it doesn't snow here."

Bob focuses his turtle gaze on her, but doesn't say anything.

Barbara the nurse, says, "I don't mean to interrupt, but we do see things like that on the psych ward all the time. People hurting themselves, but it's like they don't feel it. That's when you have to get the restraints, sometimes."

Nan brings the folding chair down square on all four legs. It makes a tinny thump. "We're not here to talk about restraints, Barbara. We're here for *information*."

Barbara raises an eyebrow.

"Okay," appeases Bob. "Okay. I know it's hard. But let's move on."

"She's a slut," says Shirley. "And a thief."

Bob blinks. "Right. I can imagine how difficult that would be for you and your husband."

Dave, next to Shirley, has the expression of a man going down with the ship. He looks at the floor.

Nan passes a hand over her face. "Can we talk about strategies now? How long is this meeting?" The other Bob nods vigorously, and Nan looks over at Marina to be her ally, their ally, to join them in figuratively casting Shirley out of the circle.

Marina makes a sympathetic face, but, in another surprising emotional turn, she sees that to cast out Shirley would be to cast out Dave as well — Dave, who is hanging on by his fingernails, who is here not for Shirley, but for himself and the daughter, if she even exists. Marina smiles at him. He blushes.

"Strategies," says Bob. "Absolutely."

"That's what *I'm* here for," says Nan in a tone some might call challenging. For the first time since Christopher's difficulties began, Marina recognizes the little burn of panic working its way into her heart. She fights it, not for Christopher, but for herself. It is vital, she realizes, not to run. She must not run.

When Nan and Marina get home, they find Christopher sitting on the living room floor with the television on, soundlessly. He is watching *The X-Files*. In silence, Scully and Mulder approach a dark shape that is seeping, and glowing where it seeps. Christopher is drawing something small and black on a small piece of paper. Next to him is a plate with the remains of dinner, one of those frozen dinners he likes so well; Christopher is a longtime fan of the microwave.

"Hey," he says, drawing.

Nan sits down on the sofa. "Is it a good one?"

"I don't know."

"Was that enough dinner?"

"Uh-huh."

Marina, in the doorway, says, "Did you miss us?" Scully and Mulder regard the glowing, seeping shape. They are puzzled.

He laughs. "Of course."

"We saw this one, Chris," says Nan. "Remember? They go into the canyon."

Christopher looks annoyed. He frowns. He doesn't ask where they've been, and Marina realizes that she and Nan have entered into some unspoken agreement not to say.

Scully gently restrains Mulder from touching the shape that might or might not be a shadow. Christopher continues to draw, watching the TV out of the corner of his eye, making a set of careful lines. Marina feels strongly that they have interrupted a private moment, an idiosyncratic state, and that they should leave him to his solitude; at the same time, she sees that that is not entirely possible anymore. His solitude is a two-way mirror now. They must watch.

Nan chucks him on the arm. "What are you drawing?"

He shrugs and folds up the paper. It's just the same way, Marina thinks, that she folded up her napkin at the meeting: hide the evidence, which is nothing, really — a crumpled rag, a sketch of, maybe, a tree. Things that couldn't be less remarkable. Christopher doesn't glow, and she and Nan are no Scully and Mulder, who are still peering at the dark shape, then discussing it. The wind blows Scully's hair.

Christopher rests his hand on the folded paper, which is resting on his knee. "I do remember this one," he says, and smiles. "It's one of the first ones."

Nan waits in the car outside Christopher's school. It is a square, squat, dun-colored building, like a parody of a school, built to be hated. It is, in fact, a very good school; Christopher was lucky to get in. Nan rolls down the driver's-side window, which squeaks and drips old rain. She never had a lot of use for school, though she liked to know things and she liked to be among gangs of kids. It was the confinement that bothered her, the tedious rituals and regimes; the rituals she had with Jonathan and Henry and Robert were so much more useful: running, pouncing, lurking. But Christopher is a good student, always has been. Neatly filling in the answers, adding up the numbers, like Hal. He labeled the subject dividers in his notebooks; he saved past notebooks in his closet. He was like that: a hoarder. He never got into fights.

Just as Nan begins impatiently tapping the wheel, the ugly doors open and the kids pile out. Skateboards, backpacks, baggy things, tight things, trinkets affixed to various junctures of self and clothing, some piercings, some ostentatious drapings of paired arms and hands: Nan feels a great tenderness for their small rebellions, which seem to her like rebellions against nothing, against a gravity that barely affects them. They can do anything they want; they already live in the land of milk and honey; distance is nothing to them, just the flick of a computer key.

But that doesn't matter now. Finally, she sees the flash of Christopher's hair in the crowd, the familiar droop of his green back-pack. She toots the horn. He waves; Tamara, beside him, waves, too. Christopher says something into Tamara's ear, and she laughs, holding a hand to her face. Her rings glint in the sun. She is nearly as tall as Christopher; the wide bell of her pant legs makes her look even taller, though also as if she's wearing a long skirt, like a pioneer girl. Tamara, like Christopher, Nan thinks, has always lived here. It probably doesn't seem like the farthest point of anything to them.

They descend the steps and amble toward the car. Tamara leans into Nan's open window and says, "He was *bad* today."

"Oh, yeah?"

Christopher is shrugging proudly.

"*Yes.* He gave, like, a lecture. A singing lecture." Tamara rolls her eyes. "The child can*not* sing."

Nan looks at Christopher, who is holding his pale face up to the sun and smiling. "Singing what?"

Tamara straightens up, laughing. "It is just too stupid." She catches Nan's eye significantly. "*Normal* stupid. No pill for that." She raps the car hood with her knuckles. "See ya, C. Bye, Nan."

In the minute that it takes Christopher to get into the car, Nan considers her options. She decides to tread softly. "Hey, goof," she says as he buckles himself in. "How was your day?"

"Fun."

Nan starts the car in a measured way. "We have to get going or we'll be late."

In the office of the psychopharmacologist, Christopher does not sing. He sits politely in the waiting room, as if he is waiting for someone else, his green backpack between his feet on the car-pet. Affixed to the backpack is a button that reads PUNK ROCK ISN'T JUST FOR YOUR BOYFRIEND — a present from Tamara, Nan guesses, wondering if this means that Christopher is now, of-ficially, Tamara's boyfriend, or if the button is simply a public ser-vice announcement.

Christopher leans over. "What if I fail?"

"You can't fail, Chris. She's just going to talk to you about the medication."

"It's fine."

"So you can tell her that. That's good news."

He nods reluctantly. "Yeah." He gazes into the nonexistent distance. A mirror hung high on the wall just catches the top of his hair, the smooth line of his forehead.

Nan reaches over to brush a stray blond lock out of his eyes. "Ten minutes. That's all."

The psychopharmacologist is named Dr. Stubbs. She is neat and angular, perhaps thirty-five, wearing a soft suit that drapes well. She has done her homework. "How's the tremor?" she asks.

Christopher holds up his hand, which is almost completely steady. "Gone."

She looks intrigued. "Gone? No, I see some."

"Just about. It's going," says Christopher.

"Hmm. Okay." She glances at Nan. "Have you noticed it recently?"

"Well, not as much, actually." Nan smiles. "I guess that's good."

"Hmm," says Dr. Stubbs. "Anything else?"

"I'm fat," says Christopher.

"Can't do much about that one," says the doctor. "It's a shortcoming. Sometimes it evens out on its own. Hearing or seeing anything unusual?"

Christopher shrugs. "Like what?"

"He's good," says Nan. "We're all much better."

They drive to a spot just outside the city where dunes sleep beside the sea. The dune path snakes through succulents, which are profusely blooming. A muzzy sun is out. Christopher walks along the slight path, careful not to step on the tumbling greenery. He was the kind of child, Nan thinks fondly, whom one never had to tell to pet the cat *gently, like this.* He already knew. She used to so love zipping him into his little jacket, over his solid small chest. Tying his shoes. Combing his hair.

He turns around. "That thing today at school," he says.

"Yeah."

"It was nothing. I told Tam not to tell you."

"Why shouldn't she tell me?" Nan hadn't been thinking about it, but now she perked up her ears.

"Because you worry too much."

Nan tries to see if his hand is shaking or not, but he has it tucked into the pocket of his windbreaker. "I can't not worry about you, Chris."

"Why not?"

The question is so absurd that Nan almost laughs, but Christopher is entirely serious. He looks almost mournful, as the succulent plants curl and lap at his feet. She answers him seriously. "Because I love you."

Nan, Marina, Christopher, and Hal play cards.

"Do you have any twos?" Christopher asks Hal.

Hal winces and lays down a two of clubs.

"*Any* twos." Christopher holds out his right hand, which is steady.

Hal flips over two more twos.

"Thank you." Christopher tidies his many cards.

It's Nan's turn. "Do you have any kings?" she asks Christopher.

"No."

"Do you have any tens?"

"No."

"Do you have any threes?"

"No."

"Fuck."

"Mom."

"How did you get so many cards?"

Marina sighs. "Nan, you're supposed to go fish." She sets her cards face-down on the table and twists her hair into a barrette. "It's getting late."

Nan extracts some cards out of the pile. "Christopher, if you don't have any kings or tens or threes, what do you have in there?"

Christopher smiles slyly. "I'm not telling."
"Twos, obviously," says Marina.

In, out.
    Nan breathes.
In, out.

Hal picks up the phone, puts it down. *And then what?* he thinks.

Marina zips her sweater to the neck. It's colder than she had thought, and wet, as always. When she gets to the corner, she stands for a minute, trying to decide which way to go. Determinedly, she heads for her studio.

Nan calls Jonathan from her office, where the drifts of paper are growing. Peta has emptied the green trash can, but left the papers undisturbed, probably thinking they're important in some way. Nan pushes them to one side of the desk and leans forward, kicking the door shut with her toe.

"Jonnie, I'm wondering if I should send him down to you for a while. Or if you should come up here."

Jonathan makes an indeterminate humming sound. "Did he ask to see me?"

"No. But he's quiet these days. It's just something I know."

Jonathan laughs. "That is pure Ashby. We *all* just think we *know.*" He begins a tune, lets it fade away. "I always think I know when an earthquake's coming."

"Psychic."

"Animal was more my thought." He pauses, slipping over various notes. "You're a good mother, Nan. You always have been."

"He's my child."

"I meant to us."

"I left," says Nan.

"What else could you do? We all left, when we could. Maybe not Robert. But even him, eventually."

"Not her."

"No." Though their tones, their intonations, are not the same, their voices strike the same notes, as always.

"Will you come?"

He sounds one note, then another.

"Will you come?"

"Nan, if I was as stubborn as you, I'd be as famous as Eric Clapton by now."

"He lost a child, too."

"That was different. That child is lost forever."

Silence.

"I'll come in a while."

Hal sits with Mary on the deck in the light gray afternoon. He likes Mary; she reminds him of his Idaho aunts, who religiously contributed bad pies densely swathed in Saran Wrap to every family gathering.

"Gingivitis," says Mary. "It's our modern eating habits. Sugar. Beef. Cornstarch."

"Do you really think so?"

Mary nods. "Especially cornstarch. It sticks." She glances at the open hand, on which rest three damp Hershey's Kisses. "Not that I'm proposing a ban."

"Do you think celery's good?"

She shrugs noncommittally. Mary, Hal thinks, would make a great criminal because she is so unlikely to be mistaken for one: tall and gentle, she seems every inch a dentist, or an undertaker. In fact, her family were undertakers, and Unitarians. Mary collects pessaries; Hal has always sensed some peculiar combination of spirit and sex in her, something slightly feral at the core. He doesn't really want to know exactly what it is. It simply comforts him to know that it's there somewhere, barking into the night.

"You look good," says Mary. "I've been meaning to tell you. Have you been going to the gym?"

"What? No."

"Well, you do." She smiles one of her grave smiles. "Maybe because Chris is home safe. You're more relaxed."

Hal wants to jump up and find a mirror but restrains himself. "I don't know. I'm not sure I really feel more relaxed yet. It's so hard to believe: that things can be one way one minute, then the opposite the next. All chemicals."

"Chemicals and history," says Mary, unwrapping a Hershey's Kiss. "Powerful combination."

"And love," interjects Hal. "Don't you think love has its effects?"

Mary holds the Kiss out to him on her long, open palm.

Christopher and Tamara lie on the floor of Tamara's room, listening to PJ Harvey. Only their heads, barely, touch. Tamara has her feet propped up on her bed, her legs sloping at a low, long angle. It's quiet between Christopher and Tamara, with PJ Harvey saying many things that seem exactly right, exactly what it feels like, what they both know, though never say. Tamara smells Christopher's sweet, cool breath. These days, the scent of him is poignant to her; it's like the scent of a wounded animal. His breath is all of him that she feels she can touch without hurting him in some funny way, so she holds his breath inside her own.

"She's great," says Christopher.

"Yeah." Tamara nods.

PJ Harvey talks about the sadness and glory of the world in many ways that all seem like different languages, including a guttural, unearthly one that Tamara doesn't know but feels she recognizes. Tamara turns her head up at an awkward angle to get a glimpse of Christopher's face. He is completely serene, listening. He reaches over and placidly takes Tamara's hand. She is the only one who can hold him inside her breath, her attention, and so she does. Listening with him.

"I've been writing to her," says Christopher.

"To who?"

"Her." He gestures with his chin toward the CD player. "I e-mail her almost every day."

"What?"

He squeezes her hand. "It's okay. I just have had a lot of thoughts that I think she'd understand so I write them down and send them off to her record company." He laughs. "I know she's not going to write me back."

Tamara sits up. "Are you fucking kidding me? You can't do that."

Christopher doesn't move from his position on the floor. His face is clear and calm. "People do it all the time, Tam. It's fan mail. Big deal."

Tamara studies his face for clues. "What have you been telling her?" she says neutrally.

Christopher returns Tamara's studious look. She knows he's deciding whether he can trust her. Tamara keeps her expression blank, as if watching a cloud pass. She keeps hold of Christopher's hand, purposely loosely.

"Well," he says, "first I told her who I was and everything, where I lived, about my parents, all that business. I told her about some of my experiences."

"Like — on the road?"

He considers the question. "That, too. Recently I've been writing to her about the sea. She knows a lot about that, you can tell. I've been telling her some things I know. Certain interesting facts. And, you know, I tell her about you, too."

"Me? Like what?"

"Just, like — special stuff. In case I'm not around and something happened to you."

"Chris, nothing is going to happen to anybody. Stop it." It seems to Tamara that his hand, which is healed but still soft, is growing warmer in hers, though she can't be sure. She imagines Christopher's long e-mails stacking up in an endless electronic queue with other fan mail, junk, weight reduction offers, LIVE GIRLS!!!, invitations to shows, whatever, and she feels as bad for him as she would for a child lost on a busy street.

"And, Chris, if you know she's not reading them —"

"I didn't say that." A mulish look crosses his face. "I said I knew she wouldn't write me *back*. I think she probably is reading them, actually. I mean, listen to this record." He crosses his legs on the floor, like *that's that*. *QED*. He nods along to the music.

Tamara doesn't point out the flaw in his logic. She feels like a scientist observing something natural but very strong, like a gas or a wave. A crack in the earth on a pleasant hillside. What is Christopher's nature, really? she wonders, gazing at the even proportions of his face. Stretched out on her bedroom floor as the glorious sad music plays, he seems to her an angel, a little bit terrible in the way that angels can be terrible, but also bringing news from another galaxy. With warm, human hands. "So, what about the sea?" she asks.

"Oh, the sea," he says, and begins to explain.

Nan, trying to concentrate on overdue invoices, hears a faint flapping somewhere, like cloth in the wind. *Snapsnap. Snapsnap.* She instinctively looks up, but, of course, nothing is there. Nothing's coming. Outside her office, the cash register trills. A paper bag rustles. That must be it, she thinks.

Dan is standing ahead of Hal in the line at the sandwich place. Today, his shirt is mauve. It rests lightly against his shoulder blades, seeming not to touch the small of his back; it moves lightly as he breathes, pays, turns to smile at Hal.

Hal, holding the several packages of his lunch, wonders at himself. What is it about this guy? For instance, right now. Though he has seen Dan's naked back, he's very compelled at the moment by the hidden length of it within the shirt: Dan's back, concealed. It is as if he is standing, blindfolded, before a major work of art. Feeling the force of the art's presence with something other than his eyes. Hal closes his eyes briefly as his fingers curl around a little bag of potato chips, his sandwich and juice. Please, he thinks. Today is the only day this week it isn't supposed to rain.

Dan leads the way to a green slice of park, and they sit on the grass together.

"Have you had any interesting cases recently?" asks Hal, unsure if mediators have cases. Maybe they were just "jobs," or, as therapists refer to them, "clients."

Dan gingerly unwraps his sandwich. Hal sees that he must have been a finicky child — shy, watchful, alert. It's hard to imagine him in a trailer park. How did he avoid getting beaten up every day?

"Well." Dan shakes his head. "You have to wonder about some of these people. No home training, my grandmother would say." He cuts Hal a bit of a sly look. "Money isn't actually everything, you know? But if there was no cash at stake, I don't think some of them would even try."

"I didn't come out here for money," says Hal.

"Really? I did. No, that's not true. I came here for something better." He laughs. "Why do we always believe north is better? Though it has been, I have to say."

"I was famous here for a while," offers Hal. "Before you were here."

"Oh, yeah?" Dan eyes him. "As what?"

"I was a big flower. And I sang."

Dan looks amused. "Like in a school play?"

"No, on stage. Years ago. I was — I was in a band." Hal feels abashed at this disclosure, not only that he had once been in a band, but that it was important to him to be seen as a man who had once been in a band. "We were called the Venus Flytrap."

Dan looks even more amused. "So you did songs about eating bugs?"

"No," says Hal. "Sucking cock, mostly."

Dan's delicate fingers pause over his sandwich. "Yes, well, of course. And you were —"

"An orchid. Sort of a Weimar orchid, I guess you'd say."

"And you quit it to become an accountant?"

"Our moment passed," says Hal. "But." He wants Dan to understand. "I came here from Idaho, on a bus. I wanted to be . . . larger, somehow. Grander. The best possible version of myself. I never really cared about theater per se. It was just this moment that happened. This opportunity to be something unimaginable by anyone I had known back home. Do you know what I mean?" He meets Dan's gaze; Dan looks interested. "It was like an instinct."

"I know what you mean," says Dan. "I keep thinking I should quit one day, do something else."

"Like what?" Hal holds his sandwich, unopened, in his lap. He glances at the position of the sun. He feels that their one sunny day is passing very quickly.

Dan laughs. "I don't know. Union organizer. Ballerina."

The people on their lunch hour begin gathering up their empty wrappers and downed Snapple bottles. Dan stretches out on the grass. The sun touches him on his face, on his neck. His breathing is even and deep, like a man asleep, but he is fully awake, his face turned slightly toward Hal.

Hal sees that he might be about to fall in love. He gives himself over to it, spreading his arms, as it were, into the open air. Dan smiles into the afternoon sun, and Hal falls faster. There have been many kinds of men in Hal's life over the years, and until this moment he thought he'd learned the ropes of difference fairly well. But he wasn't in love with any of them, so their differences were only facts. Now that he might be in love with this man he sees that he doesn't really know much about it at all. Nevertheless, he is optimistic. It feels muscular, almost, to be optimistic. It feels improbably new. Peace enters Hal's heart and lodges there.

"I always wanted to be Thumbelina," confides Hal.

"I wanted to live in Paris."

"Tell me about it," says Hal.

Nan goes into Christopher's room one morning after he has left for school. His door is only quasi-shut; it has never been his way, before or now, to hermetically seal off his space. She pushes the door open aimlessly. Inside, his room is slightly more tumbled than it has been in the past. The bed isn't made. A few of his new, wide T-shirts from the Husky Bill store are collapsed in bright circles on the floor. *Cry, the Beloved Country* is sliding down a crest of blanket at the bottom of the bed. His window is open. There's a glass of water on the floor next to his bed. She takes a sip from the glass of water, sitting down on his bed for a moment. The sky blue sheets smell innocently of him; they need to be changed. Nan thinks that that must be hard on him, to sleep alone every night. She can't remember the last time she slept alone for more than a few nights, and even then it was always in a bed to which someone — Marina — was returning. Will Christopher ever have anyone in his bed? Will it ever be a bed to which someone comes back, happy to be home? Nan doesn't know. Tamara certainly seems to want to be there. This bed on which she's sitting is a single one, with sheets she bought for him and that she will wash. She sees that he has taken down his sketches. In their place is a picture taped to the wall of a skinny, dark-haired girl — not Tamara, it's clearly a picture he ripped from a magazine — with a knowing expression and heavy eyebrows, carrying a fringed handbag. Nan doesn't like her. She doesn't like the blank wall, either, with its one taped-on magazine picture. It looks poor.

Across the room is Christopher's CD player and little speakers and a scattering of CDs. Nan realizes that the girl on the wall must be her, the atonal girl: PJ Harvey. It makes sense that she would dislike the atonal girl as much visually as she does aurally. The girl on the wall *looks* like the kind of girl who would make that kind of music and be smug about it. She looks, in fact, like the sort of skinny girls Nan used to date whose only true talent was for emotional havoc, despite self-important stabs at the other arts. Like mother, like son. Nan sighs. She isn't sure which prospect is more unpleasant: that Christopher will fall for exactly the kind of impossible girl she used to fall for, or that the only girls he will ever have will be girls in magazines. Women, she corrects herself. PJ Harvey is a grown woman. That's obviously part of what she's so smug about, as if she has just discovered the grand department store of womanhood and has only begun to shop.

Nan crosses the room and finds a PJ Harvey CD. She pops it into the CD player, turns the volume up high, then returns to the bed, where she lies down, careful not to put her boots on Christopher's sheets. She keeps her feet on the floor. She looks at the ceiling. The music begins. The first thing Nan notices about PJ Harvey is that she seems like a Patti Smith sort of person with a smaller, prettier voice. Nan always liked Patti Smith, it's true, and she remembers that when she was Christopher's age she had a Patti Smith T-shirt that she wore until it wore out. It made her feel sexy just to wear it, especially after she cut the sleeves off. She remembers how much Patti Smith knew then. She was the first woman Nan had ever seen who looked like she actually lived the life that Nan had been imagining she herself might live someday — the life of a deserter. She sounded like freedom and pain.

Listening to PJ Harvey, Nan tries to hear what it is that Christopher hears, but PJ Harvey sounds to Nan like a wailing woman at a funeral. Nan recoils from the sound, but she forces herself to stay where she is on the bed. She wants to know where he's going when he listens to this girl for hours, this girl who seems so sad. There are sounds on the record like ghosts knocking things over in an empty house. There is whispering, which Patti Smith never did. There is something like keening. Lying on Christopher's bed, Nan imagines that he leaves his body when he hears this music, he flies away with the witch girl to somewhere in the night, even when it's daytime. She imagines that this music is a relief to him, especially now, when his body is heavy and stolid; PJ Harvey is like a dark and vital dream to Christopher. He doesn't draw anymore. He does this CD instead, drawing with his mind when the witch girl is with him.

Nan doesn't like it. Desperately restless, she stays where she is, not liking it. Mostly, Nan thinks that PJ Harvey sounds like a crazy person. It's as if Christopher befriended some crazy girl, someone worse than Candy because of being smart and pretty and young. Someone who, in certain lights, is admirable and intriguing, but obviously completely out of her mind. Nan doesn't want her, with her cigarettes and her weird moods and her fringed handbag, hanging around Christopher. It's not good for him. As difficult and tedious a place as his body might be at the moment, he needs to stay in it and not go shooting into the night with this banshee. But what can she say to Christopher? Get back in your body right this second, young man, or you're grounded? Nan stares into the ceiling, which is blank, without a single leak.

The CD ends.

Now there is another blank space, like a shadow, where the sound used to be; the blank space in the room is growing. Nan rests her cheek on Christopher's pillow. Will everything be taken from her? Will the witch girl and the stupid girl and Tamara fly away with it all? On the long, pockmarked road that constitutes her life, this house is the only place she has ever wanted to stay. She will have, she knows, no other. This is the last one.

Nan stands up and rearranges the sheets into their original rumples. She closes Christopher's window as if that's what she came in for and perhaps, she thinks, it is. She closes his window to keep any stupid witches out, and to keep his soul inside.

Nan and Marina walk by the sea. Nan takes Marina's hand and holds it firmly, a gesture that comforts Marina: they've walked on this stretch of coast a hundred times. More. Marina tries to add up in her mind how many nights she and Nan have spent together — seven years, at three hundred sixty-five nights a year, give or take a night here and there. That must be, she calculates, more than two thousand nights. Well past a thousand and one. They have no new stories to tell each other, which seems comforting, comfortable.

Nan bends over to pick up a rock. "Look at this vein," she says, holding it up for Marina to see. The rock is gray-green, with a white streak girdling its middle. Nan slips it into Marina's pocket. "Art."

It's an old joke between them. Marina laughs. "I feel like I haven't really seen you in weeks."

Nan eyes the waves. "You've seen me."

"I know I've set eyes on you. I mean that we've both been so . . . busy."

"Yeah." Nan wraps Marina in a bear hug; they're both awkward in their thick jackets. Marina closes her eyes, steeping herself in Nan's familiarity. "I've missed you, too," says Nan. She kisses Marina next to her ear. "We're almost there."

"Where?"

"The end of it. He's doing so well." Nan's face is bright. She squeezes Marina. "We've all worked hard, you were right. I know you've made a lot of sacrifices, too."

Marina thinks guiltily of the gold dress, its ridiculously expensive folds, its train. A dress like that would pay for so many things: furniture, the down payment on a new car, the Christopher bills insurance doesn't meet, time off for Nan, canvas, paint, years of studio rent. And yet she wouldn't give it back. She still could — it's been less than two weeks — but she knows she won't. Even if it stays in its bag in her studio forever. She feels like a child, hoarding her princess gown, but also like a lover. The dress turns idly in the window of her secret life. "I love you," she says to Nan, and she means it. What does the dress have to do with anything that really matters?

The coast wind blows at them, pulling their hair, their sleeves. They walk down the beach. A man throws a red ball for a dog and the dog barks at it as it bobs in the waves. They go on, pushed alternately forward and back by the wind. Marina studies Nan, walking. Nan is slight, but also very sturdy; her slightness seems more the result of compression than lightness, a compact density. She walks into the wind as if leaning closer to talk to it. Her face is surprisingly, almost magically, unlined, considering how little attention she has ever paid it. From the back or even the side she could pass for a young man, or a boyish young woman. It's only from the front that she seems the age and sex she is, and even then the impression results more from the expression in her eyes than the gray streaks in her short hair. And, though Marina didn't know Nan at twenty-two or -three, she suspects that Nan's eyes seemed just as old at that age. Nan's gaze, Marina thinks, has always been exactly what it is now: level, wary, vigilant, not unkind. But knowing, certainly. An old soul. For Marina, a fair part of her attraction to Nan has always been the sense that Nan was not only six years older, but centuries. Nan has the gaze of someone who has witnessed ruins and is still trying to figure out what caused them. This quality makes Marina feel more human, more understandable: there's nothing that new under the sun to Nan. There's an almost imperceptible hitch in Nan's walk as they pass over the sand; her bad hip is getting tired.

"Let's go to the point," says Nan.

"No, I'm ready to turn around."

"Are you?"

"Yes. Come on."

They walk without speaking for a bit, each one in her own thoughts, side by side. Marina nearly confesses, then thinks better of it. What would she be confessing exactly, anyway? Shiloh? That's over now. That she purchased a party dress for an evening in the Taj Mahal to which she will never be invited? Or is there something else she should be admitting to? She decides to leave confessing for another day, when she's more clear about her motives.

"This is what I've always wanted," says Nan. The hitch in her walk is worsening, but her grip on Marina's hand is as sure as ever.

Tamara is laughing. Christopher is spinning in circles in his underwear, the music is loud, his body is soft when he collapses into her, lightly. Tamara is surprised by the softness. She hadn't expected that. His heart pounds against her chest.

Hal goes, by himself, to a dinner party in Haight-Ashbury. He brings a bottle of Australian red wine for the hostess, who has a popular radio show, a blend of alternative music and conversation about alternative books, given credibility by her past as a junkie and her present as a force in the San Francisco arts community. She organizes rallies; she organizes festivals. Her name is Mimi and she is quite tall and curving, like the neck of a swan. Her face is well creased. She only ever wears jeans. Every now and then, she has been spotted at an orgy, but only as an onlooker. Her own sexuality is vague. They became friends because she was an avid fan of the Flytrap. Her radio show back then was called *Moody Visions*. Years later, Mimi did an entire hour of tribute to the Flytrap on her current show, *From the Margins*. She interviewed Hal, played the few remaining scratched tape recordings of Flytrap concerts, got teary in her big headphones. As they worked, Hal had the sudden, wild thought that she had once been a man. He studied her throat, but could come to no definite conclusion. He found it restful, actually, not to know. It made him feel more hopeful about the increasingly practical world in which they had been marooned together — Orchidia Candelabrum and the Flytrap's biggest fan, backstage.

Hal hands Mimi the wine.

"Darling."

Kisses. Olives on the coffee table. A fire in the fireplace. The rose walls of Mimi's living room, the faintly wavy old glass in her long windows. Other guests — a local playwright; a local novelist; Mimi's sound engineer, Sam, who may or may not be her lover, Hal has never been able to figure it out; Mimi's mother, Zuleika, with those long nails; Ti-Hua, a financial reporter from the *Chronicle* with whom Hal had a brief affair. They are all Hal's clients. He tries to block out what he knows about their finances in the way that he imagines psychics have to close the door on the other side now and then. There are things over which it is sometimes better to draw a veil. He has never asked, for instance, how Zuleika, who is from Brazil, accumulated all that money in the first place.

"Where have you been recently?" asks Zuleika, turning her sharp gaze toward Hal. She has always reminded him of a ferocious bird, poised to strike. "We were all just saying how we never see you anymore. Have you become a crack addict?" This is Zuleika's way of joking.

"No." Hal hesitates. "I —"

Ti-Hua looks at Hal compassionately.

Oh no, thinks Hal. "Mmmm," he says noninformatively, eating an olive. It has a bitter, rich, briny taste; Mimi always serves the best olives, he doesn't know where she finds them.

"Oh, leave him alone." Mimi folds herself onto the sofa, which is covered in a deer pelt. She strokes the tawny fur. "Let the man have his secrets."

Zuleika smiles knowingly.

"I'm all for secrets," says the playwright, whose name is Earl. "The bigger the better."

"Exactly," agrees Zuleika.

Hal rolls another olive around in his mouth. It doesn't taste or feel a thing like Dan — he wouldn't say Dan had an olive essence — but he tries to look as if he is savoring the olive while thinking of something private and sexual. Better that they think that's his secret. He winks at Zuleika, who winks back.

"Excellent wine," says Mimi. "We're having rabbit tonight. This will be great with it."

Sam, the sound engineer, makes bunny ears with his fingers. "Mimi shot them herself."

"Yeah, right." Earl laughs uncertainly.

"She did," insists Sam in his deadpan way. "She's a great shot, didn't you know that?"

"I taught her all about it," says Zuleika. "We go to the range every Sunday."

Hal isn't quite sure that they're kidding anymore, but the wine is good, and the olives are rich, and in the wavy glass of Mimi's old windows the dinner party is perfect in a weathered way — he loves the weatheredness. He loves Mimi, whom he can easily imagine leaning out the back of her Victorian with a .22 to take out a few bunnies hopping through her massively overgrown backyard. Maybe she took out the deer somewhere, too, and then she and Zuleika skinned it and made it into a sofa. Sam would have watched, drinking a beer in his bare feet.

"She shot an intruder in this very house," offers Hal, upping the ante.

"We don't talk about that, Hal," warns Zuleika, with a stern look.

"I think the statute of limitations has run out," Mimi says and shrugs.

"Actually," says Earl, leaning forward, "there is no statute of limitations on murder."

Mimi pauses in midpour. "Really?"

Earl nods.

"So we're back to secrets then," muses Ti-Hua.

"Accountants have no secrets of their own," says Hal lightly. "We're very boring people." He realizes that the olive does indeed remind him of Dan, but not in any of its specifically sensual attributes. The olive reminds him of Dan because it seems so complete in itself. He feels almost afraid, he realizes, to love Dan; he fears dislodging the other man from his perfect state, his equilibrium of being completely Dan Jones, partially unknown to him. Hal appreciates anew the painful pleasure of worshipping from afar. Maybe he should just do that.

"I think the bunnies are ready for us," says Mimi.

"He is very fat!" says Zuleika proudly.

After the other guests have gone home (Sam, with a meaningful look at Mimi, said he had to go home to walk his dog) and Zuleika has retired for the evening, Hal and Mimi curl up on the sofa by the fire. The deer pelt is warm and furry and homey, like a pet. The one light, besides the fire, is low and far away. They have sat on this sofa so many times before, at so many gatherings, and now Hal remembers that Mimi bought it in Santa Fe, on Canyon Road. So she didn't shoot the deer herself. He is slightly disappointed.

Mimi sprawls rangily next to Hal. "I may take a break from the show for a while."

"Really?" He doesn't point out that she makes this threat about every year and a half.

"Ah, it's getting stale — you know, the underage transvestite hooker digital ambient blah-blah-blah. I'm too old for this bullshit."

"What would you do?"

"Maybe go back to teaching. I'm genius with third-graders." She gives the fire a stir with the poker.

"Sounds good." Christopher is with Nan tonight. Hal might call Dan, or he might not. For the moment, being by the fire with Mimi seems wonderfully luxurious and exactly right. This is the sort of man he is, the sort of man he's always been, sitting on the deer sofa with Mimi at the end of the party, then going home alone, or not. The rabbit was delectable, no matter who shot it.

"And you?"

"I'm not great with third grade. Middle school, maybe."

Mimi opens up her interviewer's wings, a great invisible span of patience. She doesn't have to say anything. At certain moments, such as this one at the end of the evening, Hal finds himself believing that she was, in fact, once a man and is therefore, like Tiresias, wiser than others about matters of the heart.

Hal coughs. "I don't know, Mimi. I don't know how I am. Nan and Marina are a disaster. And Marina is so impossible."

"Nan loves the chase. You know that." Mimi lights up a small roach.

"But all she wants is simple openness —"

"Oh, for God's sake," snorts Mimi. "Openness is the most intrusive possible arrangement. We all deserve our own secrets. She's terrified: what she wants is to force revelations from people who look like they have something to hide. Remember that Sharon debacle?" Mimi offers Hal the roach, but he declines. "Anyway, people who want to know everything about their lovers should be shot."

Hal is as amused as ever by what he likes to think of as Mimi's frankness. "But everything is different now."

"That's what we always think about love, too," says Mimi, stubbing out the roach. "Aren't you in love?"

It occurs to Hal that his conversations with Mimi are not unlike his conversations with his mother, in the sense that she, who seems to be so vague, usually has the upper hand and in the sense that he likes it that way.

"I am." He pauses.

Mimi strokes a ridge, a place that must have covered the backbone once, in the deer pelt. "Being in love is a story we tell ourselves about the future."

Driving back from Mimi's in the virtual Audi, Hal swings across Market, but instead of heading toward Noe Valley, he finds himself rambling up Mission Street, past Tenth, trying to remember where Dan's apartment was. A windy corner south of Market . . . a warehouse nearby. Close to the train station? Had he heard a train? Had he heard anything that night besides the wind? He turns left, turns right, passes through an alley, drives down Folsom, where clubgoers, with their bright faces, roam from bar to bar. Moss Street. Harriet Street. He crosses Sixth, letting the wheel spin. He could call Dan, but that's not what he wants to do. A current blows him east. He stops the car and looks up.

In a second-story window on the corner, Dan is reading a book. He is wearing glasses that look heavy on his face. Hal didn't know Dan ever wore glasses. There is the distant sound of a train, but Hal can't see the train station from here. Dan takes off his heavy glasses and rubs his eyes. When Hal calls Dan from the car, Dan comes to the window and sticks his head out.

"It's late," says Dan. "You can't park there."

"Should I come up?"

"Yes."

Tamara has begun to have an idea. The idea grows in her, like a plant, like one of Marina's paintings. Her idea has to do with honor. No one who she knows, young or old, ever talks in a serious way about honor, but honor, she believes, is important. Not like the flag or the army or the Girl Scouts. But the idea that a person is that person, just that one, and no other, and who that person is should be honored. That doesn't mean you *believe* everything he says (who believes everything that anyone else says?), but it does mean that if you honor that person you sort of step aside to let him pass to wherever it is he's going. You honor the motion. You honor the heart of the person who believes in that motion, because if you dishonor him you dishonor yourself, in a way. Your own right to pass, to wherever. Tamara feels serious, holding this idea, walking to school or hanging out online or helping her mother cut peppers. Her mother says, "A penny for your thoughts," and Tamara shrugs. She'll explain later, sometime.

What Tamara honors in Christopher is the fact that he is a person of two elements, earth and water. He can exist in either one, like an otter — he believes that. Or, he seems to believe it with what Tamara has come to think of as his other mind, his shadow mind. He slips between his two minds more easily than he generally lets on; it's the way he is. So when he says that he can breathe in water, Tamara knows that he doesn't mean that he can go and stick his head in a full bathtub. It's not like that, just the way he doesn't exactly think that PJ Harvey is going to write him back. He means that in his shadow mind, many things are possible, like on *The X-Files*. It could happen. In some dimension, it is happening. In this way, he also lives in two elements at once: the now and the possible. The possible simply hums closer to him than it does to most people. He's willing to listen to its special sound.

Tamara finds this gift interesting and exciting, an open field. Her parents, for instance, always want to know what's *really* happening, what she *really* feels, what this or that is *really* about. As if *really* is the end of the story. With Christopher, *really* is only one door amid an entire corridor of doors, all of them opening and shutting all over the place. Whenever he disappears through one door, he reappears at another unexpectedly, grinning at her from the entryway. Both of them breathless, laughing.

And maybe he can breathe in water, who's to say? She isn't going to *test* him. That's where honor comes in: she honors his belief, the way you have to honor the belief of people in Fiji that the water spirits desire gifts, or whatever it is they believe. You just have to toss the flower into the water with an open hand.

On a day when she knows that Marina is having lunch with her friend James in Berkeley, Nan lets herself into Marina's studio. Before the rain started, Marina had been so distracted, jumpy, and peculiarly raw. Then she got all resolved-looking and attentive. That was what made Nan really want to know. Maybe it wasn't a stupid girl. Maybe it was: a rough girl with a potholed past, not unlike her, but younger; or a smooth girl puffing out her chestful of degrees; or a wiry girl with a fortune, some Silicon Valley jackass in a four-by-four. Nan can picture only too well Marina climbing up into the big car, the door closing. Why shouldn't Marina want to be rich for once? In Miami, she almost was.

Nan doesn't have to bother being quiet with the key or anything like that; she has every right to be here, she's been here thousands of times before, she's Marina's lover. Partner, as they say, a cold and faintly patronizing term she's never liked. Though, at the moment, if anyone who didn't know her came by and said, "Hi, who are you?" she'd say, "I'm Marina's partner." As if Marina were maybe home sick and needed a certain art book from here, or her favorite sweater, and Nan came all the way over to retrieve the item for her partner. The way partners do: being helpful. Nan isn't looking for evidence of the affair; she's sure there was one; she's equally sure that it's recently over. What she wants to know is why Marina lied about it in the first place. It's not the *who* of the stupid girl, it's the *why*, and the deeper why.

Once inside Marina's studio, Nan realizes how long it's been since she's come over here. It's a total mess, as always, a tumble of junk and paint and light. The sharp smell of the paint is particularly striking to Nan, because it's the scent, much more faint, that trails Marina every day. Both chemical and earthy, it's a scent that Nan has come to think of as a quality of Marina herself, of her skin. But standing here, in this building steeped in paint and turpentine and canvas, Nan remembers that, of course, it's the scent of this place and other places like it. Another world Marina inhabits. Yet she thinks of it as Marina, as if she is at the source of Marina, drenched in Marina. In this place that used to be a church.

Nan steels herself, looking around. Did they meet here? Is Marina really in Berkeley today? Really with James? The studio doesn't say. Its disorder is perfect camouflage for anything and everything Marina might be doing or have done. Nan peers at a glass jar of kidney beans. Why does Marina have a jar of kidney beans? In the window are three seahorses taped to the glass, like specimens. That day at the beach seems like centuries ago now. If Nan had to, if she were asked by the same indeterminate passerby why she's snooping around, she might say that 1) she and Marina had an arrangement, and by violating the arrangement, Marina forfeited certain rules of conduct because she had violated Nan's trust as well, and 2) things were just different now. Like in a war. Different laws applied.

But no one asks Nan this question or anything else, no one comes to the door or cares at all that she's there. Gallingly, the room itself seems not to care that she's there, its kidney beans and boxes of cut-up stuff and baby shoes and old canvases from when Marina was working big — Nan still likes those — leaning or overflowing or sitting quietly on the floor as if waiting for someone else. Row on row of silent trees. It's like being in a forest in some foreign country; Nan worries momentarily that she won't be able to find her way out again. But there's the door. Nan tries to decide where to start. If she were to move anything, Marina probably wouldn't even be able to tell. Nan pokes through the art detritus, wondering what it all means, though none of it means anything like what she's looking for. The room is chilly, too. What does Marina do in here all day long?

Marina's cell phone is lying on her worktable. Nan turns it on, but there are no messages waiting to be retrieved. She turns it off. In the center of the worktable is a piece of drawing paper with a charcoal arc drawn on it and a smudge of something that looks like soup in one corner. A knit glove with the fingers cut off. A blue plastic frog barrette Nan has never seen in Marina's hair. Nan sighs, frustrated but also relieved. It probably was just a stupid girl, a stupid girl in a frog barrette who sang a pretty song for a few months, so inconsequential that Marina didn't want to bother her with it; they don't need any more drama, that's for sure. Life is long; relationships are complex. If they dug up every other body, or dream of a body, well . . .

Something shines. To Nan's right, on the floor, is a heap of yellow-bordered *National Geographics* and some other glossy stuff and papers. An edge of something golden and lacy is visible, poking out of a black bag. Nan extricates the bag; she can tell that it was somewhere between hidden and in plain sight. Even the tissue paper feels rich. Nan undoes the paper gently, feeling the golden, lacy thing under her hands — what is it? A gift from the wiry girl? Who would shop at Armani, so predictable.

Nan begins removing the dress, but the more she unfolds the more there is, it seems, to unfold. How could so much dress fit into one not particularly enormous black paper bag? She feels like Mary Poppins taking that hat stand out of her carpetbag as yards of gossamer and silk and who knows what unfold their glamour. Nan grapples with the folds. She recognizes a train. Is Marina planning to marry the king of Siam?

A credit card receipt in Marina's name for a stunning sum of money falls onto the floor. The wiry girl would never make Marina buy her own dress, that would be a waste of the wiry girl's prowess. The rough girl wouldn't be able to afford it. And the smooth girl wouldn't think of it; she thinks of Hegel. The dress is so fantastic and grand that Nan almost weeps herself at the sight of it; it seems like a dress from somewhere far away where everything is gold and mahogany and ivory. It makes sense that it's in the pile with the *National Geographics*. The train grazes the floor, and Nan instinctively sweeps it up, out of danger of touching the earth.

Nan, holding the intricate, excessive folds and lace of the golden dress in her arms, feels a sadness unlike any sadness she has ever experienced. The dress is ridiculous. It is extravagant. And it is what Marina wants, what she is willing to go into debt for, and lie about, and hide, and possibly never wear. Why would Marina stand at this worktable, keeping the golden dress just within reach nearby, not quite out of sight? Nan has an ominous sensation; this discovery is worse, by far, than any stupid girl. Maybe there was never any girl at all. It's as if the skirt that Nan used to loft into the tree has fallen down on her, still filled, like a sail in the wind, with its own inscrutable destiny. She still doesn't understand that skirt. But what could this dress mean, except that Marina is foolish and self-indulgent? She has always loved such foolish, foolish women. Underneath her bravado, though, Nan feels a chill. The dress, she can tell, is a dream of something. But what? For what Prince or Princess Charming — what other life — has Marina been saving it? A canvas with a half-finished tree on it leans against the wall under the window.

The bodice scratches at Nan's chin. The golden skirt cascades from the crook of her elbow. Nan has no idea how she is going to repack the thing. She hoists it over her shoulder, the bodice at the small of her back, the train nearly at her feet, the skirt at her throat. That will at least, she thinks, keep it from wrinkling. Can it wrinkle? She doesn't know. There is so much she doesn't know, has never known. Her right hip aches, as if the dress is heavy, but it's quite light. The perfect hem brushes her neck, so gently.

It's the way he walks: slightly on the balls of his feet, carefully. It's the way he sets things down: precisely, as if setting something precious into place. His handwriting is neat and curt, compact. He reads novels constantly, searchingly. At the moment, he's in a Doris Lessing phase.

"Do you like her?" asks Hal.

"Not really." Dan turns a page, intent.

There is no closet full of corsets, as it turns out. Dan's just built that way, as if for speed, though he's not speedy at all. He's poised. Hal thinks he must have floated through the trailer park, like a zephyr, his nose in a book.

"A zephyr? No, I had a good time. There were lots of kids around, and that was fun, early on. Later is when it got hard. Later I — what did you say I did?"

"Floated."

"Not like a zephyr. Like a butterfly. I loved Muhammad Ali."

"That doesn't seem like the path of nonviolent conflict resolution."

"He could talk to anyone, that man. He talked the entire world around."

It's the way he seems fondly bemused by Hal. He regards Hal as being perhaps slightly insane (in the nonclinical sense), and in

Dan's presence Hal feels, pleasurably, that he might be. Madcap. Dan's word for Hal's Flytrap past is "cosmic," as in, "You mean back when you were cosmic."

"I'm still cosmic," avers Hal.

"Oh, yes," says Dan.

Hal feels protective of Dan, who has lived alone almost as long as Hal has. But he also feels as if Dan is constantly picking him up and setting him down again, holding him up to the light, taking mental notes. Hal wonders what they say.

Jonathan slips into the house so easily and without fanfare that he seems to have come from next door instead of Los Angeles.

"Hey," he says, and he and Nan embrace tightly, unselfconsciously.

"I'm so glad you're here." Nan draws away to look at him. "You're so thin!"

"Nah." He slouches into the living room, but doesn't sit down, glancing around with interest. "This looks like Nanaw's house, did you know that?" Nanaw is their grandmother, still tiny and alive but no longer in possession of her house; instead, she sleeps in a rest home in Austin.

"Huh." Nan sees that Jonathan is right: Nanaw had an abstemious attitude toward furniture. It made the inside of the house almost indistinguishable from the outside of the house, the flatness and heat carrying through in an unbroken line: you could run straight through and out the other side, away. In lush California, the same spareness seems like an empty basket, waiting to be filled. Nan is already relieved by her brother's presence; Jonathan never fails to bring a different perspective on things. "There's a leak in the living room."

"We'll patch it." Jonathan's entire body seems to be balanced on his wide, leather belt; his ass is small and tight. He is light on his feet, moving soundlessly around the room in his high-tops. Nan was surprised that he turned out straight, and maybe a little disappointed. Women, however, go mad for him. He's like some potent, drifting scent, simultaneously enveloping and evanescent.

Women clutch the air when he's around, follow that scent for miles in their bare feet.

"Are you hungry?"

"Sure."

Both their accents are thickening. In the kitchen, Jonathan eats like a horse, the way he always does.

"Have some more greens."

"All right." He smiles his crooked smile at her. "You sleeping these days?"

"Most of the time, though I try to dream as little as possible." She gets a fork and eats some of the collards herself, hungry for the first time all day. "I should have gotten us some beer — you still drink beer?"

"I kick one back every now and then, just so I don't forget how."

"Have you talked to Henry recently?"

"No."

"Robert?"

"No."

They laugh, in cahoots, as their mother would say. "Well," says Nan. They each obey the unspoken agreement not to talk about their parents, who may be back together, or may not.

"Hey," says Jonathan. "Wow." He stands up and peers at the garden through the glass. "Did you do all that?"

"I did. It's gotten kind of shaggy —"

"It's terrific, Nan. I mean that. The last time I was here — when was I here?"

"A while ago."

"Too long." He looks at her, looks at the garden. "I'm sorry."

Nan finishes the greens. "It doesn't matter. You're here now."

Marina, pedaling home, is astonished at how cruddy she feels. She is, it has now been proven beyond the shadow of a doubt, a cruddy person. An unhappy, bored, and cruddy person. She pedals slowly, dragging out her brooding time. She doesn't even want Shiloh back. She knows it was the right thing to do. She just wants the throbbing in her head to stop, and the rain to stop, and the continual knot in her stomach to untie, and to get that fucking tree right for once, and to be back with Nan, but Nan has been ghostly serious lately. Gone very far into some garage of herself, locking the door behind her. Jonathan's being there only seems to have made it worse. It's bad enough with Nan and Hal. Nan and Jonathan are like some sort of secret-language twins, drawling monosyllables, and there is no declared endpoint to his visit. He made some plaster mess on the living room ceiling that looks like a scratchy cloud. Someone really needs to sand and paint it, but she'll be damned if she'll do it.

Christopher, meanwhile, seems not only well, but positively snappy. He's been drawing up a storm, bounding through the house, no visible hand tremor anymore, and they're all pretty sure that he and Tamara are officially together; he stays at her house too late and smirks when he gets home, like any teenage boy. Nan said she spotted a hicky on his neck. So now it's their turn, Marina supposes, now that the child is fat and shiny, to be unhappy in the pettiest of ways, the most boring, headache-inducing, middle-aged sorts of ways. She is also a cruddy person because she blames Christopher for that, too, for getting better and leaving them with their bitter, flabby problems. Worst of all, she envies him his exuberant ability to draw. He draws for hours, late into the night. She can't believe that this is what she's come to, being jealous of a fragile teenage boy drawing simple likenesses, over and over, of some pop star.

Hal sits with Dan at the table in the window in Dan's apartment. Cars rumble past below. Hal admires Dan's way of sitting; Dan seems to balance serenely on his chair, his limbs making graceful angles and spaces.

Dan yawns. "I have to call my grandmother today." He's wearing jeans and no shirt, showing off his lilting waist. He apparently doesn't mind the pervasive coolness of the windy apartment, which is furnished with things that curve and billow: a red camelback sofa, long sheer curtains, a plush ottoman with a decorative floral button in the center. Even the silverware has rounded handle edges, fat tines. The wind moves silently along the curves of the furniture, opens the folds of the curtains.

"You're such a good grandson." Hal sips his orange juice. Dan rarely mentions his mother, his father even less. They're plainly present, still living in the same trailer park, but it is Dan's grandmother, who has a small, tilted house on the edge of a lake, whom Dan calls and writes. He said about her once, "We were both always a little out there."

Now Dan gazes out the window. "I don't know. I haven't been back in a while."

"Why don't you bring her out here for a visit?"

Dan laughs at this. "Leave her lake? Oh, no. She has to see that lake every day. It's like her lover. She doesn't understand why I'm not living next door, so I can take the lake over when she's gone."

"She owns it?"

Dan shoots Hal a bemused look. "Of course not. But it's her place. When I was really small, I thought she was a witch. Casting spells on my behalf."

"Listen," says Hal. He hesitates a moment, then, awkwardly, "We're all going to Pescadero next Saturday."

Dan pours more coffee. "Who's we?"

Hal tries again. "I mean — we is Nan, Chris, Marina, and Nan's brother is in town, so I thought maybe you'd want to come along, too. You could meet my son."

"Oh." Dan looks somewhat surprised, even reluctant, and Hal hopes he hasn't timed it wrong, or done it wrong altogether. Intimacy is a high-stakes bridge game.

Dan rubs his arms, on which a few goose bumps have appeared. "Well. Huh."

"I thought, you know, it would be a way of introducing you. I haven't gone into all of it yet, but —" Hal thinks he gets it. "Are you worried about the race thing? They're not like that. I mean, of course — do you want to have this conversation now?"

Dan shrugs distractedly. He falls quiet. He gets like that sometimes, as if he's negotiating with some internal committee behind closed doors. Or maybe he's thinking of his grandmother, watching over her lake. "Why do you want me to meet your son?"

"The reason," Hal says as slowly and clearly as he can, and with no small sense of urgency, "is that I'm falling for you. I have fallen for you. I have fallen for you, Dan. That's the reason. Do you know what I mean?" Hal promises himself that he won't ask, this isn't asking, he's just explaining something about himself.

Nor does Dan answer. "Ah," he says, with a complicated expression.

The day is shining. Round yellow sun, blue sky, green trees. Marina notes the downward arc of one branch as they drive along, reminds herself to save it for later. She plans to go to her studio when they get back; her head is pounding. In the back seat, Jonathan sprawls and drawls with Christopher and Tamara. Nan is driving as if she's alone. Behind them, Hal and his date are safely buckled into Hal's climate-controlled, multiply air-bagged, whisper-quiet conveyance; the date, Marina thought, seemed like a librarian, which would be an improvement over the flamboyant narcissists Hal usually goes for. Maybe he's finally grown out of that.

"Dan seemed nice," Marina says quietly to Nan in the front seat.

"Yeah." Nan accelerates.

Silence.

"So did you get to meet her?" Christopher is asking Jonathan.

Whatever, thinks Marina, putting her head back and closing her eyes. The Honda rattles. If nothing else, she decides, they are definitely getting a new car.

As they're unloading the trunk at Pescadero, Nan notices two teenage boys in sleek black wetsuits picking their way with tan bare feet across the stony parking lot. They are carrying surfboards, which are also tethered to their ankles by long, black cords. Their ankles are delicate and wild, like the ankles of deer.

"Faggot," says one boy to the other, jostling him.

Nan hands Christopher the cooler, Tamara the blanket. Marina, in her big sunglasses, is already at the entrance to the path with Hal and Dan. Nan tries to remember if Hal ever had a black boyfriend before, then wonders why she cares. The breeze off the ocean blows Marina's silver hair around. Nan sees Marina in that golden dress, walking away from her down the beach. Instead, Nan attempts to think of Marina as a special plant, maybe a kind of orchid, the sort of plant Nan would never grow, the sort of plant she would see in a book or a magazine, lit to look like jewelry. Not an everyday plant. Not a perennial. Nan finds that if she frames Marina in this way, as a separate species (Marina asks Dan a question, and he smiles), then it is easier to give in to the desire to look at her. Even now, Nan wants to look at her; Nan wants to talk to her, and she does, minimally, but if she's going to stay it seems vital at the moment, especially after all these years, to recognize who, in fact, she's with. Which will take time. Marina, in her sunglasses, waves a little half-wave. *Come on,* she calls.

Nan closes the trunk, hefting a bag of beverages under one arm. The surfboard boys pass by Christopher and Tamara, who are both pale and large by contrast, waiting obediently with the cooler and the blanket and Jonathan, who is also pale. Nan wishes desperately that Christopher were as fleet-footed and arrogant and unheeding as those boys, clinging to the surface of the water with their tan feet. The boys trip over the hill, the tips of their surfboards, like fiberglass tails, disappearing last.

Nan and Jonathan spread out the old plaid blanket. Christopher and Tamara find a few rocks under the bluff and put them on the corners of the blanket; the rocks are damp and cold, with red and brown sand clinging to them. Marina opens up the cooler. Hal, standing next to the blanket with Dan, feels awkward suddenly, as if he, and not Dan, is the outsider.

"Do you think any of these rocks could have fossils?" Tamara asks, sitting back on her heels.

"I doubt it," says Dan. "They're not that kind of rock."

Hal is surprised and impressed. "You know about rocks?"

"From my grandmother." Dan winks. Rocks. Hal doesn't know anything about rocks. Hal hefts a round red rock in his hand; it has the knobby feel of the back of someone's head. The back of Dan's head, to Hal, is indescribably tender. Hal wants to tell Dan that. Later, he thinks. Wait. He carefully sets the rock down.

Marina sits down on the blanket and looks out to sea. Hal tries not to feel irritated with her; it's such a pretty day, finally.

The waves are high-spirited and rough, as if they've just been let out after a winter inside. They're shaggy, crazy-ass waves, and the boys fall off their surfboards again and again, endlessly.

"Look at that," says Nan to Christopher. "Look at them."

Christopher glances up from Tamara's toes, onto which he is idly pouring sand. "Surfers bite."

"Christopher." Tamara laughs.

His cheeks are bright from the wind, his voice excited. He's thinner, Nan sees, still not the way he was before but definitely thinner. He exudes something like happiness — energy at least — as he expounds, "I mean, what's the point? Up. Down. Up. Down. All they do is ride on top of the water, the water could be any-thing, it doesn't matter, they're just going for a *ride*. Like at *Disneyland*. They don't *know* anything, all they want to do is look cool. They buy certain clothes and listen to certain music —"

"So do we," points out Tamara.

"It's not the same thing," he replies, almost tersely. "We're not, like, cult members." He turns to Tamara, serious. "I mean it, Tam."

Nan picks up the round red rock that Hal left in the middle of the blanket and moves it to hold down a stray blanket edge. It has a good solid weight, that rock. She would like to tie it to Christo-pher's shirttail, for ballast.

Jonathan, cradling a pear, cocks his head, listening. "You know what I think it is? I think it's the speed. Two minutes, four maybe, that fast. Like broncos."

Nan nods, counting the boy's heads: one, two. "I'd like to go that fast."

Christopher whoops. "You could! You could!"

Marina, lying on her side, making the sand into random furrows and troughs, remembers another day when they were here, probably in this very same spot. The birthday cupcakes were all eaten; the remainder of the pasta salad was full of sand; a half-eaten hot dog rested at the edge of the plaid blanket. Nan was lying with her chess-piece head in Marina's lap, watching Christopher at the edge of the ocean, bent forward at the waist, walking in tiny steps. He was ten and still rather small for his age.

"He's so serious," said Marina that day, toying with Nan's hair.

"He's so smart," said Nan. "He tests right up there with the best of them."

Marina kissed Nan on her serious forehead. "Like you."

"Not a thing like me. I barely graduated high school."

Christopher made his way over the sand to them, holding something between his cupped hands. "Marina. Close your eyes."

Marina closed her eyes, held out her palm. One, two, three small, wet, sandy items. She opened her eyes. Three little seahorses rested in her hand in a horizontal line, each one perfect and spiny and curving, simultaneously toylike and entirely mysterious.

"Happy birthday," he said. He pointed. "That's all of us."

It wasn't clear whom he meant, but Marina decided he must mean her, Nan, and him. She stroked the small, perfect creatures with a finger. "Thank you, honey. They're wonderful."

Nan twisted her head around to study Marina's face.

"I love them," Marina said, trying to make enough but not too much of the gift. She kissed Christopher, kissed Nan. "I love them," she repeated with conviction.

Now she makes a furrow of sand, flattens and scores it with the round red rock Nan used to hold the edge of the blanket down. The rock pushes the sand into interesting, unnatural shapes; the rock makes the sand remember it. Hal is explaining something that he heard on NPR about newly discovered planets. Marina tries not to feel irritated with him. It's such a pretty day. Where did his date get that extraordinary shirt? Maybe later she can ask him, when her mood improves. What, Marina wonders, is the limit to love's bargain? Till death do you part is the easy promise; it's the living that can feel insoluble. She rolls the rock around until she finds its roughest surface, then presses that part, hard, into the sand.

It's really too cold to swim, although a few daredevils stand by the water's edge with their pant legs rolled up, wading. The sun is bright and strong overhead, making simple things gleam. Underneath the curve of the bluff, two boys and a girl — all maybe twenty, white, with dreadlocks and flapping layers of bright clothes — pass a joint around. The cloying scent wafts over.

Hal sniffs the air exaggeratedly, like a man in a cartoon. "Youth!"

Christopher and Tamara exchange a glance, paper plates on their knees. Christopher picks up the round red rock and puts it on Tamara's plate, laughing.

"Jerk," she says fondly, chucking the rock a few feet away.

"What they smoke is not what we smoked," says Nan quietly. "It's much stronger now."

Dan nods. "A different drug altogether." He pats his stomach. "I'm full. Thank you to" — he gestures broadly — "the chef."

"Jonathan made the black-eyed peas," says Nan.

"Family recipe?" asks Dan so politely that Hal is suddenly quite certain that Dan is about to break up with him.

Nan and Jonathan laugh and laugh. Dan looks at them, puzzled. Hal wants to shush them both, they're only making it worse.

"Inside joke," says Jonathan.

Dan smiles what Hal is sure is his mediator's smile. "That's family."

Jonathan, Tamara, and Christopher go for a walk, ambling across the beach and up onto a dune path. Christopher, his bright hair shining in the sun, is the tallest of the three. Nan feels an unexpected shaft of pride, and she remembers with sadness that she used to have that feeling every day. Every day. She gives in to the urge to embrace Marina, who is sitting up and eating a sandwich, watching the ocean. It literally seems to be roaring today, not a bronco but a lion. Nan rests her cheek against Marina's back, clasping Marina around the waist. Marina turns around slightly, as if to ask a question, but instead bends to zip up Nan's pullover. "There," she says. Marina's silver hair brushes the top of Nan's forehead. Nan, almost against her will, is struck by joy.

It's fun to be three, lying in the dune grass and looking at the sky. They're all giggling at the sun, squinting.

Jonathan passes the joint to Tamara. "It's a special blend."

"It's good," she says. "Can you leave us some?"

"Maybe."

Tamara passes the joint to Christopher, who takes a long hit, then closes his eyes.

Jonathan's arm is close to Tamara's arm, not quite touching it. She wants to know more about him but isn't sure how to ask. "Did you always play guitar?"

He squints at her. "Like in the womb? No. I started in grade school, I guess. Taught myself chords, kept going."

"You didn't take lessons?"

"Uh-uh." He puffs, passes it back to Tamara. "I didn't like lessons."

"Wow."

"You play guitar?"

She hands him back the joint. "No. I just listen."

"Well, that's good. Most people don't listen very well."

His wide leather belt is close to Tamara's wrist. The ropy muscle of his arm just skims her rounded one. Lying between Christopher and his uncle, Tamara has a sense not only of sex, but of rightness. Like this is where she's meant to be. Like they could go on this way, for years. "I listen a lot," she says.

Jonathan nods. "I can tell." Sweet smoke rises from him.

The sun is warm, the dune grass is ancient and tall. They're really not very far from the others. If Tamara sits up she can see the other adults on the blanket: there's Christopher's mom standing up talking to his dad, Marina resting on her side talking to the black guy. Like the three of them, hanging out together. There's the rock she threw. Tamara lies back down, enjoying the warmth of the day.

Jonathan stands up and stretches. "I'm going back." He walks away, so softly that he barely makes a rustle in the grass.

Christopher's eyes are still closed, though he doesn't seem exactly asleep. Tamara takes his hand. She's a little hungry but content. Sleep gently lifts her, carries her out on a swell.

When he lets go of her hand, he marks exactly where she is, her latitude and longitude, the date and minute and second of the day, how she's lying there and what she's dreaming. He leaves the sun with her, to guard her. It's rough and loud and then, underneath, it's colder than he thought it would be. He has to stiffen his elbows and point his toes, he has to ignore the hair in his face, he has to ignore the chill on his ankles. His eyes, of course, are closed. He opens his chest and lets his heart swim out. He doesn't tell it what to do. It stays close to him on its own, becoming accustomed, swimming away, swimming back. He opens his mouth; it's salty on his tongue. Everything comes to him. Everything is good. The clanging and the chatter, the itching and the waking, all the pulling, stop their endless assault. It's great not to be aggravated. This is the secret they've kept from him, how he can do this. He's always known he could. The same weight that pushes him down holds him up. His spiny tail flicks, uncertainly at first, then more surely. His pockets empty. He isn't surprised, except by the one thing he couldn't have known when he was a child: he wants Tamara with him. He can show her how.

It is Nan who notices first that Christopher is walking in an awkward way, very stiffly, hands at his sides, as if marching. Eyes locked ahead. He marches in this peculiar manner down the dune path, away from them, and into the sea. He walks straight into the sea, and immediately disappears.

Nan is running before she even knows she's running, struggling through the surf, pants heavy and wet and twisting around her legs, cold water up to her waist, she's grabbing at the water, grabbing for anything, salt in her eyes and mouth and ears as she screams his name, a wave knocks her over then carries her deeper into the sea. She dives blind, reaching for him.

Nothing. Water. Nan gulps air, trying to make out through her bleary, salt-streaked gaze some sign or scrap of him, but nothing. There is yelling somewhere. She dives again, reaching wide with arms and legs, pushing against the heavy, heavy water. It's her dream but with no possibility of waking. A damp strand of some plant winds itself around her leg; Nan shakes it off, heaves herself up above the water's surface, grabs air, plunges back down. She's crying, snot running down her face, everything inside her pouring out, indistinguishable from the sea, salt on salt, for a moment she wants to plunge to the bottom and let salt meet salt forever, and then she feels his foot bump her side.

Nan grips his foot as hard as she can, it's like a slippery fish, and then she finds his knee, his hip, his waist: he's dead weight, as heavy as lead. Nan pulls his head out of the water, pulling him across her chest to carry him to shore. Dan and Hal are struggling toward them, some fat man, too, the waves pushing them back. And he is so heavy, so heavy and tall, and he is pushing her under. The bead around his neck glows blue in the sun. Nan pushes up with all her strength, but even his arm flopping down nearly capsizes them both. She pushes again, she can tell that she's losing her grip, and he's not breathing. Nan punches at the sea in frustration, tries to reach around to wrench Christopher's mouth open, fails, Dan and Hal are still two waves away. Christopher's head rests hard against her collarbone, but the sea is taking the rest of him, bit by bit, and for an instant Nan hates her son for letting it take him. She is crying, sinking, and although she wills herself not to loosen her hold, the water is seeping in, trying to make her let him go. She chokes on snot, unable to breathe. Her fingers inexorably widen.

It is just then that the strong wetsuited arm of a boy who is not drowning that day reaches down and pulls the two of them across the hard fiberglass of his orange surfboard. Something on the surfboard cuts Nan's arm. The boy drags them to shore, then he and Nan heave Christopher onto the sand. Christopher lies flat, motionless. His lips are gray.

A crowd has gathered, someone says an ambulance is coming, Marina runs forward, Hal and Dan and the fat man, all drenched, are lumbering out of the surf, but it is Nan who tilts Christopher's head up, opens his mouth, pinches shut his nostrils, and blows air into his lungs. It's almost as hard to get the air in as it was to hold him in the water. Her arm is bleeding heavily. Nan takes a breath, forces it into Christopher, her own lungs straining, the sound of her breath and the sound of the wind like one sound in her ears. She takes another breath, forces it in again. Again. Again, until he spits seawater and vomit into her mouth, gags, and breathes. Her blood streaks his face.

Jonathan wraps them both in the old plaid blanket, cotton and crumbs and sand and dirt. He's saying, I'm sorry, Jesus Christ, I'm so sorry, and Nan has no idea what he's talking about as she begins to cry again, legs shaking, arms shaking, saying Christopher, Christopher, Christopher. Who is breathing raggedly, staring straight up at the sky like a blind man.

Tamara, standing on the bluff, can see the cluster of people around Christopher. She sees Nan and Hal make him sit up. Dan's sopping sleeves hang past his hands, making his arms into white flags. She hears the siren of the ambulance, which will, she knows, take Christopher to the hospital and then away. Tamara is crying but not because Christopher nearly died. She is crying because not a single one of the adults now making him breathe and move and live cares in the tiniest way about what he might actually have been doing. They think he tried to kill himself, but Tamara knows that that's not it at all. She knows that he had gathered up his courage to walk into the sea with his other mind and breathe. It wasn't easy for him; he was afraid. The cluster opens and she can see his head bent forward, his shoulders heaving, as if he is crying, too, from the failure of it.

The facts are not the point. Everyone knows the facts. It's just like PJ Harvey. Tamara understands the facts, but she thinks it's wrong, it's not honorable, to ignore the facts of what a person might want or who he might be. They're probably going to ask her questions, too, and then not listen to the answers. Two men bulked up with gear, one toting a bright yellow stretcher, run past her through the tall grass.

Summoning her own courage, Tamara starts down the dune path.

EL CERRITO

H E HATES the cinderblock. He hates the cinderblock and the scrubby view of the highway out the windows. He hates the cinderblock, the scrubby view of the highway out the windows, and the linoleum. He hates the cinderblock, the scrubby view of the highway out the windows, the linoleum, and the scratchy food. He hates the constant round of activities, the group meetings and group therapy and group dinners with the scratchy food and the scratchy movies that they then have to talk about in group therapy, enclosed by the cinderblock walls, and the linoleum floor, and the scrubby view of the highway out the windows. When they watch him take his pill, he barks at them.

Ha ha.

He needs to concentrate. It's noisy again, noisy and busy all the time; he moves from meeting to activity to whatever, blocking it all out with his hatred. It's pathetic, the way they think. Importance bites them on the ass and all they do is look around and talk and eat. Underneath his hatred, he yearns for where he was.

Somewhere vast and deep. And what was there. It was important, it knew him.

He's also bored.

He is supersonically bored, a point he has made many, many times, to no avail. He feels like the commander of a spaceship, trapped on an alien planet: El Cerrito Facility for Mental Health, the planet of retards. Everything they think about him is wrong.

They said, *We hear you like to draw,* so on top of everything else he has to sit in the small, dark, airless space they call an art room for an hour every other day. He doesn't like to draw anymore. They're wrong about that, too. With a pencil, sarcastically, he draws trucks as badly as he can. They say, *Great!*

Things happen on the TV sometimes. Stabbings and shootings, hearts breaking. Some reindeer, some snowmen. He draws what's on the TV, adding subtitles.

When his mother comes, she tries to tell him that they made a mistake before, it's their fault, experiments, they shouldn't have done it, it wasn't his fault that it stopped working, they're doing it her way now. She's not speaking to his uncle, she doesn't care how many times he tries to apologize. She tells Christopher all this as if she's giving him a present. He stares at her silently, wanting her to feel how much he hates her, and it must be working because her eyes look very tired. He told her not to touch him ever again, and she doesn't.

He pleaded with his father not to side with her, to get him out of here, this place is ridiculous, but his father, setting down the GameBoy he had brought for Christopher, said, No, he couldn't do that. He said, You almost died, Chris.

Christopher stared at the cinderblock wall behind and above his father's head. His father was the head on a nickel, talking.

Nan is right, said his father, and Christopher understood that he wasn't telling the whole truth. Christopher gave the Game-Boy to a particularly pathetic boy his own age whom he despised. That asshole had set himself on fire with lawn mower gasoline. Couldn't they see the difference?

From one little window on a scrap of corridor behind the rec room (four semideflated basketballs and a Ping-Pong table), the corner of a back of a house is visible in the distance, up a hill. An aqua fragment of pool. Twice so far, Christopher has seen a man wrapped in hoses lean over the aqua fragment, vacuuming the surface of the water. At least that's what it looked like. Christopher stood at the corridor window, watching this action that must be noisy, though he couldn't hear it. His father is wrong: he's dead now. He doesn't really have a plan, except to stay dead until he can go home. He wonders how many episodes of *Stargate* he's missed.

His mother says, I love you. We all love you.

He says, Then stop this.

He says, You're a fucking bitch. He draws a picture of that but doesn't show it to anybody.

Time goes by like an animal in the zoo pacing the same square of paddock. His hate is vast, caged. The fragment of aqua remains silent. He can tell there's nothing alive in there, no good sounds, no taste but chlorine. He'd die in there, for real, in ten minutes.

His doctor is a round woman with glasses and thinning hair: Dr. Seymour. Her manner is brusque, though she has a sense of humor, too, and a laugh like a shout.

"Mr. Ashby-Cooper." She nods in the direction of the goldfish bowl with its completely pathetic two-dollar goldfish staring at them through the glass. "Don't jump in there." It's her favorite joke; like the goldfish, it circulates often. There's no window in her office, just books and papers. The two-dollar goldfish at least has the illusion of a view.

"Okay." He attempts a smile.

"How are you feeling?"

"Great!"

She laughs her shout. "Yeah, me, too."

"Can I go home?"

"All too soon, these days."

"It's been a long time."

"It's been two weeks." She holds up two fingers. "Two, Mr. Ashby-Cooper."

"I'm cured," he says sarcastically.

She answers his sarcasm seriously. "You will never be cured. I'm telling you that right now. They might have failed to point that out at" — she taps his file with one of her stubby fingers —

"Pacific. There is no cure. There's only maintenance. And what we have you on, we know it works. It's standard."

"Tell my mom that."

"No." The goldfish bolts to the other side of the bowl. Dr. Seymour gives him her Serious Look. "I'm telling you. You're almost a man."

In the corridor, things clatter, there are footsteps, snippets of talk, a knock on the door.

Dr. Seymour sighs. "I wish we had more time."

He tries to send Tamara messages with his mind, things he can't say when she comes to visit, though he tries to look them out of the corners of his eyes. While he misses the curves and valleys of her body, he misses her mind more. He misses their music, which she never talks about, and when he brings it up she changes the subject. He wants to tell her about the underneath, that's the cool part, and he also needs to tell her what to do if certain things start happening in a certain order, where she should go, but her fucking mother is always there, watching. When he asked Tamara's mother what color her car is, she wouldn't tell him. He sent Tamara a searing look over that one, his heart was pounding, but she didn't look him back. Even with all the interference, he sometimes gets the feeling that Tamara is trying to send messages to him, too, though she doesn't say anything besides algebra class, she jammed her finger in volleyball, the weather, how is he, she's cool. One time, when her mother had already moved toward the door, Tamara touched her little finger to his and whispered, *Fiji*. He doesn't dream — he swears he doesn't — but sometimes, awake, he imagines Fiji in a way that's like dreaming. Its greens and birdsong, its waters.

Christopher watches the man with the hoses move around the aqua fragment. He leans against his arm on the window. In the rec room, someone is attempting to bounce one of the semideflated basketballs. The ball thuds squashily. The man with the hoses takes off his cap and mops his brow; it must be warm out there.

Christopher is slightly sleepy, as he often is recently. After lunch today he took a nap in his cinderblock room on the single bed with the thin sheets. Then he wandered over here, before group. He taps on the window frame, idly hating everything. A screw pops up. He touches it with a finger but is otherwise motionless, though there's no one else in the corridor. The basketball goes *thud, thud.* With two fingers, deftly, he turns the screw. It falls into his palm.

The asshole who set himself on fire with lawn mower gasoline comes out of the rec room holding the squashy basketball. His hair is still very patchy. "Going to group?"

Christopher turns only his head casually. "Yeah, I guess."

In group, while the woman with multiple personalities talks on and on in her rapid way about herselves, Christopher holds the screw lightly in his fist, as if he is holding a bee. *Bzzzz* hum the sharp threads of the screw against his palm. *Bzzzzz.* It buzzes through dinner, through *Butch Cassidy and the Sundance Kid,* through the visit with his mother and Marina the next day, who sit side by side in the old beige Naugahyde chairs like two strangers sitting next to each other on an airplane. They're fighting again, obviously, in their nonfighting way. They both look only at him.

"You seem good today, Chris," says Marina, patting his knee. "Lighter."

"Thanks." He smiles, detesting them both. *Bzzzz.*

The name of the asshole who set himself on fire with lawn mower gasoline is Nate. His parents are both professors at San Francisco State. Nate is also a cutter, which is unusual for a boy, he tells Christopher. Nate rolls his sleeve back down and resumes eating his strawberry ice cream. "I suffer from acute depression."

"Me, too," Christopher tosses off, and Nate brightens.

"Really? And what did you do? You jumped, no —"

"Drowned." The screw is in his pocket, buzzing against his thigh. "I tried to drown."

"Drowning," says Nate, exhaling the scent of milky strawberries. "Huh. Was it hard?"

"Not really. I think this is harder, this, this —" He glances at Nate as if he can't think of the right word.

"All these dumb activities."

"Right. And, you know, what's the point?"

Nate nearly squeaks. "*Yes.*" His sneakers, Christopher notices, are untied. "I've been here before," Nate confides.

"I was at Pacific."

Nate licks his spoon. "Pacific's supposed to be nice. Your folks must be rich."

"No. And it didn't work, anyway. So now I'm here." Christopher can't quite bring himself to feel bad for Nate, whom he still despises, but he does feel bad for Nate's hair, which has the stubbornly scruffy quality of something that may never grow back in the same way. He feels bad for Nate's scarred scalp. The screw buzzes in his pocket. Because of Nate's hair, he returns a confidence. "I want to leave."

"Oh, you will," says Nate.

One day, however, Christopher finds that he isn't minding, for real, about the cinderblock. He still minds about the view of the highway outside the windows, and the linoleum, and the food, and the constant round of activities, but he doesn't mind about the cinderblock. The cinderblock is nothing. Walls have to be made of some material; these happen to be cinderblock. A persistent sensation like a roving bottlebrush that has been traveling from his shins to his shoulder blades and back again disperses. The next day, he finds that he doesn't mind, for real, about the scrubby view of the highway outside the windows. He bounces the squashy basketball with Nate in the rec room, easily plops the ball through the one, low basket. It thuds on the wooden floor, then rolls to a stop.

"Good one," says Nate.

The next day, he doesn't mind, for real, about the linoleum.

Tamara frowns. "Hello? Anybody home?"

"I'm fine," says Christopher.

She leans back against the beige Naugahyde. "You look funny. Your eyes are funny."

He crosses his eyes to make her laugh, but she doesn't laugh. "Are you going to be like this forever?"

"Like what?"

"Damn. Here comes my mom. Chris, are you just fucking with me?"

It bothers him slightly that he can't quite understand what she means. Why would he be fucking with her? "No."

"Chris." Tamara kicks his chair. "Christopher. Mom. Look at him."

Tamara's mother, her bag on her shoulder, looks at Christopher, then at Tamara. "How are you feeling, Chris?"

"Fine."

Tamara's mother looks at Tamara again, head tilted. "We can't stay long today, Tam."

Tamara stands, then leans far over, pressing her forehead against Christopher's. "Christopher, listen to me," she says, her green eyes locked on Christopher's, her hands with all their rings braced firmly on his shoulders. The rings press into his flesh. "I. Love. You."

Her mother pulls angrily on Tamara's sleeve. "Tam! Tam!"

But Tamara doesn't turn away for what seems like a long time, not until a little metallic circle, maybe the size of a dime, far down within Christopher — several layers below where he thought it was possible to go — chimes. It is a very small circle, so much smaller than everything that surrounds him, smaller than any of Tamara's rings. Still, it chimes. He smiles.

Tamara, her forehead still pressed against his, smiles back. "Okay, we can go now," she says. She straightens and gathers her coat.

It's not that hard, as it turns out, to pry up a second screw. So now he has a pair, buzzing together companionably. For an experiment, he lightly taps them back into the window, and the next day they're still there, wobbly and untightened.

"Your turn!" calls Nate from inside the rec room.

The man with the hoses leans over the aqua fragment a fourth time. Christopher decides that before the man leans over the fragment a fifth time, he'll be gone. He feels very relaxed after he makes this decision. It's not that hard, he discovers, to make a swallowing gesture and then remove the half-melted, gooey pill from his mouth sometime later. It's not like at Pacific where he and Frank, the orderly, chatted for a while about guy things until the pill went down and they were always taking his blood and making him pee in a special cup, like an astronaut. Here, the orderly is a fat girl who obviously hates everybody's guts. There's a rumor that she's a patient who's never left. And it's not that hard, either, to press a note into Tamara's hand, just like at school. "See you later," she says.

He winks, like Butch Cassidy. None of it is that hard, it all flows on, except for the day before, when his mom comes.

She sits down next to him, touches his arm. He doesn't even move his arm, because he doesn't mind now. "I think they're going to discharge you next week," she says. Her shirt is rumpled; her eyes are still puffy. "They won't actually say it yet, but Dr. Seymour dropped a hint."

"Great," he says.

"Are you scared?"

He shakes his head. "I'm not scared."

She leans back in her chair, still holding his arm. He wonders what they're having for lunch today. "I might be scared if I were you. After everything that's gone on. I might . . . worry."

"I'm not worried." He wishes she didn't look quite so tired. He probably should leave her a note or maybe e-mail her, later, when they get there.

"You won't have to go back to school right away. We're going to give you time to settle in. I'll take the first week off from the store."

"You don't have to do that," he whispers. He seems to be catching her tiredness, which isn't good. He inflates his mind against it.

"No." She presses his arm. "I do. Honey, I know you think you don't need my help, but sometimes things go a different way. Chris." She leans forward. "I always thought — listen — I always thought I was a lonely kind of person, that it was just me — I thought nobody cared."

He keeps his mind as inflated as possible, lots of air between them. He concentrates on the loose screws, six of them now, buzzing against the window frame.

She looks at him seriously. "I was wrong about that. When I had you, I knew I had been wrong. I care for you. All I want to do in my life is protect you."

"From what?" He has the screws ask it, in a chorus.

A kind of shadow crosses her face. He hopes he hasn't said the wrong thing. "From . . . things that might hurt you."

As reassuringly as he can, he says, "Nothing's going to hurt me."

"Oh, Christopher." She runs a hand through her hair. "I'll be back tomorrow."

"Okay." He gives her a hug when they say goodbye and he's surprised at how small she feels in his arms. He always thinks of her as large and very solid, like a bridge, but she isn't.

Meanwhile, he feels great. Really great. He hates the cinderblock.

Later, he wills the conversation out of his mind to orbit with the rest of the clanging extraneous things, but some scrap of it remains, causing Christopher to hesitate momentarily in the shadows of the corridor. The window gleams before him. Why would she think that she could protect him? And from what? She's always facing the wrong way in the wind, his mother. He loves her, but as Dr. Seymour said, he's almost a man. He is a man. If anything, he should be protecting her.

It's this thought that almost makes him turn back, away from the gleaming, buzzing window. She's really just a scrap of a thing, a strong wind could blow her over. Though no winds ever do;

she stands her ground, staring them down. Christopher hesitates, stricken by the knowledge that she'll worry. But there are things she doesn't know, things she'll never know, and the buzzing is growing very loud. His ship is here. He feels amazing.

There is Tamara's face at the window.

Christopher goes to meet her.

BONE

THE FOREST is so old, but it seems new, as if it's not just a new year but an entirely new world. It's colder than Tamara had imagined; she's glad she brought the wool sweater and the waterproof jacket, glad she wore her hiking boots. It's high morning, but the fog is still wafting above them, reaching down here and there to touch their faces with a cold, damp tendril. The ground is soft, brown, thick with stuff. Pale green ferns spring not only from the ground, but from the crumbling trunks of trees that have fallen over and from inside trees with deep, parlor-size holes at their bases. The trees are extremely tall. Their thick red bark feels like fur. Now and then, little things patter down from them, leaves or twigs or drops of water. The forest is so vast that where light does touch it, the light seems new, as if it's never touched that patch of ground, that pale green fern before. Tamara has been to the redwoods, but never this far north. These redwoods seem different from the redwoods from elementary school, both older and closer, friendlier. Though there is no trail, it isn't that hard to make their way deeper in, toward where Christopher said he heard water. It seems as if they could walk forever this way, just the two of them. There's a strange spindly moss, like unspooled light green thread, that twines around fallen branches. Tamara thinks of it as witches' hair.

Christopher stops, head bent. Tamara stops, too. "Listen," he says.

Tamara tilts her head. "Is it the river?"

"Shhh. Listen." A bird sings in long, looping notes, like the whistle on a train. Christopher smiles. His eyes are bright and his cheeks are pink. He's wearing a red sweatshirt and zippered jacket of hers, both of which fit perfectly. He looks so much better, already, than when they left three days ago. He's carrying the backpack, which, as Tamara knows because she packed it, is heavy: there's the tent, the one sleeping bag, socks, Band-Aids and Neosporin, PowerBars and candy bars for energy, two lighters (not matches; matches get wet), water purification tablets, two T-shirts and two long-sleeved shirts, two pairs of jeans, one cup, one tin bowl, one spoon. She tried to think of everything. She keeps the money — $335 — in her pocket.

Tamara presses her face against his neck, wraps her arms around his waist. He's only a little bit taller than she is, which makes it all seem that much more inevitable: they were always the tallest kids in the class.

He kisses the top of her head. "You saved my life, Tam."

She draws away to look into his eyes; their gazes lock and hold, unbroken; he parts her lips with his tongue and they kiss for a long time in a shaft of new light. The wind blows and little things go *click, pop, clack,* as they fall down through the tall trees.

At night it's very dark. They have one tiny flashlight that they use only if they think they hear a bear. Lying inside their tiny tent in the one sleeping bag, their legs tangle and he rests against her chest, one hand beneath her shirt, on her ribs. He's humming. It's too cold at night to fuck; they've been doing it in the middle of the day, stark naked in the light, clothes tossed around on the ground. His cock is beautiful. Her bare breasts in the sun go cold and hot at the same time. Then they have to pick all their clothes back up, put them on, and continue, flushed.

"Tamtamtam," he sings. "Are you hungry?"

"We should save what we have until we can get some more."

"I'm hungry."

"Yeah, me too."

His fingers dance along her ribs, touch her belly. She really is hungry.

"Okay, we can split a candy bar. But we have to save the rest," Tamara says.

"Okay." He sits up and rummages in the backpack.

"Oh, hurry, it's cold without you."

He returns, unwrapping the bar and breaking it in half. They chew facing each other, touch chocolatey tongues.

"Gross," she says, kissing him. "That's gross."

In the morning, he leaves the tent to pee. She likes hearing the dull sound of his piss hitting the ground, though he's modest about it, always ducking behind a tree some distance away, zipping up immediately after. She waits until she hears him stop peeing, then waits a minute more before leaving the tent.

"Wow." She stretches out her arms in the wild, wet, gray air. It's like being underwater. "It is so incredible here."

He whoops, running toward her, then picking her up. "I'm so happy! This is so great!" He laughs a good, loud laugh, not putting her down. She's surprised at how strong he is; she wouldn't have thought he could pick her up at all. But he can, and hold her aloft, too, laughing.

"Hey, I think we should call today," she says, in his arms. "And we need some more food."

He shrugs.

"I'm sure they're freaking."

He puts her down, turns away, and pulls up a tent stake. "Yeah, you're right." But his tone is slightly wounded and distant, and Tamara reminds herself that he does have a problem, even if his parents' idea of how to fix it was so incredibly bad. She'd always thought gay parents would be much cooler, but obviously they aren't. He must be scared that someone is going to do that to him again, lock him up and make him a shadow. She touches his arm gently as she helps him pull up the tent stakes, but he seems pretty calm. And when she quietly turns on her cell phone later, just to see, while he's peeing against a distant tree, it doesn't work anyway. They're out of range.

Nan tells the cop to go fuck himself and slams out of the police station, punching the door with her fist on the way out for good measure, but the door is as stubborn as she is. Her hand begins to swell immediately.

Hal runs after her, stumbling down the steps, grabbing her arm as they reach the street. "Nan. Nan. We *can't* do it like this, we need their help —"

"Let go of my fucking arm, Hal." She wrenches it away from him, breathing hard.

"Nan, the man is doing his job, he's not that bad, he was just trying to tell you —"

"That asshole was *instructing* me, that homophobic piece of shit. He'd be so goddamn happy if we lost him to some — He *loves* this, Hal, he loves it that we're freaks. You know he thinks it's because of who we are, like something in the water: of course something like this was bound to happen. You tell me he didn't say —"

"That was a mistake. He apologized right away." Surprising himself for the second time that day, Hal grabs both of Nan's arms. Her arms are ropy and tense, like the legs of a wild animal as it is about to spring. Hal holds on. "Nan, now listen." He shakes her a little. "Listen to me right now. You can't roar this one down. This is large, and bad, and very, very dangerous. We cannot let it eat us first. We *have* to be rational or we will just fall in there with him. Do you hear me? We will not save him like this." He shakes her again, and because he is so frightened, he lets slip what he really thinks. "I don't know if we're going to be able to save him, anyway. But we will definitely lose him, forever, if you put your pride ahead of what has to be done."

Nan untenses infinitesimally in Hal's grasp, though her jaw remains set. "You think this is pride?"

A bit later, at his house, Hal, wrapping up ice in a dishtowel for Nan's hand, wonders if it's really possible that the Department of

Social Services could enter the picture. Tamara's father, on the phone at 7:00 A.M. this morning, suggested it, but Hal didn't think it was a very plausible scenario. In fact, Hal, surprising himself for the first time that day, said coolly that first Christopher would have to be found. He also reminded Tamara's father that Christopher certainly couldn't have gotten out without the other man's headstrong daughter, given the fact that his own plainly fragile son was in possession at the time of not much more than shoelaces. Then he hung up and went to feed the shark a little raw hamburger, which it ignored. The fish is waning again, inexorably.

The dishtowel is cold and lumpy; Hal wraps the entire thing in a plastic bag. He carries it to where Nan sits at the dining room table, holding both the swollen hand and the normal hand before her face. He lowers the swollen hand and puts the ice on it. "Too much pressure?"

"No, it's okay. I don't even need ice. I should go."

Hal doesn't say anything, holding the ice on Nan's hand.

"We should sue that place," says Nan for the thousandth time. "How could they have let this *happen*?"

"We may have to sue them, if Tamara's parents sue us." He moves the ice to her fingers.

"Why would they sue us? Did you hear from them today?"

Hal avoids the second question, venturing gingerly, "Well, if something . . . happens. To Tamara. They could sue us. Reckless endangerment or something."

"Oh, God. What about how she endangered him?"

"Nan. Come on. Parents can practically get sued these days if their kids cut class." Hal touches his hand to Nan's. Hers is ice-cold and rigid from the swelling.

"I don't know how much I think about Tamara," Nan says, flexing her fingers and wincing. "I worry more that she'll leave him by the side of the road somewhere."

Hal shivers. "I can't imagine that." Already the ice is melting, loosening in the bag.

"I still think we should sue them."

*　　*　　*

Marina sets down her brush. The tree is half-done, coming up on the canvas like a half-developed photograph, its lines and arcs and texture, all its architecture, visible now. It's like an X-ray, she thinks. How would she diagnose it? A bit too subtle, ultimately; a bit too sentimental, too. It isn't ruined, not yet. It's fine.

But then, all at once, she sees that this tree is the last. Or maybe not. But her hand has stopped.

It isn't that she believes she can bring him back by stopping, though there is something of that in it, a burnt offering. It's that she sees no way to continue from here. This form, and her life, have broken clean away from each other. She's already on one side of the divide, and on the other are seven years' worth of canvases, some bad, some good, but all irrevocably *there*, while she is undeniably here. Obviously, being here is what she needs to concentrate on; she needs to use both hands to stay.

The funny thing is that she suddenly realizes that she always knew this moment would come. She carries the canvas over and leans it against the wall to dry before she can put it away. She washes and dries her brushes and puts them away, tenderly, as if burying them. She checks that the windows are closed and locked. She unplugs the boom box. Downstairs, Turner must be etching; the familiar scent of acid wafts up. Silently, she wishes him well. She'll come back later for the dress.

She wouldn't have expected the moment to arrive in this way, but that's how it works, doesn't it? You never know in what costume it will appear. And it's something of a relief, she can see that already, because there was that flaw that she could never quite work out, though she got infinitely better, over the years, at disguising it as a virtue. As, indeed, her style. All at once she is shed of her style, thrown clear of it in the way that one of her art school professors used to call admiringly "breaking the hand." Some artists would tie up the good hand and work with the bad one, trying to break through. She could never do that, could never see the point of aspiring to it. She thought it was an affectation or a myth.

But it must not be a myth, after all, because it's happened. She supposes that sometime she should thank Christopher for that, if she ever sees him again. She has finally, unexpectedly, broken her hand. Now, according to the myth, she's free.

She turns out the old, glaring, tin-shaded light on her work-table and locks both locks when she leaves the studio. The thick church doors close behind her. Valencia Street is busy, nearly every part of it in motion.

While Hal and Marina make a healthful stir-fry that she knows she won't eat, Nan, upstairs, stands on a chair, throwing things out of the bedroom closet with the hand that doesn't hurt. When did they accumulate so much useless stuff? Earmuffs, for instance. Why would they need earmuffs? Fuzzy dice, though she kind of likes those. Scented candles. A boot box containing a heap of old, typed pages from Adam's book, which she must have said she would read. She tosses everything onto the bed: and there it is, neatly rolled up in the back. Snapping the rubber band, she jumps off the chair, ignoring the ache in her hip.

Once downstairs, she unfurls it on the kitchen floor.

"Jesus Christ," says Hal, turning from the task of chopping broccoli. "What in God's name is that?"

"Christopher made it," says Marina. "The first time out."

"Why didn't you tell me?"

Nan squats on her heels, peering at the drawing. "It didn't matter. He was here then."

Hal frowns. A piece of broccoli falls onto the edge of the drawing. "What do you mean it didn't matter? Everything matters. Everything —" He gazes down, frowning more deeply. "If that's what he feels like inside . . ." He abandons the knife.

"It's not inside," says Nan. "I think it's outside. Or what he thinks is outside."

Marina lowers the flame under the pan and moves to squat beside Nan. "If that's true, then he thinks everything is outside." She touches the spots of blood with a finger. "I can't believe that he can live at all like this."

Nan brushes Marina's hand away. "Don't touch it. I have to see."

"See what?" says Marina quietly, standing up.

"Something. I don't know yet." She holds her open palm over the paper, trying to sense the terrain.

Hal turns back to the broccoli, chopping in quick, short strokes. "You know, getting as crazy as he is isn't going to bring him home any faster."

"Look, it's not like I think this is going to tell me where he *is*," snaps Nan. "But it's the only thing we have to go on." She sees Hal and Marina exchange a glance, but she doesn't care. And after Hal has gone home and Marina has silently gone up to bed, Nan sits at the kitchen table with a cup of coffee and the landscape, tracing it with her hand, with her mind, with her mind's eye. She moves over it again and again. She catches the trail of his soul, loses it, catches it for a moment before it disappears once more.

"I could live here," says Tamara, licking her soft-serve chocolate ice cream. It's pleasingly artificial and incredibly sweet. They're sitting on the curb outside a place called Chico's Café. Nearby, a skinny kid is playing Hacky Sack with himself, bouncing the little pouch off his ankle, his knee, his elbow. He's really good. A girl with an eyebrow ring and a dog collar, wearing a tight dress that doesn't look very warm, is also sitting on the curb watching the kid, smoking slowly.

Christopher licks his vanilla cone. "This tastes horrible. Must be rotten. Don't eat it."

"I don't think soft-serve can be rotten. I don't think it's even food." Tamara catches a drip with her tongue.

Christopher throws his cone into the street, where it splats in a milky white heap. "Rotten."

The girl with the eyebrow ring laughs. "Good one," she says to Christopher, narrowing her eyes as she inhales.

"There's a movie place here. They're showing that one about Mars," Tamara says hopefully. Her shoulders ache from her turn carrying the big backpack. They found out that getting another sleeping bag would have made too much of a dent in their money, but they did get cans of beans and soup, a can opener, a little tin pot, a bottle of water, and soy dogs. It all makes the back-pack heavier, but in a good way. These days, they're always hungry.

"No," says Christopher shortly.

Tamara almost argues with him, then doesn't. It's important to keep him calm. She's noticed that he's a little crabbier in the after-noons, and they're both tired. They didn't find any river. That sound turned out to be a road, but they still walked a long time before they got picked up by a very tan woman with a long gray braid driving a truck with a bumper sticker that said I ♥ RODEO. "Where are we?" said Tamara as the woman let them out at a gro-cery store at the beginning of town. Tamara could see the end of town a few blocks away.

"Smithville," said the woman, closing the door of the truck and driving away.

Smithville is warmer than the woods, and there are a lot of kids around who all look cool. Two white guys, with red hair in pony-tails, wearing T-shirts that say REGGAE ON THE RIVER, sit down next to the girl with the cigarette as if they're her brothers. Still, Tamara misses the woods. She's always liked woods; maybe she and Christopher will live in a house in the woods someday, and speak French and make up stories about other planets. She fin-ishes her cone. "Christopher," she says firmly, "I have to call my parents."

His eyes dart around, but he says, "Go ahead."

Tamara watches him as she turns on the cell phone. It takes a minute or so for the phone to find its bearings before it beeps on. There are about a million unretrieved messages, probably all of them from her parents. Tamara touches the familiar numbers, and when her mother picks up she is surprised at how happy she is to hear her voice.

"Where are you, Tamara?" says her mother in the supercalm, therapist's tone of voice that means she's hysterical.

Tamara, eyeing Christopher, says exactly what she's been planning to say. "Mom," she begins in the identical supercalm tone of voice, "we are fine. I know you and Dad must be worried, but we're cool. We have food and everything we need and we're very safe."

"Is he sitting right there? Is he telling you what to say? Tamara, the police —"

"Mom." Tamara carefully maintains her tone. "I am not, like, being kidnapped here. If anything, I kind of kidnapped him." She giggles a little.

"Tamara." Her father is on the extension. "You need to understand this. Your picture is accessible to every police station in this country, you're on a list, and so is that —" He seems to choke on Christopher's name.

"Dad, what you need to understand is —"

"We are going to find you, Tam," says her mother. "Count on that."

"And what list? Am I a criminal here? I don't think so. I don't think you know anything about this. We're *in love*. We aren't hurting anyone. They were hurting him."

"Tamara, listen," implores her mother.

Tamara hears the muffled sound of her father beginning to cry. "I love you. I'm fine." Tamara clicks off.

The girl and her two brothers are looking over, interested. The kid bounces the Hacky Sack off his shoulder blade. His mouth is open.

"What did they say?" Christopher anxiously scans Tamara's face.

"They're freaked out. They put our pictures on some list that goes to police stations. My father is upset." Tamara glances at the heavy backpack and sighs.

"Hey, where you from?" calls the girl.

Tamara, who doesn't like her face, doesn't answer.

"Fiji," says Christopher, getting up and hefting the backpack onto his shoulders. He doesn't seem distracted or skittish anymore. He snaps the backpack straps around his waist. "We have a

few hours of daylight left. I think we can make it back in before it
gets dark."

"For real?" says the girl. "Hey, Fiji for real?"

Nan brings the landscape to work with her, taking breaks as often
as she can to stare at it. On one of her breaks, she nails it up
onto the wall in the back office, hanging it right over the bulletin board. The pushpins underneath punctuate the drawing like
braille, but what they spell out is not important: things to do, bills
to pay. It's this crazy drawing that's life or death, its dense swirls
and yellow ocean, its crows and blood and little parts where there
is much tiny, tiny writing that Nan can't decipher at all.

Peta wanders in. "What is that?"

"A thing Christopher drew the last time he was sick." Nan leans
forward to peer at the writing again, but it's futile, even with her
reading glasses.

"It's intense. Did you put it up because you miss him?"

"No."

Peta nods thoughtfully. "Did you eat today?"

"Not yet."

"I'm going to order us some lunch." Peta gazes at the map.
"Looks like those maps of the ocean floor." She wanders out, and
Nan hears her ordering in what seems to be quite a bit of Japanese
food.

Nan looks again. She is startled to see that Peta is exactly right.
How could she have missed it? That's why things seem to be lying
on the ground in that strange, untethered way; it's as if the earth
fell into the sea and broke apart. The crows, Nan understands,
have drowned, that's why they're so two-dimensional, each one
ringed by a kind of funeral wreath. Drowning has made the crows
flat. That distended yellow part is not an ocean, but the sun,
viewed from under water. It's still all folded and collapsed, illogi-
cal, but if only she had recognized it before! She never would have
taken Christopher, a boy who drew so elaborately from the perspective of someone lying on the bottom of the ocean floor, to the

edge of an actual ocean. While Jonathan may have fed him drugs (they may never speak again, she may never forgive him), and Hal enrolled him in some fancy program that almost killed him, and Tamara helped him to run off, she is the one, months ago, who rolled up his treasured drawing and put it in the back of the closet so that he wouldn't be able to find it. She thought she was protecting him from something, some dark lure. If Marina hadn't saved it, they wouldn't have anything to go on now. She tastes salt suddenly, though she isn't crying. Then she knows what she has to do.

Peta, with an apologetic expression, appears in the doorway. "Um. Nan. Tamara's dad is on the phone. He sounds upset."

Tamara's mother, whose name is Ruth, sits up very straight in her chair. "For us," she begins, glancing at her husband, "the point is to find our children. Your son" — she gestures at Nan, Hal, and Marina, who are sitting on the Mission couch — "is very ill, and our daughter" — she reaches awkwardly from her chair to grasp her husband's hand as he stands stiffly at the fireplace — "has clearly been somewhat impulsive. My own feeling is that Tam called today because she knows she's in over her head, even though of course she couldn't *say* that to us. I don't think we maybe handled it in the best way." Ruth scratches her eyebrow. Her husband, Jack, is as silent and massive as a dormant volcano. To Marina, he looks like an albino walrus: he's large, thick-featured, with pale blue eyes. He moves with the deliberateness of a big man trying not to knock anything over. His V-neck sweater has a stain on it. Ruth, by contrast, is slight, nervous, and dark, like the shadow of a larger woman. Her voice is high, higher from the current strain. Tamara plainly takes after her father physically; that must be hard, Marina speculates, to know that you resemble the more awkward parent. The gene pool never seems to divide or blend evenly.

Nan shifts uncomfortably on the sofa. "Yes. Uh-huh."

"I called the cell phone company. All they could say was that the call came from Humboldt County," offers Jack, leaning forward into the room. He shakes his head in disgust. "But that's a huge area. Who knows whether they've gone north, south, east, or west?"

Ruth squeezes his hand. "It was a very frustrating day. We are very, very . . ." She stops, frowns as if she is about to cry, then gathers herself. "We are very concerned. With this type of illness, Nan, as I'm sure you know, things can suddenly *change,* yes?"

"Yes," says Nan in a tone that causes Marina to pat her gently on the knee.

"So, what I'm trying to ascertain is about his history, which we really don't know, but which all of you are obviously familiar with." Ruth attempts a smile. "Tamara always liked you."

"She means how violent is he," says Jack heavily. "We need to know the truth about how violent this kid is."

Hal cuts in before Nan, who is now halfway off the sofa, can erupt. "Jack, I see your point, but Chris isn't violent. He's just ill, as you know, and young — "

"He used a knife," interrupts Jack, reddening.

"On himself," Hal raps back. "On himself, Jack. There is a difference."

"There certainly is," snaps Nan.

Marina feels that she should say something to support her side, but no one in the room is looking at her except Jack, now and then, with a polite smile. She has the feeling that he would probably prefer to hit all of them on the head with a hammer, and who could blame him? Their crazy son has stolen his only child. She nervously runs her hand along the hard arm of the sofa, a sofa where Tamara probably did her homework, napped, fought with her parents. Jack moves a candle on the mantel out of the way of his elbow.

Ruth says evenly, "Well, the literature isn't quite that clear, Hal, though you're right that his violence has generally been self-directed." She uncrosses her legs and, like her husband, leans forward. "But, you see, with psychosis, judgment becomes so problematic — "

Nan stands up. "What the fuck is it that you people want from us? To find him and shoot him like a rabid dog? We *can't* find him.

We are *dying* from this, can't you see that? All right, if we pooled our resources, got people working on it — we talked about this before we came over here. We're willing to pay. Is that what this is about?"

Ruth looks at Jack, who runs a hand over his big face. "If you're not willing to disclose his history, including his medical records," says Ruth in a high but firm tone, "then we're going to proceed with this as a criminal investigation."

"What?" says Nan, still standing. Marina's stomach tightens, as does her grip on the hard arm of the sofa, trying to get some ballast.

"We're going to ask the police to treat it as a criminal situation."

It's quiet in the woods. Tamara is having a dream of flying cars that's so funny she wakes herself up laughing. Her hip is resting in an uncomfortable way. There must be a rock under the tent right there. She readjusts herself around Christopher. He is wide awake, staring down at her. "Go to sleep," she says firmly. The sleeping bag tightens over her knee; the rock disappears. The tiny flashlight rests within reach, but there are no bears tonight. It begins to rain; the light, scattered drops make a pretty sound.

Nan puts extra mulch around the hydrangea. It's early morning yet. The cat from the yard next door watches her from the gap in the fence. Nan misses Hash, who is buried just a few feet away. He was a stupid old cat, and she loved him. The hydrangea is as languorous as ever, already needing to be restaked. It will have to wait. She pulls weeds here and there, checks on the daisies. Maybe she should get some special food for that plum tree. A spider scurries over the head of Sor Juana, pausing on one of Sor Juana's nostrils. Even if she had known back then where she would be today, she wouldn't have done it differently. She had to follow her fate. She felt that as strongly at sixteen as she does at this exact moment, with her wretched hip and her stretch-marked, bruised, solid archive of a body on which is written, as if she were a piece of scrimshaw, the entire history of her life: she travels light. Nan takes off her gardening gloves.

The car is all packed. Marina, when Nan quietly arose less than an hour ago, was sleeping deeply, rolled over on her side toward Nan, her small, rough hand on Nan's pillow. Nan would have kissed her but didn't want to wake her. She pulled the corner of the bedclothes over Marina's bare foot.

The rain is light but constant. It's as if the trees have turned into showerheads, releasing years of water in a steady stream. The one thing Tamara forgot was rain ponchos, so they've unstaked the tent and folded it into a canopy. Christopher is walking in the front, holding up his end; Tamara is in the back, holding up hers. Even so, her eyelashes are wet; her knuckles are wet; her feet are wet though these hiking boots are the good, expensive ones her father got her for Tahoe. In Tahoe, her feet never felt like this. She is wearing her red knit hat; the hat is wet. Christopher insisted on carrying the backpack, and Tamara let him because he's in the front; it's better for the backpack to stay under the makeshift umbrella. Maybe the bread won't get completely disgusting. She wishes it would stop raining; it has to stop sooner or later, doesn't it? Unless Noah's about to come by with his Ark.

"Chris, I think we should try to get back to that town. Just until it lets up."

He shakes his wet head.

Tamara pulls on her end of the canopy, like reins. Christopher stops. "Chris, they're not, like, all out in a posse *looking* for us. We're just on some computer thing. We're going to get pneumonia out here."

He shakes his head again, standing still, but not turning around. He's been cranky all day. He didn't eat breakfast this morning, saying the PowerBar tasted bad, though it tasted fine to Tamara. It tasted great, in fact. But then he kept after her about it, he was being so impossible, until she had to throw it away to make him happy. Now she's really hungry.

"Okay, so what's your plan, then? We walk until we die?"

He says something, but she can't hear him. "What?" She inches forward, the tent falling damply behind her. She leans around to see his face, which is wet and pale. His arms remain immobile, a strong V, but his face seems jagged, jumbly.

"It's the worms," he whispers.

Tamara looks down at the ground, but she doesn't see any worms. "Where?"

He points to his ear, raising an eyebrow. He seems very scared.

"Oh. Okay, Chris," Tamara says gently, "let me see." She stands up on the toes of her wet hiking boots and peers into his ear, silently counting, one one thousand, two one thousand, three one thousand. His earlobe is pink and cold. She tugs on it, puts her eye right up to his ear, then blows into it forcefully. "There. They're gone now."

He looks relieved but unsure. "I don't know."

"No," she says decisively. "They're gone. Let's go." She tries to take the backpack off his shoulders, but he resists.

"I'm carrying it," he says in a kind of desperate way.

"Okay. Okay, that's cool." Tamara scoonches back, holding up her end of the canopy again. Her arms are killing her. She thinks it's possible that they've walked in a circle, which would put the road over to their left. Maybe. And they can't go to town, anyway, not today. Not until he's less upset. Marching along in her cold, damp boots, she considers going in by herself. Even if she could find the road, though, what would she say to him? Wait here? And then how would she find him again? She can't leave him in the woods by himself, at the mercy of the worms, which will most likely come back, she knows that. She knew he would get a little crooked as the medication wore off, though she didn't think it would happen so quickly. Tucked in the very bottom of her pocket, next to the money, are two Valium tablets, stolen from the back of her parents' dresser drawer. She could slip one into anything, even a soy dog, with her quick fingers. She could try him on a half if the worms come back. "Are you hungry?" He must be hungry by now.

"No."

Keeping an eye on Christopher's unwavering back, Tamara moves her left arm so that it's holding up the entire back end of the tent. With her right, she reaches inside her jacket and pushes the little cell phone button with her wet fingers. The warmth of her own body inside the jacket is a comfort, as is the reassuring shape of her phone. She holds the jacket against her to muffle the sound of the thing beeping on. She waits a few minutes. Then she pulls the phone out and, incredibly, in this one spot, they seem to be in range. She wonders who she should call. The rain patters onto the phone's small, lighted display panel; it looks so happy to be of service. But before Tamara can figure out what to do with her good fortune, the wet phone slips from her grasp. "Wait — Chris." Still walking, she tries to grab the tent edge with her right hand, but it's all too obvious and already the phone is too far behind them to be picked up without him noticing. Her heart thrums.

He turns around inquisitively.

"Sorry. I just have to grab this part." She fiddles with her end of the tent, making careful note of the broken branch on the tree just in front of them, the stump next to that, the angle of the sky in this part of the forest. Trying to be casual, she looks over her shoulder, but she can't see where the phone dropped. Her heart thrums more quickly. With an effort, a deep breath, she quiets herself.

"Tam. What are you doing?" Facing forward, he pulls on the tent impatiently.

"Nothing." She quickly reaches down, pulls off her red knit hat, and drops it behind her. It sits there on the ground, perky and alone in the rain, as they walk on. "Okay, come on." Walking purposefully, she thinks of how she'll say it later when the sun's out, very even, no big deal, *Oh, damn, I lost my hat.*

Marina is so furious that she almost tears the note into pieces, but then she doesn't because she knows Hal will say, "What did the note say exactly?"

And that's what he does say, ten minutes after she calls him, as he is standing in the foyer with his coat on. She hands him the note. He reads it.

"Jesus Christ." He sits down on the bottom step, holding the piece of lined yellow paper. "I am so tired."

"Tired? I'm in a rage. Do you realize the incredible mess she's left us with? Tamara's parents are already going through the roof — we're one step away from a spot on the nightly news. While she goes off on some wild goose chase thinking she'll save the day all by herself." Marina is close to tears in her frustration. "She's so *impossible* and *bullheaded.*"

"You should know." Hal looks haggard. "You married her."

"So did you."

He smiles at that, more with his eyes than his mouth, which is trembling. "At least she has the illusion of thinking she knows what to do. I'm running out of options."

"There are no fucking options. That's what she can't deal with. She's impossible, and she's made everything a thousand times worse." Marina yanks her old floppy sweater more tightly around her. She realizes she is standing there in a T-shirt, the sweater, and her underwear. She doesn't care, except about her feet, which are cold.

Hal reads the note again. "You know." He shifts on the step. "We don't have to tell them."

"Who?"

"Tamara's parents."

"What?"

He seems to be adding a sum in his head. "I — we — can meet with them and Suarez. God knows they're probably not exactly eager to talk to her after last night. She says she'll be calling in. It's not like she's running away from *us.*"

"Yes, she is." Marina gives in to her tears, sinking down onto the stairs next to Hal. "She's left me, Hal."

They sit sadly on the same step for a while. Marina is crying, and Hal puts his arm around her. Marina thinks she has never felt so lonely as she does at this minute, lost in Nan's house with a man who's never really liked her that much but who is now hold-

ing her while she weeps. She is exhausted, and angry, and home-
sick in a vague way.

Hal hands her a tissue.

"Thanks."

He gets up to call Dan. She hears him explaining the situation.
Her feet are still cold. She puts her hands over her toes to warm
them. Her feet are always cold in San Francisco, it's the city of cold
feet. The worst part is that she knows how Nan feels, she can
imagine perfectly Nan's drive to go, her relief at finally being out
on the road, searching. It takes a runner to know one, after all.
Maybe Nan's flight is cosmic justice.

Hal returns. "He's going to try to get out of his meeting and
come over."

"Do you love him?"

Leaning his head against the balustrade, Hal says, "Yes."

"Does he love you?"

"I don't know."

Marina rests her chin on her knuckles. In a different mood,
years ago, she would have found the discovery that she and Hal
were more alike than not ironic. On this empty morning, however, it seems dangerous to her, as if the two children have been
left at home with a book of matches and a stove neither of them
knows how to light. Waiting on the stairs together for people who
may or may not ever come home.

Nan hangs up the phone, then stands outside the phone booth,
smoking. The sky is kind today, an arc of lighted blue. The smoke,
as it curls through her and then into the air, draws out with it the
noise back home: she explained, she promised, she agreed to
whatever they said. Now she wills herself to forget it in order to
clear the way for him. She's listening hard for him, imagines herself a tuning fork, pitched to his pitch. In her mind, he's like a boy
with a glass jar over his head, as exotic and terrifying fish stream
past his eyes. She was wrong, she was so wrong before, to try to
make him stay in her country. The only thing that stands a chance
of working is going to his. Wherever that is. She leans against the

dirty panes of the phone booth, drawing up tar and nicotine. They taste good, like the road itself.

She stubs out her cigarette. The old Honda, rust-spotted and speckled with dings, loyally starts right up. The road unfolds. On a hill, plastic pinwheel sunflowers spin. Her heart told her they were still north, so she went north. The 101 seemed right — bigger than Highway 1, but not as big and blaring as the 5. She doesn't feel that he's gone to the coast, not yet. Instead, she feels that he's burrowing somewhere, little animal, camouflaging himself as earth. Like her. She's tried once or twice to feel with her heart for Tamara, but nothing really arises. If Ruth hadn't been such an idiot, she would have liked to ask her, quietly, what she senses about where Tamara is. Mother to mother, Hunter to Hunter. Maybe she still can, later. In a better world, she and Ruth could have hunted together. Not that the side of the road seems to offer much by way of hunting grounds: gas stations, a Best Buy, the Tamalpais Motel, an In-N-Out Burger. Nan turns on the radio: such reasonable voices.

The car has a particular sound it makes, like a pen hitting a tin can. It hits the can faster or slower depending on how fast or slow she goes, *pingpingping*. The pen is hitting the can in a meditative rhythm at the moment, a patient, almost plodding rhythm. *Ping. Beat. Ping.* She's pretty sure it's the fan belt, though she's never had it checked out. Secretly, she has a superstitious feeling about it, that if she had the fan belt fixed the entire car would finally fall completely apart. She doesn't want to risk that, especially not now. She rolls down the window. Traffic stalls. It's so much warmer here than in the city, which always seems to perch inside a cloud. She could probably sleep outside. They could, too, if they're close by, rolled up together in a field.

She doesn't sense them close by, though; when she extends her mind-spirit into the air, she doesn't find them. She doesn't find him. The car pings in two-step time. Her runaway logic has all come back to her, like Odysseus's dog, as faithful as ever despite his master's long absence. Some of the basics, like heat and cold and hunger, pale beside the necessity to get the hell away; that's what she can imagine is driving Christopher. The other thing about runaway logic is that you tell yourself that food and shelter will appear somehow, they have to, and meanwhile you just go as far as you can. His legs are younger and stronger than hers, the legs of a young man. For this reason, she is glad of Tamara. Girls slow a person down.

Pingping. Pingping. Sports scores, temperature, the stock market, traffic over the Golden Gate and Bay bridges, a shooting in a restaurant, an actress getting married for the third time: they're all clattering numbers, dropping away behind her. Numbers are Hal's job. To her left, a vineyard slides past. To her right, a road climbs a golden hill. An expensive house tops that road, a house of glass and sharp angles, an unpeopled deck with a view of her, passing by in her pinging car. She isn't lonely, not yet. Usually, the loneliness comes later, like a blister. She flexes her toes inside her shoe; her feet are soft now, with bunions and those annoying little recurring pains in her heels. How far could she walk, she wonders, in a day? She passes a thick guy who's wearing too many clothes for the weather, his thumb out. She doesn't stop, and barely notices that she didn't stop until a few miles later. In the past, she might have stopped — she could have been him, waiting in the sun for a ride. It's since she became a mother that she doesn't.

Love and death and taxes, says the radio. Her petty obligations — the job, the mortgage — are already burned away, forgotten. She is an arrow, shot straight into the air. The vineyard stakes look like cattails, and for a moment Nan despairs: he's certainly not going to be hiding at a useless, expensive winery. No. He's gone farther. She passes the turn-off she used to take to Pacific. Settling into patient alertness, she punches in the cigarette lighter. *Pingpingpingping* goes the car.

Tamara cannot believe how incredibly lost they are. She trudges along behind Christopher, thinking how much she must look like the back end of the donkey, except that donkeys have sturdy, all-weather feet, and she has sad, soggy, heavy ones. Christopher, with a worried expression, turns around again.

"Are you all right, Tam?"

"Chris, neither of us is all right." She points at the sky. "It's *raining*. It sucks. We have to get out of the rain."

His hair is plastered onto his face. "Are you okay? Are you cold?"

"Aren't you cold?"

He shrugs. "Not really. Maybe I should carry you."

The bread is probably soaked. Every time he turns around, which is often, he doesn't take care to keep the backpack out of the rain. Not that anything is out of the rain in any substantial way. Things are only more or less drenched to the core. Tamara, exhausted, lets the canopy rest on her wet head. "You can't carry me. I'm way too big." She wishes, though, that he could carry her, just for an hour or so. If she had only remembered the rain ponchos. If she hadn't dropped the phone. Such simple things, like that rhyme: *For the want of a nail . . .*

"Yeah, I could. Come on." He holds out one arm, easily holding up his tent edge with the other. It's wild, how much energy he has. He could go like this all day, she can tell, and maybe all night, too, plunging doggedly into the dark.

"Save it for later. Chris, we have to figure out where we're going."

His face simultaneously closes up and falls inward somewhere far below. It's the strangest thing. It's almost beautiful in a way, though it also signals to Tamara that, despite what he may say, she has to get him out of the rain. Even if he doesn't feel like resting, he needs to rest. He shouldn't become agitated.

He kicks at the ground. "We just have to . . . *go on* for a while longer, just a little longer, Tam. Let me carry you."

"But, Chris, honey, where do you think we're going to get to? We're in the woods. Maybe the town isn't too far from here, but we'd have to be by the road . . ."

"Town? We can't go to any town, Tam. They're looking for us."

"Right, but — I mean, Chris, we can't live out here forever, right?" She smiles. "This isn't Fiji. It's cold. And wet."

His face does another one of its shimmies. "Trust me. We'll be okay."

Tamara can feel the rain sliding past her collar and down her neck. It seems to keep him calm to march them around; it won't be better if he starts flipping out and being terrified of worms. She also suspects that they've gone in several circles, which is bad, except that it could mean that they will come across her cell phone, glowing in its friendly fashion on the ground. It must be pretty waterproof. Or maybe he will, against appearances, get tired. No one can do this indefinitely. "Okay. But I'm coming up there."

He holds out his arm, as if inviting her inside someplace warm and dry, and they plow on together, the wet tent dragging behind them in a nylon train. It does feel better to be with him, even if they're continuing to go nowhere. Every few steps he shakes his head sharply, blinks hard, and shudders.

"Worms?" asks Tamara sympathetically.

"No." He doesn't elaborate. His arm is secure and warm on her shoulder; it buoys her, even as he shakes and blinks. Tamara silently asks herself if it's time to worry and concludes that it isn't. How would it help to worry? It's just her and Christopher, after all, out in bad weather. There are towns nearby. He's much more worried than she is. He's worried about things she can't see.

"Mmmm," he says quietly. "That's not right. That's not right. Shit."

"Chris?"

He attempts to focus on her, but he seems far away. The tent drags along the ground. How will they ever be able to use it again? Every part of it must be wet and filthy by now. "No," he says, though not exactly to her. The rain rains harder.

She calculates. It's Wednesday. Five days since they left, since she exited the house quietly out the front door, went to the bus station, and got on a bus. It was an almost empty, nighttime bus. No one asked her anything; they all seemed to have enough problems of their own. When she got off the bus and began walking toward where Christopher was, she felt very deeply that she was doing the right thing. He was dying, the other way. How could anyone who cared about him prefer him like that? She probably should have had a better plan, but it seemed like the first step had to be getting clear of that place, that prison, and into the open air, where he could get his eyes all the way open. It was her mom, inadvertently, who had given Tamara the idea to come up here. Her mom had a client, a teenage girl who had once run away up north, whose parents had found her and brought her home. *Finally,* her mom had said. *It's runaway heaven up there.*

But looking at Christopher's pale, jumbly, beautiful face in the rain, Tamara has to admit to herself that, really, it was just because she loved him so much. She stole him. It was almost true, what she said to her mother about kidnapping him: she kind of did kidnap him a little bit. And here they are, lost and wet, going in circles, as his face shimmies and breaks, re-forms and breaks again. It's starting to get dark. And still she loves him, she loves him helplessly, she always has. She would rather be with him than apart from him. They just have to get through this part. She tucks herself in tighter under his warm, solid arm. He kisses the side of her head.

"There's a house," he says casually.

Tamara stares. There *is* a house, which has appeared so suddenly that Tamara half expects to see the striped legs of the Wicked Witch of the East protruding from the foundation. It's a cabin with the front part set high off the sloping ground, on wooden stilts; there's one little boarded-up window. Over the door is a diamond-shaped cutout, but it's dark. A set of steps, covered in moss, is lying on its side on the ground. There's a padlock on the door. As they get closer, Tamara can see that the floor of the cabin is bowed. Some underlying support must have rotted away.

Tamara and Christopher stand in front of the cabin holding their sopping wad of tent over their heads. "Wow," says Tamara.

Christopher leaves Tamara to hold up the tent by herself, walks forward, reaches up, and gives the padlock a hard, twisting pull. It comes right out of the wood. He tosses it behind a post. "Okay, come on." He pushes open the door, holds onto the doorframe, and hops up into the cabin, extending his hand.

Tamara lets the waterlogged tent slide to the ground as she grabs his forearm. He lifts her easily into the dark entryway and drops the backpack just inside the shelter.

"Hello?" calls Tamara. She hopes that no dead bodies or aliens are lying around, but in the dim light from the open door she can already tell that the cabin holds nothing of the kind. It's one room with a mattress in the corner. The mattress has a tie-dyed spread on it. In another corner is a wood-burning stove; above the stove, a fat black pipe has come away from the wall, leaving a hole to the outside. Next to the stove is a small stack of wood and an axe. Next to the wood is the kind of lamp that you turn on by pulling the top away from the bottom to reveal a glowing middle. The floor does sag, as the exterior suggested. A single wooden chair lies on its side in the center of the floor, as if it has tumbled down the incline. "Someone's been here," says Tamara. "Maybe they're coming back."

Christopher rights the chair. "I don't think so. It's cool."

Tamara walks over to the stove and slides the pipe back into position. "Hey, look." She picks up a glittery thing from the floor: a silver bracelet with a little silver heart dangling from it. In the center of the heart is an enameled peace sign. She puts the bracelet on.

"Cool." Christopher smiles in a regular, worm-free way. The face beneath his face has cleared, like weather changing. He must be feeling better. "Are there matches?"

"A lighter. At the bottom."

"Should we wait and have the fire later?"

"No, I'm cold. Let's do it now, just not the whole thing."

In no time at all, Tamara has deftly built the little pyramid of wood — she's the fire-builder in her family — and Christopher has lit the flame to it, and up it blazes. They close the stove's iron door. A fetid, oversweet smell arises.

"Mouse," says Tamara.

Christopher shrugs. "We're here now." It's funny, how only the invisible things seem to bother him.

Tamara opens the lamp, which glows feebly. She closes it again, saving it. "Come on, we have to get dry." They strip, laying out their wet clothes, like the outfits of absent paper dolls, on the floor. They unpack the backpack, too, setting its contents around the room and leaning the pack close to the stove to dry out. The bread, miraculously, is only a little wet around the edges. Christopher pushes the door mostly closed against the cool outside air, leaving a bit open for light. Up above the door, there's what looks like an Ace bandage nailed over the diamond-shaped cutout. Tamara wonders why someone would do that. Was he cold? She strokes the little silver heart, then the flat enamel place at the heart's center.

It suddenly seems funny to Tamara that she and Christopher are both wearing nothing but jewelry. The leather cord with its blue bead around Christopher's neck is the only thing he has on. In the half darkness, he is large and pale with long, strong legs, a boy's round face, but a man's feet, a man's cock and balls. He stands before the stove with his hands out, his little, rounded butt a man's butt while the roll of his belly and the fat on his chest and hips seem much younger. He's like a time-lapse photograph of one person at different ages, including ages when he was, and will be, well.

Tamara wraps herself in the tie-dyed spread, which doesn't smell completely awful. She still feels a little awkward being naked with Christopher. She's not so sure about her breasts sometimes. She's glad that she and he are almost the same height. She used to say that he was like the brother she never had, but she doesn't say that anymore. With the spread around her shoulders, she moves to stand next to him at the stove, which isn't yet throwing that much heat. His body is generating more warmth on its own. Her ass is awfully cold — the draft seems to go directly there. Her head, with its wet hair, is cold, too. She touches her cool, blanketed hip to his warmer, bare one, feeling shy. She's pleased to notice that he gets a little hard and she gets a little wet, their bodies murmuring to each other in their own special language through the thin, tie-dyed wall.

"How far do you think we've walked?"

He turns his hands over and back again. "Far. To the Andromeda Galaxy, maybe." He smiles. "Psych."

"I think we've gone pretty far."

"Yeah." He shakes his blond head, drying his hair. The stove warms up a fraction. He's a strange boy, and she loves him. She couldn't love a normal one — she tried, but it was dumb. He folds her in his arms from behind, kissing her ear, her wet hair, and his cock is hard against the small of her back. He reaches under the tie-dyed spread to touch her nipples with his thumbs. The draft raises goose bumps on the curve of her waist. It occurs to Tamara that it might not be okay to do it after the worms and everything — should they stop? — but her body has already long since sped past stop, and then he's with her, all of him, his mouth on her mouth, her knees around his hips, the spread in a tangle beneath them, the dust of the floor making her sneeze even as she opens up, opens wider. She can say anything as loud as she wants to and she does.

"Tam." She is half reclining, and he is still inside her, still hard, carrying her close against him with one arm. They're both panting, skin to skin, sweating on the mattress. The stove is hot now. The room is theirs. "Tam."

They've gone very far, way past another galaxy, she knows that, but she doesn't care. Even the fat on his chest is sex to her. She touches the blue bead at his throat, licks the warm hollow beneath it. He moves more deeply into her; she holds onto him with her entire being. The little silver heart rests against his shoulder blade. This is it, this is the place, she was always supposed to be exactly here. He's like a bird from some other dimension that has flown inside her, its wings beating. She kisses his beautiful mouth. He holds her so tightly, more tightly than she's ever been held.

And even though he's spent, he doesn't leave her, he stays inside her, he pulls the thin, tie-dyed spread around them both and buries his face in her dusty, damp hair, carrying her against his chest with no sign of tiring at all, as if he could fly right away with her, holding her like that, to the next universe.

Nan watches a late-night talk show with the bedside lamp turned off. The celebrities provide the only light in the room. She can remember worse places than this; it's just a motel, and not even that cheap. Christopher's drawing is unrolled on the AstroTurf-like carpet. Someone's kids are shrieking and running up and down the corridor outside. Those kids, she thinks, should be in bed. She almost opens the door and tells them so herself. The sheets are terribly clean, the kind of scraped, much-bleached clean that never warms up. They smell of Lysol. There is a cigarette-burn hole in the baby blue polyester blanket. Nan is still in her clothes, including her jacket, zipped to the neck. She didn't pack a sweater. She didn't, she discovered earlier, pack a toothbrush either. Her mouth is full of the day. Not for the first time in her life, she wishes she were taller, as if that would help something or other. Not her teeth. Not the lack of a sweater. She just imagines, though she knows it doesn't make sense, that if she were taller she'd have a better chance of seeing him. She felt that way when she was pregnant, too, that maybe if she were taller it would be easier to tote around the sloshing, kicking weight of him. Having him, though, was the most natural thing she'd ever done in her life, an act for which her low-slung self seemed to be incredibly well suited. She delivered him in six hours. The doctor was astonished at how fast she did it. Nan wasn't. She'd always known it would be exactly like that, a good, strong, solid push from her center. And then she couldn't even feel the lower half of her body except for the shaking of her legs and the gush of the afterbirth, which she could hear splatter onto the floor. "Whoopsie," said the nurse. Hal wiped the sweat off her face with a cool washcloth. In her exhaustion, Nan began to cry, feeling that someone had cruelly taken her baby away from her, her baby was gone, she was empty now. But then they laid him on her chest.

The table is covered with papers and cups of take-out coffee. Hal brought enough for everyone to have two, which was also a bit of a strategy to keep them all in the room for as long as possible. He didn't want Suarez to duck out for coffee and get caught up in some other, more interesting crime. Hal made sure to get lots of packets of sugar as well.

Dan offered to come along to help; he and Officer Suarez, apparently, have taken an immediate liking to each other. They both dump a lot of sugar into their respective cups of coffee and drink it while it's still scalding. Hal made a special trip to some cheap place to get the scorching coffee, on the hunch that Suarez would like it and he does. He hadn't, however, anticipated that Dan would like it quite so much. Dan is already on his second cup, buoyant.

Marina stirs her coffee tentatively. "I brought more pictures. I found a few of him and Tamara together." She empties the contents of a manila envelope onto the table.

"That's good," says Suarez.

Dan nods in agreement, glancing at the spill of pictures. He casually picks one up. "They look so happy together, don't they?"

Suarez takes the photo from Dan. "Yeah, Jesus. They really do."

"What's that around Chris's neck?" asks Dan.

Suarez leans forward. "A bead. The kids wear them."

"He always wears it, doesn't he?" asks Dan. "Did Tamara give it to him?"

"I don't know." Hal feels somewhat abashed. "Marina —"

She shakes her head. "Maybe."

"Ah," says Suarez knowingly. "I bet she did." He flicks the photo. "Where's Nan?"

Dan offers smoothly, almost offhandedly, "She's on phone duty this morning. She's kicking herself for not having a cell."

Marina catches Hal's eye in a way that clearly means, *He's good.* Hal has to agree, feeling proud that Dan has taken this on for him, for them. They need help. He loves Nan, but she has some serious blind spots. He sometimes wonders if she has any conception of community at all.

"What happens now?" asks Hal. "What can we do?"

Suarez is still looking at the picture. "Tall kids. They could pass for twenty-one, easy."

"No," says Dan firmly. "They're geeks. It's not like that. They're hiding up there somewhere."

"What?" Marina glances from Dan to Suarez, though Hal, sickeningly, understands.

"Kids on the run," explains Dan gently, "sometimes do what they need to do. And if that was the case, we'd want to search in more urban areas. But I feel, though I'm new here" — he smiles, leans back — "from what Hal has said about Chris and his girlfriend, that's not what's happening."

Not yet, Hal thinks.

Dan reaches over and grasps Hal's hand. "Look at that picture. Look at them. They don't think like that."

Suarez nods, but very soberly. "Lot of land up there. And those local cops." He rolls his eyes. He is obviously pained, more pained than Hal has seen him in all the times they've dealt with him. And it's because of that simple gesture, Dan inviting him to look, really look, at the picture of the young lovers, the boy with the bead and the girl who gave it to him. *Mira.*

Dan, meanwhile, has a relaxed, satisfied air. He buttons a cuff. "What's your read," he asks Suarez, "of this criminal charge thing? Can Tamara's family make that stick?"

Suarez makes a face. "Yeah, they called me about that. Several times." He glances at the clock overhead. "You know, the girl obviously went of her own free will. But if something happens to her — "

"We understand," says Hal. "There's a lot at stake here for all of us."

"You think they're serious, though," comments Dan to the officer.

"They're serious about calling a lot," replies Suarez. "But what else do they have to do? Go up there and beat the bushes?"

Marina begins shredding the top of her Styrofoam cup.

"We'll talk to them," says Dan briskly. "Hal, is there any more coffee in that bag?"

Shiloh sits back in the frayed wing chair. "Yeah," she says dubiously.

"I mean," Marina continues, trying to get this right, "you do understand, don't you?" She fidgets on the sofa, hoping one of Shiloh's roommates — she always forgets if there are four or five, and are two of them twins? — doesn't walk in.

Shiloh carefully maintains a bored expression. "You want to hang out with me again. You want to have sex —"

"Maybe. No, no, that's not a good idea."

"Whatever. You want to roll with me." Shiloh has shifted her look a bit since Marina saw her last. Her hair is still orange, spiking all over her head, but today she's wearing a gauzy white shirt with long bell sleeves and an ankh around her neck. She seems to be slightly thinner, the planes of her face more defined. The excessive seriousness of her girlhood is just about to give way, Marina can see, to the permanent seriousness of her adulthood. She will be a serious woman.

"Yes. If it's okay with you." Marina, on a lumpy sofa that is indistinguishable from the lumpy coffeehouse sofa of their last meeting, can barely stand it, but it's still better than being at home. She tries not to look as desperate as she feels.

Shiloh sighs. "I don't know."

"Friends." Marina holds up a hand, like a crossing guard on the boulevard of love. "I'd like to be friends."

"Yeah, yeah. Sure." Shiloh raises an eyebrow. "Old friends, though, wouldn't you say? By now?"

"I guess so," says Marina, attempting a little laugh. "If you're old enough to have an old friend."

The younger woman doesn't laugh. She tucks her hands inside the long bell sleeves.

Nan drives. She drives and drives, looping off exits to swing through one or another small town, each time getting back on the 101 just a bit farther up than where she left it. Once or twice she thinks she catches something like his scent, a trace of his aura, but then it's gone again. National Public Radio follows her, like a crow. She puts up her photocopied flyers, shows them to the boys skateboarding the afternoon away outside a Walgreens. The boys shake their heads. She leaves a trail of flyers in her loops through the little towns, taped with duct tape to the sides of 7-Elevens, gas stations, streetlight poles, Wal-Marts. When the fucking vineyards give way to trees, the hair on the back of her neck stands up. He's this way. Maybe. If he didn't go south. Or east. She doesn't believe any bullshit screen-saver wisdom like THE JOURNEY IS THE GOAL. The journey is not the goal. Finding her son, Christopher Ashby-Cooper, sixteen, whom she loves to the depths of her being, is the goal.

On the outskirts of somewhere, somewhere that had a take-out sandwich place, Nan pulls off the road at a turnout. There are trees, a few picnic tables, a little stone barbecue with a handful of blackened sticks in it. Nan sits down at a table and unwraps her sandwich. It's a cheese sandwich, which seems to be all she can remember to order these days. Everything else seems too complicated. The light slants down on her. Birds play nearby, pattering through the leaves. Cars swish past from time to time. It's cool even in the sun; she tries not to think too much about whether Christopher has a sweater, or sturdy shoes, or warm socks. At least it's getting warmer. Has it really been nearly a year since all this began? It feels both infinitely longer and much shorter. Summer, fall, winter: she would have imagined he'd be almost better by now, ready to be reborn when spring comes.

She chews her cheese sandwich, drinks her soda. She has only three flyers left in her bag. At the next town, she'll have to make another pile. She takes one out to look at while she eats her lunch.

There's Christopher before he got sick, in Golden Gate Park, standing in front of the buffalo paddock. She chose it because it shows the full length of him, smiling, in jeans and a T-shirt, with his hair not so different, coincidentally, from how it was in El Cerrito — cropped short all over. The buffalo in the background are muzzy, dark shapes, like storm clouds. HAVE YOU SEEN MY SON? Under that are the city precinct's phone number and her own.

HAVE YOU SEEN MY SON? He doesn't look like that anymore, but not in a way that a stranger would be able to see. Only someone who loved him would be able to tell that he's different now, different in his eyes, different in the space around him. To a stranger, the likeness would be close enough, even with the weight he's carrying these days. On an impulse, Nan picks up her bag, the flyer, and walks into the woods. He's not here, nowhere near here: she's dead sure about that. But she feels a closeness to him in this place. The tall trees draw her toward them. There isn't a path exactly, but there is a sort of yielding part of the ground where it's easy to put her feet. She follows it to where the light seems to be getting stronger.

A little stream, not much more than a creek, wanders along in the sunlight. Nan sits down on the gentle bank, puts a hand into the stream, and lets the water run through her fingers. It's as cold as a cold penny. It soothes her hand, which still aches from when she punched the door at the police station. She wiggles her fingers, like fish. Goldfish, they'd be, or guppies: nothing special. There's a small cut on one knuckle which she doesn't remember getting. The cold water washes it clean. Nan looks up toward the sky, holding her face to the sun. She closes her eyes and sees red, indeterminate shapes. Christopher, her buffalo child, shaggy and large and precious. She is going to have to herd him into some gate, snapping at his heels. The sun warms her face, the delicate skin of her eyelids. She wants a cigarette. There are hours of driving ahead of her. For a moment, she is, quite unexpectedly, happy.

Nan opens her eyes. She studies the flyer carefully, as if she's never seen it before. She holds it between her palms. Then, with a single upward thought, she sets it into the stream. It slides just beneath the surface of the water and away, floating around a bend. Perhaps, she thinks, the otters will find it and bring him back.

Tamara perches in the doorway of the cabin, eating a PowerBar. Her bare feet dangle above the ground; her boots and socks are lying below in the sun, drying out. The gooey PowerBar is wild berry: her favorite flavor. Christopher, bare-chested, is standing on the thick branch of a tree. It took him hardly any time at all to get up there.

"Hey," he says. "Hey."

"What?"

"Look." He lets go of the trunk and stretches out his arms, bending slightly at the knees, balancing. The forest light paints him in curls and strands. His jeans are muddy from their travels, with a tear on one knee. His hair is a snarl, like hers. His eyes seem to have gotten even larger and bluer. He laughs, palms up, suspended on the branch. "Fiji."

Hal adds. The "Christopher" spreadsheet has grown complex, with subcategories and embedded files, question marks in certain columns. The "College" column, for instance. One of the few long-term things he managed to convince Nan that they should do: two of Hal's dollars for every one of hers, then a few clever investments. The basin is full and quiescent, like water in a well. The "Medical" column, by contrast, is roiled and leaky. The Pacific Institute, now El Cerrito — they have to pay the entire bill, no matter that Christopher ran away and was obviously not cured — a blank column after that for wherever they put him next. Another. A "Legal" column, just in case. A "Liability" subcolumn. Hal adds an electronic sticky to his computer screen, reminding himself to call the insurance woman again tomorrow.

The numbers are stark. Hal has seen much bigger numbers than these, of course, elephantine numbers that turned into buildings and businesses and acreage. The numbers horizon is vast, which is something he's always liked about it: everything can be counted in the end, even the sky if need be; everything, from the cosmic to the microscopic, can be tied together by numbers. Numbers are all related to one another. This quality usually gives him a peaceful feeling. These numbers are large only by contrast, in the way that an elephant standing next to your house would seem very big; an elephant on the veldt, or wherever elephants live, wouldn't be so remarkable. Still, the numbers add up to ungainly sums. They are aggressive, pushing at the fence of the "College" column.

He sees that he missed something; he adds the "Medical" column again. It comes out right, but he adds it one more time, to be sure. Same story. He sighs. If it keeps going like this. . . . He can't quite let himself consider that possibility. He makes an unnecessary double line on the left side of the "College" column. Secretly, he had intended an eastern school for Christopher, a place about which Nan could make remarks on the nature of the privileged class, et cetera, et cetera, while utterly loving it. The kind of place neither he nor Nan had even attempted, in the years when not going to college seemed like a perfectly valid choice, a political protest even. Why go to college when you could be a gigantic orchid in a little apartment in North Beach and just live? They were local heroes. Cosmic, indeed.

Hal shuts down the computer. From Mary's office next door, he can hear the whine of the drill, the soothing patter of Mary's one-sided conversation. He turns to look out the window at their nominal garden, its disorderly profusion of vines and leaves and abundant, anonymous, organic growth. Which one is the hibiscus? Something with a purple flower on it is plainly struggling to rise from the mass of greenery. Something else is spiky and tufted and numerous, in the manner of weeds. They've had so much rain, everything will be blooming soon. Hal feels for the purple flower; he was a flower once himself, too young and, in his awkward way, arrogant, to know who tended him.

Without even putting on his coat, Hal leaves his office and goes out the back door, grabbing a decorative copper platter from the foyer on the way. The air outside is cool and moist; the countable clouds are gray and thick. Hal crosses the deck and jumps down into the green; it's a steeper drop than he remembered, and his shoes immediately sink into muddy earth. He pulls the copper platter from the deck and lets it drop next to him, where it rests lopsidedly, like a burnished metal bloom, against a plant of Amazonian proportions with leaves as big as saucers and a mass of flowers at the top. That must be the hibiscus. Wading in to plunge his hands into the mass of weeds — are they weeds? is it all weeds? — Hal tugs forcefully, and a big chunk of earth comes up, roots dangling. He nearly falls over, then rights himself and tosses the earth onto the platter, where it makes a satisfying thud. He tugs up another chunk, tosses it. Earth falls into his shoes. He keeps tugging, pulling weed after weed, sweating. Maybe Nan is right that weeding is the only thing that helps when you're worried. Maybe this knowledge is what gives her that crazy courage. The copper platter fills, and he carries it over to the deck, where he empties it out. His hands are scratched; he's thirsty. He goes on.

When the spiky, tufted weeds are almost all gone, the deck piled with dirt and grass, Hal moves on to some aggressive vines that are wound around everything and have roots everywhere, like a centipede's legs. Though slender, these vines are surprisingly tough, and he has to grab them with both hands to rip them out. It begins to rain a bit, but he's warm from his exertion; he welcomes the rain, taking off his shirt.

Mary comes out onto the deck. "Hal, what in God's name are you doing?" She stands in her street clothes, by the knee-high heap of weeds, looking worried.

Huffing, pruning the hibiscus of Amazonian proportions with his hands, Hal says, "I'm okay. I'm almost done."

"It's getting dark."

A worm rests on the top of his shoe. "I'll stop soon."

She hesitates. "You're covered in mud. Hey, that's my plate."

"Go home. I'm almost done."

"Do you promise to stop in a few minutes?"

"I promise."

She leaves, and he continues, tugging and tossing, until it's quite dark, and he has to feel for the open spaces of earth. The rain stops. Hal, his hair wet, breathing hard in his pants and his ruined shoes, searches the ground for the copper plate, but he can't find it in the dark. Exhausted, he lies down for a moment in the damp earth. The sky is a black arch ornamented with little stars. Hal wishes on one or two. The deck above him to the right is piled with dirt and plants. The hibiscus of Amazonian proportions is raw-looking as high as Hal could reach. The ground is cold against his back. He can taste the salt of his own sweat in his mouth and feel the crisscrossing network of lightly bleeding scratches on his hands and chest and arms. *This is what it is to be alive,* he thinks, but also, feeling the weight of his body in the dirt, *This is what it is to be dead.* The rain picks up again, pattering onto his eyelids. Who will account, in the end, for the keeper of accounts? Into what — or whose — column will his bones fall? For all his good intentions, Hal sees, for all the bills promptly paid and taxes well calculated, he has been selfish. He has clung to his widow's weeds. He has done all the right things for Christopher, but now he sees that he also should have been willing to do the wrong things.

Grave. Garden.

Garden. Grave.

Mira.

Marina gazes out the glass doors at Nan's garden, which is soaking up the morning sun. It's still quite tidy out there, with no need of her yet. Plants are staked and clipped and pruned, or trailing down in the way that suits them. Sor Juana's blank melancholy eyes gaze benevolently at some gerbers. The plum tree has its usual gentle growth of leaves without a plum in sight. The cat from next door rolls over in a particularly sunny spot, batting at nothing. On the phone, which Marina has just hung up, Nan said that she thought she might be getting close, then coughed.

"How much are you smoking?" asked Marina.

"Not nearly enough." Then Nan repeated that she was close, pretty close, her next stop was the police station in Willits. "How is everything there? Is it okay?"

"It's okay," said Marina, in the new way of saying *okay*, which means that there has been no news, no breaks, but no bad news, either.

Shiloh appears on the porch as Marina talks to Nan. After they hang up, Marina lets Shiloh in, then delivers the Nan Report over the phone to Hal (who is in a surprisingly sanguine mood). Shiloh drums her fingers on the sliding glass door to the garden, radiating the energy of departure, like a little plane taxiing down the runway. "Come on," says Shiloh when Marina hangs up. "I want to show you something."

"I should stay here."

"No, you should come with me." Shiloh turns on Marina's cell phone and hands it to her. "You'll be back in a few hours."

At the sink, Marina opens the tap unnecessarily, dawdling, though she knows she might as well go. It does her no good at all to wander through the empty house, waiting for the phone to ring.

"Okay."

On the BART train, Marina watches Shiloh read the paper in bad light. Shiloh's face is delicate and vulnerable; her solid body trails behind her, today outfitted in corduroy pants and a shirt that says ELI on the pocket. She's a big girl in the way many younger women seem big to Marina these days — unapologetically lush, with bellies overflowing their jeans. She's also wearing a funny, aqua knit hat that comes to a peak at the top. As they head to the nether reaches of the East Bay, Shiloh shows Marina some things in the paper about Thailand, where she was an exchange student in high school. "You should go there sometime," she says. "It's unreal."

They get off the train on a dilapidated suburban street and walk a few blocks to a doorway next to a gated liquor store. Shiloh is happy, taking Marina's hand as they ascend the stairs, unlocking and pushing open the door of her studio with her hip. It's quite a

large space, divided at intervals by plywood and rigged-up curtains; there is the whirring sound of a potter's wheel. They pass
through one curtained area after another. Shiloh says hey to a
bald man doing something with plastic sheeting. Then they see a
young woman, in a gray knit hat like Shiloh's aqua one, talking on
the phone amid vast, pinkish beige canvases depicting young
women talking on the phone. Next is the fat potter, who is throwing a tall and spindly form. Then they pass two men who look like
Russian revolutionaries circa 1916 staring intently at a tiny proj-
ected image on the wall; the image appears to be that of a large
pig. An irregular clinking, ringing, almost musical sound can be
heard in their area.

One of the two Russian revolutionaries says, "Shiloh, you're up
next."

"Yeah, yeah." She doesn't stop.

As she parts the last curtain, which is a shower curtain, Shiloh
murmurs to Marina, "The picture they took doesn't even *look*
like me."

Marina silently asks herself how she feels about being here,
amid art-making's familiar trash and treasure, but the answer is
not unlike the clinking, irregular sound in the studio of the Russian revolutionaries. It's a ringing sensation neither of sadness nor
fear, but of marking time unpredictably. She has a sudden memory of what it was like to be nine, trying to draw the most beautiful tree in the world which she'd never actually seen.

"Check it out," says Shiloh proudly.

Marina's first response is surprise that one so young could produce something so antique. Has she found yet another old soul?
Her second, nearly as immediate, response is that no one must
ever see what Shiloh has so carefully frescoed onto the entire back
wall of her partitioned area: Marina. Spreading across the wall
from floor to ceiling and edge to edge is an elaborately detailed
tree with abundant green and orange and violet leaves like astonishing hair flowing upward from an equally elaborate trunk. The
trunk is made of Marina: she has been worked into the body of
the tree, like Daphne. Her breasts and legs and arms form the

curves and knobs of the trunk, surreally extended. Her shadowy face is tilted up before dissolving into the astonishing hair. Beneath the tree are seated, cross-legged, a miniature Nan and a miniature Shiloh, both gazing into the branches. Marina's bicycle leans against the tree.

It's a modern fresco — Nan is in sneakers, Shiloh has her destroyed hair — but the colors are pale and washy, like a Giotto, and the perspective has the awkward tilt of the divine. Shiloh has somehow managed to then distress the entire image so that it's semierased, almost transparent in places. It looks like the tree of life, left to wear away on a wall for centuries. Marina's face within the tree has gone a little fuzzy, as faces in distant memory do. It is her body, inextricable from the tree, that is most closely drawn. Marina can't imagine how much work it must have been first to plaster and paint this scene on the wall, then to rub it so carefully and cleverly, the partial erasure making it all seem that much more inevitable and ancient. Was it a labor of love? she wonders. Or a labor of hate? The best thing about it is that it's impossible to separate one from the other. If Marina were Shiloh's mentor, she'd say this work was a breakthrough.

But she isn't Shiloh's mentor, she's her sometime lover, and what panics her the most, of all the things that are panicking her, is the knowledge that when Shiloh leaves this place, as she surely will, she will leave Marina behind, fused with the tree forever, and with the two expectant women beneath it. Shiloh will move on to something else, maybe video. She will move to New York and get thin. She will move to Los Angeles and pierce her nose. Marina will still be rooted on a bad wall in Oakland, growing fainter by the day but no more free. The tree isn't one of Marina's trees — it's a curvy, spiky, noisy Shiloh tree. An electric guitar is caught, upside down, in one of the upper branches. Irrationally, that it isn't even one of her trees makes Marina more upset.

Shiloh says uncertainly, "I've been doing this twenty-four/seven since you left. It's not all done yet." She leans forward and rubs a spot with her elbow. "It's supposed to be an homage. To you. Marina?"

"How could you?" says Marina, shaking, furious. "You had no right." She picks up an open can of gesso and throws it as hard as she can at the wall. White hits the center and drips down.

In a room with no windows, Dan listens. There are six of them, and they're all nervous. One woman has a typed, detailed list; she's wearing a polo shirt with the company's logo discreetly etched on the left side. Her hands are stubby. She's the one, Dan can tell, who hates him the most, who hates everything about this encounter. The other people in the room eye her warily from time to time. If they could, they would be saying: *She's a bitch. She's a beast. She's a monster. This is all her fault.* Dan has no doubt that this assessment is true: every corporate maze has its Minotaur. He also knows, from reading the background, that she brings in the money. He knows that the company is on the brink of going under, that there are problems on the board, there are problems in the chips, there's a patent problem. They've already been sued once, by another barely solvent company just down the highway. The woman in the polo shirt has no expression; her hair is dry. Not looking particularly at her, Dan explains a pertinent legal fact; she rolls her eyes.

A ripple of unease and rage goes through the room, but what Dan feels is pity. To be a believer, especially now, is heartbreaking. He can imagine her cleaning out her desk, driving home in her joyless car to her blank condo in San Jose, alone, a big cardboard box in the back seat. Doesn't she read the papers? Doesn't she know what happens? Or perhaps she does but insists loudly that none of that will ever apply to her. She's a dinosaur knocking over telephone poles. He makes a tentative suggestion. She nods. He feels as if he has moved a boulder a quarter of an inch.

During the years that Dan was in therapy, his therapist once asked him what would be better, truly better, to do. This was during the unhappy lawyering years, the years of pro bono work and bad suits, bad shirts, bad ties, clients who trusted all the wrong people, including him. Every day felt like a ghastly charade in an ill-fitting costume. Anything, said the therapist — trapeze artist, poet, teacher. Dan loosened his bad tie for the fifteenth time that session (but he could still feel the polyester), and said, "I just can't be the one always bringing the hope to the scene. I want to be finding it there, even if it's only a sliver."

Today, the dry-haired woman in the polo shirt is his boulder with its one shining vein. For some reason, he thinks of that red rock on the beach the day Christopher went into the water. He thought the rock looked like a worn fragment of an ancient temple. He drove Hal back that day, understanding for the first time that Hal both did and didn't know what was going on. How endless it would be, as wide as the ocean. Hal's hair was stuck to his head with dried salt water. Impulsively, Dan reaches over and clasps the woman's stubby hand in his, which clearly both alarms her, and cracks her, just a little. "Here's why folks have trouble in this sort of situation," he begins.

Tamara wakes up on the mattress. Christopher isn't there. She checks her watch: 10:30. She shouldn't have slept so late. There's an open jar of peanut butter, with the spoon in it, on the floor; she takes out the spoon and puts the lid back on the jar. Eating a piece of bread, she pushes open the cabin door. "Chris?" she says into the sunlight.

An old man with a long white beard is sitting cross-legged on the ground in front of their cabin. He is wearing striped pants, sandals, several T-shirts layered one on top of the other, and a purple macramé bag on a string around his neck. His eyes are closed.

"Hi," says Tamara to the old man. "Who are you?"

The old man opens his eyes and smiles peacefully at her. "I don't have a name today."

Tamara, chewing her piece of bread, looks at him. His beard, she notices, is stained. "Why not?"

"I'm between names at the moment."

"Well, what was your name before?" She doesn't think he's dangerous, but she suspects, because he's so skinny, that he might be hungry. She pulls the cabin door nearly closed behind her; they don't have enough to feed strangers.

"Jupiter." He closes his eyes and flexes his toes.

"Okay." Tamara finishes her bread. "Have you seen a tall blond guy around?" She adds, "My boyfriend."

He doesn't look much like a Jupiter, Tamara thinks. Pluto, maybe. She sits down and leans against the cabin wall, trying not to worry. Christopher couldn't have gone too far; he wouldn't. What would he eat? It's getting warmer. The old man nods in the sun. Maybe this cabin was his; maybe they've been sleeping on his tie-dyed spread, looking at his Ace bandage nailed on the diamond over the door. It could even be his bracelet, though Tamara doesn't think so. She's pretty sure he's fallen asleep.

Through the trees comes the sound of teenagers, somewhere, laughing and shouting. They're probably far away, their voices carried in the strange way sound moves through these woods. Tamara can't make out any words, just the shrieks of kids on the loose. After a while, their voices fade.

UFO WELCOME AREA reads a billboard depicting a not hugely convincing spaceship blasting off. And around the next bend, under a mass of trees, CARVING FOR CHRIST is scrawled on a sign nailed to a tumbledown house by the side of a road. On the sign is a tilted yellow cross. Nan turns up the radio: a woman announces gently that it's time for the *Workers' News.* Where in God's name is she? She's been climbing for a while, past great stacks of wood in vast lumberyards, past campgrounds, past ELK CROSSING signs, past an old painted school bus without tires resting, and probably rusting, among weeds. She had never before made it this far north in her travels, though she had always thought she would. It had been her backup plan. Something about a bakery; she and Adam used to talk about it.

A little redheaded boy on a bicycle pedals furiously past tiny red shacks covered in peeling paint. Boomer's Bar and Grill. Camp Winna Rainbow. The road curves and curves. Set out in a yard are numerous carved wooden bears and dwarves and gnomes, absolutely no people walking among them, as if this is the carved things' party. A little ragged horse looks over a fence. Twilight zone, thinks Nan. He's here, somewhere. From the radio comes the sound of cafeteria workers on strike in Chicago. The road turns again and now for a while there are no shacks or gnomes or campgrounds, just trees and trees and trees, a sloping mountain in the distance covered with tall trees, trees pressed against the road's edge.

Nan, feeling momentarily breathless, stops at a turnout. Leaning against the car, she takes out a cigarette but doesn't light it. The sun is out; it's warm. The trees are ancient and everywhere, thousands of trees and Nan, with her pinging, old car. There isn't even anyone else at the turnout. She is painfully aware suddenly of how short she is, how slight. What is she going to do? She taps the end of the cigarette against her forehead. She misses the forest of Marina's body, of Marina herself, painter of trees: Nan had often felt that she was sensing her way through some dense, unknown, leafy place. A kind of hero of love, on a quest. But when she regards these endless trees, these all too real trees that may or may not be hiding her son, she remembers that the trees Marina painted over and over weren't any actual species of tree. They were metaphors. Which really don't matter at all right now. It was wrong, the way she saw things before, what she thought was so important, but still she feels lonely. The real quest is cheese sandwiches and photocopied flyers and cigarette burns in a motel blanket. Real trees just get in the way. Clear-cut them, she thinks. Clear-cut them all.

Tamara turns on the precious battery-operated lamp and sets it in the doorway, and light streams up. The old man unfolds himself and goes away as dusk falls, disappearing into the woods. For a long time there's no sign of Christopher, and then he comes back, scudding his feet in the undergrowth. Tamara, from the porch, watches him arrive. She wills herself not to say anything, yet. He has two scratches on his nose and some bulky thing concealed under his jacket.

"Here." He jumps up onto the porch and hands her a half-empty jar of peanut butter, going inside with a sigh, as if he's had a long day. "I saw a bear."

"You saw a bear? We still have peanut butter, Chris. Where did you get this?"

He shakes his head, turns around, and jumps back out the door, kicking over the lamp. Tamara retrieves it, then glances to the left, to the right. "Chris?"

The dark woods are silent.

Carrying the lamp, Tamara goes back inside the cabin and makes a peanut butter sandwich from the jar they already had, spreading the peanut butter with her finger. She thinks the other jar of peanut butter might have been a kind of joke, but she doesn't get it. Also, when she counts the money in her pants pocket, it's all still there. The Valium, however, has turned to crumbly mush from the rain. She thinks maybe she could scrape up a little of the smeary stuff from the twist of paper, if she had to.

"Chris?" She pokes her head out the doorway again, shining the light on the tree he climbed the other day. "Are you in Fiji?"

The branch is empty.

Tamara sits down on the mattress and eats the peanut butter sandwich. It's quiet. The point isn't the peanut butter, she reminds herself, trying to stay focused. The point is: Where did he go? Did he really see a bear? Is that how he got the scratches?

She is sorry, a little bit. She probably should have put the pill in something earlier. And, okay, she's scared. That Jupiter guy was creepy.

She misses her cat. On *The X-Files*, it would all turn out to be something about a spaceship or a virus or ghosts and is it *possible*? Do you *believe*? It was so goofy and scary. At the moment, the other, half-empty jar of peanut butter is what's scary, for real, much scarier than any bear, and she's failing. She tries to think of all the songs she likes, humming a few bars of each.

At an indeterminate sound, she dashes to the door. "Chris? Chris?" She can't quite bring herself to go outside in the dark, alone. There could be a bear. The lamp flickers. She closes it, but then it's so totally dark, and the total dark makes the cabin claustrophobic. Tamara allows herself their little flashlight, which she turns on and sets beside her in the doorway. That should last awhile. Peanut butter is good for you. Her father's booming voice, unbidden, rises up inside her. She hates it when he gets mad. He says, *What the hell are you going to do now?* Crying just a little, she whispers, "I don't know."

The sound comes again, a rustle and a shake, then almost a grunt, as of someone breathing out hard. "Chris?" From the doorway, Tamara peers into the clearing. She glances up. The trees are motionless, but she has a feeling he's in there, somewhere. Picking up the little flashlight, she bites her lip and hops down from the cabin. It's only Christopher, up a tree; she knows that. "Christopher, come on." She walks toward the trees, shining the little light this way and that into the branches. She thinks she glimpses a toe, but then it turns out to be just a knob on a trunk. There's another rustle, but he must have climbed high because she can't see him. She sighs. "All right," she says loudly. "All right, buttface. Don't come down. Whatever."

But she wants him to. Maybe he's somewhere around the back of the cabin. She shines the flashlight ahead of her — it's just the back of a little house, it's not haunted — and at the back of the cabin there isn't much to be scared of: a length of ladder that's broken at the top, a rotting pile of newspapers, some other junk. Propping the ladder against the side of the cabin, hoping the old wall doesn't give, she clambers up with her flashlight in her back pocket. She wedges her foot against a protruding board, pushes, and she's on her stomach against the slope of the roof. The incline isn't that steep; it's easy to get to the top and stand there and shine the light into the trees. They look empty, but she knows they're not.

Of course, she's right, because after a minute or two of standing there like the Statue of Liberty, she hears him say, "Tamara." It sounds like he's right next to her, almost.

"Where are you?"

"Guess."

He's in front somewhere, just as she thought. She moves forward, balancing easily. Her legs are strong. "I know where you are," she bluffs.

"Tam," he says, and he sounds so sad. "Tam."

"What?" She walks toward his voice. "Come down. It's dark."

"I've figured it all out now," he says. She can't stand how sad his voice is and instinctively she reaches out an arm, but she must have been closer to the front tip of the roof than she knew because the fall is very fast. She can feel the bone in her leg break when she hits. Her palms scrape the ground, and she can feel the bone come through her flesh. She can feel — a rock? an old pipe? — underneath the broken leg, smashing in. But it doesn't matter what the smashing thing is. She knows it's really bad. The wind has gone out of her. The pain in her leg feels as if it goes through the top of her head.

In the long minute or two before she blacks out, she hears the thump of Christopher landing on the ground, and then his ragged breath as he unfolds her and picks her up, cradling her head against his sweaty chest. He smells worse than a bear. But maybe he really can fly because he effortlessly carries them both into the cabin, then kicks the door closed.

"The thing is," begins Ruth. She turns toward Dan. "Do you have kids?"

"No," he says softly. It's funny for Hal to see him in Nan's house somehow. In his grace, he makes the sparse furniture seem almost large.

Ruth is pinched, miserable. Her breath is bad, Hal can smell it from across the room. "Then get the fuck out of here," she hisses at Dan. "I don't even *know* you." Jack is slumped in a chair like a massive, deflated balloon. He has barely spoken since the two of them arrived. Hal was amazed that they agreed to come at all. Pie sits on the coffee table next to mismatched plates, but none of them has even pretended to eat any.

Marina, who said several times that this meeting would be a bad idea, nevertheless tries bravely. "Fighting one another isn't going to help, Ruth. And Jack." She interlaces her fingers. "We're stronger as a team." Hal wonders if she believes this claim anymore.

Jack lifts his head. "This is a horror show." He closes his eyes.

Ruth says nothing in such a way as to communicate imminent absolute vengeance. She seems to be even more slender than she was before, like a filament that would conduct a bolt of lightning with extraordinary force and accuracy.

"He's here to help," says Hal, and even to his own ears he sounds weak. "He thought maybe we could talk."

"So help." Ruth folds her hands. "Go ahead, genius."

Dan appears entirely relaxed as he says, "Nan has gone to look for them. She left a few days ago. That's why she's not here."

Hal thinks he might truly, literally be ill. "Dan —"

But Dan holds up a hand. He sits back. Marina and Hal remain rooted where they are. As if we had committed a crime, thinks Hal. As if we're in hiding, listening to footsteps pass by.

Ruth begins to cry. "What?" she says. "What?"

Jack has opened his eyes wide. "Where is she?"

"North." Marina is almost whispering.

"I want to go." Ruth stands up, like a sleepwalker suddenly awakened. "I'm going."

Jack jumps up from his chair and puts his arms around her. "Ruthie, no." She struggles in his grasp; she hits at him as hard as she can with her slender arms; with one strong foot she kicks at the coffee table, knocking the top plates off to smash on the floor. Dan, quite quickly, places a hand over the remaining stack. Holding Ruth, Jack looks over to Marina and Hal, who immediately join in, saying no, it was stupid of Nan, she'll be back probably tomorrow, it was impulsive, they understand the impulse, but in terms of real help . . . real help, Ruth, the kind that will find them. The two of them are only kids, how far can they go? Ruth hits and smacks, she pulls at Jack's hair. He doesn't let go of her. Before too long, they are all crying, they're all so tired, they're exhausted.

Ruth is bent forward, sobbing, held in her husband's large arms like a rag doll. "I have to find my daughter."

Christ, thinks Hal, our children could already be dead, or so far gone down some rabbit hole that they'll never be found. Although he has considered these possibilities, it is not until this moment that he has actually believed that they could be true. He feels the snap in his soul of a branch, breaking. The falling cradle. He holds out a hand to Marina, who silently takes it. Her face is mottled with tears.

Hal is just about to hold out his other hand to Dan when he notices that Dan, alone among their distraught company, is not crying. On the contrary. He looks quite well. Better than well. In fact, he is eating a piece of pie. He's eating it quietly, to be sure, respectfully, but he is eating it, off one of the unbroken plates. Broken crockery litters the floor by his feet. When Dan sees Hal looking at him, he smiles sympathetically. Then he winks.

Dan sets down his plate. "Ruth, listen to me." He extends a graceful hand. He says all the right things. He is perfect. He is like a matador, cutting back and forth among the charges of their rampaging emotions, his sleeves making gorgeous soft bells. After a while, everyone is eating pie, Marina and Ruth sharing one plate.

The atmosphere in the room is suffused with the fullness and emptiness of sacrifice. It's late. They all begin to gather themselves for the long night ahead. Hal is so grateful to Dan, who has more than averted unpleasantness, he's carried them to a new place — a desolate place, certainly, but of the sort of necessary desolation adults must survive. Parents must survive. What he did to Ruth: it was almost cruel. He lanced her, like a boil. But that was necessary, too, and now Hal can see that it was the only choice because she held the center of the scene.

"I'm so hungry," Ruth says wearily.

Jack strokes her shoulder. "I'll make you an egg."

Hal is grateful; he is astonished. And yet. In Dan's place, would he have winked? What a rush it must be, he realizes, to bring people together. Especially people on the edge of disaster.

Dan is talking with Jack, knee to knee. "My brother . . ." Hal hears Dan say. "My sister." Dan has hardly spoken of his siblings to Hal at all, but Jack is nodding vigorously, listening. Marina begins picking up the broken plates. Hal looks at the carpet; he doesn't want to see Dan wink again.

Nan lets the waitress pour her another cup of coffee. The waitress has a long neck like Marina, a similar way of moving, though the waitress is much younger and her hair is jet black. It's obvious that she doesn't care about anything yet, with her bright red lips, her pen perched jauntily behind her pretty ear. Nan finishes the coffee and leaves the waitress a big tip.

It's sunny this morning. Nan rolls down the car window. The radio is on, but she can't hear it that well. She catches some fragment about a microearthquake the night before. She's well north now. Much more ghosty up here. Haunted country. She prefers landscapes where she can see to the horizon, see what's coming. Here, the density seems to offer a thousand hiding places. Which makes sense, for him; if it was Nan, she'd desert around here, too. Still, it makes her nervous. If he can hide up here, so can lots of people.

The car goes *pingping pingping.* An RV going the other way passes her. When he gets back and is well again, she thinks, maybe they'll rent an RV and take a trip, all four of them. Someplace classic and ridiculous like the Grand Canyon. She and Marina will have made up their unspoken argument by then; the dress and the stupid girl will have been returned; the car will be back in the garage, next to Marina's bicycle. The road enters a shady patch, and Nan's head clears. She's definitely getting somewhere, she knows it.

The car goes *pingthud.* It stops. Nan remains behind the wheel for a second, as if it will miraculously restart. It doesn't. She puts the car in neutral, gets out, and, with one hand on the steering wheel through the open window on the driver's side, eases it off the road. A car flies past and around the next curve without stopping. Nan retires to the warm hood of the car to wait, boots on the fender. Shit. Why doesn't she have a cell phone? Why was she born forty years too early? She still sells books printed on paper, for God's sake. She believes in motherhood. She checks her watch: 9:40. Plenty of hours left in the day to get back on track. Beneath her, the car's engine slowly cools.

After an empty hour, Nan grabs her stuff and Christopher's drawing from the back seat, locks the car, and begins walking. The next town, Poplar, is seventeen miles away. She can just about make it before it gets dark. She carries her bag on her good-hip side; after not too long, even today's tender sun begins to feel hot. The sun, she tells herself, is not there. She conjures up images of glaciers. Polar bears. Ice. She holds Christopher's rolled-up drawing in one hand, trying not to crush it. She finds herself wishing for Marina's bicycle. She should have put it in the trunk. Her bad hip smarts, as if there's a thorn in it. Snow. The inside of the freezer. Antarctica.

Something tugs from within, an interior discomfort. Nan attempts to will it away; it never occurred to her to bring tampons because she was bleeding just two weeks ago. She is as exasperated and disappointed as if she were twelve. What sort of deserter has to worry about cramps? She tries to think of it as an open bullet wound. Ladies ministering to her with gauze. Shots of whiskey. That carries her through another mile or so toward Poplar, as the sun moves higher in the sky. If only she were taller, she could cover that much more ground that much faster. She sighs, sweating, cramping. She shifts the bag to the other shoulder, which proves surprisingly more comfortable, for a little while.

The sun has done its worst and is on the downward slope of its journey when Nan hears the rumble of a car. She turns around right away, stubs out her cigarette, and holds up her thumb. It isn't a car, but a truck, and it pulls off the road just ahead of her. On the rear bumper is a sticker that says I ♥ RODEO and inside the cab is a very tan woman with a long gray braid and glasses. On either side of each lens is a string of little turquoise birds, flying on a still loop.

"Hey, young lady," says the woman, leaning across the seat and opening the door, "don't you know hitchhiking's not safe?"

Nan's hip is clanging with pain as she climbs up into the cab, pushing her bag and Christopher's drawing ahead of her. "Don't you know not to stop for hitchhikers? Could be dangerous."

"Yeah," says the tan woman wryly, "so I hear. That your car back there?"

Nan nods, exhausted. Her entire body feels bruised, and there's a familiar leaking sensation. "Do you by any chance have a tampon?"

"Glove compartment. Got another one of those cigarettes?"

Nan hands the woman a cigarette, grabs a tampon out of the glove compartment, clambers out of the truck, and hunkers behind a tree. She'll have to clean up later somewhere, though what she'd really like to do is stay right there, in the cool of the tall trees, listening for small sounds.

"Where are you going?" asks the tan woman when Nan gets back in.

"Poplar. I need to get my car fixed. I'm Nan."

"Sue." She pulls off the shoulder and onto the road.

"Thank God you came by. I thought I was going to have to walk the whole way."

"I'm on this road a lot. I've got one son in the hospital up in Fortuna, the other one in the hospital in Garberville."

"Both of them?" says Nan. "What happened?"

"Beat each other clear to shit over a drug deal."

"Are they all right?"

"More or less." Sue laughs, exhaling smoke. "They're both supposed to be out next week, and I said to the doctors, 'Hey, maybe you should keep them a while longer.'" Sue shakes her head. "No dice." The truck rattles along. Sue's strings of birds bobble lightly. "You have kids?"

"Yes. I have a son, too. That's why I'm up here." Nan fumbles in her things for a flyer. "This is him, Christopher. He's missing. I know he's gone this way, I've been tracking him — looking for him."

Sue doesn't take her eyes off the winding road. "Lots of kids up here. Most of them down in Smithville this time of year." She taps an ash out the window.

"Where's Smithville?"

"The other way. You must've passed through it."

Nan turns around to stare at the unexceptional road curving behind them. Her heart contracts. "Please. I'll pay you. Whatever you want."

"The flats are full of kids, too, and down by the riverbank — "

Nan is frantic. "Please."

Sue eyes Nan briefly. "This the first time he's run?"

"He didn't mean to. He's — not well. Not himself."

The truck rattles as Sue considers. "There's a bus . . ." she begins. One mile. Two. "All right," she says finally.

"I'll stop at a cash machine in Smithville."

"Screw that," says Sue, swerving into a turnout, then onto the road going the other way. The turquoise birds swing far out on their lines. "This is what mothers do, right? Up and down the same damn road, every goddamn day."

Hal pats the earth. It's still early in the morning, cool and quiet. The petals of the orchid are profoundly pink and raggedly oval; they look surreal, or like something cut with a child's scissors. Hal pushes the dirt into a heap around the base of the slender plant, bracing it with a little wooden stick and a bit of pink thread. The pink petals shimmy in the breeze. An old man in a hat sits on a portable stool at the foot of a grave nearby. Its headstone reads MIRIAM GREENBAUM, 1927–1998. BELOVED WIFE AND MOTHER.

"That's not going to last," says the old man. "Not that kind of plant."

"I know," replies Hal. He traces the letters on the stone with his fingers: ADAM MARKOWITZ, 1946–1985. THE MOTHER OF US

ALL. Hal had been the only one left to write it. He thought it was what Adam would have written himself, but he really didn't know. "That's an exotic," says the old man. "That's why."

"It's okay. It's pretty now." Hal sits back on his heels. There is dirt on the knees of his chinos, dirt under his fingernails.

Marina rides her bicycle over to Hal's, cornering as fast as she likes, without a helmet. Since Nan took the car, she's had to borrow the globalizationmobile once to get groceries and it's time to borrow it again. And yet — she swoops, stands to climb his hill — she doesn't think she will. There's still rice and whatever. She chains her bike to Hal's gate; she's not that late. "Hey," she calls from the entryway. "I'm here." She pours herself a glass of orange juice. "Where's Dan?"

Hal appears in the kitchen doorway, carrying his shaving kit. There's a big smudge of dirt on his pants. That's unlike him. "Listen," he says.

Marina understands immediately. Nan called from Smithville an hour ago; she must have called Hal, too. "Wait a minute."

"Marina, she has no car, that hunk of junk is never going to start again, she needs help — "

"She could *rent* a car, Hal. She's not in the middle of Mongolia — "

"That's not the point." His mouth closes in a line. This is determined Hal, tall and awkward and clipped, balding, smudged. It's as if the dirt has given him a new authority.

"My God, Chris and Tamara might not be anywhere near where Nan is. Have you thought of that?" Marina feels as if something is tilting, sliding sideways, toward a long drop.

Hal zips up the shaving kit. "But she's there. I can be there by tonight. We'll call you — "

"You'll *call* me? Is this a joke? What about all that stuff last night? Hal. I'm her lover, if anyone should be going — "

"I'm his father." He drops his gaze for a second, but only a second. "I'm Christopher's father," he repeats.

"I can't believe you would say that to me. And she's going to have a fit, Hal. She must have told you not to do this. Does she even know?"

Hals sets the shaving kit on the kitchen counter. He sighs. "Marina." He rubs his face. "Someone needs to stay at home."

Standing in Hal's narrow, shining, well-appointed kitchen, Marina has the awful thought that this was always not only where they were headed, but where they were, in fact, standing all along. He has a fragile look around the eyes, which only makes it worse. It is almost unbearable that he should be human as well; it is impossible.

"This isn't fair" is all she can manage to get out, like a child.

His eyes fill. He says angrily, "Nothing about any of this is fair. Do you want to know what's fair? *Nothing*. Not one fucking thing. I'm not fair, and Nan isn't fair, and Christopher, for damn sure, isn't fair. You're not all that fair either, are you? Do the math, Marina. Add it up."

"Is that what this comes down to for you? The math? Why don't you just wheel in biology while you're at it?" Marina laughs her mother's bitter laugh.

Hal rubs his face again, harder. "No. It's not that. It's that Nan and I have to go. We absolutely have to. Do you understand that?"

Marina shrugs, but he bears down on her. Relentlessly, he continues, "Marina, can you really tell me that *you have* to go? That you would die if you didn't? If you can say that, say it right now."

A long moment passes. This is the beginning, thinks Marina. Free fall. She shakes her head. Hopelessly, she repeats herself, she argues. "This isn't fair. It isn't."

"No." He is at once ruthless, and almost kind. "I'm going. I'll call you when I get there."

Christopher tries to give Tamara a drink of water, but she won't take it. He can't tell if she's asleep or not: her eyes are closed, though not all the way. She's drooling, just a little. He wipes off the drool with a corner of bedspread, dips a finger in the water bottle and runs it over her lips. Even in the darkened cabin — he had to close everything up so the police can't find them, so no one can find them — he can see that she's crying. The bone protrudes, jagged and white, from her shin. Her pants leg is bunched at the knee. She's sweating; well, it's stuffy in there with the door closed, he's sweating, too. The flesh around the bone looks like someone stirred it with a knife. He'd try to feed her, but all that food they got is bad, it's poisoned, that's probably why she fell. They can't eat that food. Christopher bites at the bedspread until it tears, then makes strips, like a Boy Scout. He ties up her leg: tight, tight. He has to push the bone down. Her eyes close all the way and when he says her name, she doesn't answer.

Smithville is small, with the Smithville Motel at one end and a RadioShack a stone's throw or two away at the other end. When they got there, Nan hopped out of Sue's truck at the one gas station, where the longhaired attendant promised to tow the car in before the end of the day. "It's important," Nan told him, and he nodded distractedly. She used the pay phone to call Hal. The sheriff's office, said a man on the corner, is just over there, behind the organic bagel place.

Nan stopped at the organic bagel place, which was encouragingly large and clean and bright, and got a big cup of organic coffee. Now, feeling freshly invigorated, she walks over to the sheriff's office. It's a one-story cinderblock building, not much bigger than a large garage, on a shabby street, across from a muffler and auto repair shop. A shining white police cruiser is parked outside. Inside, behind plexiglass, is a woman with dyed blond hair wearing a low-cut leopard-print top. Taped on the wall above her are posters on how to get a restraining order. "Hello, may I help you?" says the blond woman. Her face, and her bosom above the low-cut top, are gently wrinkled.

Nan is momentarily caught off-guard by the woman's resemblance to her own mother. It's like something out of a dream. Even her eyeliner, the place where it falters at the corners, is the same. "Oh," says Nan.

"May I help you?" asks the woman again, polite and faintly wary, smiling.

"My son is missing," Nan manages. "I need to talk to someone."
The woman calls over her shoulder, "Steven? Yeah." She nods,
gestures to Nan. "Come on in."

Seated at a desk behind a laptop is a sturdy young man in uniform with a big face and kind brown eyes. Cords fall from the laptop to the floor, where a Siamese cat with bright blue eyes sits. The
young man stands up, shakes Nan's hand firmly. He has badges, a
walkie-talkie at his neck, a holster around his waist. He is Officer
Mills, sheriff's deputy. Nan explains.

"Do you have a flyer?" asks Officer Mills.

Nan hands him one.

He glances at it, petting the cat, who has hopped up onto
the desk. "Okay, I'll get a Teletype from San Francisco with all
his info, and we'll do a BOLO at the start of the next shift tonight."

"A what?"

"BOLO. Be on the lookout. If we see him, and he has ID, we'll
tell him you all are looking for him."

"No . . . what? He's very unstable. Look, I brought this to show
you . . ." She begins opening Christopher's drawing, which has
sustained some damage, she notices. "This is how he thinks."

The older blond woman, from her position at the plexiglass
window, exchanges a glance with Officer Mills. Her skirt is short
and black, with a rhinestone flower at the waist.

The officer, glancing at the map, says patiently, "I understand.
Are you familiar with Welfare and Institutions Code 5150? San
Francisco must have explained this to you. He has to be a danger
to himself or others, or gravely — "

Nan's voice rises. She drops the map. "He *is* gravely disabled.
He's very ill. I'm sure he's not taking his — "

Officer Mills becomes more patient. "Ma'am. We don't know
where he is."

"He could be here. That's what I'm saying."

The cat purrs, looking at Nan with its bright blue eyes. Officer
Mills lifts the cat and puts it back on the floor. "The thing is . . .
there are two things you need to know. One is that being missing

is not a crime. We can't detain juveniles for no reason if they haven't committed a crime. I'm sure you already know this."

Nan shifts impatiently in her seat.

"Two," he continues, "and I'm sure you could surmise this as well, we're a very small outfit. I" — he points to his strapping chest — "am the only one on this shift. I'm on until nine o'clock tonight. My territory goes clear up to Two Rocks and down past Lucas. That's hundreds of square miles, most of it forested. This is a poor county. We don't have the manpower to look for Jesus H. Christ himself if you told me you saw him walking down the road. And, I have to tell you, we do get a lot of runaways up here."

The blond woman nods agreement. "Summer's even worse." An older man appears at the plexiglass window. "Hey, Joe," she says.

As much as Nan would like to punch the wall and storm out, as she did the last time, this little cinderblock office with its cat and its one laptop, its one police officer, seems to argue against it. And there is her mother, standing at the window in a leopard-print top, tapping a sandaled toe on the floor. "Well, my spider plants are doing good," her mother is saying.

Nan slumps, exhausted. "He has to be here."

Officer Mills holds up the flyer that says HAVE YOU SEEN MY SON? "Believe it or not," he says nicely, "these things help sometimes."

Hal drives. Vineyards pass silently. They're soothing to him, the rows and rows of vines, their twisted branches. They look like modern dancers, paused in formation. He is afraid, and tired, and determined. He feels as if it would abrade his eardrums to listen to anything more than the low whoosh of the car driving on. He almost feels as if it's the car that's driving, heading inexorably north. He's sorry about Marina, but she's wrong: what he and Nan began, they must carry. Marina can walk away, and from what he knows of her, she probably will; what has she ever committed to except paint? He has time to think of one thing, and one thing only, though it is also awful to think. He tried to explain all this to Dan, but the connection was bad; he'll have to try later. He really can't think about Dan at the moment, either. He allows himself the comfort of trying to calculate how many vines per half mile, then multiplying by the number of miles that pass per vineyard. It's not an accurate number, but that doesn't matter. The rows of vines feel like years, like graves. He presses the accelerator.

Christopher stands in the doorway of the cabin, watching. His hands are bloody from changing the bandage; he had to tear up more bedspread. She didn't wake up. He told her all about the sky and what was written there, what she needed to watch out for, the massive orange shit of the bear. She didn't even turn her head. Her breath stuttered. He grips the doorframe, scanning. He can close the door in a second, he can hear everything for miles.

The colors of Christopher's aquarium have always seemed too supersaturated to Marina, like wet candy, but this afternoon she feels a proprietary tenderness toward them as well, as if they were her own budding ideas. Since she stopped painting, the visual world has become denser and more intense to her, pressing at her. It feels as if it's painting her rather than the other way around. The fish in their saltwater kingdom streak her eyes with their bright colors, their wild shapes. The tangs are like surreal suns. They leave impressions on her sight, spangling her vision.

Marina taps the squid into the tank and watches as it descends past the indifferent bamboo cat shark, who stares at her glumly through the glass. The other fish, each one more alien and lovely than the next, are sleek and bright, sated. They've already eaten. The shark, however, is wan. His strange eyes are dull. Marina drops in another squid. The shark makes no move toward it. Marina checks the temperature of the tank, but it's exactly warm enough. An angelfish dips down, skims the shark's untouched meal, then floats away. The little shark is so glum; she pities him. She's furious with Hal for leaving, she's furious with both of them, but she doesn't want the shark to die while he's gone. That would just add to everyone's misery. She checks the encyclopedic *Care of Saltwater Fish* book that's stashed near the tank. It states, unequivocally, that sharks are pure carnivores, but if that's true then why won't this shark eat even the most tempting bit of meat? Every species has its oddballs. Marina goes into the kitchen, opens Hal's refrigerator, and finds a plum. She cuts it up. With a palm full of plum, she returns to the tank, then drops in a small bit of plum flesh. The shark bites it right away. Marina drops in another. Plum juice trails through the water, dissolves. The shark chases the piece of plum to the gravel; the piece of plum disappears. Leaning over the tank, Marina drops in two pieces of plum at once. *Snap snap* goes the shark. Marina rains down more plum until the creature's small teeth are purple with plum meat and the water is ever so faintly stained. Her palm and fingers are sticky, purple-black. The shark, she notes proudly, looks happier already. It actually begins to swim a little. So there's that, if nothing else, Marina thinks. Poor shark. Poor everyone.

Marina presses her palm to the glass, leaving a plum-colored imprint so light that it's barely visible.

Nan spends the afternoon walking the town edge to edge, putting up her flyers with duct tape. What the hell would she have done in a place like this? She noticed right away that there wasn't a bookstore, though probably there was a hulking mall out on a strip somewhere. She would have ended up tending bar, waiting tables. Making just enough to keep herself in motorcycle parts. She picks up a cheese sandwich at the organic bagel place, and it has mung bean sprouts in it. Smithville is that kind of town: mung bean sprouts but no bookstores. A towheaded boy in baggy pants flies past her on a skateboard. Nan flexes her hands. The bad one is still a little stiff. She opens both her hands, studies her palms. Which crease had Quince said was her lifeline?

She passes the Smithville Motel twice. Hal's car isn't there yet, of course. It will be very late by the time he gets up here. She warned him that the road winds quite a bit. Nan wonders if Sue is sitting at one son's bedside, or the other's. Holding their hands and giving them hell. Somehow she imagines Sue in both places at once, her arms, lined with turquoise birds, stretching from one

town to the other. Nan sends out her spirit to look for Christopher, but it comes back empty; with every step, the arrow in her
hip bites deeper. She checks for her car at the gas station, but now
no one's there at all. She writes on the back of a flyer, *Where the
hell is my car?*, and slides it under the door. She checks into the
Smithville Motel on her third pass, more for something to do
than anything else. There are two queen beds with flowered, polyester bedspreads; a television with an HBO card tented on top;
and two white molded plastic chairs. It's dark in the room until
she opens the heavy, flowered curtains. The walls are faux red-
wood paneling.

She sits down on the bed for a minute, then lies back with her
feet on the green carpet. It could be that she falls asleep because
when she sits up again the sun has gone down. She feels that she
has dreamed, but she's not sure of what. She tells herself that she
isn't hungry, she should go out and walk some more. She turns on
the television, turns it off. She's very hungry. She leaves the motel
and walks down Smithville's main street. The sky over the trees on
a distant ridge is mauve, like a tie-dyed sky. There is a half-moon.
She stops at a place called Chico's, where kids, smoking and hanging out and playing Hacky Sack, line the curb in front. A girl in a
dog collar and a tight dress that's too old for her is laughing. A
gangly boy is bouncing a Hacky Sack off his elbow. They all look
innocent and dangerous, and none of them is Christopher. One
boy, whose round face is scarred either by horrible acne or perhaps a burn, sits slightly apart, holding a mandolin. He has a peculiar, slack expression. There's lost, thinks Nan, and then there's
lost. She goes inside.

Chico's has burritos and spaghetti and pizza and an impressive
variety of beers on tap. Nan orders a Belgian beer and a burrito.
She sits down at a table next to the window, drinking her beer. After quite a long time, the teenage girl behind the counter calls Nan's
number. The teenage girl is wearing a glittery top and low-riding
pants; Nan wishes that that were her problem: a daughter who
dresses like a slut. She even, for a moment, wishes she were that
girl, entranced with herself in glitter. Like Marina. How nice, she

thinks bitterly, to have that kind of time. She eats her burrito, which has olives in it and is actually good. Through the window, she watches the boy with the mandolin, who smiles in his slack, scarred way at every passerby. Behind her, two neatly dressed men are eating spaghetti. One is saying, "When I fly into Amsterdam . . ." She supposes it's true that it's all drug dealers up here — what else is there to do? Nobody in this town cares about a bakery. She knows she needs to go outside and interrogate those kids, but a fatigue has overtaken her. She goes back to the counter and orders a cup of coffee. The girl in the glittery top says, "I have to make a new pot."

Nan sits down again. She feels so strange. It's not the beer, which she didn't even finish. Her head hurts. This place may have been where she thought she was going once upon a time, but she doesn't want to be here now. She doesn't want Christopher to disappear here, lost behind the mauve sky. She feels quite certain that if they lose hold of him in Smithville they will never find him again. Outside, the girl in the dog collar and the tight dress stands up from the curb, makes the peace sign, and walks away into the night.

Nan is still waiting for her coffee when her mother sits down across from her. No, she reminds herself, it's the older blond woman from the police station, now with a denim jacket over the leopard-print top. "I'm Karen," her mother says, extending her hand. She squeezes Nan's hand affectionately. "How are you holding up?"

Nan shrugs.

"Listen. It's hard. We get so many like you, and Steve and I always feel so bad about it. We did find one girl last year, managed to get her home, but then off she ran again. Guess she wanted to see the world." She gazes at Nan compassionately. "I just feel so bad," she repeats.

The cup of coffee finally arrives and Karen nods the girl to bring another. "You have any family up here?"

Nan shakes her head. She has a deep desire to keep Karen talking, about anything, to keep this woman sitting across from her for as long as possible. She is so lonely and tired. She's always been so lonely and tired.

Karen stirs sugar into her cup. "Kids'll break your heart. God knows I broke my mother's enough times, doing every single thing she ever told me not to. It was like everything she wanted me to do was a *menu* for me to do the opposite. Your son ever run before?" Karen asks delicately.

"Sort of. Just once."

"Mmm. Mmmm." Karen shakes her head. "That must be hard."

"I don't understand it," Nan finds herself saying. "It doesn't make any sense."

Karen's eyes, Nan sees, are green. The day's make-up is almost all worn away. Her lashes are naturally pale.

"I mean," Nan goes on, "it's like he walked off a cliff. Like I turned around for one second . . . but I didn't *even* turn around, I was standing right there. It's more like the ground gave way. For no reason at all."

Karen nods. "Honey, you can't blame yourself. You just can't. If I had a nickel for everything I should have done . . ."

"Do you have kids?"

Karen laughs. "No, not me. I was like that girl from last year. I wanted to see the world." She finishes her coffee. "I need to get home. Steve's a good guy," she says reassuringly as she stands up. "He'll keep your boy on his radar."

"Thanks." Nan puts an amount that must be enough money down on the table and stands as well. "I need to get some rest myself."

As they step outside Chico's, the scarred boy with the mandolin smiles at them. "That's Pumpkin," confides Karen in a low voice. "He's always around. Good night."

The mauve sky has deepened to dark blue. Nan watches as Karen walks away. It's so strange to Nan: how can this woman be tending spider plants in a leopard-print top in Smithville when her doppelganger, with skittery eyes, is still trapped in that little, overfurnished living room in Texas? The physics of it, or something, is all wrong. After a minute, instead of going toward the motel, Nan trails along in the direction Karen is going, hanging far back, though Karen doesn't turn around at all, walking confidently down the little main street. She makes a right. When Nan makes the same right, she finds herself on a street of ragged bungalows. Then, after a left, on another street of ragged bungalows. Reggae music lopes out of a nearby window. Nan is dying for a cigarette, but refrains.

Karen, in sandals, ascends a street with a fairly steep incline. Nan stays well behind. Karen's dyed blond hair is bright, and the brightness seems to Nan to have something to do with happiness, something she's never been able to understand. Her mother was always changing shades, ash to summer sun to goldenrod, as if changing her identity without leaving the house. Each color would look good for a while. Now, watching Karen move briskly up the hill, Nan longs to ask her what the secret is, what Karen found when she roamed the world. And why she stopped. Toward the top of the hill, Karen opens the gate on a split-rail fence around a pretty peach bungalow. Karen must have her porch light on a timer because it's on, as if the house is expecting her. Nan can see that there is a white wicker loveseat on the porch, and that stained-glass wind chimes in the shapes of stars and crescent moons hang from the porch ceiling. Karen sits down on the loveseat, kicks off her sandals, rubs one heel. On that porch, nothing at all is happening. A wind chime rings.

Nan, standing in the dark street midway down the hill, is dumbstruck. Is that it? Is happiness as small a thing as that? She turns away, not the Hunter at all, but the gawky child, terrified that Karen might see her frozen there, yearning and exhausted.

Marina leaves Nan's silent house, unchains her bike, and flies downhill in the night. She has her cell phone, but when she gets to Shiloh's she suddenly decides to turn it off. Fuck them. She doubts Shiloh will even let her in anyway. This ride is just exercise, something self-lacerating to do with her free time.

Shiloh is laughing as she opens the door. When she sees Marina, she says, "Oh."

"I —"

"Yeah, you." Shiloh sighs, then turns around, leading Marina to the backyard, where various young people are occupying bits of salvaged furniture. They look like deposed royalty to Marina, the grandeur of their youth scattered about like bolts of raw silk on a metal desk chair, a ratty bright green beanbag chair, a raw wood glider, and an overturned plastic bucket.

"Nicholas," introduces Shiloh. "Rachel, Jade, Hannah, and T."

Hannah and T are entwined on the raw wood glider. Hannah has long, long, wavy brown hair and a Vermeer face; T is squat and strong, her platinum hair streaked with dark roots. She's wearing Shiloh's ELI shirt and a thick ID bracelet.

Hannah, reclining against the wooden glider arm with her legs across T's lap, baldly looks Marina over. "Hello."

T nods, unsmiling.

Nicholas, a fawnlike young man, is occupying the bucket. Nicholas's hair is the same platinum as T's — did they go to the same salon? are they related? — but, curled up on the overturned bucket, he's as soigné as she is sturdy: a bucket nymph. Rachel, a bald Asian girl, is wearing an extraordinarily tiny camouflage skirt held together with staples; Jade is bright white and cheery, busty in a cut-up T-shirt, lounging in the beanbag chair with an electric guitar that isn't plugged into anything. They are all annoying, and quite beautiful.

Marina waves awkwardly. "Hey." This visit was obviously a mistake. Shiloh sits down in the beanbag chair with Jade and keeps her eyelids low. No one offers Marina a seat.

Nicholas stands up on top of the bucket and begins tip-tapping his little feet. "I. Am. Going. To. Be. Famous."

From the glider, Hannah and T laugh. T throws a paper cup at Nicholas's ass. "Nicky, shut the fuck up."

Hal stops for dinner at a place with a jukebox where everybody is fat. It looks just like Idaho. He hates it and quickly eats his turkey burger and fries.

Nan takes a wrong turn and walks a long way up some other hill of bungalows, then turns down the hill, but that's somehow in the wrong direction as well, and Smithville, it turns out, is bigger than she thought, with few streetlights. The night feels like some dark cotton batting she has to struggle her way through with no compass or map. She feels as if she's lost inside some portion of Christopher's drawing. Locating the half-moon, she turns toward where she thinks it would be relative to the motel, but instead she ends up in the parking lot of another motel that isn't on the main street. Tired, irritated, she sits down on a dark curb and smokes a cigarette, like one of those kids outside Chico's. An image of Karen's breast under the leopard-print top drifts across her mind hazily.

Nan is about to stand up when she notices a man reaching into the dumpster by the side of the motel. He's tall and broad and soft, like a bear recently emerged from hibernation. He's barefoot, and his hair is so matted and dark with grime that there is quite a stretch of time — at least a minute, maybe two — when Nan doesn't recognize him. Then she does, and is about to jump up and call his name, but an instinct keeps her crouched, watching. Her hands and feet and the tips of her ears get hot. If he were to run, she wouldn't be able to catch him. And this man by the dumpster, she understands, is fully capable of running far, and fast. Without moving, she turns her gaze up one side of the street, down the other; no cars approach. The muscles in her legs twitch, ready to jump. Her hip feels perfect. Still, she holds back: she's smaller, alone. She strategizes, hands clenching and unclenching. They're going to have one chance.

He forages in the dumpster, reaching in with one arm. He pulls out what looks like a grapefruit, a can of soda. He sets them carefully on the ground. He pulls out something in a cellophane package. Nan studies his feet. Where are his shoes? In the half light of the moon, she tries to see if his feet are cut or bruised; his jeans are torn in several places. Although she can't actually smell him, she knows that he smells very bad, of sweat and shit and the road. She knows how he smells because it's akin to how she smells herself, three days past her last shower, blood still streaked on her thighs, pressed against the side of the motel. He doesn't glance in her direction, absorbed as he is in his task. He sets half a candy bar next to his other finds.

The door of one of the rooms opens, and he efficiently wraps up the stuff from the dumpster in a piece of green nylon he seems to have brought along for the purpose. Nan cautiously watches. He disappears around the back of the motel. Nan follows him, walking very lightly in the dusk. Behind the motel, she trails him down a street she hadn't noticed, then across a small field. The woods are surprisingly close and dense. Christopher, his green nylon sack hanging from his hand, cuts determinedly across the bit of field, bobbing down for a second into a small ravine, then rising up again. Tall and solitary though he is, the dark is heavier here and the moonlight weaker. Nan has to squint to make sure she's following her son and not a stray shadow. Her glasses, she remembers, are in her car, on the dashboard. She should have a string like Sue's. God knows where her car is. He keeps his head down as he walks, and she's not sure, but he seems to be humming. He enters the forest.

Nan stays back until he's well in, then follows him. Now she's certain she can smell him, his particular Christopher scent mixed with suffering and filth and earth. His form is somewhat indistinct in the woods, but he crashes through the undergrowth unselfconsciously, humming into the night air. She pities his poor feet, scraping across the forest floor. She picks up her own and sets them down like an Indian, noiseless. She's sure that she can smell him. The half light deepens to darkness as the forest thickens, and she stops, sniffing, listening. He crashes along to her right. She turns in the dark, toward him. The sensation is not of seeking, but of being pulled along, as if she is on one end of a rope and he, heavier and stronger, is tugging from the other end. Her breasts tingle and seem to swell, almost painfully, as if about to leak milk. She remembers that mammalian scent.

The crashing sound stops. The moon seems to be gone. There is a kind of thud and scrape and then a sound that Nan can't identify at first because it's so out of place. Then she realizes that she has heard the sound of a door opening. The door is very slightly ajar; a dim sliver of light leaks out along its edge. Nan crouches down on the ground, waiting until her eyes adjust, but even when they do it's so dark that the light seems to be a cut in the night itself, a tear in the dense black stuff that surrounds her. Also, it's peculiarly suspended above the ground. It makes Nan think of spaceships; she squints again, peering harder; finally, she just discerns a small, square, apparently windowless structure. The door closes, and the hovering light winks out. Nan slows her breathing almost to a halt, but there is no sound at all from the square structure, which seems to be little more than a greater depth in the darkness, a deeper, colder place. Nan waits for a long time, her breasts aching, and crouches in the silence, but the door doesn't open again.

Nan is sitting in a molded plastic chair by the empty desk of the Smithville Motel around 3:00 A.M., drinking coffee from a paper cup and eating an Oh Henry! bar, when she sees the headlights of Hal's car and then Hal, in a zipped plaid jacket, getting out of the car. He locks it by remote, looking up at the sign. Seeing her through the window, he waves energetically, relieved. She always knew about fate, but she never knew what a sense of humor it had, arriving in Adam's backyard in the form of a gay nightbird-accountant from Idaho. She didn't even think he'd jack off that day, she was really sort of bullying him, in her grief. He was too much of a sissy to say no. Or so she had thought.

She stands up as he comes through the door. She is exhausted. Her hip is throbbing. She is so glad to see him.

"Nannie," he says. "Dear God."

"I found him."

They embrace.

From inside the middle of the night, from far within the dark tunnels, Tamara knows that Christopher is holding her in his arms. Some rotten, acrid thing is at her lips; she tries to push it away. Even being a little bit conscious is unbearable; there is more pain coming from her leg than she thought there was pain in the world. And it smells. Water is filling the dark tunnels. She's moving out, along them. She's so thirsty. But he holds her, he holds her more tightly than she's ever been held in her life, he rocks her. Because of how fiercely he grips her, she finds she isn't scared of the rushing, the force of it. It's easier than she thought, to go away to Fiji.

In the dark, Marina strokes the small of Shiloh's back, where her labyrinth tattoo is. She imagines she can feel the raised whorls of inky blue; she finds the unmarked dimple in Shiloh's skin that constitutes the labyrinth's center. "Why did you let me in?"

"I don't know." Shiloh sounds sullen. She turns over and moves a thumb just inside Marina.

"Your friends don't like me."

"Hannah and I just have a lot of history. She knows me way too well."

Shiloh moves deeper. Who is the shark? Who is the plum? With the lights out, Marina can't say. Shiloh kisses the back of Marina's neck, then bites her a tiny bit too hard. What Marina was hoping for from their encounter was, more or less, to lose consciousness for a while. She wouldn't mind if Shiloh drew a little blood. But as Shiloh makes a sound that isn't quite a sound, she moves over Marina with a delicacy, an anticipation of Marina's desire, that leaves Marina feeling almost frighteningly awake. Despite Marina's best efforts, Shiloh apparently has learned her well. Every touch is like a point made in an argument. The girl is smart, and something worse: Marina has the dark feeling that Shiloh knows more about why she's there than she does but isn't going to tell her. That will be Marina's punishment. *Tell me,* begs Marina's body. Shiloh refuses, making her come to her.

"So, do you think she's sleeping with the stupid girl again?" asks Hal, dipping a corner of toast into egg yolk. The diner clatters busily. It's very early in the morning. Marina didn't answer the phone last night, though, as Hal said, it was awfully late.

Nan makes a dismissive noise. Her hair is wet from the shower

Hal made her take, though the fried eggs he made her order are going cold. "I don't fucking care. Probably. Maybe." The waitress refills their coffee cups. "It's irrelevant."

"Well, today, yes, but — "

"No. Every day. Forever." Nan eats a teaspoon of cold egg. "Drop it."

"I don't understand you."

"Understand me later."

Hal finishes his egg, his toast. One of them, at least, has to have eaten. The sheriff's office will be open in a few hours. Hal wants to get out of Smithville as soon as possible, preferably by sundown. "He's going to hate us for this."

Nan frowns. Hal would take her hand, but he can tell she's barely holding herself together as it is. "I know that," she replies. "But if we lose him up here, he could be gone forever. These woods go on for miles."

Marina is still dreaming — some place with too many doors, tunnels filled with water — when Shiloh nudges her with the cell phone. "You got a message last night."

Marina sits up, listens. "Oh, Christ."

Shiloh drives Marina home in a car (a rather nice, suburban sort of car, Marina notices through her anxiety) that belongs to one of her roommates. Shiloh opens the trunk and hands Marina her bike. "See you later."

Marina nods distractedly, lugging her bicycle into the house and leaning it against the wall in the entryway. She dials Dan, not knowing who else to call. "Meet me at Hal's. I have to feed the fish."

Christopher, his arms around Tamara, is asleep.

Steve scratches the Siamese cat behind the ears. Karen is smiling sweetly at Nan, clearly under the impression that Hal is her husband, or at least her boyfriend.

"Okay," says Steve. "But I'm going to have to call the highway patrol and see if they can spare me a man or two. It can take a little while."

"How long?" Nan wishes that Hal would speak up instead of staring around with that woeful expression.

"Depends. I'll call you. I hope not too long."

"Now," says Nan. "Now."

"We know where you mean," offers Karen. "That's that place where Birdsong and them camped out last winter."

Steve nods.

"It's not really so far," reassures Karen.

"She knows that," says Hal testily.

It's quiet in the woods. Maybe a leaf falls. The sun shines through trees it's shone through for ages. The cabin door is closed.

Nan and Hal lie on Nan's bed at the Smithville Motel. The heavy, flowered motel curtains are open to the parking lot outside. Anyone looking in would see a couple — a tall, balding man and a small woman with short, gray-streaked hair — lying on a double bed in a plain room, talking. Nan picks up the phone once or twice to make sure it's working. Christopher's drawing is unrolled on the wood-laminate table.

"He'll call," Hal says. "It's only noon."

"He has one more hour. Then we're going back down to that office."

"All right. It's okay."

Nan is rigid on the flowered bedspread. Hal holds her sweaty hand. "I miss him," he says.

She relents slightly, grasping Hal's hand. "Me, too. I miss the way it was. I still can't believe it. And not to him. It shouldn't have happened to him."

"It shouldn't happen to anybody."

"I don't care about *any*body. I don't love *any*body. You don't either."

"That's true. Do you remember that this is almost exactly what we said about Adam?"

Nan shrugs, looking surly or possibly tender, Hal isn't sure which.

"Did you know there was a sister?" says Hal.

"Yeah, Joanie."

"No. Another one. Edie. They never talked about her."

"Why?"

"He wouldn't say. He didn't tell you?"

"No. What? A sister?"

"Maybe he made it up, I don't know. It was toward the end." Hal laughs a little. "Adam." He turns on his side. He looks at Nan and sees the last twenty years of his life in her house. You, he thinks. Cowpuncher.

Nan turns her head to look at Hal and sees the traces of his beauty. She will watch the rest of it fade away. You, she thinks. Flower.

They lie there together on the flowered bedspread, talking of nothing, until the phone rings.

Marina lets herself and Dan into Hal's little yellow house. She thinks she left her watch there when she was feeding the fish yesterday — her third lost watch this year. "Are you hungry?" Marina asks Dan. "I'm starving."

"Just toast would be great." He sits down at the wenge wood dining room table, looking uncomfortable. "This is such a nice house," he says uncertainly. "I don't know why Hal and I never come here."

"Maybe he likes yours better." Marina takes the bread out of the silver breadbox. It is a nice house, it's true; poking around curiously in the well-stocked cabinets, she allows herself the fantasy that Christopher will begin here when they bring him back, that she and Nan might be in their own house alone for a while, sorting through the mess they've made. Because it is, she can see now, quite a mess. What was it that she ever thought she could know through sex?

Dan wanders toward the back. "I love those fish."

"I cured one of them with plums last night," calls Marina, rescuing the toast from burning. "I think he must be a vegetarian."

There's a silence, then, "Marina, what happened to the rest?"

Marina drops the toast she's buttering. "The rest?" She hurries to Christopher's room, where Dan is standing by the tank, hands on his hips.

He moves aside to reveal the shark, seeming quite lively and, somehow, pleased with itself, swimming briskly around a clear tank that is entirely devoid of any other fish. Its eyes are bright. The water is burbling at exactly the right temperature. The lovely plants are suspended, plump, colorful. The bright-eyed shark glides smoothly from edge to edge, happy and alone. There isn't a trace of the other exotic specimens, not even one scrap of yellow or purple hanging from the shark's strong teeth.

"Oh, no," says Marina. The massacre will be counted as her fault, she knows it already. It won't matter that the shark is obviously feeling much better.

The two of them watch the shark in silence for a minute or two before Dan says, "I've been thinking I might go back home for a while, visit my grandmother."

"Really?"

"I don't know," he says moodily. "I haven't decided. I can't decide. Do you know what I mean?"

"I do," answers Marina, watching the frisky shark. "I guess you know when you know."

Nan leads the men to the gap in the trees. Hal, Steve, and two good-size guys from the highway patrol follow her single file, hushed, into the forest. She has no problem finding her path of the night before; it's as if she's been walking it every day of her life. When they get within sight of the cabin, Nan pulls Steve aside. "I'm going in first," she whispers.

"That's not — "

"No," she says. "I am."

Steve studies her face, then motions the two highway patrol guys into positions at the sides of the cabin. He nods at Nan.

Hal, pale but determined, approaches with her, crouches down with her when they see the cabin, which is entirely quiet, its door shut. In the daylight, Nan can see the diamond over the door and, in the leaves, a yellow sock too small to be Christopher's. Except for the single yellow sock, the property looks as if no one has been there for centuries. The forest, plainly, is taking it back. A squirrel sits on the roof, worrying at a nut. Nan reaches within herself for the wolf, but the wolf is gone. In the wolf's place is an emptiness, a space of neither hope nor despair.

Hal whispers, "Are you all right?"

Nan nods.

"Do you see where the lock's been pulled off?" he murmurs. "We'll be able to get in."

"Okay."

"Nan?"

"No, I'm ready," she finally whispers back, finding her voice.

They walk quickly but softly up to the cabin. Steve watches; the men watch. Nan and Hal pause together at the high door.

"Go," he says, boosting her up.

Nan balances on the narrow sill a second before pushing open the cabin door. "Chris?"

Hal clambers up beside her, huffing. "Christopher."

It takes a minute for Nan to understand what she's seeing in the gloom. On one side of the room, cans and empty wrappers and rotting food, spoils of the dumpster. In the sagging center of the room, some tie-dyed thing torn into strips, heaped up in bright, dirty profusion. On the other side of the room, on a mattress, Christopher, feral, holding Tamara in his arms and blinking in the sudden light. He is bare-chested, barefoot. There is an extremely bad smell.

He holds a finger to his lips. "She's sleeping," he says, very low.

Nan goes cold.

Hal peers. "She is," he says.

Nan looks, sees that Tamara's chest is, indeed, just barely rising and falling, but she can also see that there is a tourniquet made of tie-dyed fabric on one shin, and that the horrendous smell in the room is emanating from the mattress where Christopher holds Tamara so tenderly in his arms. He strokes her matted hair. "I have her," he says.

Tamara moans. From one loosely wrapped layer in the bloody tourniquet, bone protrudes.

"Oh, Lord," says Nan. "Oh, God." The girl's skin is a bad color, not the color of death, but close to it. "Tamara? Tamara, can you hear me?"

Hal steps forward. "Christopher, she's sick."

Christopher clasps her more tightly to him, but still with a great tenderness, a lover's gentleness. "Get away from us."

Nan holds out her arms. How long have they been in here like this? How much more time does the girl have? "Chris, it's us. Please. We'll take care of her."

"No." He cradles Tamara like one who is prepared to cradle her forever. The girl burrows into his neck, eyelids fluttering. He takes her hand and Nan sees her weakly grip his in return. Something in Nan gives way. All this time, though she could hardly admit it even to herself, she has been as terrified as anyone else about Tamara being at the mercy of his rage. That kind of violence she understood in her marrow. But it never occurred to her that the greater danger might arise from being at the mercy of his love.

In the end, the two good-size guys from the highway patrol can't hold him, and Steve has to call for even more help, until the woods are full of men running, shouting, the crackle of walkie-talkies, paramedics carrying Tamara on a stretcher out of the woods, a truck with enormous wheels fighting its way in, front fender strewn with branches. Nan and Hal call things out to Christopher that he probably can't even hear where he is, fighting his worst nightmare made real. It's so much worse than she had imagined that Nan almost tells them just to let him go, let him return to earth or sea or air. But she doesn't. She stands by with Hal, who is crying, watching seven strong men restrain their son. At one point she thinks she feels little birds brush her face, but it's only the wind. She and Hal ride in the truck to the hospital.

Through the blur of excruciating pain and the strange, mottled light, whatever they put into her arm that momentarily brought her into consciousness and is as quickly carrying her out of it again, Tamara sees with crystalline clarity that they are never, ever going to let her see him again. Not even once. Not even to say goodbye. Like the snapped bone in her leg, the break is complete. She's out of the forest. Streak of sky. One leg dissolves, then the other. The ambulance doors close. She can't even cry, and she will love him for the rest of her life.

WALNUT CREEK

THE SHEETS are freezing and wet and they hold him tighter, it feels, than his own skin. He tries to twist, to turn himself inside out, and disappear through the portal at the top of his head, but the cold is even more brutal than the restraints. The portal is frozen shut. His balls, his ass, the insides of his thighs, are so cold they hurt. His feet aren't wrapped, but the air hitting the numerous scratches on them hurts them, he's sure they're bleeding again, they'll flood the room with blood. "My feet," he says to the nurse, who is reading a book in a chair beside him. She glances at his feet, touches them with her hand. She touches his neck.

"You're fine." She returns to her book.

He turns and turns inside, he turns his heart around and around as if it is the lid on a jar. He turns his kidney. He turns his spine. He makes his jism flow up, toward his lungs. The nurse turns a page. Nothing else happens. The wet sheets are freezing. His organs slow in their revolutions, then still. His jism flows back. His breathing slows. It's the Ice Age. The cold is global, voiceless.

STRING

A thread on the dress has come loose. Marina can't believe it. All that money, she's never even worn it anywhere, and there's a gold thread coming unstitched just where the bodice meets the skirt. The thread is ominously long, as if it has worked its way out on its own since she's been gone and will, magically, only get longer even if she never takes the incandescent creation out of its tissue paper again. It's clear that if she doesn't bring the dress to whatever incredibly expensive tailor repairs dresses such as this one, she will surely come in one morning to find that the dress has become a heap of gold and silver thread, like Rumpelstiltskin in reverse. She will have paid a ridiculous amount of money she doesn't have for a handful of pretty — albeit very pretty — string.

The air in her studio is stale. She opens a window, which sticks. Her own canvases look strange to her, like the photographs of friends from high school. Whatever passions once accrued to them seem far away, barely remembered. Her trees lean against the wall, clustered in groups or alone, but all unaware of her. Like the dress now lavishly spreading its splendor across her worktable, the trees have some inner life of their own of which she is not a part. They're not waiting for her to come back particularly. The end of winter, then spring, came and went, and the trees went on without her. If she left and didn't return for another season or two it wouldn't surprise Marina at all to find that the paintings had simply gone blank, the images migrated to a better artist's studio. Gazing at her own canvases, Marina wonders if she will ever paint another tree, or, indeed, anything.

What is she supposed to be doing? What task or feat? Marina gives the thread a little tug. The dress under her hands is rich, diaphanous, complicated. She could never make anything like it. She's become fluid with paint; with everything else, like sewing and cooking and gardening, she's clumsy, awkward. She used to love her semitransience — going from residency to short-term teaching post to fellowship — because it made her look terrific with a hot plate as opposed to hopeless in a regular kitchen. Marina quickly sheds her jeans and sweater and bra and zips herself into the dress. She adores the dress to an unreasonable degree. She can feel its excessive beauty on her skin even though she can't see herself in it. Her feet in their thick brown socks peek out from underneath the shimmering skirt. She clears a space on her worktable, finds a piece of clean drawing paper, and sits down on it. She dangles her legs in the glowing folds. Her shoulders feel naked. The stray thread at her side feels like a hand on a ticking clock.

Nan waits in line at Celestial Coffee. The meditative young man, today wearing a T-shirt with a rainbow on it, says to her when it's her turn, "Coffee, black, right?"

"No. Green tea."

"Right on," says the meditative young man. "Polyphenols."

"Yeah." Nan takes the cup. "Thanks." On her way to the store, she takes the lid off and blows on the tea in a perfunctory way. It's a foggy, cool summer morning. She doesn't think green tea ever gets that hot, it's too green, but blowing on it gives her the illusion that it's coffee. Less caffeine is supposed to help with the hot flashes, and it might, a little. She took a book about it home from the store.

"Hey," says Matthew. When Peta left to live in India for what she said would be the rest of her life, Matthew, her roommate, took over her job. He's plump, high-voiced, and very conscientious. "I sorted the mail."

"That's great, Matt. Did UPS come yet?"

"No. Should I call?"

"No, no. They'll be here." Nan surveys the store, which is placid in the morning light. Matt has a nice eye for displays and faceouts. The books look simultaneously scrubbed and brushed and tasty, ready to be taken home by the armload. The postcard rack is amusing and sensual. The New Arrivals table is up to date. Matthew told her brightly that he's wanted to work at a bookstore his entire life and, this morning, she can almost see what he means. The books appear every season, undaunted, persistent, shedding their boxes. Some are perennials, some annuals. It was good that conscientious Matthew was able to weed through them this spring, because she'd barely noticed what was coming in, even though she'd ordered them. "Did Christopher call?" She unwraps a piece of nicotine gum.

"Not yet. Do you want me to call there?" Matthew picks up the phone.

Nan laughs and hands Matthew a five. "Go buy us some muffins." The nicotine gum is as awful as ever. It never tastes any better.

Christopher usually calls in the morning before his shift in the kitchen starts. There's a lot of prep to do for twelve people, apparently much chopping of vegetables and peeling of garlic. He's not yet one of the ones who go to the store, but he doesn't seem to mind. The house, the small grassy yard, and the house dog, whose name is Bleach, are enough for him. He has recited the house routines to Nan until she knows them as well as he does: breakfast, kitchen prep, lunch, cleanup, group, free hour, dinner, television, lights out at ten. Tuesdays and Thursdays, Dr. Blanchard, the psychologist; every other Wednesday, Dr. Magathan, the psychopharmacologist. No food in the rooms. No roughhousing with Bleach, he has a bad leg. No hiding the remote. Sharps — razor blades, kitchen knives, scissors — are permitted, but counted every night. If you have a problem with another resident, bring it up in group. On Saturdays, the GED tutor comes to work with Christopher and Drew, who is twenty-nine. On Sunday mornings, you can go to church if you want, Julie will drive you. On this roster of rules and privileges, typed and photocopied and taped up in the hallways and kitchen and living room and TV room of New Day House, they have hung their lives.

Nan could call Christopher, but, carefully, she doesn't. Dr. Blanchard feels that it's better for Christopher to be the one who calls sometimes, who holds up his end of the connection, who understands that your mother and father and the other people who love you like to hear from you. What he calls "tasks of daily living" are important to Dr. Blanchard, who wears a hearing aid in his left ear; they are a running theme in his conversation.

Nan turns on the computer. Today is an ordering day, and there's a rep at three, and they've been withholding too much tax from Matthew's pay, she has to figure that out with Hal. ONWARD, says the screen saver, which Matthew changed for her. She throws away the piece of nicotine gum and drinks her green tea. It tastes bitter.

Hal makes the bed. The sheets are lilac, three-hundred-thread-count, and though they look quite lovely and ethereal pulled tightly over the mattress, Hal is sorry to erase the impression of Dan's body. Their nights together these days are rare, their days together rarer still. It seems clear that they've reached the end of the episode, they're simply telling the last beads now. They were connected by the crisis, but the crisis is past; it happens that way sometimes. Dan keeps saying he's going to go to Florida, but he hasn't done it yet. That will be the end. Hal fluffs a pillow in its soft lilac pillowcase. He tucks in the blue cotton coverlet all around. He should really put another blanket on the bed — it's summer, and he'll be cold, sleeping alone. Maybe he should repaint this room. He picks up his black leather backpack from the chair.

In Christopher's room, the fish tank is dry and clean. Morning light, uninterrupted, shines through it. Beneath the tank table is a cardboard box containing the filter, the heater, the pump, the thermometer, the hydrometer, a half-empty bag of salt mix and various other accoutrements. Hal means to donate it all before Christopher comes home, but that won't be anytime right away. Hal tries not to think too much about the money. It's still less, considerably less, than the hospital, but even with insurance New Day House will thin the College column. *Mira.* He has to focus on what's important. Howard from the aquarium store took care of things, as smooth as an undertaker, disappearing in his van with the lively shark neatly stowed inside in a large Styrofoam container. Hal misses the shark, a little bit, but there are other fish in the sea, and for the time being that's where they'll have to stay. He can't say he's sorry not to have to sacrifice live glass shrimp anymore. He never did get used to that. Really, it would have been better to thank Marina. She was just the catalyst. Since he got back, he feels that the passing world of ambition and desire is much less complicated than he once thought, but also that his skin, literally and figuratively, is thinner. He falls asleep early, worn out from the daily press of ordinary looking and touching. All he wants is to hold his son, whom he almost lost.

On the dining room table are Dan's cereal bowl, Dan's coffee cup. Dan, always polite, had jumped up to clear them, but Hal said, No, leave it. Now, keys in hand, Hal doesn't clear away Dan's dishes. When he closes the front door he likes knowing that Dan's bowl and cup are there on the table, that they'll be there when he gets home.

Drew and Christopher chop vegetables. A mound of carrots rises at Drew's place, a mound of potatoes at Christopher's.

"Nevada was pretty good," offers Drew. "Warm, cops don't hassle you too much, plenty of places to pitch a tent. There was a great Denny's near Reno where you could order one cup of coffee and sit all night."

"Yeah," Christopher says knowingly, as if he's been there. Drew's been so many places, seen so much, had such incredible hopes and dreams and experienced amazing coincidences. He's wiry, with long black sideburns and one drooping eye. He knows about all kinds of machines.

"See, the thing is, you have to get in with the locals. Then they'll look out for you. I had this one guy over at the gas station could tell you *everything* that was going on in that town. Fix any car on earth, too. Good man." Drew crunches on a carrot.

"I like the woods." The world briefly tilts, then rights itself again. They told him the vertigo might go away, but it hasn't. The tips of his fingers and the tips of his toes hurt. He wiggles his hands and feet, which sometimes works.

"Woods are good, too." Drew crosses his arms, chewing. "Got to be careful of snakes, though."

"Yeah. And bears. Probably you should have a gun. Do you know how to shoot a gun?"

"Used to build 'em." Drew picks up his knife and begins chopping again. "I built guns in Alaska." Drew scratches a spot on his neck that's already raw. They've had Drew on a few different medications; the current one, he says, makes him itch.

Bleach trots into the room, swinging his bad rear leg, and sits down next to Christopher's chair. Christopher rubs Bleach's ears, then drops a piece of potato onto the floor for him. Bleach sniffs it, picks it up in his mouth, trots lopsidedly over to the stove with it, and spits it out again.

"No dog will eat a potato," says Drew authoritatively. "Except if it's a french fry."

"Yeah, I know." Bleach returns to Christopher's chair. "I just wanted to see what he'd do." Bleach hasn't spoken to Christopher since that once, a few days after he arrived, but Christopher hasn't entirely given up hope.

"Did I tell you about my six Mississippi uncles? All of them river rats?"

"Yeah, but go on." Christopher sweeps the carrots into one big aluminum bowl, the potatoes into another, and sets both bowls on the counter. He gets the big wooden bowl of garlic and puts it on the table between him and Drew.

Drew turns melancholy. The drooping eye seems to droop more deeply. "Nah. Never mind."

"Come on." Christopher thought the uncles were from Alabama, but it doesn't matter.

"I think I feel too sad today to do that." Drew stops peeling garlic to take a folded piece of newspaper from his jeans pocket. "Chris, what's this word? Where I put a star."

"*Realignment.* It means that something — okay, here it's political parties, it's in Germany — something where it was set up one way, now it's moved and it's going to go another way. Like . . . tires, right? People realign tires."

Drew looks at the piece of newspaper. "So they roll straight."

"Exactly." Christopher feels proud. He likes it when he can tell Drew something he doesn't already know. "Do you know who PJ Harvey is?"

"P. T. who? Is that a cartoon?"

"No, she sings. She's a singer."

"Is she pretty?"

"Yes." An image of Tamara, unbidden, flits across Christopher's mind. They won't talk to him about her except to say that she's back home with her family and he's not allowed to call her. Ever. He hasn't told Drew about her yet. He doesn't say anything about her in group, either. He keeps her, small, whole, and smiling, inside him; he talks to her in his mind at night. "She's very pretty but in a way that's hard to explain."

"Uh-huh." Drew is unperturbed. His melancholy gone, he cracks garlic skins efficiently. "I know the type."

In the early evening, Marina helps Nan around the garden. She weeds this and that while Nan mulches.

Nan says, "Where's the rake?"

Marina gestures. "Over there. In the grass."

Nan retrieves the rake, tidying the mulch. "Do you think we should put in tomatoes?"

"I don't know." Marina reaches back to the fence for a weed. She thinks it's a weed, though it's awfully pretty. Figure, ground: she's never been as good at distinguishing those as she should be. The evening air is nice but chilly. "Maybe we should go to the desert this summer."

Nan is bent over, peering at the tomato stalks. "Maybe. Depends."

Marina sits back on her heels. Everything always depends, depends on a seed or a shoelace — she reties one of hers that's come undone — or a thread. She never has liked that gloomy nun statue, either. She's had her fill of nuns. "Did you talk to him today?"

"Yeah, he sounded good." Nan's feet are planted firmly in the earth as she bends, inspecting leaves. "He's responded so incredibly well to this drug, I think he's more scared right now than anything else. I was thinking we might get him a dog when he comes back."

"Maybe," says Marina. She pats the grass beside her. "Come sit down a minute."

Nan stretches out beside Marina in the grass. She's a little sweaty, her forehead damp. After a minute, Nan puts her head in Marina's lap. Marina blows lightly on Nan's face. It is a beautiful face to her, even now. Its lines are like a pattern drawn over and over in water, constant, flowing. Nan's skin is the skin she knows best. Marina kisses Nan on her sweaty forehead. People do go on.

"I'm sorry," Nan says, eyes closed. "I was out of my mind." She takes Marina's hand and kisses it. "Your hand has gotten so soft," she says regretfully. "Listen." She twists her head to look at Marina. "I needed to save my son."

Marina pushes a bit of hair behind Nan's ear. "And you did." It's her own fault, from one angle. She never tires of wishing for moments like this one, when the wild unicorn rests its strange chesspiece head in her lap. Shiloh is no different, only younger. "I'm sorry, too."

Nan doesn't ask Marina what she might have to be sorry about. The unsaid words are what they have, in a way — a slender sequence of them, their value lying precisely in their not being spoken. Marina's mother and father stayed together the same way, wrapped round and round each other with invisible thread. Everyone was just too tired to keep fighting. Sitting in the garden, Nan resting so docilely with her in the grass, Marina sees a kind of grace there, where before she had seen only deceit. What is love but a series of small decisions made under impossible circumstances? One by one, they add up to years. The stone nun isn't so bad, really. The tree that's never flowered or plummed is still there. The two of them are the figures; everything else is ground.

"I want these hands rough again," says Nan, rubbing one of Marina's between her two small, strong ones. "I don't know you with these soft hands."

"Don't you?" says Marina.

Dr. Blanchard cups his bad ear. It's a mystery to Christopher why he sometimes appears with the hearing aid and sometimes without it. Drew says Dr. Blanchard is faking the whole thing, it's just a kind of disguise, like the bow tie. Christopher isn't sure.

"Think of a tree," responds Dr. Blanchard. "No, scratch that. Think of a river. Are you thinking of a river?"

Christopher nods, not thinking of a river.

"What does it look like?"

Christopher is startled. "I don't know. It's deep, I guess."

"Okay, so this deep river —"

"That's not what I asked you," interrupts Christopher. "I asked you why this happened to me." He shakes his head to clear a wave of dizziness.

"I'm trying to tell you. So, there's a river, it's wending along —"

"No!" Christopher jumps up. "*Fuck the river.* I don't want to hear about the river."

Dr. Blanchard looks up, cupping his ear. "Could you sit down?"

Christopher sits down, frustrated.

Dr. Blanchard begins again. "When you were homeless —"

"I wasn't homeless. We had this great cabin."

"Your girlfriend almost died. Your father told me if they had gotten there hours later, maybe less, she would have been dead."

Christopher hates this particular line of reasoning. He says what he always says. "But she didn't die."

"Why didn't she die?"

"Because I took care of her. I wrapped her leg up."

"No." Dr. Blanchard is patient. "She didn't die because she got the medicine she needed." He says these words as if he's never said them before. "She had an accident. That's all. It's like if the river —"

"Aaagh!" Christopher jumps up again. "Why don't you answer my question? Do you think I'm an idiot?"

"Christopher, you have to sit down."

Christopher sits down. "I have another question."

Dr. Blanchard cups his ear. "Shoot."

"What if there was a kind of person who had, like, skin and eyes and ears and a nose and everything, but there was just maybe *one different* part, one extra thing that he could do, and it wasn't a big problem, it was just this . . . like being psychic. People pay other people to be psychic. It's not a problem."

"She could be dead." Dr. Blanchard fixes his pale blue eyes on Christopher's.

"But she *isn't.*" Christopher feels extraordinarily frustrated. Any minute now, Dr. Blanchard is going to go back to the thing with the river. "I would *never, ever* have let her die. It was just because of the other stuff."

"So you would have gone into town and gotten an ambulance for her? Told doctors? The police? Her parents?"

Christopher is miserable. He's explained a thousand times. Aren't they supposed to be concentrating on the future? "There were —"

"You didn't do it, Chris. You didn't help her."

After his ridiculous session that told him nothing, Christopher goes in search of Bleach. Julie is sitting in the living room with Pete and Edna, playing Scrabble. Drew is at his job at Kinko's. Mary is at her job at the Gap. Miranda is at her job at Ben and

Jerry's. Michael and Lucia, the other two counselors, are off at some kind of training: How to Annoy Crazy People, maybe.

"Hey, Chris," calls Julie, "want to play?"

"No." He wanders around until he finds Bleach sitting on the porch, watching the almost nonexistent traffic on the quiet street. "Julie, I'm on the porch." He can see the three of them through the window, happy with their little wooden tiles. Julie, who is pretty, waves.

Bleach is a large dog only in spirit. He pants, smiling through his whiskers, one white paw hanging over the top porch step. Christopher sits down next to him. "What kind of dog are you, huh?" He scratches Bleach's ears. "Are you a freak? Are you a psychic dog? Are you a psycho dog?" Christopher picks up Bleach's left ear and stares down into it. The whorls of Bleach's left ear are pink, with delicate nodules and concavities and the tender dim chute that leads into his brain. "What's going on in there?"

Bleach licks Christopher on the eye.

It would be so cool if Bleach would say just one more thing, give him a clue. What Bleach said the first time — *Patagonia* — wasn't all that helpful, but Christopher thinks that's because he hasn't cracked Bleach's code yet. Why would Bleach be talking about a kind of clothing? That fleecy stuff. A man with black hair walks by, and Bleach stands up, his bad leg suspended, barking indecipherably.

"It's okay," Christopher reassures the black-haired man. "He won't hurt you."

The man looks with interest at the house and walks on. There's just that one little NEW DAY sign, but still, it sounds like a cult. Bleach sits down, ears up. His fur is slightly abrasive on Christopher's fingertips, but Christopher ignores it. He's disappointed because he did really want to know why. Dr. Magathan doesn't mind telling him why this, why that, how many milligrams, what the funny feeling in his eyes could be. Dr. Blanchard likes to play games: think of a river. Who cares? Bleach is the only one who knows the truth, which is that something awful happened somewhere. First the world got so much better, brighter, and bigger, then it got incredibly worse. It wasn't anything like a river. If he could find his drawing — where *is* it, anyway? — he could explain, he could show them.

This quiet street is so retarded. From here, if he were allowed to, he could walk to his mother's house or his father's house or Tamara's house in less than half an hour. He doesn't want to go to any of those places. He wants to go somewhere else, far away, where it's quiet and there aren't so many people in his face all the time. He wants to live among trees.

He lifts Bleach's right ear. It looks just the same as the one on the other side: the whorls, the nodules, the dim chute. *"Bonjour,"* he says to Bleach's right ear, experimenting to see if Bleach talks another language in that one.

Bleach licks him on the eye.

Results inconclusive, Christopher writes invisibly, on an invisible chart.

Hal brings Christopher a book.

"What's this?" asks Christopher. "*The Long and Winding Road.*"

"It's about someone kind of like you," says Hal. "I think he was much worse off, actually, but he did experience some of the same things, and this is the story of how he got better. He was a Beatles fan."

"How old is this book?"

"Well, he is older than you, but it's not that old a book. He's much better now." Hal smiles encouragingly, making himself sit back on the plaid sofa. He doesn't know if he'll ever succeed in liking New Day House, though he keeps trying. If only they'd been able to take Christopher back at Pacific. New Day, with its afghans and posted rules and old cooking smells, feels like junkies and Vietnam vets and hopelessness. He can't stand that guy Drew with the sideburns who looks like he just got out of either jail or the carnival or both. That limping dog. Yet he reminds himself that this place is better, this place is progress. He couldn't bear ever to see Chris again the way he was at Walnut Creek. It's miraculous that Chris is only puffy, pale, and faintly stiff in his movements, rocking in the rocking chair in New Day's living room, his bare, healed toes tapping the floor. It's miraculous that the worst thing that can be said about him at the moment is that he seems to be growing a mustache and beard. A layer of blond fuzz is sprouting on his upper lip and jawline. Hal fears that in some way he's imitating Drew. With any luck, Drew will leave soon, graduate to living on his own, preferably in another state, in a place where there are no telephones.

Christopher rocks, holding the book in his lap. "Listen," he says. "I don't cry anymore."

"Maybe you're not sad," offers Hal. Christopher looks at him skeptically. "Let's ask Dr. Blanchard about it."

"Whatever."

"In the book," explains Hal, "the guy talks about his experience as being like a road, like a journey — though you know the drugs then were so much worse, don't be scared by that stuff — and he talks about what was helpful and what wasn't, what kind of people he met. He draws, too. Some of his drawings are in there."

Christopher, with an obstreperous expression, opens the book to the plates of drawings. He sighs. "They're all roads," he says querulously.

Hal doesn't know what to make of this complaint. "Right. That's what I said. He felt like he was on a long road. But he's good now, his life is good."

"Can he cry?"

"It doesn't say."

Christopher closes the book, rocking up onto his toes and staying there. He wiggles his hands. Hal knows the compulsive wiggling isn't New Day's fault, but it's just part of the whole thing. Why *doesn't* he cry? And why must they have rocking chairs?

Christopher angrily scratches at his blond jawline fuzz. "That is just *bullshit.* Nothing is *like* anything. No one is understanding me. I don't want to hear about some loser who listened to the Beatles a thousand years ago." He hands Hal back *The Long and Winding Road.* "How are my fish?"

Hal blanches. He had promised himself that he wouldn't lie because Christopher is a person and the fish were his and he has a right to know. When Hal's father was dying, they didn't tell the old man how bad off he really was until it was almost too late. Hal still hasn't entirely forgiven his mother for that. Hal says, "Oh, they're great. One of the angelfish died. But the rest are in great shape."

"The blueface?"

"No, uh, the other one. The blueface looked sad for a while, but it seems to have recovered." He hands the book back to Christopher. "You keep this, okay? You might want to read it later."

"I doubt it." Christopher takes the book politely, as if Hal were handing him a Christmas sweater with a big garish Santa on it. He holds the book, closed, in his lap. He closes his eyes. Dr. Magathan has said that the fatigue will diminish eventually. Looking at his son in the rocking chair, Hal thinks, Who is this man? Hal has read *The Long and Winding Road,* which had the virtue of depressing him minutely less than the other books he's read on the topic; in the end — after various schemes to bring down the U.S. government and problems with people who were really robots and writing constitutions for several countries that had not requested new ones — the hero went into the family business, a travel agency in Schenectady. He wrote that he liked helping other people on their journeys. Yet another reason never to go to Schenectady, Hal thought, but what if Christopher could become a C.P.A.? Cooper and Cooper. Or Cooper and Ashby-Cooper, to keep Nan happy. Three generations of accountants. It happened all the time, not only curses running in families, but gifts. Christopher always did very well in math. Hal was surprised to find that he liked the idea. It could be that their stories, father and son, weren't so disparate, after all. Hal, too, had had his wild illusions, his own long and winding road.

As if he has read Hal's mind, Christopher opens his eyes and says, "You know what I've decided I want to be?"

"No, what?" Hal is pleased to see Christopher not rocking, both feet on the floor. Pretty soon, they'll be able to sign him out for day trips. They could take a walk together to the barber.

"A cop."

Nan watches Marina get dressed. The little teaching job seems to be benefiting Marina, it was nice of James to hook it up for her. Just a figure drawing class, but Marina says it's helpful to go back to basics and the students are good. The money helps. Some days, she says, she almost remembers wanting to work. Almost. Equally lovely, however, to Nan is the development that, though the job doesn't require it, Marina has taken up the practice of dressing for class. At school, she wears a smock over her outfit. Maybe it's a response to all those years of wrecked studio clothes, the stained jeans and T-shirts and sweatshirts, thrift-store detritus suitable for dust and paint and stretching canvas, for climbing ladders and hauling things up the old church stairs.

Now, taking her time, Marina dresses. Nan rests on the bed, watching. She had forgotten this particular pleasure. Nearly as enjoyable as the sight itself is remembering that she can enjoy it, that there is time now for ordinary, pleasurable sights such as this. As a child, because she was the only girl, she was the only one who got to watch her mother get dressed, who got to hand her things and zip her up and run into the cloud of her perfume after she left. In the mirror of her mother's dressing table, they were together, her mother applying the concealer, Nan leaning against the elaborate gilded curve of the white headboard, carefully keeping her sneakers off the pink bedspread. What, Nan wondered even then, was the secret of that femininity? What did her mother think about all day?

This morning, a towel lies on the plain white sheets of the plain wooden bed. Marina, her hair damp and curling, puts cream on her legs, her arms, her belly. There are good muscles in her arms and along her back, but to Nan they seem only to be in service to the curve of Marina's waist, like a vase holding a flower. She's long-waisted, long-necked; in the middle of her back is the pucker of a scar where a mole was once removed. Marina's ass is pale, low-slung, and no more taut than riding her bicycle requires. She's not a gym-goer. Her feet are small. Her legs are somewhat short, but slender, with a slight bow to them. Her breasts have retained the roundness of one who hasn't nursed a baby; Nan is proud of them. She is proud of Marina's small nipples, of the dark rose of their aureoles, that suckle only her. For Nan, Marina's breasts are like buried treasure; she'd veil them if she could. While each part of Marina's body is beautiful to Nan, she feels that they all meet and part at that curve of Marina's waist, that Marina's entire body begins and ends there, on that bend. There has always seemed to be something self-contained about Marina's body, as discreet as a leopard. If Marina had wanted to have children, it would have been all right with Nan, but she hasn't. The warmth of her body is singular, private. Their secret. That stupid girl, Nan thinks smugly, might have been able to watch Marina get undressed, probably quickly, but she never, or rarely, had the privilege of watching Marina get dressed, slowly.

Marina puts her hands on her bare hips. "Did they say it might rain?"

"I don't know."

Marina takes a bra and a pair of underwear out of the top drawer of the dresser. "I don't think it will rain." She puts on a pair of dark gray socks. From the closet, she draws a loose, silk, light gray blouse of professorial modesty. She puts it on and buttons it. "To here?" she asks Nan. "Or here? We should get a mirror in this room sometime."

"There." Nan points to the higher button.

The hem of the blouse skims Marina's thighs. She is forever buying things just a little too large so that her collars are always slightly too wide, her sleeves slightly too long. She rolls up one sleeve of the blouse, then the other, to right below the elbow. She tousles her damp hair, drying it. She puts on a pair of black trousers, zips them up, holding the blouse at the waistline. "These?"

"The other ones," says Nan.

Marina steps out of the black trousers and into a different, wide-legged pair of charcoal trousers. She tucks in the blouse. She buttons the trousers. "These are better."

"Yes."

Marina slides a black belt with a silver buckle through the belt loops and buckles it. Except for her hands and forearms, her face and throat, she is entirely covered, a smoky column of silk and light wool, as if she had sketched herself. Nan thinks of Marina's body beneath her clothes. "C'mere," says Nan. "You have a thread." She pulls the stray, or it could be a strand of Marina's hair, from the back of the blouse's collar.

"Am I tucked in right in back?" Marina looks over her shoulder.

"Yes." Nan pats Marina on her charcoal hip. "You're perfect."

Marina finds her boots and steps into them, zipping up one, then the other. "I have to meet with a student for a little while after class." She makes a face. "Just for an hour. I promised."

"Yeah, okay." Nan, stung by doubt, maintains an even non-expression. "Do you want to have dinner?"

"Oh, definitely." Marina gives her hair a shake, taps her boot heels on the floor. She picks up the damp towel. "It won't take that long."

Smoothing her trousers so that they don't wrinkle, Marina kneels on the narrow wooden bench, hands folded, forehead pressed against her hands. She avoids looking at the altar. She doesn't really know how to do this, it's not as if she ever paid attention, the nuns always hated her. Still. She tries to clear her mind of that day's class, the lines and curves and angles, the scratch of pencils, the foot of the model none of them could get right. Its excessive length had led them all astray. Her muscles ache, as if she's been teaching dance for the last three hours. Sometimes she does, in fact, literally move their arms and fingers with hers: *Here. And here.* She tries not to take the charcoal from anyone's hand. Shiloh isn't in the class; she's already far past these students, past ungainly parts and well into the fluid dream of the whole. Shiloh left the gesso splotch in the center of the fresco; she likes the damage of the splotch. She seems to feel that it's a kind of tattoo. A digital image of the splotched fresco is going to be the cover of Wet Mink's first CD, which they're going to finish this summer. Nicholas knows someone who's going to help them distribute it. Shiloh promised to erase Marina's face altogether.

Marina prays, or tries to pray, more fervently. The large foot of the model intrudes. The church is cool and dark, the wooden pews scratched. Two women sitting up near the front are speaking in whispers. "Ay, Dios," clucks one softly. Marina wonders what God they're invoking. She imagines that it's a daily one, worn, like the wood of the pews, as familiar as the beads of the rosaries they're loosely turning. Central, constant, barely noticed. Her own God seems a little more mercurial than that. She's not sure that she has the right location equipment. Maybe she should be opening her arms in a V above her head, standing on a deserted hilltop at the full of the moon. But she doesn't have time to find that hill, or wait for the moon. She's in Oakland, and she wants to get home in time for dinner. There is, of course, a smudge of charcoal on her blouse. With an effort, she once again clears the large foot of the model from her mind.

Tapping her thumbs against her forehead, Marina prays for no more lives. She had a few before Nan, though those passed much more quickly and lightly, butterfly lives. She prays not to slip the bonds of this one, heavy though they sometimes are. She prays, indeed, for them to get heavier, to hold her as tightly as possible. She prays for Nan to hold her, and for Hal to hold her, and for Christopher to hold her, twining around her with their six arms, like Shiva. Marina offers up her own painting in exchange for just this one life. She offers her hands. She offers her eyes.

Christopher, bored, lies on the living room floor idly turning the pages of *The Long and Winding Road*. The rug is gross. Pete probably didn't really vacuum it, even though he said he did. Dinner is soon, but not soon enough. He can't believe the guy put his sorry-ass drawings in the book. Still, Christopher thinks gloomily, at least this guy has his own book. Something of his own, that no one can take away from him or change behind his back. Nearby, Edna, with that wild look in her eye, is knitting and humming.

"What time is it?" asks Edna.

"Quarter to six."

Edna nods, humming.

Christopher turns a page with his elbow to see if he can. He kind of can. Underneath his elbow, he sees the word *Patagonia*. It's in a sentence: "That was the spring that I met up with some hippies in Patagonia." Christopher can't believe it. Patagonia is a place?

"Edna, where's Patagonia?"

She considers. "I don't know." She resumes her knitting. It's long, whatever she's making.

Bleach walks in, sits down, and looks Christopher in the eye. Christopher begins to tremble. Before Patagonia was a brand, it was a *place*. He would have known that if he'd just thought about it a little harder; he really has to pay more attention. He flips intently through the pages in the book; it seems to be somewhere in South America. People there wear serapes. Maybe that's where the awful thing happened, maybe that's the source of the awful thing, like the epicenter of an earthquake. Is he supposed to go there? Or did Bleach mean something else? He stares at the dog, who has gone to sleep.

"It's six, isn't it?" says Edna, laying aside her needles. "Chris, isn't it six?"

Hal decides to woo. It comes to him in a second, effortlessly, like the sun coming out or a bird flying past the window. He is buying sweat socks on his way home from work when it happens, swish, plunk, there it is: he will woo. After the last year, why not woo? His regular heart is skeptical, but his orchid heart agrees.

"Twenty-two fifty," says the girl behind the counter.

Hal gives her the money and takes his bag of squishy white sweat socks with green toes. Leaving the sports store, he is confident and happy. He buys a bottle of Merlot from the wine store that he calls the wine museum. He goes into the florist and buys six violet roses, two birds of paradise, a handful of irises, baby's breath, and a large daisy. He leaves the florist with his bouquet, which is sizable and ungainly, wrapped in silver paper. Ducking into a drugstore, he picks up a glasses string for Nan; she'll never get it for herself.

A few doors down from the drugstore is a store that sells clever baubles and trinkets from France. None of them is quite right, though. They're expensive, but they look cheap. Hal leaves that store. He passes a pet store where puppies are sleeping in the window, but he can't give so aggressive a present. It would be too obvious that Hal is really the puppy, wagging his tail. In another store that sells slightly less clever, but better, baubles, Hal finds a smooth vase made from horn. He's always felt that horn is good luck, it's just his personal superstition. And Dan is, in fact, a Capricorn. He buys the vase. Carrying the sweat socks, the Merlot, the bouquet, the glasses string, and the rather heavy horn vase, Hal is beginning to feel burdened, but he isn't done. The gifts for Dan are his first wooing notes, and he wants to strike the right ones. He wants to show Dan that he understands him, to seduce Dan with recognition.

He wanders up and down the street, in and out of stores. Cream-colored chaps: no, that's so eighties. Kilim-covered bookends: no. A hookah (same store): no. A green bird in a cage made of crystal teardrops: no. Cashmere everything: no. A magnificent encyclopedia: almost. The man selling the magnificent encyclopedia flutters the pages enticingly. "Everything under the sun is in here," he coos. Hal declines. The bag with the vase in it is wearing a ridge in his hand. He's getting hungry. A boxed set of Mozart arias: no. He begins to despair; he's about to fail at giving a gift for the second time in one week. Perhaps a good shirt? That would be a mistake. He shifts the bag with the vase to the other hand. Toward the end of the block is a little place packed with chinoiserie: vases and jade, fat Buddhas. Hal roams the aisles with his packages, using two fingers to pick up and put down lacquered and ivory objets d'art, all costing more than they should. The bouquet in silver paper threatens the delicate items on the higher shelves.

"We're closing," says the young Chinese woman behind the counter. She leans on the glass, waiting.

At last. Hal spreads open a silk fan. It's black, with black wooden ribs. On the outside of the fan is a heron in full flight, its delicate feet extended, poised over a much smaller hill with a river winding into it. There is also a round moon. The inside of the fan is sheer night-colored silk. The heron and the moon can be seen, like a transparency, on the other side. He hurries to the counter to buy it.

Later, as he drives below Market to Dan's apartment, his wrapped presents on the back seat, Hal turns on the radio. Someone is wanting someone else who doesn't want her, apparently he wants somebody else, but the beat is brisk and the first someone doesn't really sound all that unhappy. When Hal gets to Dan's building, he sees that Dan's lights are on. Dan is home.

For a second, Hal almost turns back. He is silly with his flowers and his fan and his vase, piled up in the back seat of a station wagon. Wooing is a power trip, essentially. He should go back into therapy. In the rearview mirror, his presents are hopelessly lovely, like girls waiting to be asked to dance. There are too many of them. He can barely carry them all.

And yet he does, though he has to ring Dan's apartment with his elbow, holding the fan in his teeth.

Dr. Blanchard passes by Christopher in the hall. "Hello," he calls out. "See you tomorrow!" He isn't wearing his hearing aid. Christopher makes a note of that. He's very excited, now that he understands a little bit. The first step was to begin a new drawing. He found some paper in the kitchen. Then he drew a picture of what could be Patagonia, he had to estimate, with some lines coming out of it for energy, and Bleach's head connected to the lines. He and Tamara had thought it was Fiji, but it wasn't, it was Patagonia. The next time he sees her, he'll tell her that. He wishes he had something better than a pencil; he'll ask Marina tonight. He looked up *Patagonia* in the old paperback dictionary by the Scrabble set, but *Patagonia* wasn't in there; he made a special note of the fact that it wasn't in there. Now, turning toward the wall, he writes down that Dr. Blanchard isn't wearing his hearing aid, and the date and time. Julie, wearing her black hair in two braids banded both at the top and bottom with red rubber bands, comes by to remind him that they're all going to the park.

On the way, Drew pokes him. "I fucked her," he tells Christopher in a low voice, nodding toward Julie.

Christopher looks at Julie. It could be true. He looks at Drew, who is grinning and scratching the raw spot on his neck. The raw spot is worse. They sent him home from Kinko's. He makes a note, mentally, of what Drew said, though he doesn't think it's that important and he might not even write it down. He wiggles his fingers, blinks some of the dizziness away. "Isn't Dr. Magathan coming today?"

"Next week," says Drew, keeping his eyes proprietarily on Julie's ass.

The park is very random. Christopher checks it for patterns, but he doesn't see any in the grass or the trees or the distribution of patches of sun. There doesn't seem to be any particular order to the people, either, or to who is eating and who isn't. No bears. He sits down on the grass, feeling fairly relaxed about the situation. It is a nice day.

Edna empties a paper bag and puts it over her head.

Julie removes the bag. "It's okay, Edna. We're all here together." She picks up Edna's sandwich from the grass and hands it to her. Edna puts it in the pocket of the winter coat she always wears, though that pocket already seems to be pretty full. Edna crams in the sandwich. Christopher can't believe that Edna has kids when she's such a nut — she really does, they come to see her, four grown women with Edna's eyes. What kind of mother could she have been? Where is her husband? He can't imagine his father, or even his mother, in a skanky coat like that, hiding from the air in a paper bag. On Mother's Day, Edna's daughters all brought her the same bouquet of flowers. They must have gone to the same store. After they left, she threw all the bouquets away.

"Are you going to eat that?" Drew has designs on Christopher's roast beef sandwich.

Christopher considers, then gives Drew half. Drew is always hungry.

Pete, who reminds him of one of his tangs, is holding his flat face to the sun. Edna unbuttons her coat. Julie sits cross-legged, eating her sandwich and writing on a pad, her black hair shining. Seeing Christopher looking at her, she smiles, then returns to her pad. He almost takes his list out of his pocket to show her, then doesn't. His half of a sandwich tastes good, and he wishes he hadn't given Drew the other half, but it's too late. Drew has already moved on to the cookies.

"Have you ever been to Patagonia?" asks Christopher.

Drew squints. "Patagonia? Oh, sure. That's in Texas."

Drew probably didn't fuck Julie, either. Christopher is relieved. The grass under his hands is soft. The cookies are good and sweet, with lots of chocolate chips.

A tall woman with cornrows and long legs sitting nearby says to a man in a baseball cap, "Tiara is not going to have it together by next week. No way."

The man, who is lying down on the grass, says, "We don't really need her to do the presentation. We could do it today if we had to."

"I don't know about that," says the tall woman. She looks at her watch. They gather their things and leave the park. Christopher watches them cross the street, then turn a corner, the woman striding easily with her long legs. She seems as if she would know about Patagonia. He should have asked her. Would Tamara like Patagonia? He'll have to find that out, too. He hopes it's a warm place. Tam likes warm places. This time, though, he might have to be the one to get her, to pack what they'll need. They'll definitely have to get a new tent.

Christopher finishes his cookies and stands up. "I'm going to walk around the park," he tells Julie.

"Sure. Great day, isn't it?"

He can see written on her pad the words *Clozapine, atypical,* and *compensated.* Some numbers and slashes. It seems to him that her notes might be a clue; he memorizes the numbers, but not in a way that Julie can tell what he's doing. He blinks twice, to set them.

The park is quite small. Christopher paces it slowly, paying close attention. A purple bench. A white plastic bag on the grass; Christopher puts the plastic bag in a trash can. Two birds twittering near a stick. *Why?* says his left foot. *Why?* says his right foot. And why him? And what next? There are stores across the street from the park, and a café, and people in the café. He could be in there, too, free and easy, if someone would only tell him what it was all about. He counts the women and men: about equal, no help there. It's very frustrating. If he were a cop, he could find out a lot more. He'd have all that computer stuff they have, and a gun, too. But why hasn't Bleach said anything else? And what if he isn't there when they get back?

Halfway around the park, Christopher sits down on a purple bench that's just like the other one. The bench is warm. Julie waves; he waves back. His fingertips aren't hurting him at the moment. Sometimes these days, he gets a little tired. He remembers Dr. Friend talking to him about stress, how stressed did he feel today? The next day? The next day? Dr. Blanchard asks him that, too, cupping his ear to hear the answer. Maybe they know each other. He asks himself how stressed he feels, then waits. He doesn't have to cup his ear. About halfway, he decides. Of course, he could be much less stressed if someone would give him a straight answer for once. It's a sad day when a dog tells you more than your own parents.

Christopher grips the warm purple slats of the bench. He takes out his piece of paper, writes down the numbers he saw on Julie's pad. Taken together, the facts he has so far don't add up to much. The only really good thing on the paper is the drawing of Bleach's head. Marina would like that part. The sky over the park, over the city, is vast and calm. He imagines himself floating there, looking down on everything and understanding it all, finally.

A yellow ball with blue stars lands on the bench next to Christopher. He picks it up. A few feet away, a small Asian boy in a fuzzy red jacket laughs and jumps in a circle, as if Christopher has told an excellent joke. The Asian man with the boy holds up his hands for Christopher to throw the ball back. Christopher tosses the ball to the man, but just as the ball leaves his hands he glances at the fuzzy red jacket of the boy. Fear tightens around him, a fear he doesn't quite understand yet. But he knows enough to be very afraid of what he sees. On the boy's red jacket, in bold white letters, it says *Patagonia*.

Nan salts the chicken salad while Marina sets the table. Marina is wearing a sleek black dress that Nan likes; she likes Marina's hair pinned back that way, too. Somehow it seems more silver, elegant, brushed close against her head.

"How was it today?" asks Nan, stirring the salad. She tastes it, peppers it. Better.

"I'm going to have to make a no cell phone rule," says Marina. "One of them was actually talking to his friend in another class — poli sci, I think. Can you believe that? Between the cell phones and the headphones, I could lose my mind." She gets three glasses out of the cabinet. "I thought maybe it was just the summer kids, but James said they're all like that now."

"Different generation." Nan puts the chicken salad on the table. Heat rises to her face. She sweats. "Can you open the door?"

Marina slides open the glass door for her. The cool from the garden rushes in, soothingly. That might be the major crop she's growing out there these days: cool green for her mercurial system. Nan finds it funny to imagine that some of the women she slept with in her life are probably doing the same thing, rushing to roll down car windows or throw open doors, switch on fans. So much for heat.

"Someone fell through for the fall. A little bit more advanced class. James asked if I wanted it." Marina surveys the table. "Do we have any wine?"

"Hal said he'd bring some. So do you?"

Marina rubs her arms, staring out at the garden. "I don't know. Maybe. I mean, I should take it, it's a pretty good gig."

"You don't have to." Nan puts the bread on the table. She's still too hot. Marina looks cool, black and silver against the glass; she's years from this internal leaping tiger. The bare backs of her knees are delicate. Does Marina love her anymore? Nan puts the butter next to the bread. "Are you hungry?"

"Sure. Can I close this now?"

Nan nods, sweating. She's starving. She wishes Hal would hurry up. "Are you going to your studio tomorrow?"

"No," says Marina shortly. Then, surprisingly, she slides her hands up Nan's sleeves, pulls Nan close, closer, almost too tight. "You're an oven." Her cool fingers touch Nan's shoulder blades. She presses her pale cheek against Nan's flushed one. "I love you, Nan."

Nan feels deeply afraid. The heat rushes away, like water running down a drain. "I love you, too."

"Ah," says Hal, appearing in the doorway with a bottle of wine. "Marriage."

A while later, over peach pie, Hal says, "I don't want him to get stuck there. *Halfway* means 'halfway *to* somewhere.'"

"Where?" asks Marina, tapping with her fork at her uneaten crust. Though she did, Nan noticed, pick out all the sweet peaches.

"Listen, he could still go to college." Nan sips her mint tea. It tastes like boiled paper. "Not this year, obviously, not with his class, but it's not out of the question."

"It's true," Hal agrees. Since Christopher got back, Nan has been struck by how much he and Hal resemble each other. Their foreheads are identical; their voices have much the same timbre. They are the same height. Hal continues, "Dr. Blanchard said he thought Chris could handle it, eventually. I wanted to talk about it with Chris, but Blanchard said to wait."

"You know, though, there's still the Tamara problem," says Nan. "He was asking us about her the other night."

"It was hard," says Marina.

"Lord." Hal looks grave. "He didn't say anything about that to me. If he goes anywhere near that girl, they're going to shoot him."

A silence falls over the table with its half-eaten pie, its familiar mismatched mugs. The one time Tamara's parents permitted Nan to see the girl in the hospital, Tamara folded her hands over her stomach in the blue and white gown with the knowing expression of someone who had fucked and fucked the son of the penitent, exhausted mother standing in front of her. Tamara wouldn't speak a word, like a prisoner of war.

"He still loves her," says Marina. "Is that so crazy?"

After Hal leaves, Nan tells Marina to go ahead up, she'll take care of the dishes. Marina's slender black form, her bare legs, ascend the stairs. Nan rinses a plate, puts it in the dishwasher. Rinses another. *Still loves her.* So she *is* back with the stupid girl who is . . . what? Demanding. Complaining. No: being lovely, as smooth as silk. Consoling. Murmuring. Nan rinses a glass and sets it on the upper rack. She won't even try to compete with a murmuring girl, there's no percentage in that. She's no murmurer. And what can it matter, anyway, some stupid girl, after what they've been through in the last year? It seems so irrelevant, like a soda commercial. She can't save Marina from herself. She just barely saved Christopher, though she isn't sure for what, or if she really did. Nan lays the salad tongs in with the glasses. She wishes Christopher weren't quite so handsome. Even at this age, love's choices baffle her. What she had wanted to say to Tamara, as to her mother, was unsayable: *Girl, he almost killed you.* But love, or something, is not only deaf, but mute. Nan puts the forks in the machine, tines up. She feels as if she's spent her whole life crashing into dark forests after love. She's done with questing, with tracking. This time, let love walk out of the trees to her.

Shiloh is aggressively scraping the damp paint from the canvas. Aqua, lavender, and rich black are all over the floor in splats and swirls. Shiloh, in her sports bra and running shorts and peaked knit hat, is happy, scraping and tossing, stepping in the paint on the floor, giving a little shake with her plush hips now and then.

Some music is playing in her space, very low; the Russian revolutionaries and their pig aren't next door today.

"I thought that one had some interesting ideas in it," Marina says, sitting with her back to the fresco, with its gesso splotch at the center. "I actually had a thought about that problem —"

"No," interrupts Shiloh exuberantly. "I have a way better thing I'm going to do, and then the resin will make it pop, Hannah was showing me —"

Marina interrupts her back. "Shiloh, resin is such a cheat. I don't let students use it."

"I'm not your student." Shiloh wipes the sweat off her brow with the inside of her elbow, breathing hard. "I like resin."

Marina gives up. Shiloh has two thousand theories for every square inch of canvas, and this one is going to have something to do with the obsolescence of certain kinds of technology, also gender, global warming, and decay. She doesn't tell Shiloh that the fresco is the better work, because that's the one she wishes Shiloh were scraping off. Or painting over, with a gallon of plain white paint.

"What are we listening to?" asks Marina. The music is foreign-sounding, with a propulsive beat and jangles and a high, fractured voice riding over the top.

"That's me. That's Wet Mink." Shiloh smiles beatifically, aqua paint in her orange hair. Her hazel eyes are clear and bright.

Marina guesses that it might not have been such a good plan to break up with Shiloh here, in her painting space. Her thought had been that it was better than being at Shiloh's house, where her roommates were always around, or in a ghastly public coffeehouse like before — she couldn't face the woman with the sketchy mustache again — and then she would just leave, and Shiloh would be able to sit quietly in her own territory, with all her work around her. Last time, the girl had found comfort in that, in working. Which seemed like the right message to send, besides being the only thing Marina really has to give her.

In the flesh, however, she seems to be unable to do it. After all this time, she still can't quite leave this room with its ambitious orange-and-aqua-headed spirit in a sports bra. Her will is apparently as broken as her hand. Shiloh looks so happy, paint-smeared, dancing to her own undanceable music. She looks so optimistic. For a minute, Marina almost believes that this new, vast idea of Shiloh's will work. Resin does make things pop, giving even mediocre canvases a dense, slick, important surface. And Shiloh isn't mediocre. Marina envies Shiloh's fervent willingness to start over, to toss away worlds at the drop of a concept. What must her parents be like?

Shiloh bounces around, scraping, in her peaked knit hat. "The edge," she sings. "You fucking angel." After a while, the canvas becomes nearly empty of shape and form. Clouds of unbounded color hover in the large square. Shiloh merrily brandishes the scraper. The tape comes to an end and clicks off.

"Things like this . . ." Marina begins.

"Not again." Shiloh slowly runs her thumb along the handle of the scraper, pushing black and lavender paint to the floor. "Why don't you just sit here and watch me paint and skip the broken-record speech?"

"Oh," says Marina quietly. It's wretched, suddenly. She sees that she has been wrong in a completely different way. She might not be a painter at all, but a voyeur.

Shiloh begins putting things away — the scraper, the empty canvas. "Look, I know you love Nan. I know I'm not real to you. I'm not, like, a gardener."

"Oh," says Marina again. How long has she been unhappy? Her eyes hurt.

Hal books a boat. Mary told him about it, which surprised him: a dentist in a boat. He couldn't quite put the two together, but she assured him that it was wonderful, she loved it, the skippers were all very nice. Hal was content not to know anything more about Mary and the nice skippers and the boats than that. He likes the simple, doable action of booking the boat; you call, a boat appears, like magic. Reading his credit card number into the phone, it makes him feel as if winning Dan's heart might be possible as well. He buys new khakis for the outing.

The boat is pretty. The skipper's name is Luisa; she is also pretty, and as fit and burnished as the boat. She tells them that her brothers and sisters skipper the other five boats and then she tells them to relax, enjoy the view, the wind is good today. She goes into her little house with the wheel in it and waves. They chug out into open water.

Hal doesn't particularly like or trust boats, he hopes they don't end up drowning, but Dan smiles, getting up from his deck chair and embracing the bay with his face to the wind. He walks around the deck easily, peering over the side at the wake behind them.

"What's it like down there?" calls Hal from the deck chair. The wind is loud. He hopes he isn't going to be seasick. Baysick.

"Deep," says Dan. He ambles around the deck, hands in his pockets, the plumb line of his back to Hal. It seems to Hal that the wooing is not going all that well so far. Perhaps he's out of practice. Dan laughed and exclaimed over the presents, but when he told Hal that he shouldn't have it almost sounded as if he meant it. His eyes over the fan were only playful. They had perfectly nice sex and then went to sleep. Hal feels as if Dan is a safe and he's a safecracker, listening hard for that little click but dialing past it every time. He doesn't know the combination. Or why Dan is still there, if he doesn't want to be. And, like a safecracker crouched over a safe in the middle of the night, Hal senses that the clock is ticking. Dan will fly, not today, but soon, if Hal doesn't find the right number. He has a new understanding of what makes Nan such an edgy lover.

Dan sits down in the deck chair next to Hal and crosses his legs. "Hey."

"Isn't this boat great? I've never done this in all the time I've lived out here."

"No, me neither. Look at the city. It's like it could disappear any second." The buildings do seem weightless against the clear sky.

"Well, it has. I was here for the last big earthquake. I was walking Christopher to a birthday party, actually. He felt it before I did. He was already crying when it hit."

"Closer to the ground?"

"Maybe. He was just a very sensitive kid. I grabbed him and we ran to stand in the nearest doorway, it was one of those places that sells religious stuff. All the plaster Jesuses fell off the shelves. I covered his ears, I don't know why. It was truly terrifying."

"Did you have all that stuff you're supposed to have, the canned goods and the water?"

"No. We made it over to Nan's and ate all the ice cream before it melted. Chris thought that was great."

"But you have it now."

"No," says Hal. "I don't." He smiles, remembering that day, which was terrifying but also strangely lovely, the three of them suspended in time, eating ice cream, as sirens sounded in the distance.

"I have it all. The flares, the water, the beans. My grandmother made me promise. She's always sending me clippings from the newspaper about horrible earthquakes around the world." Dan laughs. The boat pushes through a small wave. "I feel cheated that we haven't had one yet, like I don't really live here until I've felt one."

"You probably have. There are little earthquakes all the time. They had one on the peninsula last week."

"Oh." Dan looks disappointed. "I wish I'd known."

"There'll be more, don't worry," reassures Hal. Is that what Dan wants? An earthquake? If only they were predictable.

The boat slows. Luisa waves happily from her little house as if to say this is normal, this is part of the ride, everything is good. Is it? The swell becomes more palpable, lifting them and setting them down again on the water. The red span of the bridge arches delicately from point to point. Hal's nausea isn't too bad. He made them a reservation for lunch at a seafood place, continuing the nautical theme. The bay is sort of like a lake.

Dan turns his head to look at the water. His sweater is a fine weave of green. "Pretty."

"Do you love me?"

Dan's gaze barely flickers. "Are you sure a lover is what you want?"

"What do you mean?" His heart is a sinking ship.

"I mean there's you, and Nan, and Christopher. And that girl. And her family."

"And Marina."

Dan stares at Hal as if he's an idiot. "Marina? Hal, come on. That's what I'm saying."

Hal begins to grow angry. "I don't understand what you're saying. Don't you come with people, too?"

Dan looks at the bay again. The city shimmers alongside it. "Is this Paris?"

Hal glances. "How the hell should I know? No. Yes. There are *planes*. Just put me out of my misery. Do you want me as your fucking lover or not?" He wishes he weren't shouting, but maybe the wind will muffle the noise. And what was that crack about Marina?

Dan continues to look at the bay as if reading it, page by page. The boat rocks. Luisa, in her little house, slowly spins the wheel, eyes discreetly fixed on the horizon. Minutes tick by. Finally, Dan turns to look directly at Hal. His small face is intent. "Does this look like Paris?" he says. He gestures at the waves all around them. "Do you see me standing here?"

Christopher ties his shoes. He brushes his hair. He likes his own eyes in the mirror. He touches his beard; it feels good, like short fur. He touches the blue bead on the leather cord around his neck. It's a privilege that they gave it back to him. In Walnut Creek, he couldn't have it. He flexes a bicep: still there, pretty good one. He closes one eye. His face jumps, looks the same, only closer.

There's a tap on the door. "Christopher?" It's Michael. "Are you ready?"

Christopher puts on his sweatshirt and opens the door. Michael is short and squat, but he talks and moves quickly, like a bouncing ball. He bounces down the hall, down the stairs, out the door, to the van. "Big day." He isn't kidding. Little things mean a lot to Michael. Christopher opens the van door and gets inside. He waves goodbye to Bleach on the porch. Bleach sits on the top step in his usual way, one white paw hanging down.

"How's it going?" asks Michael.

"Okay." Christopher touches the blue bead. He isn't afraid.

"Edna taking your kitchen shift?"

Christopher nods. As they drive along, he sees that there are so many people on the street, all on their way somewhere. To work, it must be. They have on sunglasses and jackets, dresses and suits. Some are talking on cell phones. Michael goes over a hill and stops at a stoplight. Christopher glances to his right and sees his school. Even though it's summer, a few kids are standing in front, talking to one another. Summer school. His French teacher, Madame Pinkney, walks up to them and hurries them inside. He sinks down, though they can't see him in the van. He doesn't recognize any of those kids anyway, maybe they're new. Probably beginners.

"How old are you?" Christopher asks Michael.

"Me? I'm thirty-three. And never been kissed." Michael winks.

"I'm seventeen," says Christopher. He had his birthday in Walnut Creek.

"Yeah, I know." Michael drives on, his small feet bouncy on the pedals.

The parking lot is enormous and the grocery store is enormous, like an airplane hangar. Michael hands Christopher the list. "You keep us honest. Julie said no more Fritos."

"I like Fritos."

"Well." Michael winks again.

Michael gives Christopher a cart and takes one for himself, leading the way through the big doors that slide open as they approach. Inside, Michael says, "Remember, our budget is $425.75. We usually just start on the right and work our way over." To the right are fruits and vegetables, piled high, and there on the top of the list are the fruits and vegetables: a dozen apples, six heads of lettuce, four cantaloupes if they're ripe, and on down to eggs, which Christopher can see already are in the next aisle. His left hand is tingling, but not too much. He can read the list.

"Geronimo," says Michael, waiting for Christopher to go first.

Christopher likes driving the wide cart. It must be a little bit like driving the van; he wonders if you need a special license to drive a van. He could knock things over with the cart if he wanted to, but he doesn't. His other, more important piece of paper, the one with Bleach's head in Patagonia, is in his back pocket. He drew the little boy on there so that he would remember if he saw him again; he could take out the paper and compare them on the spot. He hefts in two bags of apples, stuffs three heads of lettuce into one plastic bag, three into another. How much food would two people eat in a week? Two seventeen-year-old people in another country?

"This is how you tell if the cantaloupes are ripe, Chris." Michael shows him the flat button on the bottom. "See? This one isn't ready." He picks up another melon, pushes it. "This one's good." Michael hands it to him. Christopher can feel the thick button yield. His fingertips are okay today. He puts the cantaloupe in his cart, then a few more ripe ones. They cost seventy cents a pound today.

"Now what, Chris?" Michael waits, short and squat, behind his cart, like a ball that has rolled to a stop.

Christopher checks the list. "Tomatoes."

"How much can we spend on tomatoes?"

"Um. About ten dollars."

"Great." Michael bounces on his toes.

The lights in the grocery store are awfully bright. Christopher has to squint as he and Michael move through dairy, past the mammoth freezer cases, where Michael tosses in an entire extra carton of butter pecan ice cream. "For Julie," he says with a wink. "I'll pay." Christopher is relieved to see that there are no people or animals frozen there, no distressed faces pressed against the icy glass doors.

"How are you doing? Are you tired?" asks Michael. "Do you think we got enough eggs?"

"No. Yes." Both of their carts are filling up. Michael showed him how to move the more delicate items to the front so they don't get squashed. Michael seems to be really into this whole grocery thing, that must be why it's part of his job. Taking a bag of frozen french fries from one of the cases, Christopher imagines that the new kids at summer school are asking the way to the Champs-Elysées about now, asking if it will rain, asking if Marie-Hélène has her red umbrella. His advanced class, before he left, was reading *L'Ecole des Femmes*.

"Get three," instructs Michael. "We're having the barbecue on Friday."

The rice aisle is easier on his eyes. He has to concentrate, but it's not so hard. He doesn't know why Pete had acted all superior in the past about being the one to go. Pete's moving to an apartment in the East Bay this weekend. They're supposed to help him take his things. He's been acting superior about that, too; he says he has a girlfriend, though she's never come to the house. *Orzo*, says the list. What is orzo? Michael points it out, explains how you cook it, how easy it is.

They're sailing through tea and coffee like a grocery cart convoy — Johnny loved to convoy — when Christopher spots a small, redheaded boy sitting in a cart by himself. There are some large boxes of cereal and Pampers in the cart, a container of Reddi-Wip. The boy's little legs are dangling through the spaces at the top of the cart. He is sucking both his thumbs. Christopher looks around, but he can't see any parent with the child. The aisle is empty except for the boy, Michael, and himself. This is worrisome, but worse, much worse, is what is written on the little green jacket the boy is wearing: *Patagonia*.

Christopher stands very still in the aisle, trying not to panic. Michael, ahead of him, is pulling different kinds of tea from the shelf. "Chris, do we need chamomile?" he asks, holding up a box.

"Sure," Christopher manages, though he doesn't look at the grocery list. The boy burbles through his thumbs, kicks his legs.

Christopher's heart aches. He suddenly understands: this must be how they mark them. What should he do? Who knows better than he does how hard it will be? The boy's skin is soft and fine, perfect; Christopher is terrified for him. He moves his cart next to the boy's. How heavy could the boy be? That little green jacket is like a jacket of fire.

A woman with a baby on her hip passes Michael and puts a frozen pizza in the cart where the redheaded boy is perched. "Hello," she says to Christopher, shifting the baby to the other hip. She kisses the boy. "Sweetheart." He burbles, waving his damp thumbs. She whirls him away.

Christopher's legs are shaking, and he tries to hide it, but Michael can tell. "What's up, Chris?" Michael drops some boxes of tea into his cart.

Christopher has a watery feeling in his head. He would rather *not* believe what he's seen, but how can he ignore the evidence? He feels so sad. "That little boy," he ventures to Michael, gripping the rail of his cart.

"In the cart?"

"Yes. He was by himself." He can't bring himself to say the word *Patagonia*. He touches the blue bead, which barely helps.

"Just for a minute," says Michael reassuringly. "He's all right now."

Nan sits next to Christopher at the barbecue, holding her paper plate on her knees. Hal had a date. Marina went to an opening. "Chris, I think you should shave the beard. It's scruffy."

"No, it isn't." He eats some beans in his clear-eyed way, casually opposing her. She supposes she should be grateful for that. Also that he smells sweet and clean, that his blond hair is cut, that he is wearing sneakers and socks.

She can't help herself. "You look like your uncle Henry did when he was following the Grateful Dead."

Christopher shrugs, spooning beans.

Nan retreats momentarily, eating her hot dog, which is rawish on one side, burned on the other. Pete, who's a manic-depressive, is in charge of the grill. He doesn't look quite as much like a serial killer as he usually does, with his flat face and missing finger, and, truthfully, Nan envies him. This barbecue is for Pete's going-away. He leaves New Day House tomorrow. He leans into the smoke, assiduously tending the meats and veggie burgers.

The other residents of New Day mingle freely with one another and the counselors, the two groups, in jeans and hooded sweatshirts or light sweaters, indistinguishable. They've rigged up a stereo so that music plays out the back windows. A large woman in a winter coat and that little counselor, Michael, are two-stepping on the grass. Dr. Blanchard, in a long-sleeved Sierra Club jersey, is standing by the grill, cupping his ear and talking to Pete. The old white dog that Christopher likes is roaming around wagging its tail, pausing at an abandoned plate to eat a french fry. Christopher's friend Drew is telling what seems to be a big story to a small group on the deck; they're all drinking longnecked near beers. A man who looks much like Pete, but who has all his fingers, is sitting and laughing with the group on the deck. He's Pete's brother, Larry. It's freezing, of course, but at New Day they like to observe holidays and customs by the book: in the summer, people barbecue. She can only pray that Christopher will be gone from here before Christmas.

Nan doubts that such gatherings will ever seem natural to her. She has tried very hard, especially recently, to understand her son, but she can't bring herself to concede that these are his people. He's passing through. That's as far as she can go. And isn't that her job? To hang with all her weight on the other side of the rope? He's only seventeen. They have years ahead of them. She squeezes his arm. "You look good, Chris. I'm so proud of you."

"Yeah." He shuffles his feet on the grass. "What's the most foreign place you've ever been?"

"Turkey, I guess. Before you were born."

"Was I born in Patagonia?" he asks intently.

Nan glances over at Dr. Blanchard, who is taking a burger from Pete. "Of course not. You were born here, in San Francisco. You know that. What are you talking about?"

"Are you sure? Think about it."

Nan lowers her voice. "Chris, are you taking your medication?" The doctors have told her it's "an uneven process," but how uneven did they mean? The yard is bounded by a simple wooden fence, not unlike hers. The street is less than fifty yards away.

He dismisses her question as if it's absurd. "Of course. Every morning. They watch me. I'm just trying to figure something out."

"Like what?"

He clams up, holding out a piece of burger for the dog, who licks it from his fingers. He scratches the dog gently behind the ears, and the dog pants happily. "This is a really great dog," says Christopher.

Nan knows it's irrational, but she suddenly feels suspicious of the little white dog. She stares hard into the dog's eyes, searching. There's nothing there but dogness, and cataracts. Relenting, she slips the animal a bit of bun. "Would you maybe like that sometime? A dog? Not right away. But in a while." Isn't a dog a task of daily living?

Christopher brightens, dims, brightens again, chewing on a thumbnail. "Wow. I guess it would depend on what kind." He eyes the New Day hound. Nan thinks of how many residents must have touched that dog, held that dog in states of mind she can't even imagine. She's sure the dog knows more than she does, more than they all do. And there it is, still alive, trolling the barbecue for treats. What is its name again?

"I was kind of thinking the pound. Mutts are best. But" — she pats his knee, he seems a little agitated — "it was just an idea, honey."

Christopher seems to be concentrating, weighing various considerations. "I like dogs," he finally says.

Nan is glad he isn't asking about Tamara tonight, she really doesn't want to have that conversation again. No matter how many times they explain it to him, he circles back around, like a homing pigeon. The word *never* seems to have disappeared from Christopher's vocabulary. She can't tell if that's an effect of his illness or his age.

Dr. Blanchard appears, smiling, with his paper plate. "May I join you?" He commandeers an empty folding chair. "Terrific party, isn't it?"

"Sure. How long has Pete been here?" asks Nan.

"This time? Oh, about eight months. He's done extremely well." He scoots his folding chair closer to theirs, on his good-ear side. "Chris, don't you think so?"

"He's a jerk," comments Christopher.

"Did you bring that up in group?"

"He's *leaving*. When's the cake?"

"Bring it up in group," presses Blanchard easily, almost off-handedly. Nan admires his stamina, though maybe he had two good ears when he started this job. "And how are you?" He turns to Nan.

"Me? I'm good. Yourself?"

"Well, I'm all right. I went for a hike today with my wife. It was just lovely. We stopped for lunch in Marin on the way back."

"Expensive up there," says Nan politely. Christopher, between them, is fidgeting, pulling at the leather cord around his neck.

"Expensive everywhere." Blanchard chuckles. "It's ridiculous. We would have loved to live up there, but it's impossible."

"Yeah." Nan can't think of anything else to say. She likes Blanchard, whose first name is Rick, but she can't call the man who holds her son's life in his hands by his first name. She doesn't want to know about his hikes or his adventures in real estate.

"Where do *you* want to live, Chris?" asks Blanchard, eating a piece of watermelon and carefully depositing the seeds on the paper plate. "Ever thought about that?"

Christopher frowns. "Maybe . . . in the country?"

Edna, standing by the sheet cake that Julie is about to cut, takes off not only her winter coat but all her other clothes as well. Her large underpants fall to the grass.

"Oh, dear," says Blanchard, leaving his paper plate, with its five watermelon seeds, on the folding chair.

When Nan gets home later on, the house is quiet. She hangs her jacket on the banister. She takes off her shoes. She listens to the messages. Marina will be late. Whatever. It's been a long day. Nan would like to have a cup of coffee the way she used to before bed: last, sweet coffee of the night. Holding her hand over the warmth. Making a cup of mint tea instead is just depressing. She wanders through the living room, the dining room, turning on lights, then turning them off again. Hating Marina, she leaves a light on in the hall for her. This is my house, she thinks with some surprise. She actually managed to buy this house, a long time ago now. In the kitchen, she reaches into the back of the freezer, behind some frozen chicken, and finds the pack of cigarettes, wrapped in tinfoil. She takes out one cold cigarette, lights it off the stove, and sits down at the kitchen table. It's like smoking a black icicle. It tastes good.

The kitchen is its regular, scuffed self. There's a splatter of soy sauce on the table. She never, ever thought she'd stay this long. Or that her last time on the road would be what it was. She won't go again. Nan inhales, exhales cool smoke. Edna's body was big, striated with wide stretch marks on her great belly and flopping breasts. You could see where four children, like four little glaciers, had moved through her. Her pubic hair was sparse. Her thighs were very thick, dimpled. The residents, and even some of the counselors, gaped, but Nan felt that she understood Edna perfectly. Edna was showing them her life's work. If Nan were just a slightly different sort of person, she'd do the same, walking right down the middle of Van Ness Avenue. Showing the world to the world. Nan takes a last, deep drag on the cigarette, then stubs it out in the sink, satisfied.

Marina meant to stay only a few minutes at the opening — she hates openings, including her own — but she fell into conversation with her old sort of friend, sort of rival Greg, and she had a second glass of wine, and the work on the walls began to look better than it had when she walked in. What she had thought was boring now seems to her provocative, possibly mythic, though not attached to any specific myth. She didn't mind running into people she knows. Someone had a baby. Someone else just got back from Cuba. The walls of the gallery have been painted a very pale, crystalline blue; the art floats on them, like strange buoys.

"And what have you been working on?" asks Greg, his eyes darting around. Having already been twice as venomous about the show, twice as cleverly as Marina, he's bored.

"Nothing," replies Marina. "I'm not working at the moment."

"Oh." Greg is clearly uncertain what to say next, and confused about whether honesty has won or lost Marina that conversational point. "Is that . . . a good thing?"

"I don't know." She smiles at him. "It just is."

Greg takes in this information, poking at the lemon in his sparkling water with the little straw. "I guess a break is always nice," he offers vaguely. "Did I tell you I'm backpacking into the desert next month? I'm going to plan a major project there."

"Great," says Marina. "When do you come back?"

"No idea. When I'm ready. Isn't that what Guggenheims are for?" He smirks.

Not for the first time in their long acquaintance, Marina thinks how deeply she dislikes Greg, how transparent his power plays are. He's such a creep. When they were in art school together, he believed everything their professors said and was always eager to change lightbulbs for the shorter of the female faculty. She's happy that he's bald now. "Why the desert?" she asks, dodging the Guggenheim bullet, and meaning why the desert for the next epoch of his greatness as opposed to, say, the feet of the Sphinx or the top of the Empire State Building.

He answers a different question. "Lindsay and I split up. You didn't know?" His eyes dart more quickly. "It's all gone. That's what my project is about."

"What?"

"What happens." He waves his hand nervously. "To things. Did you hear Roberta got a Prix de Rome?"

"I'm sorry," Marina attempts, meaning the split with Lindsay.

"Oh, Rome can have her." He looks at his sparkling water with the shredded lemon. "I'm going to get a drink."

When Marina leaves the gallery, she doesn't call Nan to come get her as they had arranged. Instead, she walks awhile. She walks awhile more. The cold streets are as dark as a confessional booth, but she finds she has no desire to confess. She doesn't call home. Instead, she looks into darkened store windows, restaurants full of strangers. At a small, undistinctive place, she goes in and eats a mediocre bowl of mussels at the bar. In the mirror behind the bar, she can see the companionable, familiar curve of her own forehead, the way her hands move. Maybe she should cut her hair, or grow it, or whatever those things are that people do. What do people do? That's what she and Greg really should have talked about. Maybe she'll send Lindsay a note this week, though she hasn't seen her in years. Lindsay was always the better artist in that couple. Marina finishes the mussels and calls a taxi; it's much later than she thought. Once home, she ascends the stairs quietly. From the kitchen comes a faint, dark, familiar scent. Nan has had a cigarette, obviously. The bedroom is silent. Marina undresses and slides into bed beside Nan, whose breathing and posture take the form of sleep, but not entirely convincingly. Marina draws close. "Nan?"

There is no answer. As if in her sleep, naturally, Nan turns and shuffles to the far side of the bed so that no part of her touches any part of Marina. "I'm sorry it got late, I took a walk," whispers Marina, but there is only silence, punctuated at regular intervals by Nan's breath. Marina gives up. The slender strip of sheet between them has become so uncrossable that it might as well be the Sahara. Marina notices that the sheet hasn't been changed in a while. She wishes she had asked Greg how he's planning to survive, where he's going to pitch his tent, and how he's going to withstand the loneliness. Nan is ten times more stubborn than any desert, and Marina is no camel. She's very parched already.

Turning over on her side, away from Nan, Marina feels the great weight of all the arguments they haven't had, all the objects they haven't thrown, all the furious, cutting things they haven't said. It's as if it's all stacked up between them, like furniture, in the dark. So much heavy, invisible clutter, and the two of them on either side of the heap, both refusing to toss so much as a dirty plate. Ruth would do a better job of it. But for them: Stalemate. Checkmate. Cold war. She probably should have told Nan about the dress, too. They could have lit a match to it together, watched it become a lavish, brief bonfire before turning to ash. At least then they could have shared that sight. But how can they burn anything now, when everything else is finally not burning? Marina closes her eyes and does her best to sleep.

Hal rolls over next to Dan under the orange silk bedspread. The room is bright with morning light. He always likes the mornings at Dan's. Maybe that's why they end up there most of the time, especially since he doesn't have to go home to feed the fish anymore. Hal drapes an arm over Dan's chest. He is happy. Dan's curtains billow at the window, and suddenly Hal sees Marina there, on the other side of the pane, tapping. This vision shakes him, but it is Dan, only Dan, who murmurs, "We'd better get a move on."

Christopher, sitting on the edge of the bed to tie his shoes, wishes he would see another bear. He liked the bear. He thinks it's possible, looking back on it, that the bear meant that there were bears in Patagonia, but he isn't sure. Its golden brown fur was shining. It stood up. Christopher ties his shoe, listening for the jingle of Bleach's tags. It's very curious that Bleach hasn't said anything else, not even when the two of them are all alone in the yard or sitting on the porch watching the street. It makes Christopher upset in some way he can't explain that Bleach just walks around like a dog all the time, not saying anything, though looking as if he might at any minute. Christopher keeps a close eye on him. When he gets a chance, he studies Bleach's eyes, which are complicated. He's read through the part in the book about Patagonia a few times, underlining. Things are much clearer to him than they were before. He knows what to do.

Chopping vegetables, he and Drew discuss the three branches of government. It's on their GED test, which is Saturday. Drew, Christopher can tell, is nervous about it. Drew isn't a big fan of government generally; he hacks the yams into large, ragged chunks, asking, again, why there are *three*, why not four, why not twenty? "Since they can use all the help they can get," Drew comments sarcastically.

Christopher, mincing garlic, says he doesn't know why, it's just traditional.

Drew, hacking, squints knowingly. "Huh," he says.

The kitchen, with its giant pots and pans and skillets, is pleasant. There's one knife that's Christopher's favorite, one with a nick in the handle. He likes its heft and feel, the sharpness of its blade that works so efficiently. He likes to cut up more vegetables than they even need. It makes him feel rich. Also, it impresses Julie, who will say something about there being enough for an army and then be surprised, later, at how everything gets eaten up.

"Where's Bleach?" asks Christopher.

"Vet." Drew moves onto onions, which never make him cry.

Christopher has his suspicions, but he doesn't say anything. He has to be a little careful, even with Drew. Drew doesn't seem to do research the way he does. Christopher has never seen him write anything down.

"Think Pete's bored yet?" Drew sends onion bits everywhere.

"Bored?" It hadn't occurred to Christopher that Pete could be bored, or that anyone could be, out in the world where everything is.

"Oh, sure. It can get real dull out there, the same old grind. Making copies. I liked the lawn crew job, but then that ended. I hate television. I like to *go around*, you know? I'm a wanderer, like you." Drew eats some onion, not crying.

"Yeah." Christopher fingers the nick in the handle of his favorite knife. It's smooth and worn, like something that's been there a long time. He didn't make the nick, but it fits his thumb. It would be nice to come downstairs every morning and work in this kitchen, pick up his knife with the nick in the handle. It would be nice to know that the knife was waiting for him, strong and useful, nicked from years of service. The knife kind of reminds him of his mom, the way it gets things done, the way it's always there. The way it can bite, too, you have to be careful with it. But still. He likes the knife. He likes to think of it as his. "What are the three branches of government?"

"The *Nina*, the *Pinta*, and the *Santa Maria*." Drew smiles, his teeth full of pearly onions.

Nan rubs the scar on her arm that the surfboard made at Pescadero. The scar is white, about an inch long. It falls across a spot right above her wristbone, randomly, like a twig or a leaf on the grass. The crosshatchings of the stitches are quite faint already; soon the mark of that cut will be a simple white line, a single brushstroke.

She picks up the garden hose and waters the plants, the little tree, still dressed in her clothes from work. Water spatters her shirt. There are things she wants to say to Marina that she'll never say, and the thing she most definitely will never say has to do with the way Nan can't draw, never could. What she would like to say to Marina is this: *Draw me a boy. Draw me a house. Draw me a tree in the yard. Draw me an ocean, draw me a boat, draw the boy in the boat, draw the boat sailing past the house. Draw the boy in the tree.*

But of all the things she could ask for, that's the most foolish, the least essential. It won't fix anything. Never has.

She can't do it. Could she ever do it? Marina puts down the bit of charcoal. The classroom is empty, with easels askew everywhere, a candy bar wrapper on the floor along with the little stretchy earpiece cover from a Walkman. The windows are open and letting in warm East Bay air. Marina is sweaty, tired. Her right shoulder aches. After making corrections for three hours, she suddenly had a burst of frayed energy. An impulse flowed down her arm, like a hunch, and so as not to scare it away she picked up a stub of charcoal from a student's tray, tore a piece of drawing paper from a pad, and moved. Without will. A few minutes went by, a tenuous shape began to form, and then, like the capricious counter on a Ouija board, the motion stopped. Nothing happened. It's as if her hands have been cursed with a special kind of paralysis that permits her to use them in every regular way, except to draw or paint.

She wonders if this failure is her punishment for dragging on with Shiloh, who seems to have absorbed all the painting energy that has fled Marina. Shiloh's body of work gets bigger all the time, like a constantly expanding universe. Marina tries not to resent her. She really has to break up with her.

Gathering her things for the train ride home, Marina resolves to talk to Nan. She has the sudden idea that if they could talk, if they could really get to the heart of it, then not only would their relationship improve, but the curse would lift. No more secrets. Maybe her hands are registering a protest; maybe they're trying to speak. She and Nan have barely had *any* decent conversations in months. Even having one would be a start. As she waits on the platform for the train, she rubs her aching shoulder.

When she gets off the train, the streets of the Mission are as profuse as ever: two little boys handing out Jesus pamphlets at the BART station, white kids with messed-up hair lingering in cafés and taquerías, salsa music on a car radio, the night fog coming in, and the suede mountains in the distance making all of it seem benevolent, enduring. Marina has always liked the jumble in this part of town, the constant striving activity and community combined with the sense that at any minute it could all topple over and spill out, as if it were an overloaded boat. Before Nan, she didn't have this local abundance; the places she had lived were either much smaller or much more diffuse, and she was generally on her way out of them, half dreading and half hoping to be followed. She passes the busy laundry, the pawnshop that's never open, a church that always is. Five dark-eyed little girls in school uniforms are sitting on the church steps, singing a J. Lo song.

When Marina gets home, Nan is paying bills in the living room, with her reading glasses on, and drinking green tea. The glasses string Hal gave her arcs delicately against her neck. They kiss hello in the usual way. Nan frowns at a bill. Marina, in a chair opposite Nan, puts her big work bag down on the floor and takes off her shoes. "Nan," she begins.

"How was class?"

"Fine."

"Where's the calculator?"

"I don't know." Nan, Marina notices, has gotten so much more solid. She isn't any bigger physically — if anything, she's smaller and more wiry — but she displaces air in a different way. She sits more solidly. She moves more solidly, more deliberately. The few lines in her face have set. Her jeans are the same size they've always been, but her body beneath them is more still. She's like a spool of thread wrapped tight. The salt and pepper in her hair has gone more salt; her hair is quite short these days, the nape of her neck bare and strong. The glasses string makes her look older. "Nan."

"Yeah." Nan doesn't look up, or even raise a hat above the wall to draw gunfire.

She is indeed, Marina thinks, the most stubborn person alive. Feeling tired, Marina continues. "The thing is, I feel like I don't know where you are."

"I'm right here, Marina. Where I've always been." Nan deliberately puts down her pen and sits back on the sofa, waiting. The lamplight glints in her glasses.

"No. Or maybe it's where we are. I don't know where we are anymore. Do you know what I mean? We're — gone, somehow. There's this space."

"Space?" Nan tilts her head, as if Marina has introduced a very interesting concept.

"Space," Marina says firmly. "Come on. You know what I'm talking about. At night."

"Like the other night?" Nan's tone is cool.

Here, Marina knows, is the difficult moment. They haven't spoken of it all this time; neither of them has spoken of it. But to reduce it to Shiloh would be wrong as well. Marina tries to steer a course between the Scylla and Charybdis in their living room. "The other night, I took a walk after the opening. That's it. And it isn't the point, Nan, you know it isn't the point."

"So what is the point? What are you trying to tell me?" Nan crosses her legs. "I'm listening."

"Are you?"

"Yes, I am. Look at me. I'm sitting right here."

Marina feels strangled in some way that she can't articulate, throttled by invisible ropes. Beneath Nan's solid wall of reasonableness, she senses a question, but the hell of it is that she can't quite make it out to answer it. Nan is guarding her question like a dog with a bone; she has buried it very deep. "I love you, Nan. I want us to be together. I want to stay here. That's what I'm trying to tell you." Isn't that what Nan wants to know, at heart?

Nan takes this statement in with barely a shift in her position, as if reaching up to catch an easy fly ball. "Then give her up," she says quite clearly. She leans forward, writes a check, licks the seal on an envelope, and closes it. To Marina, it is as if Nan has firmly shut a window and, on the other side, turned her chess-piece profile to the glass. Marina knows what her next move is supposed to be — weep with contrition, smash the window, grab the stubborn queen — but her hands remain still at her sides, unable to move.

Nan, on the sofa, is just as still. They hold each other's gaze, motionless.

Hal opens the door to his house, the little yellow house he has loved so well, and finds he doesn't love it anymore. Something has fled it. The air inside is empty. He puts his black leather backpack down in the entryway, glances at his face in the entryway mirror, considers dinner, notes the light blinking on the answering machine, tosses the mail on the dining room table, but none of these ordinary actions satisfies. Their gravity is wrong. They don't hold him. He feels like an astronaut, bouncing across the moon. He also feels in some way that it's because the fish are gone, even though they didn't really do anything except cost money and look exotic. It wasn't as if you could pet them. None of them had real names. Still, without them circulating silently in the other room, without their expensive fish food stinking in the fridge, the house seems flat. Maybe he should go out to dinner.

Hal walks out of the house, walks back in again, shutting the door with a bit of a flair. *Honey, I'm home.*

Nothing in the house responds. It's as if the house has gone deaf, or decamped, though there are all the doors and windows in their usual positions, there is his good furniture, there is the 1975 poster of the Venus Flytrap from when they played Berlin. There he is in 1975, glittering, with his ass hanging out in German.

It's a curious thing. Where did his house go?

So this is love, he remembers, this missing. This is the fullness of absence, of skin in need of skin. This is the wealth of yearning. He sits down in a good chair in the house he doesn't love anymore, feeling rich with want.

Marina wanders purposelessly around her messy studio. She should call Shiloh, but she doesn't. She could call a friend, call James, call Nan at the store. She owes a call to a student. There are always things to take care of. Instead, she stares out the window at the street. The three little seahorses are still fixed to the glass in their old tape. She touches them one by one; they're delicate, spiky, dry. Carefully, she lifts them in their winding sheet of yellowed tape from the window and lays them on the sill. They look like three fossils. Everything comes in threes for her, always. Why is that? The tiny, blind, rococo horses offer no explanation. Maybe she's just a restless soul; maybe she'll wander forever. Maybe she's the fool who always takes the fall when the thing gets lost or broken. *Things like this:* she thought she understood their terms, but it's clear that she had no idea what the terms really were. Maybe she should have dug deeper, gotten a good look at the roots. Maybe she should have said more, or less, or sooner, or later. Maybe she should have grabbed on, in the moment before they went under, and held it tight, the way Nan held Christopher that day at Pescadero. It's just that she doesn't know when that moment was; the moments recede endlessly, dissolving. All she knows is that at some point they both let go. Christopher took all the fight they had, as was his right. Isn't that what kids do, take the fight out of their parents? For a second, this thought consoles Marina. She is truly a parent, after all.

In the burning house, what do you save, the painting or the cat?

The marriage or the boy? Everyone always knows everything already, and nothing at all. In the burning house, she made her own instinctive grab; Nan would surely say it was the wrong one. She couldn't get the tree right when she was ten either. For more than seven years, like some girl in a fairy tale, she's been drawing her failure, over and over. Poor seahorses, she thinks, regarding them on the sill. Their spiny tails curl jauntily, as if they're bobbing in the ocean, but they're nowhere near it.

Nan, standing in the garden, drops a match into the tin bucket. Though she carefully wadded up the paper, the flame doesn't catch and she has to drop in another match. This time it goes: the whole country or realm, all the gold, the mountain ranges, the rocket, the crows. The strange sea catches fire. The mountain ranges blacken and crumble. The blood burns.

Christopher tries to call Tamara, but the number's been changed. The new number is unlisted. They don't have the Internet at New Day, but that doesn't matter. He gets the hint.

The days tick by, interesting and boring. The nick in the knife greets him every morning, and he chops fields of vegetables into bowls. He goes to the grocery store again, without incident, and even leaves with change. They add it to the budget for the next week. Michael teaches him how to make a cake from scratch. A new resident comes in, a very pale girl who stays in her room all the time. First she says her name is Dinah, then she says it's Trish. In group, she asks them all to please call her Patricia, with four syllables, then folds herself up on top of her chair like a strange colorless bird perched momentarily on a fence. Her voice is high and tense, and she eats a lot of sandwich cookies, crumbs falling onto her sweatshirt.

Christopher passes the GED; Drew fails. They're going to let him try again in six months, though Drew, winking, doubts he'll be here that long. Christopher wishes New Day had cable, so he could watch *X-Files* reruns. Dr. Magathan comes and goes.

Dr. Blanchard cups his ear, interrupts Christopher less. Bleach is Bleach.

The paper with his new drawing on it is gray and soft from being folded and unfolded so often, and dark with detail. If he had something better than a pencil, he could draw much more clearly, but he can still make it all out. There's a big question mark in the middle, surrounded by swirling lines. That's where they took his brain and gave him this other one that isn't quite the same, like someone else's shoe. Until they give him his own brain back, he's going to have to make do with this one, the way Bleach does with his bad leg. When he tells Dr. Blanchard about his fake brain, Dr. Blanchard says a lot of people like Christopher feel that way. Like him? wonders Christopher. What is that? Switched-brain people? Patagonian people? He knows the other word. It just isn't very specific, and Dr. Blanchard says that's true, it isn't, but it's the word they have.

Christopher tells it to Bleach as they sit on the porch, watching not much traffic pass. Lifting Bleach's ear, he also tells the dog about how he's starting at a Ben and Jerry's in Russian Hill next week. He'll have money. They all talk to him a lot about that, about having his own money. You'd think sad-ass Ben and Jerry's was paying him a million dollars. He taps his fingers on the porch. His fingers don't hurt at all anymore. Inside the house, the phone rings. Julie leaves the living room to get it. One thing he's sure of: it's not Tamara calling for him. It never will be.

Picking up Bleach, Christopher walks away. He walks off the porch, and out the little gate, and down the street, and around the corner, to another street. From there, he turns onto another street. Bleach is furry and warm and unruffled, looking around at everything. He doesn't have his collar or leash, but it doesn't make Christopher tired to carry him. It's funny being outside, as loose as a leaf in the wind, with no one watching him or trying to tell him how to do things. His legs feel rubbery, as if he just got off a boat after a long voyage. The sidewalk is surprising, and the houses, and the stores. A family of tourists, with water bottles and fanny packs, pass by him, talking in another language. He almost understands it, even though it's not French. Bleach stares at the family knowingly.

After a while, Christopher finds himself on a wide boulevard with a lot of cars on it, but the more he walks, the less rubbery his legs feel. In fact, they feel very strong, as do his arms. He shifts Bleach to the other arm: it's easy. The other people on the street are wearing windbreakers, but he's fine in his T-shirt, the dog warm against his ribs. He feels as if he could walk for days. When he passes a Ben and Jerry's, he's reminded that he has no money, but he's not hungry. He's happy. He's happier than he's been in a long time, just walking around with his strong legs and his strong arms. He wishes he had remembered to bring his knife with the nick that fits his thumb. He scratches Bleach behind his ears, smiling, and Bleach smiles back at him. He could be about to say something, outside, away from everyone else.

A woman carrying a grocery bag passes by. "Cute dog," she says. "Is he hurt?"

"No," says Christopher, moving on. Like before, it's important to keep moving. It is a long and winding road: you can't stop.

The road goes up, then down. Cars stream by. He keeps his head down, walking straight on. He thinks he hears Bleach whisper, though it could be the wind, which is getting stronger, cooling his face. All this world out here. All this time unfilled. It's almost sad, somehow, as if the world itself is lonely and walking on it is the only thing to make it less alone, less flyaway. His feet in sneakers make no noise, holding the world down step by step. The light dims slightly, but there, ahead, is the bright curve that means water, and before the water, trees. Land's end. He's been there a million times. Christopher speeds up to get there, looking both ways as he crosses the boulevard, then heads into the trees.

He puts Bleach down, and Bleach sniffs, pees, trots along with him, tail up. The woods smell like eucalyptus and pine, and the path is soft earth. A great peace comes over Christopher; his thoughts can perch freely in the trees. He takes out his paper with his drawing on it and holds it up to the light. This is it, all right. Or one of them. The mythic counterpart to Patagonia. And, as if to prove it, a man and a woman walk past him on the path, both in blue jackets that say PATAGONIA. He isn't surprised. He's getting closer. It's funny, in a way. He laughs, shaking his head. He stretches out his arms, breathing in. Life is good.

Christopher and Bleach amble up the path, around a bluff or two, past silver trees and brush and wildflowers. The air grows damper, cooler. Bleach, swinging his bad leg, disappears from the path, then returns, burrs in his fur. He barks at a bird. A constraint, one that Christopher had somehow forgotten, lifts, making him even stronger. This is how it was before, this *relief*, though this time it's better. He wasn't as strong before. His feet strike the earth perfectly, tapping out a warning to the other Patagonia, the real one far below, as if they are digging a hole to China. He's so happy. He half expects Dr. Blanchard to come around the next bend, cupping his ear and nodding, yes, see, it's what he's been telling Christopher all along, that this moment would come. Bleach bounds away into the undergrowth. The white tip of his tail moves among flowers, then is gone.

Christopher's path turns and twists, leading him, with his perfect feet, to a bluff above the water. He doesn't need to look on his drawing. He sees the ocean, vast and deep and full, stretching from end to end in his vision. In the distance is the bridge, the hills beyond. It's cold now, and the sky is going gray. It's the end of the day. It's land's end: everyone he loves and everything he knows is behind him. He breathed, that other time. It was after, on the beach, that he couldn't breathe and wanted to die. It's just been one hassle after another ever since. Christopher walks to the edge of the bluff. Bleach, back from his own adventure, trots out from the scrub and sits down on the bluff next to Christopher.

A small blond boy with red cheeks darts up to Christopher and Bleach. "Puppy!" cries the boy. He hovers over the dog, excitedly waiting for permission.

"You can pet him," says Christopher.

The boy, perched on the edge of the bluff, pats the dog with enthusiasm. Christopher kicks a loose stone and it tumbles down. He watches it ping into the little waves. Then he sees that on the blond boy's fleecy vest reads PATAGONIA, in red letters. Christopher is startled, then realizes that that's exactly it. That's why he's here. That other time, he was still a boy. Now he's a man; he knows about regret. Two women, one carrying a little fleecy hat, are far off down the path, heading toward them, calling out to the boy, who ignores them. His fair hair blows in the breeze. Bleach, one paw hanging over the bluff, isn't saying a word. The boy laughs against the sky.

Down at the bottom, before it begins, he will hold the boy against him, lung to lung, keeping him warm. He will tell the boy everything, he'll show him all there is to see. Christopher doesn't feel one bit unsure: he's got it figured out, at last. He pulls his drawing from his pocket and tosses it into the water. Walking forward to the edge, Christopher picks up the boy, feeling extraordinarily strong, like the strongest man in the world. He looks thoroughly into the boy's face, into the blue rings around the pupils of his eyes, and lets the boy look back into his.

One of the women begins to run.

The air is cold.

Bleach stands up.

The running woman shouts a name — Odah? Noah? The boy turns to the sound of her voice, Christopher's foot slips, and they both fall heavily to the ground. The child begins to cry.

"Oh, shit," says the woman, panting, picking up the boy and inspecting him. "Are you all right?" The boy wails, heartbroken, squirming. "You're all right. It's okay." She turns to Christopher uncertainly. "Did you hurt yourself?" Christopher shakes his head.

The other woman reaches them and peers over the cliff. "Jesus Christ."

Christopher feels tears starting in his own eyes. He looks at Bleach sniffing along the edge of the bluff, and he is so sorry, so incredibly sorry. His extraordinary strength ebbs. It's evening. It's over, for now. One ankle hurts. He's cold, and he's hungry, and he wants to go home. He can see the huge cartons of ice cream already, all the frozen multicolored drifts along the cardboard sides and his own arm reaching in, digging.

The two women hold the crying boy between them, comforting him, but he cries all the way down the path, reaching back in the dark for something they can't see.

Nan reaches for Marina's hand and holds it tight. She hangs up the phone. "He's back," she says, desperate and relieved. "He came back on his own, with that old dog." She exhales, cries a little. "Oh my God."

Marina looks at the cold spaghetti in the colander. "What does this mean?"

Nan seems dazed. "It was — a moment. A bad moment, but Blanchard said it's excellent that he was able to make the right call."

"So he's back," says Marina.

"Yes, thank God, he's back. We'll all be together again."

Nan stops bleeding. The string of the tampon is white, as is the tampon itself when she pulls it out, as white as snow, which is strange, because just yesterday she was bleeding a lot. Maybe that was the stress. Or maybe it's some biological game of hide-and-seek: as soon as she actually gives in and keeps tampons on hand, her body ceases to bleed. If she threw all the tampons away, she'd probably gush. Returning to her desk, she wonders why she never had another child. It had never even occurred to her, she was so involved with Christopher, and it was so hard, sometimes, even back then. One thing after another, daily life with all its questions and snot and kisses, just getting him to bed intact was a major accomplishment. And she loved him so. She still does. But now her body is beginning to snip off the possibilities, one by one. It shouldn't be surprising, but it is. Why is it that the most ordinary human events — birth, grief, age — are the most astonishing? As if no one ever before had a child, loved, got old. ONWARD, says her computer, as if there were a choice.

Hal pokes at the ground with a finger. The empty seed packet, turned upside down over a little stick, has a hopeful photo of bright red and yellow flowers on it. Of course, he planted at the wrong time, but he thinks he sees a bit of green, coming up out of the earth. He sits back on his heels. How long it has taken him to understand what anything really costs.

Dan calls his grandmother. She's all right, she says, except for her eyes and her bones and her heart. She's been listening to the radio. She had a nap. The lake was filled with yellow birds this morning. How is Teabag? asks Dan. Teabag is the cat. Well, she says, Teabag is fine. Dan tells her he'd like to come visit soon, and bring someone with him.

Someone? says his grandmother. Who's someone?

Dan says his name is Hal, then falls silent.

Hmmm, says his grandmother. She coughs. The lake was filled with yellow birds this morning, she tells him. She had a nap.

Marina locks her bike to a dead fire hydrant outside a nameless warehouse down by the train station. The big black metal doors are closed but, when Marina pulls, unlocked. Music thumps from the inside. A thin girl wearing a man's shirt with the sleeves cut out and VIVE LE PORN spray-painted across the front is sitting at a folding table near the door with a cashbox and a rubber stamp. On the cashbox is a sign saying ALL PROCEEDS GO TO WENDY'S FAMILY. SUGGESTED DONATION $5. Marina puts a ten into the box and offers her hand to be stamped. A battered guitar is displayed on the folding table; all around it are candles, flowers, joints, cards, and a few packages of condoms.

Though it's still daylight outside, it's as dark as a club inside the room, with people milling around, and cigarette smoke, and onstage a woman who looks to be about Marina's age, but with long, tattered black hair and arms full of tattoos, striking a hard chord.

"This is for Wendy," rasps the woman, "because she knew how to *make the rock.*" She slams into a song as if crashing a car into a wall. In the crowd, a face is momentarily illuminated by a match, but it isn't Shiloh. The atmosphere in the room is murky, sparky. A heavyset man standing near her is crying; tears are running down his large, unshaven face as he pumps his fist in the air in time to the music. A young man in a tattered dress holds up a digital video camera, filming the woman onstage, who is taking off her shirt.

Marina feels a bit as if she might have journeyed to hell, or some other underworld shore, except for the fact that the ambience is also undeniably sweet. When the woman with black hair finishes her song, sweating in her bra, she says, "If anyone wants to get up on stage, that would be cool," and three tender-faced women with side-parted hair, all carrying guitars and wearing black T-shirts, immediately volunteer, each one kissing and hugging the black-haired woman like a sister. When they begin to play, they sound like singing mice.

Where is Shiloh? Maybe she already left. Marina hitches the paper bag she's carrying onto her other shoulder, not that it's particularly heavy. She could leave. Then, from a table to one side of the room, Shiloh waves, beckons. When Marina goes over, she finds Shiloh sitting with T and Hannah and Jade at a table cluttered with beer bottles and ashtrays. Hannah is whispering something to Jade, who is giggling. On stage, one of the tender-faced women says liltingly, "This next song is about vampires."

"Your roommate told me where you were," offers Marina tentatively.

"Okay," says Shiloh, gesturing expansively for Marina to sit down. This is her terrain, after all. She can afford to be generous.

Hannah moves over reluctantly.

Marina ignores her, turning to Shiloh. "What is this?"

"It's for Wendy. Of the Wild Asshairs. She died in a motorcycle accident." Shiloh adds proudly, "Everybody loved Wendy."

"Where's Nicholas?"

"Los Angeles. He just signed a massive deal."

"Are you kidding?" Marina can only imagine him tip-tapping on his plastic bucket, like a child. Except that he isn't a child, of course. He's a man.

"No, for real. He's totally going to help us out."

Marina puts the bag on the floor, between her feet. Shiloh is looking girl-tough, with slicked-back hair and a motorcycle jacket. Despite the outfit, she still looks like a nice girl. She was an avid equestrian once, with her own horse, and first-place ribbons. Marina has always thought that it was this background that lent Shiloh her perpetual, clear-skinned innocence, her unshakeable naturalness, even here in this dark, smoky warehouse. Shiloh always seems capable of riding off into the sunset, with a bag lunch. Marina likes that about the younger woman; she believes it will keep her safe. She hopes it will.

Marina has a beer, picks off the label like a teenager. Shiloh puts her hand on Marina's knee under the table, claiming the proprietary rights of the wounded party. Bands come and go. A black woman with a great corona of violet hair plays the theremin, as intent as a priest saying Mass. Members of some bands stick around stage to play in other bands. Shiloh and her friends gossip, laugh. "Drum kit was *everywhere*," says Shiloh. Jade and Shiloh braid Hannah's hair into myriad long, slender plaits that swing around her Vermeer face, tying them with everyone's shoelaces, which T cuts up with her pocketknife.

Shiloh and Marina hang out together in the noise. Marina silently catalogues her sins, leaf by leaf. For a while, Shiloh rests her head in the curve of Marina's neck, drowsily, though the music is crashing and burning. She lights a cigarette. Marina thought you couldn't even smoke in bars anymore, but maybe it's different when it's a kind of funeral. Everyone in the room did know Wendy, that becomes clear, who was plainly no spring chicken when she died. In fact, Marina learns, she was thirty-nine, and had just gotten clean the year before. She had a son, who's there somewhere, and he's great, Shiloh says, she used to babysit him. From time to time, people stop by their table to say hey or bum a cigarette. More than once, someone earnestly presses Shiloh's hands and says how sorry he or she is, and how is Shiloh doing? Shiloh graciously accepts their condolences.

"Did you know Wendy well?" asks Marina, after the woman with the corona of violet hair has come by to say how sorry she is and leave one of her band's homemade CDs.

"Sure," says Shiloh. "She was my first lover."

Marina attempts to calculate the respective ages, then gives up. "Jesus."

"What?" Shiloh is genuinely surprised. "Didn't I tell you that?"

Hannah glances over, interested.

"It's just —"

"What?" Shiloh seems curious, but also, perhaps, the tiniest bit pleased to have found an edge, at last. She leans back. "Everybody knows that, Marina. Like, everybody here. She wrote an entire *song* about it. Wet Mink is doing it as a tribute tonight."

Hannah leans in, braids dangling. "It's called 'Who's My Bitch?'"

Shiloh unzips her motorcycle jacket. "Didn't you see this picture? It's from my shrine." Transferred onto her T-shirt is a photo of a much younger Shiloh resting, laughing, in the arms of a woman who is older than Shiloh, but younger than Marina is now. The older woman has a waifish face, intelligent eyes, and hair so blond it looks silver.

"I never noticed it," says Marina slowly. How ridiculously perfect. She was no dark despoiler of youth, but only, as always, a late arrival. A bad copy. Wendy's silver hair was longer.

Shiloh is dumbfounded. "It was right there the whole time."

"It was," concurs Hannah importantly.

"Let's go outside," says Marina, standing up. Shiloh rolls her eyes.

Outside, they both blink in what's left of the light. Shiloh leans against the warehouse wall, yawning. Wendy pixelates across Shiloh's chest.

"Why did you even come here?" Shiloh, against the wall, is annoyed. "You didn't know Wendy."

"I came to see you."

"Why?"

"I know it's hard for you to understand, I know I've been impossible, but, I —" Marina flounders.

Shiloh sighs. "You know, I don't know why you sleep — sorry, slept — with me when you think I'm such an *idiot*. I do understand. Your whole thing over there came apart. That's why I made that painting: I know you."

"What?"

Shiloh shivers. "I *know* how awful it is when the thing splits. God, Marina, do you see all these bummed-out people here tonight? Do you see this T-shirt? We're *family* here. The Wild Asshairs were huge for all of us. How it is in your world is how it is in my world, too, and it's really hard." Shiloh, her face half in shadow and half in light, has a profoundly regretful expression. "Bands break up all the time."

"I didn't know."

Shiloh shakes her head regretfully. "They do, Marina. Jesus."

Marina pulls the gossamer dress out of the bag and thrusts it at Shiloh. "Here. I brought this for you. To keep. From me."

Shiloh is puzzled, pulling at the golden folds and threads. "What the hell is this?"

"It's a dress." Marina steps forward, arranges it, and eases it over Shiloh's head. The shining, strapless bodice tears immediately, gaping over the photo transfer of Wendy and Shiloh.

Shiloh laughs, bursting from the dress, her boots already making hay of the gleaming train. "This is so fucked-up."

An extremely pale, very tall woman rushes up, carrying a bagged instrument that looks as if it might be an oboe. "I'm here! I'm here! Wow, that is awesome. Did you get that at the Salvy?"

"No." Shiloh looks at Marina as if trying to make her out. "It's a hand-me-down." She thrusts her arm around the tall woman's shoulders, and the two of them walk into the warehouse.

After a few minutes, Marina follows, slipping quietly to the back of the room. She never has heard Shiloh play. She should at least do that.

Onstage, Shiloh, in the T-shirt with Wendy's picture, the shredding gossamer dress, and boots, is fastening her guitar strap. She sounds a wild chord, then leans into the microphone. "Fuck love, man," she says, "as long as I can rock."

Hal packs a box. It's a box of books, the easiest thing to start with, and, besides, he has only one box. He's going to have to get more. It surprises him how few books he has, though. What has he been doing with his life?

"Oh, I always wanted to read this," says Dan, holding up a book. "I've read all his other ones."

Opening a kitchen drawer, Marina pulls out the biggest knife they have, the one they use to cut the Christmas turkey. She carefully touches the blade: it's sharp. The cool evening breeze comes in softly through the open glass doors. Marina walks into the garden. Starting from what she knows is the wrong end, she first snips off some leaves and tiny branches, maybe even the beginning of a flower. It falls to the grass. The small outlying branches are easy, but the closer she gets to the slender trunk, the more she has to saw, firmly at first, then with both hands. The cat from next door watches her indifferently. It's an odd thing, she realizes, sawing, that destruction can feel not unlike creation. Every cut she makes seems to have meaning. She digs at the roots with the knife blade, cutting where she can. When the little tree goes over, she slices the trunk at the middle first, as if it were a loaf of good bread. She's sweating. She's ruining the knife. She tries to break the trunk over her knee, but it's too green to snap. It only bends, stiffly. Marina crouches down, whacking at it with the ruined knife. She feels closer to the tree than she's ever felt. She sees exactly the element that was missing from her composition all these years, and where the line should have gone.

Nan leaves work and drives home.

Nan and Marina stand in the yard in the dark. To Nan, Marina smells like smoke and beer and wherever it is she's been, wherever it is she's going. To Marina, Nan looks like a shadow, kicking at the pieces of tree on the grass. She loves her entirely.

"Why did you do it?" asks Nan in a quiet voice. Her hands remain open, unfisted, and empty.

"I couldn't look at it anymore. You'll plant another one."

"That's not the point."

"No. The point is that neither of us could ignore this."

Marina tries to see Nan's expression, but Nan is turned away from her.

"I think the cab's here," Nan says. She can't say anything else.

Nan, hands in her pockets, walks with Marina out to the street. The cab door closes. Marina taps a finger on the glass. Nan goes back into her house and shuts the door.

On a bright, hot fall day, Christopher packs to go home. His father and Dan are coming to get him, but he wanted to do this part by himself. He rolls up pairs of socks, folds underwear. Every now and then he gets a glimpse of himself in the mirror, his bearded, square face.

Dr. Blanchard raps on the door. "Do you need anything, Chris? Tape? Twine?"

"No, I'm okay." He pauses. "If you were me —" He pauses again.

Dr. Blanchard cups his ear. "Yes? If I were you?"

Dr. Blanchard, thinks Christopher, will always be here. Up and down the same stairs, sitting in his same office with the fringed cushion on the patient's chair, listening to all the strange stories. Christopher doesn't understand how he doesn't get bored, being lied to so much. Still, Christopher likes him.

"If you were me," continues Christopher, "would you get a dog?"

Dr. Blanchard rubs his nose thoughtfully. "I, uh, I think I'd wait to see if I still wanted one in, say, a month or two."

Christopher nods. "Yeah, that's what I thought." Dr. Blanchard stays a few minutes more, then they shake hands goodbye. Dr. Blanchard isn't a hugger.

Christopher tucks his newest drawing inside *The Long and Winding Road*. On another piece of paper, he writes Drew a funny note, folds it, and sets it on top of a pile of uncut potatoes. When he's all packed he carries his suitcase downstairs to the porch, where Bleach is watching the street, one paw hanging over the top step. Christopher sits down next to him, scratching gently behind Bleach's furry ears. He whispers something to Bleach. His father and Dan pull up in the car. He can see their two heads through the windshield, his father's face behind the steering wheel lifted to greet him. Christopher waves.

CODA

HAL SETS the table. His silverware and Dan's are jumbled together, Hal's elegant, slender forks and knives mixed with the
odalisque forms of Dan's flatware. It's all a bit like Jack Sprat and
his wife, but Hal doesn't want to separate the sets. He places a
long, cobalt-handled knife alongside a zaftig fork and spoon.
Three plates. Three glasses. He calls Dan to remind him that they
need mustard for the salad dressing. Christopher's boots are lying
in the foyer, half-unlaced. Hal puts them in the closet. The sound
of the rush-hour traffic on Market Street floats in through the
open windows. It will be awhile still before Nan brings Christopher back, but Hal has fallen into the habit of leaving dinner
warm in the stove and reading the paper in the living room, exactly as his mother used to do — still does, though no one else is
coming. Hal turns a page, content.

Nan and Christopher gaze at the jellyfish. It's getting late, they
need to go, but they're both taken with the tenuous, translucent
beings falling endlessly through the water. The aquarium seems to
have glammed up recently. The jellyfish hall is called "Living Art."
There are actual, huge, ornate frames around each of the jellyfish
exhibits, with Da Vinci and Van Gogh reproductions set nearby,
for comparison. "Sea of Love" plays over a loudspeaker. Written
on the floor in light, in a spiral, it says: THE TIDES ARE IN OUR

VEINS. Crowds of children, as always, press their hands against the glass, trying to touch all the alluring, strange creatures. "Giant clover balloon!" screams a little girl, laughing, her fingers splayed against an exhibit with dark purple water.

A little boy with lights winking on his sneakers runs by, trailed by a man in a white turban pushing an empty stroller. That's a good innovation, Nan thinks, keeping their footsteps from ever being invisible. It's as dark in there as ever, the better to illuminate the extraordinary features of the jellyfish. There are jellyfish like lightbulbs, brown and white jellyfish in a clump like a big brain from outer space, jellyfish that seem to be lined with neon, jellyfish of incredible delicacy with infinite wisps of tentacles trailing upward through water filled with thousands of tiny white dots, jellyfish like bonnets.

"I wish I could draw," says Nan. "Chris, you should draw them."

"I wish I still had my fish," he says crossly. "I don't want a drawing of them."

"She was trying to help. Come look at these."

They walk over to a tank full of minuscule jellies that resemble stars. A small girl holding a stuffed dolphin stares, transfixed. Christopher smiles at the girl and at the starlike creatures, smoothing his beard. Tall, he stands far from the glass so as not to block anyone's view. He's paunchy, but strong in the arms from scooping ice cream and carrying crates. He's wearing a T-shirt that says RAINFOREST CRUNCH. His hair, in the last year, has darkened almost to brown.

"How are things with Maggie?" he asks.

"Oh, that's not really happening anymore." Maggie, who had an open face and honest blue eyes, told Nan everything. Nan was bored; it was worse than being alone.

Unselfconsciously, Christopher takes Nan's hand. "Are you getting tired?"

She is getting tired, but she doesn't want to go, not yet. He doesn't have very many days off; he seems to like to stay busy. "Do you want to see the otters?" she says.

"Okay." He tilts his head, as if listening to something.

Nan shifts her weight off of her right hip, which is twinging. A man wearing a sweatshirt that says MONTEREY looks at them curiously, which bugs her. Can't a grown son hold his mother's hand? "Okay, let's go," she says, but doesn't move. Instead, not letting go of Christopher's hand, she remains in the hall of jellyfish. They are beautiful dresses. On either side of Nan and Christopher, from floor to ceiling, the beautiful dresses fall and fall, fall and fall again, imprinting complex shapes on their faces.

On the way home, Christopher turns around to watch the 101 drawing away behind them. He turns back, fiddles with the radio until he finds a station he likes.

Tamara touches the little silver heart with the enameled peace sign at the center. She feels a forest in there, and a path to a house.

Marina pays the check. Jonathan, already on the street, winks a friendly goodbye and eases away. His resemblance to Nan lies not in his eyes or his hair or his features, but in his light, swift way of moving and one or two notes in his voice. He's coiled tightly inside, as she is. It's why he speaks so softly. When Marina and Jonathan have a meal now and then — no particular reason, are you free? — they never speak of her, and never ask if she has called the other. In this way, they comfort each other.

The waitress looks out the window after Jonathan, twirling one of her curls. Marina finds a pen in her bag and begins doodling on a napkin. The pen is almost empty; it scratches as much as it inks. She should get some new ones for her trip. Will she come back to Los Angeles? She has to, of course. She's hardly prepared to relocate to Egypt permanently, it's just a fortieth birthday present from her mother, who seemed to have no trouble understanding why a woman would want to go to the desert alone for a while.

Marina will leave tomorrow. She pushes at the napkin with the bad pen, scratch-sketching little waves. They peak and fall, peak and fall. Just so, she thinks, she'll draw them in the sand.